PRAISE FOR CARLENE THOMPSON

IF SHE SHOULD DIE

"A gripping suspense filled with romance. Ms. Thompson has the reader solving the mystery early in the novel, then changing that opinion every few chapters. [An] excellent novel."

—*Rendezvous Review*

"With engaging characters and intriguing motives, Thompson has created a smart, gripping tale of revenge, anger and obsession."

—*Romantic Times Bookclub*

"*If She Should Die* is a riveting whodunit!"

—*The Road to Romance*

"In the tradition of Tami Hoag or Mary Higgins Clark, Thompson has created a gripping page-turner. The storyline is engaging and the characters' lives are multi-dimensional. This is literally a book the reader will be unable to put down."

—*Old Book Barn Gazette*

More...

BLACK FOR REMEMBRANCE

"Loaded with mystery and suspense . . . Mary Higgins Clark fans take note."

—*Kirkus Reviews*

"Gripped me from the first page and held on through its completely unexpected climax. Lock your doors, make sure there's no one behind you, and pick up *Black for Remembrance*."

—William Katz, author of *Double Wedding*

"Bizarre, terrifying . . . an inventive and forceful psychological thriller."

—*Publishers Weekly*

"Thompson's style is richly bleak, her sense of morality complex . . . Thompson is a mistress of the thriller parvenu."

—*Fear*

SINCE YOU'VE BEEN GONE

"This story will keep readers up well into the night."

—*Huntress Reviews*

IN THE EVENT OF MY DEATH

"[A] blood-chilling . . . tale of vengeance, madness, and murder."

—*Romantic Times*

DON'T CLOSE YOUR EYES

THE WAY YOU LOOK TONIGHT

ST. MARTIN'S PAPERBACKS TITLES
BY CARLENE THOMPSON

SHARE
NO
SECRETS

Carlene Thompson

St. Martin's Paperbacks

In Memory of Sue Casto Handley

Thanks to Pamela Ahearn, Stefanie Lindskog,
Jennifer Weis, and Keith Biggs

Special thanks to Debbie and Morgan Long,
owners of The Iron Gate

AUTHOR'S NOTE

In the past, I have used imaginary West Virginia towns as settings for my novels. This time, I used my own hometown of Point Pleasant, West Virginia, located on the point where the Kanawha and the Ohio rivers meet. For fictional purposes, I enlarged the population and created a few sites that do not exist here, including Photo Finish, Heaven's Door, and most important, the haunting hotel, La Belle Rivière.

Sometimes, though, when I'm driving north at night along the Ohio River, I look up, and, through the fog, I could almost swear I see a graceful, ephemeral shape that strongly resembles a beautiful white Georgian hotel hovering slightly above the ground like a palace in a dream.

SHARE
NO
SECRETS

PROLOGUE

Julianna Brent stretched languidly on the cool satin sheets, uttered a tiny moan of remembered pleasure, and opened her amber eyes to the cobalt blue showing through a three-inch part in the draperies. It wasn't morning yet, but soon morning with all its stark brightness would glare upon the world, killing the aura of romance. She remembered a rhyme her mother had recited at bedtime when she was little and now she said it aloud:

> *Good-bye to blues,*
> *Farewell to pinks,*
> Adieu *to purples,*
> Au revoir, *my greens.*
> *When this day is done,*
> *And stars come anew,*
> *I'll see the rainbow orbs,*
> *Again in my dreams.*

Julianna giggled at the simple poem and breathed deeply, inhaling the scent of burning jasmine candles placed around the bed. She loved the smell of jasmine and the way the light dipped and sparkled in the candles' cut glass containers. A flicker fell on the crystal figurine of a young, long-haired girl in a flowered gown given to Julianna when she was seventeen by her friend Adrienne. Julianna treasured the piece of Fenton art glass and christened the girl Daisy, a character in the Henry James short novel *Daisy Miller* she'd read in senior English. Julianna always brought the figurine with her. Along with the candles, "Daisy" made this beautiful but impersonal hotel room feel as if it were hers.

And *his*.

She picked up a fluffy pillow and pressed it to her face. The smell of him clung to the satin pillowcase, a smell clean and manly, arousing, and capable of provoking a hundred romantic scenes that made her body come alive again although by now she should be weary and eager to go home.

But she didn't want to go back to her lonely apartment. She wanted to lie here and fiercely clutch the ecstasy of the morning to her as if it would be for the last time.

A chill ran over her. *For the last time?* What had made that portentous phrase pop into her blissful thoughts? Premonition? Certainly not. Julianna didn't believe in premonitions, much less one so ridiculous as the fear of never seeing him again. It wasn't an omen. It wasn't an augury. Those were words from her mother's vocabulary to describe her mother's beliefs. No, the phrase had merely been . . .

A *warning*.

Yes, a warning. After all, extramarital affairs were tricky, and this one was even more so. It had the potential to make more than her lover's wife unhappy. It had the potential to be dangerous. Caution was absolutely crucial, and her lying on this bed as dawn grew brighter was certainly not an act of caution.

But Julianna was exhausted. Satiated, but exhausted. Yesterday had been long, wearing, and disappointing. She'd only gotten a couple of hours' rest before she came here to meet him. If only she could go back to sleep for just a little while . . .

Julianna felt her eyelids drooping. Would it really be so bad, she wondered, if she grabbed some rest? The hotel was empty, closed for almost a year. There was only Claude Duncan, the caretaker, who would be lucky to shake off his hangover and make his lackadaisical rounds of the hotel by mid-morning.

Julianna drifted one layer deeper into the world of sleep. The room began to fade as her thinking became cloudy. Slowly, she felt her dream of the meadow coming alive again.

For the last month, she'd dreamed every night of walking in an endless meadow of white, pink, and yellow flowers. She'd told her mother, Lottie, about it and been surprised at the look of worry on the woman's face. "What is it?" she'd asked. "What's wrong with my dream, Mama?" Lottie had smoothed Julianna's shining hair and, as always, astonished her daughter with her vast knowledge gleaned from a trove of esoteric reading. "In mythology," she'd said, "a meadow is a place of sadness. A Greek philosopher wrote of the 'meadow of ill fortune.'" Lottie had shaken her head. "The dream is not a good sign, Julianna. I beg you to give up the path you've taken with this man. It can only bring you unhappiness, my darling, and maybe much worse."

Her mother's words had troubled Julianna, but she had not given up her lover. After all, her mother was basing her feelings only on a dream, and dreams didn't necessarily mean a thing. When she was awake, she'd simply put the dream out of her mind. But when she slept, the dream always returned. Just like now.

Julianna didn't hear the hotel room door open softly. She was unaware of someone stealthily crossing the soft blue carpet to the bed and staring down at her—staring at the lush spill of auburn hair, the creamy complexion, the rounded shoulder and full breast exposed above the satin sheet. The stare burned as the hatred behind the eyes grew more vicious with each second.

Deep in Julianna's brain, an alarm flickered to life. She opened her eyes. Her lips parted, but surprise stilled her voice. A thrill of fear running through her, she started to rise, her hands fluttering upward as if she could ward off the malevolence hovering above her.

She was only dimly aware of an arm reaching toward the bedside table beside her. Then, before she could utter a word, a ceramic lamp crashed on her head. She fell backward, her eyes closing as unconsciousness mercifully sheltered her from the horror that followed.

Five minutes later, Julianna's assailant glanced away from the bed. The small crystal figurine of Daisy still stood placidly on the table, only now splatters of blood streaked her delicate flowered dress. The assailant gazed for a few satisfied moments at the lovely, still woman on the bed, then glided across the room and out the door, leaving Julianna to wander forever in her beautiful, endless meadow.

ONE

I

The Iroquois Indians called the river "the Ohio," which was translated by the French as "the Beautiful"—*la Belle Rivière*. Later, linguists argued that the name really meant "the Sparkling," "the Great," or "the White." Perhaps other translations were more accurate, but to most people who lived along the Ohio, the river remained "the Beautiful," an apt name that would follow it throughout history.

Adrienne Reynolds stood on a low rise overlooking the river. Behind her loomed the long, white, Georgian lines of a hundred-year-old resort hotel named la Belle Rivière, more commonly referred to by the locals of Point Pleasant, West Virginia, as The Belle. She removed sunglasses protecting her sea-green eyes from the bright morning sun and looked downward at the hotel's best-known attraction, its majestic view of the wide Ohio River.

Adrienne loved the river. As an artist, she was always intrigued by its colors. They varied from a muted emerald when the waters were low and tall grasses could be seen swaying beneath the surface, to the café au lait or "milky" tone achieved during light rains that gently eddied sediment, to dark chocolate when storms roiled the murky mud of the riverbed. She especially liked the Ohio on cool summer mornings like this one when fog gracefully rose from the river, parting now and then to let glittering sunbeams spear the glassy surface of the water. She looked behind her and saw that already sunlight sparkled off the glass cupolas atop the four-story hotel overlooking its namesake, La Belle Rivière.

Adrienne had been born and reared in the West Virginia town of Point Pleasant set in a lush rural landscape and only two miles away from the Belle. She'd never dreamed of leaving the area for places known to have more excitement, but right after college, she'd followed her young husband, Trey Reynolds, to Nevada where he'd created a lounge act and managed to hang on to it for almost five years in a minor Las Vegas casino. Although Adrienne loved her husband, she hated her new home. Every day she looked with desolation at the flat expanse of hot sand, the prickly cacti, the parch-skinned lizards scurrying around her front yard, and the endless sky. Local people described that sky as vibrant turquoise. To her it looked like a piece of bleached denim with a burning white hole that passed for the sun. Her husband never knew how often he'd just cleared the driveway on his way to the casino for rehearsal before Adrienne had burst into a storm of homesick tears for the wide Ohio River and the lush blue-green hills of Appalachia.

When Adrienne had become pregnant, she began supplementing their scanty, irregular income with her sketches and paintings. Their daughter Skye was five by the time Adrienne was getting a small start in the local art world when, in an unexpected and crushing blow, Trey had been demoted to an even less popular club farther away from the hallowed "Strip" where everyone wanted to be. "I don't think there's anyone in the audience under eighty," he'd complained to her in a lost, hopeless voice. "Half of them sleep through the songs. *Snore* though the songs! It's humiliating. And I'm not making enough money to keep three of us going." He'd sighed and stared into the distance. "I *won't* put my family through this. We're going home. I'll join Dad's business."

So Trey Reynolds had abandoned his limping, ego-crushing casino career and they'd moved back to West Virginia. Adrienne had known what a blow his failed entertainment career had inflicted on Trey, although she'd been amazed he'd managed to hang on to his lounge act for as long as he had. For her part, though, she'd been overjoyed to return to her and Trey's hometown of Point Pleasant. Within a year she'd begun selling her work at a nearby Ohio gallery called the French Art Colony and teaching art at the local branch of Marshall University. Her happiness had increased tenfold. And even now, her enchantment with the area remained, particularly on a beautiful morning like this one at the old hotel she loved, although Trey was no longer here to share the beauty.

Soon the temperature would rise, probably to the low eighties according to the forecasters, but now the dampness from early morning fog turned Adrienne's long, honey-brown hair wavy and sent a ripple of chill bumps along her arms beneath her denim jacket.

"I'm opening the thermos of coffee," her fourteen-year-old daughter Skye called. "You want a cup? I'm freezing!"

"You didn't have to come out here with me so early."

"I love it out here just past dawn with all the mist," Skye claimed enthusiastically. "It looks like Camelot, or some of the places in my old fairy-tale books. What about the coffee?"

"Yes, please." Adrienne stood on the bank for a few more moments, savoring the atmosphere, before the smell of strong coffee reached out and lured her like the Greek sirens calling to the sailors. Skye held out a cup, Adrienne took a sip, and smiled. "You used the good stuff."

"Royal Vintner, your favorite."

"Have you misbehaved in some way you're about to confess?"

Skye looked reproachful. "Of course not, and besides, I'm too old to *misbehave*. You make me sound like I'm seven."

Adrienne raised an eyebrow. "Pardon my demeaning language. Have you raised hell in some way you're about to confess?"

Skye burst into laughter, her adolescent face beautiful in the gentle sunlight. "No. I'm not you, Mom. I'm not already raising hell at age fourteen."

"Neither did I."

"That's not how Aunt Vicky tells it."

"My big sister was Miss Manners all her life. I don't think she ever did one thing wrong."

"But you were your parents' favorite."

"Only according to Vicky. If they were alive, they'd tell you a different story." Adrienne looked around, squinting slightly against the sun on the mist. "Lights are still flashing down on the road. I think that wreck is a really bad one."

"Maybe someone was trying to pass in the fog."

"You're not supposed to pass at all on that strip of highway, fog or no fog. Too many curves."

"I hope no one got killed. But you'll get the scoop later today. Dating the local sheriff has its perks, Mom." Skye gave her a mischievous look. "Just how serious are you two?"

"This coffee is great but you still look cold, Skye," Adrienne said briskly. "Why don't you get your sweater from the car?"

"No sharing of secrets about Sheriff Lucas Flynn this morning even when I made a pot of your favorite coffee?" Skye's hyacinth-blue eyes, so like her father's, danced beneath long lashes. "He's awfully nice, Mom, and Daddy would want you to be happy."

Trey would also want me to be in love, Adrienne thought sadly. He would want me to feel joyful and passionate, not just safe and comfortable like I do with Lucas. But she said none of this to her daughter. "Oh well, I'll try to pump more information about the romance later," Skye relented cheerfully. "Now I need to find Brandon. I hear him barking in the woods."

"He probably had a mad urge to pursue a squirrel that

would scare him to death if it turned on him. Honestly, I've never seen such a cowardly one-hundred-pound dog."

"Mom, Brandon is a lover, not a fighter."

"Whatever you say. You go save Brandon before he's attacked by a chipmunk, and I'll get my camera and sketchpad out of the car. I only have three weeks to get a painting done of this place before it comes tumbling down."

"Before Ellen Kirkwood has it knocked down," Skye said bitterly. "What a waste. Are you sure Kit can't do anything about it?"

Kitrina "Kit" Kirkwood, Ellen's daughter, had been one of Adrienne's two best friends most of her life. Kit—smart, fast-talking, opinionated—was violently opposed to the destruction of the Belle, but the hotel belonged to Ellen, who was adamant. Kit told Adrienne she'd lost the fight to preserve the place she loved and had thought one day she would inherit. So she wanted Adrienne to do a painting of the hotel, something Kit could hang in her elegant downtown restaurant, The Iron Gate.

"I don't see why Mrs. Kirkwood is so amped about pulling down the hotel," Skye continued to grouse, reaching for the sweater she'd earlier said she didn't need.

"Ellen's convinced it's cursed. Her mother harped about it to Ellen all her life. And to be fair, there have been a lot of strange accidents and deaths here. But Jamie's drowning in the pool last year was the end for Ellen." Adrienne thought of the beautiful four-year-boy Ellen Kirkwood had adopted when he was a baby. "She couldn't bear to look at the place anymore."

"Her husband doesn't want her to tear it down."

"Gavin doesn't own it, and I don't think he has much influence with Ellen, either. Or Kit, even though she and Gavin are on the same side for once."

"Why doesn't Mrs. Kirkwood just sell the Belle?"

Adrienne raised an eyebrow. "Honey, it wouldn't be sporting to sell a cursed hotel."

Skye grinned. "Yeah, real unethical."

"We shouldn't make fun of Ellen," Adrienne added guiltily. She'd always liked the woman in spite of her peculiarities.

"Making fun just a little bit won't hurt," Skye said. "It kind of takes the sting out of knowing this great old place will be sticks and stones in a few weeks."

"You're right." Adrienne sighed. "I hear Brandon. He's in the woods off to the left."

"And I'm off to the rescue. Be back pronto."

Actually, Adrienne was glad for the temporary solitude. She needed to concentrate on finding the right perspective from which to do her preliminary sketches. It would take several tries, some of which would be interrupted when her daughter and dog returned. She'd have been happier to leave Skye and Brandon at home for the morning, but Skye had insisted on accompanying her, and when Adrienne had balked at bringing Brandon, Skye had put up a guilt-inducing argument about how he hardly ever got to run as much as he should. He was, after all, at least ten pounds overweight. A romp in the woods would do him good, Skye had said convincingly. Unfortunately, his "romp" had turned into an allout rampage.

Adrienne reached inside her car for the Olympus Epic Zoom 170 Deluxe camera she'd just bought last week. She'd done practice shots, but these would be her first serious photographs with it and she was looking forward to seeing how the hotel looked caught by a 170 mm 4.5X high-performance zoom lens. It seemed powerful to be so light and convenient to carry.

She took random shots around the hotel, catching the long porches stretching the length of all four floors that had allowed guests to stand outside their rooms and view the river. She photographed the tall glass cupolas, the red shingled roof, the big clock tower with its Roman numerals, the iron weather vanes topped by black roosters. The vanes sat motionless. A brisk breeze would have quickly chased away the fog, Adrienne thought, but for now she liked these shots with the mist shrouding the hotel like a veil, even if the pictures probably wouldn't be much help when she worked on the actual painting.

Finally, the fog began to clear a bit in spite of the still air of the morning and Adrienne decided to get started. She'd selected a sketchpad of rough paper and a 3B graphite pencil for her preliminary sketch. She went to the east side of the hotel, where the morning sun shone brightest, sat down on a piece of wrought-iron lawn furniture, and stared up at the hotel, drawing pencil poised.

Sunlight shimmered through the remaining mist, giving the hotel a magical look. Skye was right, Adrienne thought. La Belle Rivière possessed a fairy-tale air, evoking the beautiful women who'd once walked in graceful gowns down the wide first-floor porch steps onto the lush green grounds. Their handsome companions, men in excellent suits with exquisite manners and equally exquisite bank accounts, would have accompanied them. Adrienne sighed at her vision of the hotel as it must have looked in the early twentieth century.

But just a few years ago, the place had still retained its grandeur as well as its reputation as one of the most beautiful resort spots in the country. The hotel had drawn everyone from statesmen, to movie stars, to foreign royalty. Ten years ago, it had been the site of a high-fashion shoot featuring local girl turned haute couture model Julianna Brent. How beautiful Adrienne's girlhood friend Julianna had looked in sumptuous evening gowns as she posed at the hotel, a landmark Ellen Kirkwood had maintained with all the diligence its builder, her great-grandfather, could have desired.

Adrienne's reverie snapped when a sharp caw broke the morning silence. She looked away from the cloud to a telephone line, on which sat three shining black crows. One cawed again, its sound strident and irritating. The lookout crow, she thought, signaling to the other members of its group. A murder. That's what a group of crows was called. Not a flock. Not a gaggle. A *murder* of crows.

Another bird landed on the telephone line. He looked bigger than the usual crow, more like twenty-five inches long rather than the average nineteen or twenty. Two more arrived. They sat close together on the telephone line, all seeming to glare at her with their hard little eyes.

An old riddle about crows she'd learned in childhood came to Adrienne's mind, and she caught herself saying it aloud:

> *One's unlucky,*
> *Two's lucky.*
> *Three is health,*
> *Four is wealth;*
> *Five is sickness,*
> *And six is death.*

The last word pulled her up sharp. A *murder* of six crows sat on the telephone line, and six meant *death*. Abruptly she felt colder and reached for the cup of coffee sitting next to her on the bench. But it too had turned cold. She set it down and grimaced. Then she shook her head, annoyed with herself for being fanciful enough to let a few birds spook her. She'd never liked crows, but they were hardly a danger like the ones in Hitchcock's movie *The Birds*.

"Get lost," she called to them. One cocked its head and threw her an especially sharp caw. "You're not scaring me, you know," she went on. "You're just getting on my nerves."

"Caw. *Caw. Caw!*" all six returned loudly as if understanding her and indignant at her attitude.

"Cram it!" she yelled, then glanced sheepishly around, hoping Skye hadn't been near enough to hear her. She sounded crazy out here bellowing at birds. Adrienne looked back at the hotel, determined to ignore the noisy, glistening little creeps on the telephone line and get back to the business of capturing the hotel's essence on paper.

But she felt peculiar, as if she were being watched. Well, she was, she thought. The birds had her in their sights like prey. But as much as she disliked crows, she knew it wasn't their beady gaze making her uneasy. She glanced toward the woods and caught a flicker of movement. It must be Skye or Brandon, she reasoned. But neither of them would dart from tree to tree, lingering for a moment behind each.

"Who's there?" she called. No answer. Brandon was too exuberant for hiding. Besides, he wasn't over five feet tall as the flickering figure seemed to have been. And Skye would have answered her. So would the caretaker Claude Duncan. Perhaps it was a teenager lurking around, although it seemed too early for that kind of nonsense. Still, there had been the car wreck close by. Maybe someone had been drawn to the scene, then wandered up around the hotel, which was off limits without permission from Kit or Ellen Kirkwood.

Adrienne caught a flicker of movement again. Uneasiness flowed through her and impulsively she picked up her camera, taking several shots. If they discovered that someone had broken into the hotel and stolen or damaged furnishings, she might have caught an image of the thief or vandal.

She sat still for a few more minutes, camera poised. Then the idea that whoever was lurking in the woods might do her or Skye harm abruptly popped into her mind. Her nerves erupted to life. Something was *wrong*.

"Skye, come back right *now*!" Adrienne yelled shrilly at the exact moment a nearby Skye shouted, "Brandon, come here!"

"Skye, let the dog go and come sit with me! I think someone is in the woods."

"Yeah. Me and Brandon." Adrienne could hear the exasperation in Skye's voice. "I'll be back as soon as I get him."

Adrienne was annoyed that the girl wouldn't do as told, but at least she was safe and she was close by. It probably *had* been Skye she'd seen darting through the thinning mist,

Adrienne reasoned. The fog and the loneliness of the abandoned La Belle Rivière had unnerved her. Besides, all of her life she'd experienced dark premonitions and not one of them had come true. It was always the unexpected disaster that jumped up and slapped her in the face.

Assured that charging into the woods after Skye would be foolish, Adrienne forced down her uneasiness. Tucking the camera into a slit pocket in the flannel lining of her jacket so she wouldn't lose it, she shifted her gaze far to the right where a six-foot-high white lattice fence enclosed an Olympic-sized pool. It had been drained over a year ago, when Ellen Kirkwood closed the hotel, but Adrienne could still almost feel the tingle of its cold water on a blazing summer afternoon.

She and Kit and their friend Julianna Brent had spent endless hours poolside, Julianna always earning the most attention with her astonishing body clad in one of her many skimpy bikinis. Adrienne smiled at the thought of the venomous looks Julianna had drawn from so many females, while the males gazed at her with expressions varying from shyness to pure lust. Not in the least reserved, Julianna had loved every moment of the fascination she caused. If either Adrienne or Kit had been jealous of her, the feeling was overwhelmed by their pride at having a gorgeous friend everyone knew was destined to someday smile from the covers of national glamour magazines.

On the warm summer evenings after an afternoon of swimming and sunbathing, the three of them had ridden around town in Kit's red convertible. They'd flaunted their tans in cutoffs and halter tops, flirted with boys congregated on street corners, and endlessly listened to Julianna's favorite song, "Sweet Dreams" by the Eurythmics, which she played at ear-shattering volume, singing along with Annie Lennox. Those were the summers when Kit, Julianna, and Adrienne were sixteen and seventeen. They were great summers, Adrienne thought. Probably the best, most carefree times of the three girls' lives. And all those good times seemed tied to the doomed hotel La Belle Rivière.

Okay, now you're being morbid, Adrienne thought as she felt depression descend. It's stupid for me to get so devastated over a building scheduled for demolition when everything else is so good in my world.

A crow cocked its head and looked down at the mumbling woman with unmistakable ridicule. At least it seemed unmistakable to Adrienne. She glowered back. She'd talk to herself if she liked. Then all six birds flapped up from the telephone wire when an explosion of barking ripped through the quiet morning.

"Brandon!" Skye shouted. "Don't you dare go in that hotel!"

In the hotel? Adrienne thought. At this time of morning, every entrance door to the hotel should be shut and locked.

More barking from Brandon. More yelling from Skye. "No! You're wet and dirty! We're gonna get killed if you go in there—" A moment of silence except for the birds fluttering back to the telephone line. Then a familiar, "Mom, I need you!"

Adrienne dropped her sketchpad and pencil and headed to the west end of the hotel, from where Skye's voice had come. She was glad she'd worn running shoes because the grass was laden with dew. "Where are you, Skye?"

The slender girl with her long pale blond hair and fashionably torn jeans appeared at the corner of the hotel. "There's a door standing wide open on this end and Brandon ran inside. Mrs. Kirkwood will *kill* us if he does any damage!"

"He's not destructive," Adrienne said in relief when she reached her daughter to see the only problem was a runaway dog. "He won't hurt anything."

"But he's acting weird."

"He's just acting like a high-spirited dog. Don't get so worked up, Skye. We'll find him."

Good grief, Adrienne thought in irritation. Skye acted as if Brandon were a six-week-old pup. But she understood the girl's protectiveness. At her tenth-birthday party, Skye's father, Trey, had presented her with Brandon, already full grown and rescued from the dog pound less than twenty-four hours before he was to be "put down," which made him even more precious to the animal-loving girl. That night, Trey had been killed in a motorcycle accident. In a way, for Skye the dog had become the last precious legacy her father had left to her.

Adrienne entered the side door behind Skye. It was dark, but Adrienne saw a panel of switches in the dim morning light coming through the open door. She flipped two, and bulbs sprang to light beneath crystal fixtures on the ceiling.

Brandon barked in the distance. "Hurry up, Mom! If he jumps in that fountain in the lobby—"

"The worst he'll do is bump his head. The fountain is empty. You're acting like a hysterical mother, Skye. Settle down."

They entered the lobby in time to see one hundred pounds of shining black and white hair charging up a winding staircase to the second floor, barking for all he was worth. Odd how slowly Brandon ambled across the backyard when she wanted him to come in for the night, Adrienne mused. She'd thought he was getting arthritis, but today he moved like he'd been shot out of a cannon.

"Brandon, come back here!" Skye shouted.

"Save your breath," Adrienne said. "He's not coming back on his own."

"But what about that caretaker guy?"

"If he's upstairs, he'll catch Brandon. Claude certainly won't hurt him."

Skye took the stairs two at a time. Adrienne suddenly felt every one of her thirty-six years as she tried to keep up. I need more exercise, she thought. Jogging, aerobics, yoga. Learning to use the Pilates machine she'd just bought. It all sounded exhausting.

The second-floor hall was dimmer than below. Only one light glowed beneath a crystal cover midway down the hall, and a strange, sweet scent filled the area. Skye stopped. "What's that smell?"

Adrienne sniffed. "Flowers. Jasmine." She sniffed again in slight alarm. "I also smell smoke. Maybe we should go back downstairs—"

Brandon let out three deafening barks. Skye darted down the hall yelling the dog's name. He barked again.

He wouldn't be leading us into a fire, Adrienne thought, panicked nevertheless by her daughter's headlong rush toward the barking. "Skye, wait!"

The girl halted almost immediately, but Adrienne could tell it wasn't in response to her command. Skye stared into one of the hotel rooms from which flickering light spilled into the dim hall. Her lips parted and she said softly, "Brandon, come here," as she knelt and held out her hand.

Adrienne reached Skye's side. She looked into the room and saw candles flickering on the dressers. The heavy, sweet scent of jasmine floated from the wax. Brandon sat stolidly near the foot of a bed. That was all Adrienne could see. Brandon and the foot of the bed covered by a lush bedspread of ivory brocade. What the dog stared at near the head of the bed escaped her range of vision. But she had the strange sensation that she was supposed to go into the room. Something *waited* for her in that room.

The feeling grew. I should pull my daughter away from the door, Adrienne thought as dread grew in her mind. I need to get Skye away from here because nothing good lies on that hotel bed Brandon is staring at. Nothing that Skye should see.

But Skye rose and strode into the room before Adrienne could grab her shoulder. Skye jerked to a stop about five feet away from Brandon, her eyes widening as they fixed on the bed. Brandon looked up at her and whined. The frozen look on Skye's face and the dog's pathetic whine drew Adrienne into the room almost against her will. She stopped at the foot of the bed, staring, unblinking, disbelieving.

Two thick pillows in creamy satin pillowcases rested against the padded headboard. A woman's head lay against one. She was deathly pale, but her expression was peaceful, the lips shut, the eyelids closed, the long russet-colored hair smoothed like silk away from her face. The hair had been combed behind the right shoulder but spread over the neck and down over the left shoulder, partially obscuring her cheek and neck until it fanned out where the top of her left breast disappeared beneath the bedspread.

In the wavering candlelight, Adrienne caught the flicker of a barrette on the left side of the woman's hair, near her temple. It was nearly two inches long, made in the shape of a butterfly with tiny chips of blue, green, and pink Austrian crystals sprinkled on the gossamer wings. Adrienne had seen the barrette a hundred times and she suddenly knew with sick certainty who lay pale and stone-still in that lavish bed.

Julianna Brent. The Julianna whom Adrienne had known since childhood. The beautiful Julianna who used to smile and flirt and throw back her head and sing with the pure joy of life. Later, Adrienne recalled the one inane thought that tolled through her mind during the awful moment when she felt as if she were free-falling through space . . .

Julianna Brent would never again sing along with her favorite song, "Sweet Dreams."

2

Brandon started toward Julianna, edging toward a woman he knew well, who always petted him and lovingly rubbed his ears. But Skye grabbed the dog's collar and held him back. "No, Brandon," she said tonelessly. "We mustn't disturb her." She looked up at her mother with huge eyes. "It's Julianna, isn't it?"

Adrienne nodded slowly. "I think . . ." She swallowed. "I'm afraid it is."

"Oh God, Mom. How? Why?" Skye took a deep breath. "You probably should check to see if she's really dead."

"Honey, she must be," Adrienne said softly. To her own ears her voice sounded as if it were coming from far away. "She's not moving and she's so *pale* . . ."

"But you can get real pale from blood loss and shock. I learned that in my first-aid class. She might just be hurt." Skye made a hesitant move toward the bed. "If you don't want to touch her, I'll check and see if her heart's still beating."

"No," Adrienne said quickly. "I'll do it. You stay back and hold on to Brandon."

Adrienne moved in a state of blurry shock to the right side of the bed, the toe of her shoe banging against a heavy glass bottle. A wine bottle. Shards of cream-colored ceramic littered the floor. She realized it was the base of a lamp when she saw a battered shade and an electric cord on the floor.

Adrienne looked down at Julianna's white face, marred only by a small cut and a faint bruise on her forehead. She started to touch Julianna's neck to feel for a pulse. When she gently moved aside the hair, though, she saw a large, ragged hole just beneath her left ear. Blood saturated the back of Julianna's auburn hair and soaked the pillow, already turning to a dull red. Adrienne shuddered and paused. She fought the hot water rolling into her mouth and concentrated.

The hundreds of murder mysteries she'd read in her life, along with having dated the local county sheriff for over a year, had taught her she shouldn't disturb the crime scene in any way, shouldn't touch Julianna more than she had already. But she needed to know for certain if Julianna was dead, whether or not to tell the people manning the 911 emergency number to rush an ambulance to a dying woman and to instruct her about what to do for her friend until they arrived.

She pulled back the bedspread, light cotton blanket, and

satin sheet. Julianna lay naked to the waist beneath the bedding. Adrienne lifted Julianna's left arm. It was cooler than her own but felt soft, indicating the muscles beneath were still pliable. Julianna was not yet in rigor mortis. But when Adrienne pressed her fingers to the woman's slender wrist, she felt nothing. She shifted her fingers again and again, searching for, praying for, a beat, even a flutter of a pulse. Nothing.

"Mom?"

"She's dead," Adrienne said flatly. "I'm almost certain she's dead."

"Oh no," the girl quavered. "How?"

"There's a hole in her neck. She's been stabbed with something. There's lots of blood. You can't see it from where you're standing."

Adrienne took a step away from the bed, still looking down at her friend. Then the shock that had so far kept her calm surged from her body. Her hands turned icy as the floor seemed to shift beneath her. Her legs felt weak.

"Oh God—" Adrienne choked, then began to shake violently. In an instant, Skye stood next to her, enfolding her in her sweater-clad arms, holding her up. At five feet five, Adrienne was the exact height of her daughter, but at the moment, she felt small and shattered beside Skye's youth and strength.

"Mom, I'm so sorry." Skye's voice trembled. "She's been your friend forever."

"Since we were six. She was so beautiful. And fun. Even then."

"I know." Skye patted her back, going on mechanically. "I thought she was terrific. Everybody did."

Adrienne clung to her daughter, eyes tightly shut. Then she opened them and looked around in confusion. "What was Julianna doing here? The hotel's empty. Why would she be sleeping in this place?"

Skye shook her head. "I don't know. Maybe she thought

it was fun, or she wanted to spend the night here because the place is going to be torn down. You know how crazy she could act sometimes. Daredevil crazy. Fun crazy."

"No, that's not what happened. She wasn't alone," Adrienne stated with abrupt certainty. "She didn't come here to spend the night alone. She could be reckless but she wasn't a fool. She would have known a deserted hotel could be a magnet for vandals."

Adrienne's gaze shot frantically around the room. She noted again the wine bottle and the pale yellow wax poured into the pretty faceted glass jars Julianna's mother used for her candle-making business.

"Julianna wouldn't have lain here alone surrounded by candles her mother made and drunk champagne until she passed out for the rest of the night," Adrienne went on, more to herself than Skye. "She would have known someone could break in and hurt her."

"Maybe she felt safe because of the caretaker."

"Claude Duncan?" Adrienne emitted a dry little laugh. "Claude's father was the manager of the Belle and ran this place with military precision for thirty years. Claude is next to useless. Ellen Kirkwood only kept on Claude as caretaker after Mr. Duncan died because, by then, she'd closed the hotel and Claude couldn't do much harm. But Julianna knew Claude and wouldn't count on him for protection. He's usually dead drunk by ten o'clock."

"Well, then . . ." Skye looked at her blankly and lifted her shoulders in bafflement.

"Maybe she was here with a man," Adrienne said with certainty. "A lover."

Skye's eyes widened. "A *lover*?"

"The candles. The wine. And she's naked but wearing some mascara. And expensive perfume. L' Heure Bleue by Guerlain."

"But that's weird, Mom. If she had a lover, why would they need to come here? She lives alone."

"She lives in an apartment building where other people could see a man coming and going."

"So?" Skye paused. "Oh, she was with someone she didn't want anyone to know about." She frowned. "But if Julianna was here with a man, then *he* could have—"

"Killed her."

Skye drew a sharp breath before lowering her gaze to the floor. Adrienne suddenly realized the girl had never looked directly at the body after that first staggering glance. And her own face was almost as pale as Julianna's was. Much of the time, Skye acted and sounded like a young woman. But she's only a girl of fourteen, Adrienne thought, furious with herself for even momentarily forgetting. And I'm not taking care of my child in this crisis, she ranted on inwardly. Instead, *I'm* leaning on *her*.

She put her arm around Skye's shoulders and said in what she hoped was a confidence-inspiring voice, "Come on. We're getting out of here, going to the car, and calling the police. They'll know what to do."

"Should we just leave her?" Tears welled in Skye's eyes. "I mean, it just seems like she shouldn't be all alone and . . . I don't know . . . defenseless."

"Honey, there's nothing we can do for her." And no one can hurt her any more, Adrienne thought, but didn't say so. The pain of those words would be too great. With her thumb, she gently wiped a tear from Skye's cheek. "Put on Brandon's leash."

Skye immediately attached the leash to a docile Brandon's collar. "Mom, he was acting so strange. He led us right to her. Do you think he sensed that she was up here?"

"No. Not on the second floor. Something else set him off." Whoever I saw in the woods, Adrienne thought with a jolt. Whoever gave me that creepy feeling they were slinking around watching. For once her premonition of danger had been right and she felt as if ice water were trickling down her back. She grabbed Skye's hand. "Hurry. We're not staying in this room a moment longer than we have to."

Adrienne's agitation was contagious. Skye's tears vanished, she gripped Brandon's leash, and they made a beeline for the open hotel room door. Then Brandon balked. He sat down and growled. "Oh God, *now* what?" Adrienne gasped, almost breathless with nerves.

Skye leaned forward just enough to peek through the open door into the hall. Her body tensed. She drew back, shut the door quietly, and looked at her mother. Her lips had turned the same porcelain white as her face and she seemed to be all huge, terrified eyes. "Someone's out there." Adrienne stared at her. "Someone's coming down the hall to this room carrying something like an ax."

"An ax?" Adrienne gaped, quelling a wild urge to laugh. "Skye, an *ax*?"

"I *saw* it! At least it was some kind of weapon that looked like an ax." Skye was not prone to exaggeration and she suddenly sounded like a terrified little girl. "Mommy, what should we do?"

Adrienne went blank. She'd known fear before, but it had never been imminent. The threat of injury or death had never borne down on her with the immediacy of this moment. She was totally unprepared and completely panicked.

Brandon looked up at Adrienne with his clear, amber gaze and growled softly again, almost as if he were saying, "Snap out of it!" She drew a deep breath. Then, mercifully, her emotions seemed to shut down and a strange calm came over her. "Lock the door," she said evenly. "We'll push this dresser in front of it. Then we have to get out of the room."

"Get out? How?"

"Jump from the porch."

"Jump?" Skye's voice cracked. "We're on the second floor!"

"We'll make it."

"What about Brandon?"

"There's just dirt and grass beneath us, not concrete. He'll make it, too."

"Mom, he can't. He'll get hurt!"

Adrienne looked fiercely at her daughter. "Skye, Julianna was *murdered*. Don't you understand? She's still warm. Her killer might not have left. That could be him coming down the hall. Now help me push the dresser in front of the door to slow him down and then we're going to jump, dammit, Brandon or no Brandon!"

The girl looked cowed but immediately turned to the long, mahogany dresser behind her. Adrienne went to the other end and they pushed it hard until they'd scooted it directly in front of the door. Before Adrienne had time to draw a deep breath, the doorknob, just visible above the dresser, turned violently.

She and Skye stared at it, frozen. Brandon let out another low, menacing growl before the knob turned again, then rattled as the person on the other side shook it. "Who's in there?" a ravaged voice demanded. "Open the goddamn door or I'll break it down, I swear!"

"Now we jump," Adrienne said, heading for the French doors that opened onto the porch.

Skye hung back. "Mom, I'm afraid."

Something hit the door hard. Perhaps a man's shoulder. The door shuddered. "Next time it's comin' down," he shouted savagely.

"Oh God," Skye whispered.

Adrienne took her hand and pulled her toward the porch. "Don't think. Just jump. It's our only chance."

Brandon lagged behind, clearly confused, growling and barking. The door shuddered in its frame again and Adrienne waited to hear wood splintering as the madman outside attacked the door. The scene was absolutely bizarre, but actually happening. She'd never been more frightened in her life.

Still holding Skye's hand, Adrienne hoisted herself up onto the porch railing and slung her left leg over the side.

"Come on, honey," she urged, pulling on Skye. "It's not that far down."

Skye climbed up but her body was so rigid, Adrienne feared the fall would have an even more serious impact than it would if she were relaxed. But who could be relaxed in this situation?

"Don't look down, sweetie," Adrienne told her. "Just let yourself go."

"Mom, I c-can't," Skye quavered. "I've always been afraid of heights. I just *can't.*"

Brandon jumped up and placed his front paws on the railing. "Look, Brandon's not afraid." Another hard shudder on the door. It sounded as if the lock were giving way and it had come open enough to bang against the dresser. "Skye, you *must*. It's our only chance."

"*No.*" She violently shook her head. "No, no, no—"

More shouting. Then a second voice. Adrienne pulled at a resisting Skye. The pounding on the door stopped. Adrienne heard something like arguing. Then a familiar voice. "Adrienne? Is that you in there?" Adrienne went still, sitting half on, half off the railing, clutching her terrified daughter's sweating hand. "Adrienne, open the door! It's Lucas!"

TWO

I

Adrienne couldn't let herself believe she'd actually heard the voice of Lucas Flynn, the county sheriff and the man she'd been seeing for a year. Then he called to her again. Brandon barked joyfully and ran to the door while Adrienne nearly tumbled off the rail back onto the porch in her surprise and relief.

Skye still clutched her hand. "It's a trick!"

"I know Lucas's voice, Skye. So does Brandon. He's at the door with his tail wagging."

Skye looked at her dog, bouncing in front of the dresser that blocked the door on which Lucas still banged. "Adrienne! I saw your car. I know you're in there!"

"Yes, I'm here. And Skye," Adrienne called breathlessly as she crossed the porch. "Someone's out there with an ax."

"It's me, Miz Adrienne," Claude Duncan, the caretaker, yelled almost pleasantly in a razor voice. "Didn't know you was inside. Thought it was the murderer. Miz Julianna's in there dead, you know. Found her less than a half hour ago."

Adrienne and a slightly less rigid Skye began pushing the dresser aside. "Oh God, Claude, why didn't you say it was you?"

"Didn't want the murderer to know who I was."

This made sense only to Claude. After all, he'd just been trying to break into the room and then the jig would have been up. But such was the way Claude's mind worked.

Adrienne and Skye moved the dresser, opened the door, and finally got a good look at Claude Duncan. He stood wavering, wearing the hood of his windbreaker tied so tightly around his face only his bloodshot eyes and three-day growth of beard showed. He reeked of bourbon. Even at the best of times, Claude was no genius. Now he was clearly badly hungover. And he did hold an ax. Skye had been right about their "assailant's" weapon.

But Adrienne looked at him only a moment. Then her gaze flew to Lucas. A heavily muscled man of six feet two with earnest dark gray eyes and what some people called a lantern jaw, he was an imposing figure in jeans and a T-shirt. In uniform with a gun at his side, he was downright intimidating. His broad forehead was creased with worry, his rough sandy blond hair rumpled as if he'd run his hand through it, as Adrienne had seen him do a hundred times when he was concerned or distressed. He pulled her into his arms.

"Are you all right?"

"Yes, now that you're here. Skye and I were so scared."

He squeezed her, then turned to Skye and hugged her, too. "You're white as a ghost, princess." Then he looked at the bed, his expression appalled. "Good God. It's Julianna Brent."

"I *told* you," Claude announced hotly. "I *told* you she'd done been murdered!"

"I thought we were going to get killed, too," Skye said. "Mom and I were going to jump off the porch to escape Claude and his ax."

Lucas whirled furiously on Claude, who looked startled and backed up a step, blinking rapidly. "What are you doing with that damned thing, anyway?" Lucas shouted.

"Protectin' myself!" Claude blustered. "I don't have a gun like you cops!"

"You don't need a gun!"

"No, sir, I surely don't," Claude returned sarcastically.

"Just 'cause we got us a killer roamin' around don't mean an innocent guy like me needs somethin' for protection. What was I supposed to do if the killer was in here waitin' for me when I came back? Kick him?"

"That's the point. You shouldn't have come *back* to this room alone," Lucas said in loud frustration. "Are you nuts? You should've waited for me."

Claude stuck out his chest. He was only twenty-nine, but he looked much older because of his sagging eyelids and puffy features. His complexion had turned a sickly yellow and glistened with perspiration. "I'm caretaker here. This place is my responsibility."

"Well, no one expects you to give up your life for it, which you could have done." Lucas's tone had softened. After all, anyone acquainted with Claude knew that reasoning with him was a lost cause. He hadn't been the smartest person in town even before the drinking had taken its toll. "Think of Mrs. Kirkwood, Claude. She would be devastated if anything happened to you."

"She *is* a kind lady," Claude said earnestly, looking half sick at the thought of his own murder and half pleased at Ellen Kirkwood's resulting grief if such an appalling thing should happen. Adrienne could tell he'd imbibed even more than usual, probably at the thought that the Belle would soon be a memory—as would his job, such as it was.

She looked at Lucas. "How did you know we were here?"

"You must have seen the big car wreck when you came up to the Belle. I was there. The commotion woke up Claude—"

"Like to scared me to death," Claude broke in excitedly. "I was outta my cottage lickety-split. Then I saw a side door open on the Belle. I came in to see what was goin' on. I found—" He nodded at the bed where Julianna lay. "Couldn't believe it! But I didn't do nothin' to her. I mean, I didn't move her or nothin'. I just ran right down to where the wreck was. Knew there'd be cops. I started yellin'. They told me to go away. Then Sheriff Flynn came. I told him what was up here. Then I raced right back up to guard the scene. Like on TV. I thought you were the killer come back, Miz Adrienne. To dispose of the body, you know. I didn't mean to scare you."

But Claude no longer looked defensive or even abashed by his ludicrous behavior. He'd probably be bragging about his quick-wittedness and heroism for months to come in every dive bar in town.

Lucas shot a professional look at the bed, although Adrienne knew him well enough to see pity and repulsion in his eyes. "Claude says she's dead."

"I'm almost certain she is," Adrienne said tentatively. "I know I shouldn't have, but I touched her. Just her neck and her wrist. There's no pulse. She's still warm. Her neck . . ."

"Someone slashed her throat?" Lucas asked in a carefully controlled voice.

"No. Her neck isn't slashed. There's just a hole. Like someone jabbed her with something. An ice pick, maybe. There's a lot of blood." Adrienne's own throat tightened. She tried to swallow and couldn't. Her voice wavered. "I didn't touch the . . . wound."

"All right, everyone out of here," Lucas abruptly ordered in a commanding voice. "Go outside, but don't leave the grounds. I'll have questions after I've gotten some EMS people and the coroner up here." He looked at Adrienne. "I'm sorry, but you and Skye might have to stay a while. Got two people dead in that car wreck, so everything will be slowed down."

"It's okay." She tried to manage an air of bravado. "We have a thermos of coffee." She began to tremble again. "We'll be fine."

"I'll take care of 'em," Claude stated.

Lucas looked grimly at the man exhaling liquor fumes. "You just go back to your cottage, stop drinking bourbon, have at least two mugs of strong coffee, and for God's sake, quit swinging around that damned ax! You look like a lunatic in a horror movie."

"I wasn't *swingin'* it," Claude returned petulantly.

"You were when I was coming up the hall. Now get outside and put down the damned thing before you hurt somebody."

"Well, hell," Claude muttered. "I was just protectin' myself, like I said. You cops wanna have all the weapons and leave us civilians with just our bare hands for defense. You see where that got Miss Julianna."

"Shut up, Claude," Lucas said mildly, almost automatically. Adrienne smiled at Lucas weakly in a failed attempt to look brave, took Skye's hand, and led her daughter from the room. Brandon, for once, followed meekly behind as if he were always the obedient and well-trained dog. Claude brought up the rear, muttering heatedly about his constitutional right to bear arms.

Outside, Adrienne had to use every bit of her willpower to keep from breaking into a run. All she could think of was getting herself and Skye away from the new nightmare world of la Belle Rivière where beautiful Julianna Brent lay dead with a gaping hole in her neck, and a jumpy-eyed Claude Duncan followed them still wielding his ax.

2

On television, the lead cop viewed the body of at least one innocent victim each week. He looked at it coolly and often made a clever remark to his partner before beginning the dispassionate routine of his investigation. But it had been a long time since Sheriff Lucas Flynn had seen a body, and as he looked down at the pale, beautiful corpse of Julianna Brent, he felt anything except dispassionate and clever.

Everyone had cleared the room fifteen minutes earlier. He'd made the necessary calls on his cell phone, then took a few minutes to clear his head from dealing with the carnage down on the narrow road where a pickup truck had managed to wipe out a small car, and brace himself to deal with more carnage in this elegant hotel room.

He turned off the small chandelier and stood stock-still in the room, barely breathing, absorbing the ambience. The morning fog had burned away and bright sunlight pressed against the windows, but it was blocked by drawn brocade draperies. The only light came from candles that had burned low. The room was filled with the scent of jasmine, now too strong to be as pleasant as it would have been a couple of hours ago. One candle flame flickered against a glass figurine of a girl in a ruffled gown standing on the bedside table next to Julianna. The sparkle of the opalescent glass finish made the figurine seem to waver, as if alive.

Lucas moved closer to the bed and sadly looked down at Julianna. Her perfect face looked unearthly, almost angelic, and the candlelight brought out the sheen of her copper-gold hair spread over her creamy shoulders. He knew that beneath the closed lids, the eyes were the color of sherry, large and long-lashed. She'd fastened those incredible eyes on him just last week as she leaned across his desk and told him she thought she was being followed, watched, stalked. She'd said she was in fear for her life. And he had done nothing.

Shame washed over him as he stood looking down on that lovely face still holding on to a vague flush of life. Three summers ago, before he was elected sheriff, he'd been walking down Riverfront Street with an annoying guy who'd decided they were best friends and tagged after Lucas whenever he saw him. While the guy jabbered, Lucas's attention had been drawn across the street to a tall, willowy woman with a cascade of copper curls and a pair of skintight jeans. "Julianna Brent's back in town, actin' like she's the queen of the world," the guy had said in a snide voice. "Always did think she was better than everybody else, but she fell on her pretty face. Serves her right."

Lucas, having lived in Point Pleasant only four years at

the time and still considered a newcomer, was forgiven for
not knowing Julianna's story. The guy had launched into the
saga with nasty vigor. "Her daddy run off and left her and
her younger sister, Gail, when they was little. The mother,
Lottie, went crazy. Or crazier than she already was. She had
some bad experience up to the Belle that people say gave her
mind a turn, but I couldn't get the straight of it. Anyway, she
never mistreated the girls or nothing, but she made a fool of
herself on a regular basis. Came to town near naked one
time. Said it was too hot for clothes.

"Julianna never seemed one bit embarrassed about the
runaway daddy, the crazy mama, or the tumbledown shack
she called home," the guy had gone on with gusto. "Carried
herself like a queen and people let her get away with it because she was so beautiful. When she was eighteen, she ran
off to New York and damned if she didn't make it as a model
like she always said she would. She was hot stuff for a while,
so my wife tells me. I don't keep up with the fashion world
myself." At that he'd guffawed and jabbed an elbow in Lucas's ribs.

"So she's just back here visiting?" Lucas had asked.

"Hell, no. She got messed up on drugs. My wife says all
them supermodels do." Lucas pictured the guy's wife—a
brawny, glowering woman who worked at the local Farm
and Feed Outlet—and doubted that she was an expert on the
inner life of supermodels. "Julianna was using cocaine and
maybe heroin. The wife says they snort the heroin so they
won't have track marks. So Julianna got all screwed up,
freaked out on one of them fashion shootouts, then couldn't
get work 'cause she was unreliable. She went into rehab,
then came back here to *rest*. That's what she said. *Rest*. So
while she was here, she met this artist guy, Miles Shaw.
Long hair, weird clothes, highfalutin' ideas about art. You
know the type. Doesn't really work—just paints pictures. He
used to date that Kirkwood woman that owns The Iron Gate.
I always thought she could do a lot better. Anyway, after they

broke up, Julianna married Shaw and stayed here in Point Pleasant. But she's still wild. I hear stories."

"What kind of stories?" Lucas asked.

"Just *stories*," the guy said darkly, clearly not knowing anything concrete or he would have gone into every detail. "The other sister, Gail, seems fairly normal if not too friendly. She's a waitress at Kit Kirkwood's restaurant and dates that cop Sonny Keller. A deputy. Pretty steady guy. But Julianna's another breed. The wife says she makes up stuff so she'll seem more interesting. I think she'll end up just like her mama."

Lucas hadn't actually met Julianna until he'd started dating Adrienne. The few times they'd run into each other at Adrienne's home, Julianna had been charming, extroverted, a bit flirtatious, and in the process of divorcing Miles Shaw, who was not taking the breakup gracefully. If he hadn't fought Julianna so hard, Adrienne had told Lucas, they would have been divorced a year ago because Julianna had become bored with marriage to a talented man who would rather paint than spend a night on the town, and who wanted to keep her all to himself. Possessive, people said about Shaw. Lucas had thought that with a wife like Julianna, who wouldn't have been?

There had been public trouble between them only once, though. One Saturday night, Julianna had summoned the police when a drunken Miles had hammered and shouted and cried at her apartment door. The next day, when Lucas talked to him, he'd acted genuinely humiliated and contrite. His record showed no similar previous behavior. Lucas had been glad when Julianna didn't pursue further legal measures against her husband because he was certain she'd somehow provoked Shaw's uncharacteristic outburst. A long time ago, Lucas had been deeply in love and flatly rejected. He knew how Shaw must have been feeling.

"How did she die?"

The female voice cracked like a whip behind Lucas. He

turned to see Ellen Kirkwood standing in the doorway, her face rigid, her gaze fierce. Behind her hovered her husband, usually the picture of handsome confidence but now looking almost meek with slightly hunched shoulders and eyes fixed on a point beyond Lucas's shoulder.

"Julianna Brent was murdered, Mrs. Kirkwood," Lucas said quietly.

"I *know* that. Claude called me."

"He shouldn't have."

"Well, he did. *How* was she murdered?"

"We're not sure yet." The woman started forward, making for the body, but Lucas held up his hand. "Please don't come into the room. We have evidence to collect."

"It's *my* hotel," Ellen Kirkwood said challengingly. "I should think I have access to my own hotel."

Lucas kept his face bland although her tone rankled. "I'm sorry, Mrs. Kirkwood, but this is a crime scene. I can't let you in here even if this *is* your hotel."

"Ellen, *please*." Gavin's usually energetic voice sounded thin and fatigued. Lucas had a feeling he'd been arguing with Ellen all the way to the hotel. Damn Claude for calling her, he thought. And damn Gavin Kirkwood for not keeping his wife away from the hotel. "We have to let the sheriff do his job," Gavin continued, stroking his wife's thin arm. "He has to find out who murdered this woman."

"You keep calling her *'this woman.'* You know very well who she was." Gavin flushed. Mrs. Kirkwood's fine-boned, thin-skinned face seemed turned to stone, and her wintery gray eyes were hard as flint. "Do not talk to me like I'm a child, Gavin. I simply want some answers. I have that right."

Lucas took a deep breath. "You certainly do, ma'am, but as of now I don't have any to give you. I can't even tell you how she was murdered except that there's a deep puncture wound in her neck." Gavin closed his eyes as if he were queasy. "We haven't found a murder weapon."

"Do you know who she was here with?" Ellen demanded.

"Who she was, shall I say, *sleeping with* in my hotel?"

"We don't know that she was here with anyone."

"I should think that would be obvious. Don't you, Gavin?"

Gavin Kirkwood jerked slightly, looking trapped. "How should I know, Ellen? Dear, please let me take you home. We shouldn't be here."

"He's right, ma'am," Lucas said firmly, wanting to shake Gavin. The man, as always, looked debonair and acted completely helpless. "There is nothing you can do, and I don't have any information to give you, yet."

"Ellen, please calm down," Gavin pleaded. His handsome face had a sickly gray pallor beneath the perpetual tan. "You have to remember your heart. You're not supposed to get upset."

Ellen waved her hand impatiently. "I know I'm not *supposed* to get upset. I don't need you to tell me that constantly. But I can't help it. My God, Gavin, there's been a murder!"

Lucas, reminded of the woman's ill health, pushed down his anger at her haughty tone and tried to soothe her. "We'll be doing the best we can, ma'am," he said kindly. "We'll find out who killed her and why. We just need a little time."

"Time." Suddenly, energy seemed to drain out of the woman. Her posture slackened, making her look at least two inches shorter and frail. The skin loosened around the aristocratic bones of her face, and her eyes grew vague, almost dreamy, as she looked around the room. "Time won't help," she went on in a voice like a frightened, haunted child's. "Have you forgotten where you are? La Belle Rivière. It's cursed, this place. Julianna's mother knows it. Lottie. We were childhood friends, did you know that, Sheriff? And this place nearly killed her. Now it's killed her daughter."

"This place is over a hundred years old," Gavin said tentatively. "Naturally people have died here. It doesn't mean the hotel is haunted, Ellen."

Ellen dismissed his words with a wave of her thin hand. "I know it's not unusual that people have died in a place this old. But there have been too many deaths." She fastened her unnaturally pale eyes on Lucas and he felt as if someone were closing a cold hand around his heart. "You see, la Belle Rivière is one of those cursed places on earth where death has found a haven. I wanted to destroy it before it could kill again, but I was too late." She glanced at Julianna's chilling body and gave another long sigh. "And I'll probably always be too late, because la Belle will probably destroy me before I can destroy it."

3

Almost two hours had passed before Adrienne and Skye finished the waiting, the questioning, and arrived back at their home on Hawthorne Way. When Adrienne pulled into the driveway, the slate-blue and stone house looked strange to her, like some calm haven she had left days or even weeks ago. She was surprised when they walked inside and she could still detect the faint scent of the rich coffee Skye had brewed that morning.

The house had been designed by an architect and built for her parents in the sixties. It was one story and had been sleek, even glamorously modern. Then her parents had built an addition in the seventies, another in the eighties, and the last in the early nineties. The additions had been the inspiration of her father, who had no architectural talent but a determination that the additions be built to his capricious specifications.

The resulting house now conformed to no particular style. It jutted at various odd angles, each addition looking like a branch growing haphazardly from the trunk of a tree. Her mother had made attempts to soften the lines with carefully placed shrubbery and lush rhododendron bushes, but the greenery could only do so much in the way of improvement. Most of her neighbors on Hawthorne Way were glad that at least the unfortunate house stood on over an acre of ground, far enough away from their own carefully designed upscale homes so as not to be too great a residential blemish.

When they died within months of each other four years ago, Adrienne's parents had left the house to her and her sister, Victoria. Vicky lived in an elegant Colonial three miles away, but neither she nor Adrienne had wanted to sell, so Adrienne and Skye had moved from their cramped, square little cottage into the whimsical expanse of the family home and loved every misshapen line of it.

Inside, Adrienne locked the front door, which normally she never did when she was home during the day. She felt shaky, weak, nervous, and slightly disoriented, as if she'd been up for twenty-four hours straight and run a marathon as well. She couldn't ever remember feeling as physically drained as she did at this moment.

Skye looked at her helplessly. "All I want to do is lie down on the couch, but I feel like we should be doing something important."

"Such as?" Adrienne asked tiredly.

"Calling Julianna's mother?"

"The police will inform Lottie Brent. I couldn't bear to tell her anyway," Adrienne said. "She adored Julianna."

"What about Julianna's sister?"

"I think the police or Lottie should tell Gail. She's never liked me," Adrienne said. "She thought I was jealous of Julianna. I believe hearing the news from me would be even worse for her. She's so different from Julianna."

"But she likes Kit." Skye's eyes widened. "Mom, when we saw Mr. and Mrs. Kirkwood at the Belle this morning, Mrs. Kirkwood said she hadn't talked to Kit. Maybe Kit still doesn't know what happened to Julianna and it would be awful if she heard from someone else."

Adrienne stood quietly for a moment, thinking. Or rather,

dreading. Skye was right. She should be the one to tell Kit of their friend's death. But it wasn't just a death, which would be bad enough. It was a murder. How could she break the news to Kit without upsetting her too much? There was no way. Besides, Kit had always been the strongest of the three of them. She could probably handle the tragedy better than Adrienne was doing.

Adrienne glanced at her watch. It was just after eleven. Kit would be at her restaurant getting ready for the lunch crowd. With almost dragging steps, she went to the phone and dialed the number of the restaurant. After two rings, a cheerful, young female voice said, "The Iron Gate. May I help you?"

"I'd like to speak with Ms. Kirkwood."

"I'm sorry but she's not in. May I take your name and have her call you back?"

Adrienne knew Kit often used this excuse when she was too busy to come to the phone. "My name is Adrienne Reynolds. I'm a very close friend of Kit's and there's something important I need to tell her. Even if she's busy, please ask her to come to the phone."

"Ms. Reynolds, she's *really* not here. I've worked here a year and I've never known her not to be in at this hour, but she called in and said she had something to do and she couldn't come in until this afternoon." The girl's tone was sincere. "I'm sorry. I can leave a message for her."

"That's all right. I'll try her cell phone. Thank you . . ."

"I'm Polly. You're welcome. And good luck."

Adrienne tried Kit's home number and connected only with the answering machine. She left a message asking Kit to call her back. She then tried Kit's cell phone with no luck.

"She's certainly incommunicado," Adrienne said, looking at Skye. "That's not like her."

"Maybe she just decided to blow off the day—go shopping or something without being bothered."

"Go shopping on a day when the restaurant is open?

I don't think so. She believes the place will fall apart if she's not there supervising everything."

"I guess she doesn't feel that way today. You don't think she's sick, do you?"

"She'd be home." Adrienne thought. "Ellen has probably called her by now and Kit is with her mother but not answering her cell phone."

Skye looked at her gloomily. "This morning Mrs. Kirkwood looked so awful and she barely talked to us. What happened today sure isn't going to convince her not to tear down the Belle."

"It's like one final sign that the place needs to be destroyed if you believe in portents and omens and things like that."

"Mrs. Kirkwood does."

"With a vengeance. And frankly, after today, I know I'd never be able to enjoy the place again."

In fact, Adrienne had a slightly ill, repulsed feeling, as if she'd participated in something foul and shameful. Her fingers still tingled with the sensation of touching Julianna's cooling skin and of looking into that beautiful face stilled by death.

But she had to think of Skye. She could not let herself fall apart and leave Skye to process the shock of the morning all alone.

Adrienne forced a smile. "There's no way we're going to be able to turn this into a nice afternoon, but in spite of everything, I'm hungry. How would you like some chicken salad sandwiches on the terrace?"

Skye looked relieved, as if she'd been afraid her mother was simply going to collapse, and she managed an imitation of her usual exuberant tone. "I would *love* one."

"You know, Vicky and I ate chicken salad sandwiches all the time when we were young," Adrienne said as Skye followed her into the periwinkle-blue and yellow kitchen with a giant red begonia hanging above a window. "Mom said we were addicted to them."

"At her parties, Aunt Vicky serves fancy food that doesn't nearly fill me up."

"You've become a regular at the parties she gives now that Philip has decided to run for governor."

"Aunt Vicky gets pretty mad that you don't come to them."

"I'm a disaster at political social functions. I have a tendency to say exactly what I think to the wrong people. I don't know about Vicky, but I'm sure Philip is relieved that I don't come."

"He lets a kid like me come, but I think that's because Rachel insists. She thinks the parties are *really* boring. Her boyfriend Bruce comes, but he talks to everyone just like Uncle Philip does. She says I keep her company. We giggle about everybody."

"How polite of you."

"Well, not to their faces, Mom!"

"I didn't think so, or you wouldn't be invited so often. Philip wouldn't let anyone mess up his events, no matter what Rachel wants."

"Rachel says what Uncle Philip really wants is to be president of the United States someday."

"He always has. But I don't think Vicky especially wants to be first lady. When they got married, she thought she'd enjoy the campaign life. I believe she's changed her mind, though. It's a much bigger strain than she thought it would be."

Their usual easy chattiness soon died, however. Time once again seemed suspended for her as she and Skye sat under the big oak tree overhanging the flagstone terrace. Skye watched a mother robin bringing worms to her squawking babies in a high nest. "I hope none of them fall on the terrace stones when they start trying to fly."

"That hardly ever happens."

"It did two years ago," Skye pointed out. "Remember those awful noises the mother bird made when she saw her baby dead? She sounded like she was crying. Wailing." Skye shivered slightly. "I'm going to put my inflatable pool float on the stones right under the nest. That way if any of the babies fall, they won't get hurt."

"That's a good idea," Adrienne said, noting her daughter's preoccupation with death. First she'd brought up the death of Ellen Kirkwood's adopted son Jamie last summer, now the baby robin. But who could blame her? No fourteen-year-old should see the horror Skye had seen this morning.

Adrienne had just forced down another bite of sandwich she didn't want when a girl's cheerful "Hi, you two!" startled her into dropping her food.

"Rachel!" she exclaimed in surprise and pleasure. She hadn't seen her niece for a couple of weeks and didn't hear her light footsteps as she approached them on the terrace. "Shouldn't you be slaving away at the *Point Pleasant Register*?"

"They have this silly idea they can put out the evening edition without me." Rachel tweaked Skye's hair and grinned at her. "Did you add blond highlights?"

"No, the sun did."

"They look fabulous. I wish my hair was as light as yours."

"It's almost the same color," Skye said. "Just a couple of shades darker."

At twenty, Rachel Hamilton was tall and slender with long ash-blond hair, large dark blue eyes with sweeping black lashes, flawless skin, a beautiful smile, and cheekbones a model would envy. In fact, she'd been offered modeling jobs, but she'd always declined. She was far more interested in sports—particularly tennis, at which she excelled—and college, where she was a journalism major between her junior and senior years. This summer she had an internship at the *Point Pleasant Register*.

Skye idolized her elder cousin. Rachel was a heady mixture of beauty, brilliance, athletic prowess, and sophistication. Although Vicky always said Rachel's "terrible twos" had lasted for four years until school captured her interest and abruptly stopped a long bout of sulking and tantrums, Adrienne never remembered Rachel going through an awkward stage physically or socially. Ever since she was six, she'd been lovely and poised, the perfect daughter for Adrienne's politician brother-in-law, Philip Hamilton. But perhaps Rachel's greatest charm was the fact that she seemed unaware of how special and accomplished she was. Her manner was casual and unassuming, completely without pretense.

"How about a sandwich? I made too many." Adrienne held out the plate and Rachel took one. "So, how is my sister? I haven't talked to her for a few days."

Rachel shrugged. "Mom's all caught up in Dad's campaigning. Things are really hectic. The house is like Mission Control at Cape Canaveral." Skye giggled and Rachel grinned at her. "Of course, the election is over a year away. I can't imagine what home life will be like this time next summer. Thank goodness I'll be gone."

"But after your college graduation you'll be free to go on the campaign trail with your mom and dad," Skye said.

"I guess I could." Rachel looked into the distance, prankishness in her eyes. "Or I might run off to Cannes or Venice with some completely unsuitable guy. A devilishly handsome gigolo with no regard for the flag, apple pie, or the American way. He'll just want to sunbathe and go yachting and take me to elegant gambling casinos every night and drive my parents totally crazy!"

"Really?" Skye asked in wonder.

"No, not really." Adrienne smiled. "Rachel would never do anything to displease her father, and believe me, *that* would displease him!"

"An understatement if ever there was one," Rachel agreed. "But it'd be fun to do something shocking sometime."

"Wait until after Philip wins the election to do something shocking," Adrienne advised. "If you do something to screw up the campaign, you might find yourself written out of the will. Besides, I think your father has his heart set on you marrying Bruce Allard."

"Oh, Bruce," Rachel said without enthusiasm. "Four years older than I am and son of one of the town's *finest* families. The perfect catch."

"Well, he *is* cute," Skye offered.

"But boring," Rachel stated.

Adrienne peered over the rim of her coffee cup. "Just because he doesn't dream of casino-hopping doesn't mean he's a bore. He works at the newspaper, the same as you. You must have things in common."

"Bruce's father *owns* the newspaper. He's just marking time there because his father wants him to have a taste of 'the real world' before he takes over someday. Not that he has the slightest interest in newspapers. He talks about the stock market all the time. *All the time.* He thinks art is a waste of time, Aunt Adrienne. He can't dance. And he wants six kids." Rachel turned horrified eyes to Skye. "*Six kids!* What about my waistline? My *thighs*? I'd always be in maternity clothes and have a permanent spot of baby spit-up on my shoulder." She clapped a hand to her heart and looked upward. "Oh, heaven help me, marriage to Bruce is just too unbearable to even contemplate!"

Skye burst into laughter, as Rachel buried her head in her arms in mock despair. Adrienne knew Skye felt included and like a grown-up when Rachel discussed boyfriends with her. And although Rachel had made fun of what seemed to be a very nice and proper young man, Adrienne didn't feel guilty for laughing along if Rachel could get even a smile out of Skye on such a sad day.

After the excitement of the morning, Brandon had been nearly comatose on his giant plaid dog cushion in front of the living room fireplace. In the winter, he lay for hours staring steadily at the flames and sparks behind the screen. In the summer, he lay for hours staring into the empty fireplace. Skye insisted that at these times he was having deep thoughts. Adrienne thought he was just acting weird to get attention. However, he was extremely sociable and had roused himself at the sound of a guest's voice that had floated into the house through the open terrace door. He lumbered outside, already growing stiff from his morning of unaccustomed rowdiness, sat down beside Rachel, and offered her his paw.

"How do you do, sir?" Rachel gravely shook his paw. "You look especially spiffy with that red bandana around your neck."

"He was bathed and groomed at Happy Tracks yesterday," Skye said, smiling. "The groomer always ties on a bandana, but it got a tear in it this morning when he was running through the woods at the Belle."

Adrienne looked at Rachel. She rubbed the dime-sized strawberry birthmark beside her right earlobe, a mark she usually hid with concealer. She only touched the mark when she was nervous, but her expression showed no surprise, and Adrienne suddenly understood the reason for her niece's midday visit. The *Point Pleasant Register* editor, Drew Delaney, must have found out that she and Skye had been the ones who discovered Julianna's body and sent her over.

"Rachel, let me guess," she said casually. "Mr. Delaney is at la Belle Rivière as we speak."

Rachel nodded reluctantly, then added with some aplomb, "He *is* the newspaper editor. Where would you expect him to be when there's been a murder?"

"Exactly where he is. But he told you to come here and find out what you could from Skye and me, didn't he?"

"Yes." She colored slightly, then gave her aunt a sincerely regretful look. "I wish I could tell you that I argued with him about trying to get information from you, but I didn't. The murder of Julianna Brent is the biggest thing to happen in Point Pleasant all year. I'm ashamed to admit this to you because I liked Julianna although I hardly knew her, but I'd like to get a scoop on this. Bylines on stories about an event this sensational could get me a great job at an important newspaper next year."

Adrienne didn't approve of the journalistic imperative to dig for a story no matter who had to be pumped for information, but she admired Rachel's forthrightness. "Did the sheriff tell Delaney about Skye and me being there?" she asked.

Rachel shook her head. "It was that caretaker. Somebody Duncan. He called the newspaper this morning."

While they were being questioned, Claude Duncan had retreated to his cottage on the grounds. Adrienne knew he'd called Ellen Kirkwood, who'd showed up shortly afterward with her husband in tow. The busy-bee Claude had also called Drew Delaney, she thought in annoyance.

"Duncan said you and Skye were there, but he wanted to make it clear that *he'd* found the body and that you and Skye just got in his way while he was trying to protect the crime scene. He wanted to come in for an interview and photos." Rachel smiled. "Drew said the next murder might be Sheriff Flynn killing Claude Duncan."

"Dealing with Claude will take every ounce of control Lucas has, but I have faith in him," Adrienne said. "He knows Claude isn't the sharpest knife in the drawer. Lucas was remarkably patient with him this morning even though Claude was a handful."

"He sounds crazy." Rachel paused, her expression changing to one of sympathy. "I know Julianna had been your friend for a long time, Aunt Adrienne, and Skye liked her so much. Finding her body must have been awful for you two."

"It was." Skye's voice had become small and frightened. "She was lying on the bed looking so beautiful and peaceful." A shallow wrinkle appeared between Rachel's eyebrows as she clearly concentrated on every detail of the scene. "The sheet was pulled up to her shoulders. She could have just been sleeping. But Mom said there was a big hole in her neck—" Skye drew a deep breath and turned pale.

"That's enough," Adrienne said firmly. "I'm sorry, Rachel. I know you're trying to do your job, but we're in no shape to talk about this. I don't think Sheriff Flynn would even want us to be discussing it with the press right now."

"He'll have to talk about it sometime."

"Yes, but not right now. The murder only happened a few hours ago, Rachel. Give the police time to sort out what's happened."

"I'd rather get the story before they've had time to put their own spin on it."

Adrienne looked at her niece disapprovingly. "Rachel, you can't believe Lucas Flynn would manipulate evidence in a murder case!"

"Well, maybe not Flynn." Rachel sighed. "Look, Aunt Adrienne, I didn't mean to step on any toes where the police are concerned. I know you have a connection with them—"

"This has nothing to do with Lucas."

"Okay." Rachel held up her hand for truce. "I just want to get the story accurately and as quickly as I can. I feel bad for Julianna, but I have to look at this thing from the standpoint of my career. I'm sorry if I offended you by not being as softhearted as you'd like me to be, but in this situation, I have to be a professional first."

"I understand, Rachel," Adrienne said mildly. "But being a compassionate human should run neck and neck with being a professional. I hope you never forget that."

Skye, who had been looking uncomfortable, as if she expected her mother and her cousin to get into an argument, suddenly said, "Didn't Aunt Vicky get married at the Belle?"

"In a church, but her wedding reception was in the grand ballroom," Adrienne corrected. She smiled at the memory. "Mom had taken me downtown to Miss Addie to get my hair trimmed. Judging by the results, Miss Addie had been sipping whiskey in the back room for her nerves. She just ruined my hair. I looked like a complete dork and I was *so* jealous of Vicky that afternoon! But I was proud, too," Adrienne went on. "Vicky and Philip looked like movie stars. There was a professional photographer, of course, and thank goodness for him because Dad took about a hundred photos and every one of them was either blurry or cut off the top of people's heads. I'll get out the album and show them to you later, Skye. The professional ones, I mean. The photographer really did justice to Vicky and Philip, *and* to the Belle. The ballroom looked like it belonged in a palace. There was even a fountain of champagne."

Skye looked starry-eyed. "Nothing that fabulous will ever happen to me."

"Of course it will," Rachel said, smiling and looking slightly starry-eyed herself. "From what Mom says, it really was a magic day."

"Even though a lot of people believe something is wrong with that place because there's just one disaster after another at the Belle?"

"I don't believe in curses or anything occult," Rachel stated. "The deaths and accidents at la Belle have just been the result of coincidence." She took another sip of lemonade and announced, "I'm going out there as soon as I leave here."

"I don't think that's such a good idea," Adrienne said.

"Why not?"

"Because of the violence. Someone was murdered there, Rachel. You shouldn't be around that kind of scene."

Rachel looked at her defiantly. "Aunt Adrienne, I'm a reporter. It's my job to be around that kind of scene. Good heavens, what do you expect me to do when I have a full-time job and my editor orders me to cover a homicide story? Shudder and say I won't work on any stories that are upsetting?"

"No. But you're not a full-time reporter yet. And this was the murder of someone you knew."

"Barely. I wasn't friends with Julianna like Skye. And I'm less than a year away from being a full-time reporter. And I'm going to be a *good* one. A *great* one."

"She's going to win the Pulitzer prize," Skye informed her mother with pride. "That's the best thing a reporter can win."

"Well, that's wonderful, Rachel, but you're only twenty. You don't have a lot of experience and for now—"

A cell phone rang, cutting off Adrienne. "My phone," Rachel said. "They probably need me at the newspaper."

"Rachel Hamilton." Her face lit up as she said, "Hi, Drew! What's up?" Within a few seconds, her smile faded. "But I was planning to go out to the Belle. I'm at Aunt Adrienne's and I was leaving in a few minutes." Another short silence. "Plans for the county fair? Who cares about that?" Silence. "Well, I know *some* people care about it, but there's been a *murder*. And you want Bruce to cover it? I know he has more experience than me, but his writing isn't as good as mine." Skye gave her mother a portentous look as Rachel's face set in hard lines. "No, I'm not countermanding your orders. I'm just, well, giving you my point of view." Silence. "Okay. I'll meet with the chairman of the fair planning committee in twenty minutes. But I still think—"

She held out the phone and stared at it. Obviously, Drew Delaney had hung up on her. Her face grew red, her eyes angry. "Damn," she muttered. "Bruce. He wants *Bruce* to check out la Belle this afternoon. Bruce can't write his way out of a paper bag. I can't believe Drew won't let *me* cover this story!"

"Is Drew the gorgeous guy you said looks like George Clooney?" Skye asked innocently. Rachel flushed and gave her a look that clearly told her to shut her mouth. "Gosh, I'm sorry you can't do the story, Rachel," Skye said lamely, to cover her gaffe.

"It's not your fault." Rachel jammed her cell phone into her purse. "I just thought Drew had more faith in me."

"Bruce is a full-time reporter," Adrienne said, searching for a way to appease the furious girl. "You're an intern who will be leaving in a couple of months. Drew is probably thinking of whom he has to work with for the next few years. He'd rather ruffle your feathers than Bruce's."

"Or else he's playing up to Bruce because his father *owns* the paper. I don't like to think Drew would let that influence him, but maybe so," Rachel said, her spirit suddenly gone flat. "According to Mom, you know Drew a lot better than I do."

Adrienne felt color rise to her cheeks. How long ago it seemed she'd had a teenage romance with Drew. How she'd daydreamed about him, pined for him with all her teenage devotion, spent days sunk in angst because he didn't seem to know she was alive. Then suddenly, when she was a junior and he was a senior in high school, he'd begun dating her. She'd thought she was madly in love with him. No, she'd *known* she was madly in love with him, known it without an ounce of adolescent delusion. They'd even talked of marriage someday soon.

Right after he'd graduated from high school, he'd left for college in New York City, bidding her a tempestuous farewell. She'd been heartsick and lived for his letters and phone calls. But the calls dwindled from twice to once a week, then stopped altogether. Impersonal postcards replaced the long letters. Through friends Adrienne learned he spent Christmas in New York and by the next summer, he'd charmed his way into the inner circle of an affluent family and married the lovely daughter. Adrienne had been crushed. Furious. Devastated. And she was embarrassed to think that even now, the memory of Drew's desertion brought a sharp prick of pain, even though another disastrous marriage to a minor Broadway starlet had followed what turned out to be his first failed attempt at nuptial bliss. After the last, he'd returned home just eighteen months ago to a job as editor of the *Point Pleasant Register*.

Adrienne knew Vicky had probably told Rachel old stories about Drew in order to underscore his feckless nature and tendency to use his considerable charm to flatter and get what he wanted from people. She doubted if Vicky's point had been made, though. Lately, Adrienne had wondered if

Rachel were developing a crush on Drew. And the girl had certainly come to think she was an indispensable asset to the newspaper *and* to Drew Delaney. Adrienne doubted that anything Vicky could say would change Rachel's mind in the slightest.

"Well, I have to get on to this earth-shattering story about the county fair," Rachel suddenly announced, standing up. "Thanks for lunch."

"It wasn't much and I'm sorry it had to spring from such awful circumstances," Adrienne said.

Surprisingly, Rachel cocked her head, the anger vanishing from her gaze. "Well, at least Kit Kirkwood won't be losing her inheritance in the next few weeks. The cops certainly won't be quick to allow the destruction of the site where a world-famous model was murdered, and Ellen Kirkwood isn't in the best of health." She lifted her shoulders. "Who knows? Kit may end up with la Belle after all."

THREE

I

When Rachel left, Skye loaded the dirty dishes in the dishwasher and wiped clean the kitchen counters without being asked to, a sure sign that she was still in shock. Afterward, Adrienne announced she needed to lie down for a while, and Skye curled up beside her on the bed as she hadn't done for years. Brandon abandoned his plush cushion in the living room, stretched out on the floor beside them, and in two minutes began snoring loudly.

Meanwhile, Skye stared at the ceiling, clearly suffering the same nervous weariness as Adrienne, but unable to sleep. "Do you think Rachel loves Drew Delaney?" she asked after a few minutes.

"I hope not. He's old enough to be her father."

"You used to date him. Rachel told me."

"I dated him about a century ago."

"And then you met Daddy."

"I already knew Daddy. I just didn't know how much I liked him until he finally asked me out. We got married a year later."

"So you *really* liked him!"

"Yes. I really *loved* him. I always will."

"Me, too." Skye reached out and touched a strand of Adrienne's hair, twisting it gently around her finger like she'd done since she was a toddler. "Mom, I think there's trouble between Aunt Vicky and Rachel. They fight a lot."

Adrienne sighed. She was desperate for a nap, a brief escape from the horror of the morning, but now was not the time to push away her daughter. "I think Vicky is having trouble with Rachel becoming an adult. She's twenty. In less than a year she'll be a college graduate. And she's so independent, so self-sufficient. I think Vicky is upset about losing her little girl. She tries to cling to her, and the harder she clings, the harder Rachel tries to pull away. So they end up arguing."

"Oh. I guess that makes sense. But Mom?"

"Yes?"

"I'll never want to pull away from you. I'll always want to be just as close as we are right now."

Adrienne smiled. "I wish that were true, but a day will come when you'll find hanging out with me to be a colossal drag. But it's natural, honey. It's just part of growing up. I promise to handle it a little better than Vicky is doing." She paused. "At least, I'll try."

"I don't think I'll ever want to stop hanging out with you." Skye yawned hugely. "I'm having a good time talking to you, but I'm so sleepy I can't keep my eyes open. Can we take a nap together?"

Adrienne smiled. "It would be my pleasure, sweetie."

2

Adrienne awakened with a heavy, dazed feeling, as if she'd taken a sleeping pill. She glanced at the bedside clock and saw that three hours had passed. Skye lay curled into a fetal position beside her, and Brandon still snored by the bed. Adrienne wanted nothing more than to go back to sleep, to block out the afternoon, but she knew if she slept more now, she would never sleep tonight. Reluctantly, she quietly got up and padded into the kitchen to brew a pot of coffee.

The coffee did little to clear her head, but she was at least capable of coherent speech when Lucas Flynn called half an hour later. "How are you doing?" he asked.

"I feel like I've been run over by a truck, and the bad thing is, I don't think the reality of the whole thing has even hit me yet."

"Losing anyone you love is bad, but it's even worse when the person is young and vibrant and, worst of all, a murder victim. You have all that rage on top of the grief."

"I felt rage when Trey died, but it was different. I was mad at him for being so stupid as to ride a motorcycle he couldn't handle. Julianna didn't do anything stupid."

"Didn't she? She wasn't spending the night at the Belle of the hell of it. It's pretty evident she was having an affair."

"I didn't know anything about it, and Julianna wasn't one for keeping secrets."

"Well, she had at least one she didn't share."

Adrienne knew he was right, but she didn't want to admit it to the county sheriff no matter how obvious it was. Instead, she said, "You sound tired, Lucas."

"I am. That's the problem with being a sheriff in a relatively quiet county. Not a lot of murders, thank God, particularly not like this one. I've lost my stamina."

"Have you found out anything about who might have been with Julianna at the Belle?"

"No. Of course, the trace evidence is still being checked, although in a hotel room, working with trace is a nightmare, even if the room hasn't been officially rented for a year. Also, there are no fingerprints. None. Someone spent a lot of time wiping down that place."

"What about Claude?" Adrienne nervously carried the receiver of the cordless phone to the front window and looked out at the paperboy jamming today's edition of the *Register* into the paper box at the end of her driveway. "Could he have murdered Julianna? I mean, I know Claude wasn't having an affair with her, for God's sake, but he could have been jealous of whoever was. He could have murdered her to punish her."

"I'll admit he makes the perfect suspect. Erratic, unstable, possessive. Mrs. Kirkwood shouldn't have kept him around, even if he did take over just as the Belle was closing and there wasn't much damage he could do to the place, not that she cared anyway. But you saw him this morning. Do you think he was alert enough to wipe away all the fingerprints? And why would he even bother? There's a logical reason for him being there. Besides, Claude has an alibi. He got lucky last night at that topless bar just out of town, the Cat's Meow. Met a young lady named Pandora Avalon."

Adrienne stopped pacing. "Please don't try to convince me that's her real name."

"No. It's Maud Dorfman. Anyway, the forty-four-year-old Miss Avalon went home with Claude for a night of unbridled passion. She swears she was at his cottage until the sound of the crash woke them. According to her, she got out of there as fast as she could, leaving Claude heaving into the commode from downing too much bourbon the night before. She said, and I quote, 'I never saw nobody puke so hard. I thought his damned stomach was gonna spew right up outta his mouth.'"

"I always thought Claude would be a fun date," Adrienne said drolly.

"Yes. Along with his ax. The idiot. Anyway, I don't think he was in any shape to have killed Julianna, much less brushed her hair and posed her so carefully on the bed before he came reeling down the hill to get me at the site of the wreck."

"Do you think there was any connection between the wreck and the murder?"

"No. Two fifteen-year-olds were illegally driving one of the cars. They caused the wreck and they both died. The three people in the other car were seriously injured. None of them claims to have known Julianna, not to mention that two of them are Amish. The Amish aren't known for lying, *or* for čovering for murderers, if you're thinking the driver of the car they were in could have been the killer."

"That leaves Claude. Do you believe he's completely in the clear?"

"I don't think he killed her, but I have a feeling he may know more than he's saying. Unfortunately, I'm not allowed to arrest people based on my feelings."

"You should speak to someone about that."

"Maybe your brother-in-law. I'm sure he's going to be our next governor."

"I hope so. Otherwise, Vicky's going to have a tough time over the next few years. Philip doesn't take defeat well. He's one of those golden boys who almost always get what they want." She sighed. "That was a bitchy thing to say."

"It was truthful. I can't say I'm a Philip Hamilton fan, either, but I'll probably vote for him."

"Not because of me, I hope."

"No. Because he's the lesser of two evils."

Adrienne laughed. "I guess you should know. After all, you used to work for him. Still, I'll pass along the compliment."

"I worked for him many years ago when I was young and stupid. I've always hoped people would forget about my tenure with the Hamilton camp. Besides, nowadays he's not crazy about me, either. He was dead set against my becoming sheriff."

"He can't charm you. Philip doesn't like it when he can't charm people. Then he can't use them, and using people is what he does best." Adrienne paused. "Clearly the nap I took with Skye didn't do much to improve my disposition."

"You've just lost one of your closest friends. It'll take more than a nap to make you feel better. And to make things worse, we can't find Julianna's mother."

"Lottie? She's missing?"

"She hasn't been home all day, and no one we've talked to has seen her."

"My God! Do you think something happened to her, too?"

"There's no sign of violence at her place."

"But it's in the woods not far from the Belle. She could be anywhere around there, hurt, maybe even dead."

"We've been searching the woods. There's no reason to think she hasn't just gone wandering. She does that sometimes." Adrienne sensed that Lucas wasn't as calm about Lottie as he was trying to sound. "How's Skye doing?"

"I'm not sure. She seems all right, given the circumstances, but kids can keep a lot to themselves. When Trey was killed, she was sad but calm for over a week. Then nightmares, storms of sobbing, and depression started. It was nearly six months before I got back my sunny little girl."

"Poor kid. Now this. I know she liked Julianna."

"What wasn't to like? She was beautiful, fun, a former model, for heaven's sake. Julianna and Rachel were Skye's idols."

"Rachel is probably the better role model. She seems like an exemplary girl. Julianna, on the other hand . . . well, no disrespect, but with her problems with drugs—"

"*Former* problems," Adrienne said stiffly, immediately defensive about her friend. "Julianna worked hard at getting herself straightened out and she never returned to her old life for fear of messing up again. I admired her tremendously for that. I think everyone should."

"Yes, I suppose so. But I need to warn you and Skye not to tell Rachel or anyone else the details of the crime scene. You haven't already, have you?"

"No, although Rachel was here at lunch."

"Good. You know the drill—we like to keep some things secret so that when the nuts come in and start confessing, we can trip them up on details."

"Yes, indeed. I know the drill from all my reading of murder mysteries. And Skye will keep her lips sealed if she knows the order has come from you."

"Good girls."

"Women. Smart, savvy women. Both of us."

"Yes, ma'am!" His laugh sounded weary and strained. "I'm going to let you go, now. Talking about what happened can only be making you feel worse. Watch some television or read if you can. And try to get a good night's sleep. I'll call you tomorrow."

"Thanks, Lucas. I'm sorry for my bad temper when we had to stay at the hotel so long this morning until you could question us."

"You never need to apologize to me." Which was true, Adrienne thought. Lucas was always kind, always patient, always earnest, always doing the exactly the right and responsible thing. A good, steady man. "Love you, Adrienne. Good night."

" 'Night, Lucas," she said quickly, wishing she could say, "Love you, too." But she couldn't. She hung up the phone feeling frayed and mean, unworthy and ungrateful. But at least she hadn't been dishonest. Small comfort, she thought miserably. They should put on my tombstone, "Adrienne was a bitch, but she had integrity."

"Oh, for God's sake," she said aloud. "Now you're wallowing in self-pity."

"Mom, what are you talking about?"

Skye stood at the entrance to the living room, looking rumpled and depressed.

"I'm indulging in self-analysis."

"Oh." She yawned. "That's weird."

"Tell me about it." Adrienne put the phone receiver back on the cradle. "Neither one of us finished even one sandwich earlier. Hungry?"

"Yeah. But I don't really want to hang around here. The house seems lonely and sad this evening. Could we go to Fox's for pizza?"

Adrienne thought of the warm little restaurant with its huge portions of food, and occasional spirited performance on karaoke night. "That's a wonderful idea." She glanced out the window. "But a storm is predicted, although everything looks fine now. Get your windbreaker. And don't wake up Brandon. He'll want to go with us."

"I'm going to be too fat to get into my jeans tomorrow," Skye announced an hour later before she popped a bit of pizza into her mouth.

"You could use a couple of extra pounds, kiddo. You're getting taller but not putting on weight." Adrienne frowned. "You're not doing anything unhealthy to keep your weight down, are you?"

"You mean like throwing up after I eat?" Skye made a face. "No way. That's *so* gross. Besides, Fox's Pizza Den has the best pizzas I ever ate. It would be sacrilege to eat one, then throw it up."

"I'm glad you think so," Adrienne said, biting into what she swore was going to be her last piece.

It was karaoke night and an intrepid soul approached the microphone. After some adjusting, unnecessary blowing into the live mike, and murmuring "testing, testing," he gradually slipped into a rendition of "You've Lost That Lovin' Feeling" by the Righteous Brothers. The longer he sang, the more confidence he gained and the louder he got. Unfortunately, he couldn't sing. At all. Although the guy was clearly pouring his heart into the song, he was slaughtering it.

Skye and Adrienne struggled not to giggle. Finally Skye got enough control to ask, "Do you remember a couple of months ago when Julianna talked you into getting up there?"

Adrienne rolled her eyes. "Unfortunately, yes. She was driving because I drank beer and way too much of it. Please don't remind me."

"I can't help it." Skye's eyes twinkled. "You were singing that disco song—"

"Gloria Gaynor's 'I Will Survive.'"

"You were flinging your arms around and making all

these faces! And your *voice* . . ." Skye nearly doubled over with laughter. "Mom, you were just *awful!*"

"Thank you, sweetheart. It's so considerate of you to bring up one of the most mortifying nights of my life."

"Maybe it was mortifying for you, but everyone else was getting a big kick out of it. Especially Julianna. She kept nudging me, trying to get me not to laugh. I couldn't help it, though. I'm sorry. But when you announced you were going to sing *another* one, I started thinking maybe we could never come here again because of the big embarrassment factor."

"Thank goodness Julianna came up on stage." Adrienne smiled, abashed, at the memory. "She had to literally push me away from the microphone and insist that it was *her* turn." Adrienne shook her head. "And darn it if she didn't do a great job with 'Wild Horses.' "

Skye smiled. "You were mad as all get out for a few minutes, but you got over it quick. And Juli *was* good. People kept asking her to sing other things, but she wouldn't, not even when a guy tossed a whole *dollar* up on the stage!" She giggled. "Juli took that dollar over and put it in the can for donations for the volunteer fire department and then carried the can around until she got everyone to do the same." Skye's remembered pleasure lasted only a minute before her face abruptly fell into sad lines. "I'm gonna miss Julianna so much."

"Me too, honey. We had a lot of fun together over the years."

"I wonder if Kit knows about Juli yet."

"I'm sure she does by now. I'm also sure she's at her restaurant, but I don't want to bother her there. I'll bet Kit's been with her mother all day, trying to calm her down, and now she's bone tired."

"Mrs. Kirkwood looked half-dead when we saw her going into the hotel to see Lucas. And Julianna's body. Mr. Kirkwood looked scared." Skye reached for another slice of pizza and began picking off pieces of sweet pepper before she asked reluctantly, "Do you suppose Julianna was at the Belle with him?"

"Who? Gavin Kirkwood? Good heavens, why would you think that?"

"Because I know he fools around with other women. I heard Kit telling you about it. I wasn't eavesdropping, really and truly. Kit was just talking loud because she was mad and I was in the next room. Anyway, she said her mother shouldn't have married a guy fourteen years younger than her, and that her mother shouldn't have let him adopt her—Kit—so she had to go around with his last name, and that he married Ellen for her money and that he had affairs all the time."

Adrienne listened, fascinated. "Wow, you heard a lot and remembered every bit of it."

"Mom, you know I want to write murder mysteries. I have to pay attention to details. For my writing, you see."

"Certainly you do."

"Anyway, Gavin is pretty good looking for such an *old* guy," Skye went on in a professional voice. Adrienne smothered a smile. Gavin Kirkwood was only forty-five. "He'd have keys to the Belle, and like you said, Claude's an awful caretaker, so it would be really easy for Mr. Kirkwood to sneak in all the time. And you said Julianna was probably with some married guy."

"I shouldn't have said that about a married man."

"You were too upset to watch what you were saying. But I know about things like that, Mom. You think she was having an affair."

"Really? I'm fascinated." Adrienne took a sip of iced tea. She'd lost her appetite and left the rest of the pizza for Skye. She went on, being careful to make her voice neutral. "Did Julianna ever say anything to make you think she was involved with Gavin?"

"No. And I don't like to think she'd do something that would hurt Kit's mom. But at one of the parties at Aunt Vicky's house, I saw them talking together a lot. Mr.

Kirkwood kept touching Julianna's arm. Rachel said to me, 'I wonder what he's got on *his* mind?' " Skye leaned forward and whispered, "She meant *sex*," she explained to a mother she clearly thought was not as worldly-wise as the sophisticated Rachel.

"Oh, I see," Adrienne managed solemnly. "Did Julianna seem to especially like Gavin?"

"No-o. Not really. She treated him pretty much like she did everyone else—nice, friendly, interested in what they were saying even when I knew she was bored." Skye paused. "She didn't act that way around Margaret, though. She didn't like Margaret, Mom, and Margaret didn't like Juli. Maybe she was jealous of Juli, although she doesn't like Rachel, either. I don't know how anyone couldn't like Rachel. She's *so* great."

"Maybe," Adrienne said distractedly as she thought about how Skye's closeness to Rachel could cause a problem. "Honey, you know you shouldn't tell Rachel anything about Julianna, about how we found her. The clasp in her hair, the candles, all that stuff."

"I already told her a little bit at lunch."

"But that's *all* you can say. No more."

Skye drew back, appalled. "But she's my cousin and my best friend. I tell her everything!"

"She's also a reporter, Skye. She'd probably tell her editor, Drew Delaney, and they might decide to put the details in the newspaper. The police don't want that. Lucas is counting on us to keep this information confidential."

"He is?"

"He definitely is. He told me so."

Skye sighed. "Okay. If it's that important to Lucas, I won't tell anyone, even though it was so weird I'm just bursting to tell *someone*."

"Only talk to me when you can't hold it in anymore."

"But you don't know anything I don't," Skye complained. "Somebody else might know who could hate Julianna enough to kill her, then fix her up so nice."

"That's for the police to figure out, not us," Adrienne said firmly, feeling a chill as the whole morning came flooding back to her in wretched detail, including the fear she'd felt before they found Julianna. "Now promise me."

"All right, I promise." Skye looked sulky as another local person dared the microphone and began a wrenching version of Chris Isaak's "Wicked Game." By the end of the song, Skye's pique seemed to have passed. She looked at Adrienne, her forehead scrunched in thought. "You remember this morning when I was in the woods with Brandon? Well, I think someone else was there, too. I didn't really *see* anybody, but I sort of *felt* somebody."

"Felt somebody?"

"Yeah. You know how it is when you feel someone watching you, then you turn around and someone *is* looking at you? It was like that, only I didn't see anyone. I'm not saying this right."

"Yes you are." Adrienne's heart had begun to drum uncomfortably. "I had the same feeling. I even thought I saw someone dodging behind trees, trying not to be seen. That's why I kept calling for you to come back. I was uneasy." Adrienne trailed off, then grabbed her jacket hanging on the back of her chair, dug her hand in the pocket, and withdrew her camera. "I took pictures of what I thought was a person so if it turned out the hotel had been vandalized or robbed, a photo could help the police identify someone."

"That was *really* smart." Mr. "Wicked Game" had now begun a version of "Where the Streets Have No Name" that Bono of U2 would never recognize. "So if the person who killed Julianna was hiding in the woods, you might have a picture of him!" Skye's expression froze. "Mom, a murderer could have been right there in the woods with Brandon and me!"

Adrienne nodded, not wanting to reveal her horror to Skye, who suddenly looked frightened. "Honey, I'd like to take the film in to Photo Finish tonight. It will be developed and ready for pickup by morning, and I can give it to Lucas. Do you mind if we leave now?"

"No. I'm too full for more pizza. Let's go before the storm starts."

Adrienne rapidly paid their bill and Skye waved to the restaurant's owner before they ran out the front door. Adrienne looked up in dismay. The sky had turned from the cornflower blue of the afternoon to a dark heliotrope. She drove quickly downtown, but the street in front of Photo Finish was blocked because it had just been repaved. She had to park around the corner and halfway down the next street. When she stepped from the car, wind whipped her long hair and she gathered a handful of it and tucked it beneath the collar of her jacket.

Adrienne looked up at the sky. "We're really in for it tonight."

"If there's thunder, Brandon will be scared to death," Skye said loudly above the noise of the wind.

"Brandon is a one-hundred-pound baby. He'll get in the bathtub if he feels a storm coming. I don't know why he thinks he'll be safe there."

"He must have heard you should get in a tub if a hurricane is coming. Or is it an earthquake?"

"It's a tornado."

"Oh. Whatever." They hurried past Criminal Records and Skye glanced in the big front window. "Mom, there's Sherry and her mother!"

"Sherry?"

"Sherry Granger. I told you about her. She sat next to me in history last year. She's semicool."

"*Semi*cool?"

"Yeah. I think there's real hope for her this year since her braces came off and she's gotten her lisp under control. Can I go in here while you go on to Photo Finish? I've been saving for a CD by Matchbox Twenty."

Adrienne didn't like the idea of having her little girl out of her sight on this particular evening, but a chilly rain already pelted her shoulders. Skye had just gotten over a particularly stubborn cold that had lasted two weeks. Adrienne didn't want her daughter to get sick again because she'd dragged her around in bad weather.

"Okay, go in, but stay with Sherry and her mother. If they leave before I come back to get you, wait in the store for me."

"All right."

"Don't leave the store after you get your CD and head for Photo Finish in this bad weather."

"I won't."

"And Skye?"

"*What?*" the girl asked, annoyance edging her voice.

"If you get a rap instead of a rock CD, I'll make you ride out the storm in a tent in the backyard."

Skye giggled. "No rap. I don't like it any better than you do. See you in a few minutes."

Adrienne watched as Skye dashed into the store and made for the lucky Sherry, who apparently was evolving from semi to totally cool. Sherry looked delighted to see Skye and the two girls hugged. Both of their mouths began to move rapidly and simultaneously as they exchanged apparently earth-shattering news. Goodness, Adrienne thought. Had *she* ever been so young and joyous? Yes. She, Julianna, and Kit had acted just like Skye and Sherry.

Adrienne pushed on, hoping the darkening sky held on to the rest of the rain until she'd dropped off her film, then went by to pick up Skye. But just as the thought formed, thunder rolled low and threatening. A perfect end to an awful day, Adrienne thought dismally. She feared lightning, and Brandon became crazed at the sound of thunder. No doubt he would keep her and Skye awake for the rest of the night.

She turned a corner and started down the side street where Photo Finish nestled between two empty stores halfway down the block. The town of Point Pleasant's business district had been shrinking for about ten years. Her father, who had been on the city council, fretted constantly about owners of downtown buildings who continued to raise rents, encouraging businesses to abandon them for spots in the mall just outside of town. Dad had good reason to worry, Adrienne thought. This street was deserted, even though it was a Friday night when most businesses stayed open until eight o'clock.

The wind blew a Styrofoam cup against her leg. A raindrop smacked her in the eye. "Damn!" she muttered, wiping at her closed lid. Now she'd have a half-moon of mascara below her eye, not to mention that the water had hit with enough force to actually hurt.

Adrienne stopped for a moment and fumbled in her purse for a tissue. Just as she found one, she heard footsteps behind her. Walking fast. Now *running*.

Instinct and leftover panic from the morning made her whirl around. Wind blew her hair across her face, completely blinding her. Her heart beat furiously. She shouted in a high, thin voice, "Who's there?"

Grabbing at her wind-tossed hair with one hand, Adrienne clutched her purse with the other, intending to swing it as a weapon. But she didn't get a chance. Someone rushed at her, powerfully spinning her around and throwing her facedown on the sidewalk. Breath rushed from her lungs. Dazed and terrified, she kicked backward, but the attacker's weight rested high on her back, out of range of her flailing legs, pinning her arms. Thunder rolled again, closer and louder. Then a hand grabbed her hair, lifted up her head, and slammed her forehead onto the concrete sidewalk. The sound of the storm dulled and Adrienne's sight went from gray to black.

FOUR

I

"Adrienne! Are you all right? Adrienne, wake *up!*"

Trey. She had overslept and her husband was trying to wake her because the baby needed to be fed. "I'm up," she mumbled. "You hold Skye and I'll get her bottle."

"No, Adrienne. You're confused. It's Drew. Drew Delaney."

Drew? She opened her eyes to a blurry face hovering above hers. "What are you doing here? Where's Skye?"

"You're lying on the sidewalk in the rain. I don't know if you fainted or you've been attacked, but you have a hell of a knot on your forehead and you're bleeding. We need to get you to the hospital."

Adrienne tried to sit up. A wave of nausea flattened her. "I'm dizzy."

"No wonder." Drew pulled a cell phone from his jacket pocket. "Don't move. I'm calling an ambulance."

"I don't want a scene. And I have to find Skye."

"Only you would be concerned about making a scene right now. And we'll find Skye." Water dripped off his thick, dark brown hair onto her face as he called 911. As soon as he finished, he removed his jacket and slipped it under her head. "What happened?"

"Someone came up behind me and knocked me down, then banged my head on the sidewalk."

"It was a mugging. I've been raising hell with the city

council for a year about the lack of lights on this street."
His large brown eyes were filled with concern. "Was Skye
with you?"

"No. She went in . . . I can't remember the name. The
music store."

"Criminal Records?"

"Yes. I told her to wait for me there while I went to Photo
Finish. Drew, go make sure she's safe. She's about five feet
five and has long blond hair—"

"I've seen her with Rachel at your sister's parties, but I'm
not going after her. I'm sure she didn't leave the store if you
told her not to, especially in this rain."

"But you could look for her."

"I am not deserting you here in the dark and the rain, so
quit arguing."

"Oh no," Adrienne moaned as hot water poured into her
mouth. "I think I'm going to be sick. Don't look at me."

"Oh, for God's sake, Adrienne. Ever since you were a
teenager, you've been worried about the impression you
make. Now isn't the time for your silly vanity."

A rush of indignation chased away her nausea. *Her* vanity? Cockily handsome Drew Delaney was accusing her of
vanity after all these years?

"You have always been *such* a jerk," she said furiously.

His mouth quirked. "I do try."

"You succeed quite well."

"Still feel like you're going to throw up?"

"No."

"Then keep thinking about what a jerk I am. It seems to
be working."

Adrienne closed her eyes. Her head throbbed and she
couldn't shake her confusion. And worry. Skye would wonder what was taking her so long. What if she decided to
come this way in spite of her mother's orders?

"Drew, I have to see about Skye," she said.

"You are not going to move."

"I can't leave her in that store. Someone attacked me. They might go after her next."

Drew sighed. "I know the manager of the store. I'll call and tell him to keep her there until someone comes for her. Maybe Vicky or Rachel."

"She'll be terrified if someone shows up instead of me."

"She's not a hysterical ninny, Adrienne. We'll just say you fell, twisted your ankle, and you had to go to the hospital to make sure you didn't fracture it. How's that?"

"Well, okay," she said reluctantly. "But she's not to hear anything else. Nothing about an attack on me."

"Talk about your hovering mothers," Drew said, rolling his dark brown eyes with those incredibly long lashes she remembered from high school. She closed her own eyes. Long lashes. What a thing to notice at a time like this, she thought. Maybe she had brain damage.

The next half hour blurred into a whirl of pelting rain, and people in slickers bending over her and firing questions about her quality of vision, the level of her pain, if she remembered where she lived, shouting their inquiries as if she were hard of hearing. She was loaded into an ambulance and carried at breakneck speed to the hospital where she was hauled onto a table beneath blinding lights. People shouted more questions at her, then shouted orders to each other. If I survive this, Adrienne thought dryly, fifty percent of my hearing will have been destroyed.

When the doctor and nurses finally gave her a brief respite from their loud ministrations, Drew walked into the examining room. "The lengths some people will go to in order to get a little attention," he said dryly.

"Yes, I really wanted to create a scene like this one," she said, trying to match his tone. "Did you locate Skye?"

"Sure. I couldn't rouse anyone at your sister's house. Rachel says that place is usually like a hotel—people everywhere. Anyway, Skye remained in the store like you wanted, with her friend."

"Sherry Granger."

"Yes. I talked to Mrs. Granger, who was properly horri-fied by your predicament and full of concern for Skye. She promised, per your orders, to tell Skye you sprained your an-kle, which I don't think a bright kid like Skye will believe for one minute. Anyway, Mrs. Granger is going to take Skye home with her and Sherry and keep her until further notice."

"That's great. How can I thank you, Drew?"

"Give me all the details about your finding Julianna Brent."

"No way."

Drew gave an exaggerated sigh. "Damn. I only saved you so I could get the story."

"You're a real prince."

"You've always thought so."

Adrienne looked up at him and managed a smile. When he smiled back, she saw that the lines around his eyes had deepened, and he had the beginnings of folds from his nose to his mouth. But he was still heartbreakingly handsome with that thick, wavy dark brown hair, lightly touched with gray at the temples, the devil-may-care gaze. She wondered if the years had been as kind to her appearance as they had to Drew's.

"Is something wrong?" he asked abruptly.

"Uh, no," she stumbled, embarrassed, and closed her eyes. "It's just my head. It hurts."

"No wonder. Heads don't take well to being slammed against concrete." He reached out and gently touched her temple where blood had run into her hair and dried. She kept her eyes closed but a tiny sensation almost like a thrill ran through her at his touch. "I was scared half to death when I found you crumpled and unconscious on that sidewalk in the rain," he said softly. "You looked so small and pale. Then I turned you over and saw the blood—"

"I'm back!" the doctor boomed, shattering the deli-cate moment. Adrienne didn't know if she was angry or relieved. "We're sending you off for a CT scan right now, Mrs. Reynolds. Going to see what's in that noggin of yours."

"Secrets of the universe," she said dryly.

The doctor's laugh crashed around her. "Good. I've got quite a few questions no one can answer."

"Can she have something for her headache?" Drew asked.

"No medication until we've assessed the damage," he blasted.

"Then how about a little quiet?" Drew asked. Adrienne opened her eyes to see the doctor's head whip toward Drew, who smiled winningly. "You've got a nice voice, Doc, but you need to turn down the volume."

"Oh," the doctor said, stiffening as he turned slightly pink. "Must be left over from when I was lead singer with a local band."

"Not the Ravens!" Drew exclaimed.

"Why, yes. You remember us?"

"I never missed you when you played around here. You were great!" He held out his hand and shook the doctor's. "This is a real honor."

The doctor smiled back happily, the earlier insult over his loud voice already a memory. Drew had mended the doctor's injured feelings with three simple sentences. His charm remained fully intact, Adrienne thought. It was a winning charm. It could be a dangerous charm.

"You don't have to stay here at the hospital, Drew," Adrienne said. "This could take hours. I'll be fine."

"I'm staying."

"Drew, really—"

"I'm *staying*."

Adrienne sighed and gave up, too tired, shaken, and sore to argue. Besides, even though she hated to admit it, she felt mystifyingly comforted to know that Drew Delaney was watching over her.

2

Kit Kirkwood looked into one of the small upstairs dining rooms and smiled. The room felt both elegant and intimate with its highly polished wooden floor, warm paneling, and the fireplace above which hung a painting of a beautiful woman playing the piano. Celtic music played in the background. "Sit down and have a drink with us, Kit," someone at a table full of people asked. She smiled and shook her head. She was too busy.

As if responding to her thought, someone materialized beside her. Kit looked up to see Polly, the hostess. "Yes?" she asked, already knowing there was a problem.

Polly had two vertical lines between her dark eyebrows, a bad sign. "I'm sorry to disturb you, Ms. Kirkwood, but there's a problem. We have reservations for two parties at the same time, both wanting the same table. All the tables are taken right now!"

"Polly, how did you make a mistake like that?"

"I didn't!" the pretty hostess said in hot indignation. "I've had this job a year and I've never made a mistake. *Never!*"

"Then what do you think happened?" Kit tried to calm her voice. It was eight o'clock, she had a splitting headache, a restaurant full of hungry people, a boyfriend waiting to have dinner with her, a temperamental chef threatening to quit, a mother at home in a state of mental collapse, and her own feelings bruised and battered by finding out one of her best friends was dead. No, *murdered*. Her stomach muscles clenched.

"So, what should I do, Ms. Kirkwood?" Polly went on relentlessly. "The Hansons are here with another couple and it's Mrs. Hanson's birthday. They've ordered a cake for after dinner. The Morgans are furious. They have that gorgeous nephew of Mr. Morgan with them and Mrs. Morgan is dressed to beat the band in a dress with a neckline cut halfway down

to her navel. I'm sure she's after him, even if she's twenty
years older than he is. That woman has no shame. But she
always urges Mr. Morgan to give a *really* generous tip, so
she's not *all* bad."

Kit took in the barrage of information as she passed a
hand over her forehead and looked into the young, clear eyes
of Polly. Gossipy or not, Polly was right. She didn't make
mistakes. Someone else was responsible for penciling in two
reservations for the same time. Maybe even Kit herself.
She'd been fairly distracted lately.

"All right." Kit forced herself to sound coolheaded. "Because there are four people in the Hanson party, one having
a birthday, we'll seat them. Put them at the upstairs table by
the window overlooking the courtyard. That party is almost
ready to leave."

"That's what they really wanted," Polly added helpfully.

"Good. Meanwhile, take the Morgans to the bar. I want
them to have free drinks. And Mrs. Morgan loves piano music. Alfred is supposed to start playing in ten minutes. Have
him play anything Mrs. Morgan wants. Tell him I said *not* to
act like he minds if she sits on the bench with him after her
third martini."

"Even if she sings along?" Polly managed to wail in a
whisper. "Alfred *hates* that!"

"He'll have to hide his feelings if he wants to keep his
job. And have Troy check on them regularly."

"But Troy is a waiter. He doesn't tend bar."

"I know that, Polly, but Troy could charm Attila the Hun.
He can keep the whole Morgans party happy until a table
opens up." Kit gave the pretty young woman a dazzling
smile. "Get to work, Polly. If anyone can successfully juggle
these people, it will be you. All seven of them."

"But not eight," Polly said in spite of the compliment.
"Alfred is gonna be *pissed* if Mrs. Morgan sits with him."

"Alfred isn't a customer, and I'm sure he can bear up for
just one night." Kit put her hands on Polly's slim young

shoulders. "March, young lady. You have your orders."

With a sigh, Polly headed back to the entrance area where seven people had begun to quarrel with each other over who should be seated next. New arrivals looked at them warily. Kit detested scenes like this in her restaurant. Her headache kicked up a notch.

"Uh, Ms. Kirkwood?"

She whirled to look at a very young, skinny busboy with flaming cheeks and too much gel in his spiky hair. "What is it?"

"Well, I was out back—my regular smoke break, mind you—I wasn't goofin' off, and I saw this woman roamin' around out there. I think I've seen her before. Maybe she's the one that brings those scented candles you sell. in the foyer. Tall and real skinny—looks like the wind could blow her away. Old clothes, hair comin' down from a bun. I asked if I could do somethin' for her, and she said, 'No one can help me now.' She looks sort of crazy—"

Kit pushed past him and headed through the noisy kitchen to the back door. The phrase from a Keats poem, "Alone and palely loitering," popped into her mind when she saw Lottie Brent seated on a wrought-iron seat for two beside a small tree strung with white lights glowing like miniature stars in the darkness. The woman stared to the right at the small gazebo and the crowded tiki bar. "Lottie?" Kit asked gently as she sat down on the bench beside the woman.

Lottie Brent gave Kit a startled, slightly discomfited look, then stared straight ahead. "My goodness, I didn't think you would be summoned to my side."

"People have been looking for you since morning."

"I didn't mean to cause worry for anyone." Lottie was nearly seventy but had the sweet, lilting voice of a young girl. And although she hadn't gone past the eighth grade, she spoke with a beautiful lyric quality Kit had always loved. "I didn't want to talk to anyone," Lottie said. "I had to think.

I've walked around all day. Then I decided I wanted to sit in your enchanted garden. I didn't mean for you to even know I was out here, but I felt drawn to this place. I *had* to come. It's so lovely in the evening, like something out of a fairy tale."

When Kit constructed the half-acre garden linking the main dinner restaurant with the smaller and informal lunchtime building known as the Grill, people had laughed at her fanciful inclusion of the gazebo, a wishing well, a patio surrounded by tiki torches, and a stereo system that played spirited dance music for those who chose to drink at the outside bar. Once she'd finished construction of the "garden," Kit considered the expense well worth it. Nobody laughed at it anymore. People came long before their reservations to wander through the little park and admire the many light-draped trees, to have a drink at the horseshoe-shaped bar surrounded by tiki torches, and to drop coins in the small wishing well—money collected every month and donated to the animal shelter. In summer, customers even stopped near the front door to talk to Sinbad, a huge white cockatoo who sat regally in a big wrought-iron cage as he acquired an impressive vocabulary from his visitors. Kit had paid a fortune for the bird and Sinbad acted as if he knew he was worth every cent of it.

Kit looked covertly at the woman. Lottie was thinner than the last time she'd seen her. She had dark hollows under her eyes, and the thin white scars clustered on her temple seemed more noticeable than usual in spite of the paleness of her complexion.

"Sinbad is looking quite impressive," Lottie said finally. "Smooth, shiny feathers and a noble posture."

Kit forced her voice to sound light. "He *should* look good. He spends half his day preening and looking in his mirror. He's the vainest bird I have ever met, not to mention a huge flirt."

Lottie smiled. "You could always lift my spirits with your nonsense, Kitrina. But he *did* whistle at me."

"See? He has excellent taste in women. He *never* whistles at Mrs. Morgan. He can spot fake breasts and bleached hair a mile away." This time Lottie giggled softly. Kit laid her own hand over the woman's, which was dry and cold in spite of the warm evening. Lottie quickly pulled the cuff of her long-sleeved cotton dress over a wide, rough scar on her wrist, a wrist Kit knew had one time been bound by rope. "Why don't you come in the restaurant?" Kit asked. "I'll fix you something to eat."

"Thank you, Kitrina, but I'm not hungry."

"Can I bring you something to drink?"

"Maybe a cup of tea, but not right now." Lottie's grip tightened on Kit's hand. "You know, of course, Julianna is dead."

"Yes," Kit managed, barely above a whisper.

"She was murdered." Lottie's voice was tranquil, as smooth and rich as velvet. "I knew this tragedy was coming. *Today.*" Kit raised her eyebrows. "Oh, I know folks say I'm crazy with my premonitions and predictions. I always watch for signs of God's will manifesting itself in the softness of the night, or during the tumult of a storm, or in the burning sun of the day, so people think I'm losing my mind. But when your mother and I were young, she lived at la Belle with her parents and I lived in the cabin so near." Kit knew her mother's and Lottie's histories well, but she let the woman continue uninterrupted.

"We became friends, Ellen and I. We were so close, just like you and Julianna. Your mother understood me. She listened to me. We shared the bond of feeling, of sensing, that there was something wrong about the hotel."

"It's just a building, Lottie," Kit said gently. "Bricks and mortar and wood."

"And something else, dear. The place has a spirit. A building should not have a spirit, but that one does. One that is *bad*." Lottie paused, and began to clutch Kit's hand so tightly it was painful. "Kitrina, whether you believe me or not, God *did* warn me near dawn that something bad was to become of Julianna in la Belle."

Kit didn't believe in the supernatural, yet talk of signs and portents of approaching disasters made her nervous. All of her life she'd listened to her mother's growing, disturbing belief in the paranormal, particularly when it came to the hotel, and lately Ellen's preoccupation with it had made her certain the woman was losing her grip on reality. Now Lottie was on the same jag and it scared her because, in many ways, Lottie meant even more to Kit than her own mother. "Are you sure you didn't dream it, Lottie?" she asked almost desperately.

"No, dear. Don't look so alarmed. And please don't react like most people do. You never were like most people. Not you or Julianna or Adrienne. I believe that's why the three of you were such good friends. You were like-minded, each one of you special, and therefore drawn together by your sympathies of thought and feeling. And none of you believed I was crazy." She stared intently into Kit's face, her once beautiful amber eyes dimmed and clouded by early cataracts. She needed surgery, Kit thought, but Lottie didn't have the money and would never let anyone pay the medical bill for her.

"While it was still dark this morning, I was awakened by an owl," Lottie began as if merely continuing her last sentence. "It was very close, very loud. I sat straight up in bed, took a deep breath, touched my locket with Julianna's portrait inside, and a feeling washed over me. It was a mixture of dread and fear. And helplessness." Her voice rose. "I got out of bed and tried to think of ways to help my baby." She sighed. "But there was no help for her. Not in life, at least. Perhaps she has found peace in death."

Kit let the silence hang a minute while Lottie dabbed at tears and coughed behind a thin, embroidered handkerchief. But even in her extreme distress, she possessed an air of patience and serenity. Kit had always admired Lottie's self-possession. She was so different from Kit's own mother, Ellen, who over the years had turned cowering and anxious when she wasn't being high-handed and strident.

"I thought Julianna might be where she's been going often lately. La Belle. There's a badness in that place. I've always felt it. Real, dark, tangible *evil*. It comes creeping like a mist and slips right into your soul before you ever even realize it. I warned Julianna about it a hundred times, but she wouldn't listen. She gave me a kiss and said 'Thank you for worrying about me anyway, Mama.'" Lottie smiled faintly in memory. "Then she went off and played loose with danger."

"Yes, Julianna was always a risk-taker," Kit said faintly.

Lottie went on as if she hadn't spoken. "But when the owl awakened me this morning, I knew her fate was sealed. I feel it's my fault," she ended on a quavering note. "I failed my own daughter."

Kit felt silly but still couldn't help asking, "When you had your intuition and you knew she was at the hotel, did you realize she must have been meeting a man there?"

Lottie remained silent.

"Lottie, if you know who she was with, you must tell the police."

A wary look crept into Lottie's faded eyes that made Kit uneasy. "The police will deduce for themselves that she met a man in that place. And they will blame Miles Shaw for what happened to her."

"Maybe they should. He was still in love with her. He would have been wildly jealous of any new man she was involved with."

Lottie shook her head. "No, dear. I know you used to care for Miles, so you must realize he's a gentle, sensitive man."

Kit's face flamed at the mention of her old feelings for Miles. She had loved him deeply, but he hadn't returned her affection with anything except friendship. She also knew that Miles had become Julianna's from the moment he met her. He had been wildly in love with her. And Lottie was wrong. He wasn't really gentle, at least not on the inside. He was full of turbulent passions. Maybe enough passion to kill Julianna for leaving him and becoming involved with another man.

"Lottie, the police will definitely look at Miles as a suspect," she stated. "He's probably their main suspect. He's Juli's ex-husband and he didn't take the divorce well."

"I know all that, dear. And I know Julianna was meeting a lover at the hotel. She shouldn't have been seeing this person. It was wicked of her—the only deliberately selfish, cruel thing I've ever known her to do. But I *know* her killer wasn't Miles. Still, I cannot go to the police."

"If you know something, why can't you go to Lucas Flynn? He's reasonable. He'll listen."

Lottie touched Kit's hand. "Dear, there's so much you don't know. And so much *I* do."

Kit stared at the frail woman, dumbfounded and a bit afraid, when the back door of the kitchen opened. A busboy yelled, "We need you, Ms. Kirkwood."

"In a minute!" Kit snapped impatiently.

"It's awful important."

Lottie smiled graciously. "You go tend to your business, dear. I'm really too tired to talk anymore. I'll just sit here a little while longer, collecting my thoughts. I'll be fine."

"I gave Gail the night off," Kit said, referring to one of her waitresses and Lottie's younger daughter. "Shall I call her apartment and have her come get you?"

"No!" The single word ripped through the night. Lottie took a breath and said with forced calm, "I mean, that's not necessary. She'll be sharp and impatient with me because I've been out wandering all day. Really, Kitrina, I'm quite all right."

Kit was not a physically demonstrative person, but she leaned over and placed a light kiss on Lottie's forehead. That's when she saw the rusty smears of dried blood on Lottie's dress collar and across the shoulder seam. She also smelled l' Heure Bleue, the expensive French perfume Julianna always wore while Lottie refused to wear scent of any kind. Kit's heart leaped painfully in her chest, but she kept her voice tranquil. "I'm going inside now, but I'll be right back with a cup of tea."

As Kit walked into the restaurant, though, she thought about the blood on Lottie's dress and the scent of Julianna's signature fragrance, l' Heure Bleue, that clung tenaciously to Lottie's neck and face. Lottie was fastidious about her clothes and person. The scent and the stains couldn't be left over from yesterday.

With a chill, Kit realized that Lottie had been in the hotel with Juliana that very morning.

3

Claude Duncan's flaccid body seemed to sink into his ancient couch, his legs splayed, his right arm dangling over the side. A coffee table sat near him, laden with newspapers, candy wrappers, two empty pizza boxes, dirty paper napkins, and a notebook in which Claude had been attempting to write his novel. He was now on page 20 after two grueling months of work. A half-full bottle of bourbon stood by the couch.

On the small television across from him, a spaceship landed on an alien planet from which a distress call had been picked up. Claude loved this movie and had sat raptly through it countless times, always imagining himself as the handsome and heroic ship's captain, but tonight he was oblivious. He'd accompanied a particularly greasy pizza with four cans of beer, then topped off the meal with two candy bars and several shots of bourbon. He'd gone to sleep feeling satiated and happier than he'd been since the death of his mother.

And why shouldn't he sleep well? After all, things were

finally going his way. He no longer had to worry about losing his job when the Belle was torn down. He didn't have to go through the humiliating process of trying to find another job, of appearing polite, intelligent, and bright-eyed to potential employers who for some reason he couldn't fathom always looked at him like he was something nasty on the soles of their expensive shoes. No, sir. Claude Duncan didn't have to go job hunting. Claude Duncan had it *made*.

For a while he'd been troubled by the fact that his good fortune depended on taking advantage of a tragedy. His mother had died when he was twelve and her memory wasn't so clear to him anymore, but he did recall that she'd been pretty, kind, religious, and had tried to teach him never to profit from other people's bad luck. And that's exactly what he was doing. Profiting from bad luck. His father would never do such a thing.

Whenever Claude thought of his father, his stomach tightened with anxiety. His mother always said her husband was a good and fair man, but whose moral principles only a saint could live up to. She'd said it sweetly, but Claude had sensed gentle criticism in her words. Other people told him his father was admirable and a perfectionist. No one had ever said, more accurately, that Mr. Duncan was acrimonious, unreasonable, demanding, self-righteous and self-pitying. No one said he'd complained bitterly and loudly about the low intelligence and easy corruptibility of his miserable excuse for a son. Mr. Duncan's outbursts on this subject usually came late at night, in the little cottage, away from the fine hotel guests. But Claude, not as lucky as the hotel guests, had always been exposed to his father's contempt, although he'd never been able to analyze the problem clearly enough to put it into words, even to himself.

But for months now, since the elder Duncan's death, the harsh edge of the world seemed to have softened for Claude. Now he never looked up to see his father's disappointed, contemptuous blue eyes boring into his. He never went to bed at night feeling like a slimy, repulsive mistake that had wandered into his father's perfect world. He never lay in bed wide-eyed into the night wishing he could awaken in the morning and magically see a new boy in the mirror—a handsome, highly intelligent, confident boy whose dazzling smile, piercing eyes, superior height, and wide shoulders, all mixed with an easy charm, naturally won his father's respect. Life had calmed and steadied for Claude since the death of his father. After the initial shock of the man's quick demise from a severe heart attack, Claude had felt almost giddy with relief. He knew his near joy was shameful and he would never admit it to *anyone,* but it existed nevertheless. Still, he often escaped his fatherless but still boring life by taking refuge in his "hero" dreams.

Shifting slightly on the old wreck of a couch, Claude Duncan drifted into his favorite state—sleep—and began to dream. To his frustration, though, he could immediately tell this wasn't a "hero" dream. True, he was aboard the huge spaceship he'd just seen on television—a cold, gray thing hurtling through an eternity of darkness with him deep in its metal bowels that dripped water condensation and occasionally rattled hanging chains with hooks used for unloading cargo. But in his dream, even though he was the captain, he was disoriented and terribly uneasy.

And he was not alone.

In his very own spaceship, Claude's tall and muscular body sat huddled in a corner, arms clutched around his middle, his teeth beginning to chatter, his eyes darting fearfully around in the gloom. He knew people above were counting on him. They *always* counted on him, and why not? In the past, he'd never failed to invent a brilliant solution to whatever horrors space threw at them. Except for now. This time, to his complete shock and shame, all he could do was mutter over and over, "Monster under the bed," in a little boy's voice. "Don't look at the monster under the bed/No, no, wish the monster stone cold dead."

He squeezed his eyes tight. Tighter. So tight that lights began to dance behind the black shutters of his eyelids. He let out a tiny, pathetic moan. "No. Please. I'm the captain. I didn't do nothin' bad."

"Didn't you?"

His body jerked, then went perfectly still. Was that voice in his dream? It had to be. Vaguely, he knew this was *all* a dream, although it wasn't his typical spaceship dream. And someone new was in this dream with him. It wasn't one of his crewmen or anyone he could reach out and touch. Maybe it wasn't even a some*one*. Maybe it was a some*thing* that flittered around him with the speed of a mosquito or hovered above him with the large, silently beating wings of a dragonfly.

He tried to call for Ripley, his second-in-command—tall, resourceful, and smart even if she was a woman—but she only called back to him in a garbled tone, "Get out of there! It's coming!"

Claude thrashed in his tormented sleep. "It's coming!" he mumbled loudly. "It's coming!"

"Yes, it is," a calm voice interceded, a voice whose placid tones did not fit into the dream. "But you shouldn't be afraid."

"I *am* 'fraid," Claude wailed, still flailing, so drunk he couldn't wake up. "I'm *'fraid*!"

"You're afraid of the unknown. But the unknown isn't always bad." A strong hand closed around Claude's left forearm and held it tight. "Poor muscle tone, Claude. You don't work out."

"I work! I work plenty doin' ever little thing I'm s'posed to!"

"Now, that's not quite true, is it?" Dimly Claude felt something cold and sharp slip into the tender skin on the underside of his elbow. Then fluid coursed up his arm, pinching like ice, then moving like quicksilver, warmer, faster, shooting through him like something magical.

"What're you doin'?"

"Giving you an injection to make you feel calm."

Even in his befuddled state, Claude realized something awful, something fatal, was about to happen to him. He began to thrash weakly. "Gotta get up!" he abruptly shouted, his senses flashing back in a burst of panic. "Gotta get up! Gotta get *up*!"

He leaned forward, trying to struggle off the couch, but something pushed him back and held him down. He shook loose and tried to rise again, but his body wouldn't cooperate. The hands let go of him and he fell backward, sliding between the edge of the couch and the coffee table. He struggled to draw breath, feeling as if someone were sitting on his chest. "You're not from this world, are you?" he gasped out, saliva dripping down his chin.

"You've never known anything like me."

"It's the Belle. It brought you here a long time ago."

"Yes. I belong to la Belle."

Claude rasped in another breath and felt warmth between his legs. In shock, he realized he'd wet himself and felt absurdly embarrassed.

His companion leaned over him. "Have a little accident, Claude?"

He tried to focus on a face but he was too dizzy. Besides, he thought, it probably had no face behind that strange veil of netting it wore. He wasn't imagining it, and the veil clinched identification for him. It was a supernatural *Being*, hiding a horrible face behind a sheet of net, trying to beguile him with a soothing voice that could become brusque and slashing in a moment, a voice that expected to be obeyed, just as Daddy's had.

And predicted cruel punishments for when you didn't behave. Predictions that always came true.

By now Claude was so drowsy he barely felt the Being sprinkle the remains of the half-bottle of bourbon on him, lightly at first, then letting it stream over his face and shoulders. A few moments passed. Then more liquid flowed, surely more than could have been left in the fifth of bourbon. His now fear-dried tongue actually darted out for one last taste of the sweet nectar.

And while his tongue was out, diligently exploring for the liquid Claude Duncan valued more than blood, the Being struck a long, wooden kitchen match and stared down at Claude's drenched body, scummy beard, darting tongue. "How about a song?" the Being asked. "I know just the one."

By now, Claude was too terrified to think rationally. He simply lay limp, a sack of blood and bones, and trembled. It wasn't supposed to go this way. *Finally I had it made*, he thought with vague petulance. *Things were turnin' rosy for me. It wasn't supposed to go this way!*

The voice began to sing like Annie Lennox: "Sweet dreams—" Then it broke off. "Recognize the lyrics, Claude? Julianna's favorite song. Sing along with me," the Being invited airily as it moved backward, then threw a lighted kitchen match onto the alcohol-soaked face of Claude Duncan. Then another, then another. "Sweet dreams are made."

The Being vanished. In a few moments, a not-quite-dead Claude managed a couple of tortured wheezes meant to be screams. But his voice was lost in the terrific heat. Still tossing matches, the Being blithely abandoned Claude and his home. Finally, when Claude was no longer moving or even recognizable, the Being continued to sing "Sweet Dreams" until its voice faded into the cool darkness far beyond the blazing hell of the caretaker's house.

FIVE

I

"I can't spend the night in the hospital," Adrienne explained to a very young nurse with soft blue eyes that reflected every insecurity in her heart.

"You lost consciousness for a while, Mrs. Reynolds," she replied in a good imitation of firmness. "In cases like yours, we insist that you spend the night in the hospital for observation."

"What is your name?"

"My name?" Dismay flared in the girl's vulnerable eyes as if she thought she were going to be reported. "Ah, Miss Leary."

"Well, Miss Leary, if someone sits by my bedside all night, will I be safe from slipping into an irreversible coma?"

"A nurse's presence always helps," Miss Leary said mechanically, clearly missing Adrienne's sarcasm. "You're just getting yourself all upset, Mrs. Reynolds." Miss Leary stood helplessly in front of Adrienne, who had begun to untie the strings on the back of her hospital gown. Frustrated and unreasonably angry with everyone on the hospital staff, Adrienne was at the point of ripping off the worn, flimsy garment. The emergency room was freezing. She wanted her clothes. "If you're cold, Mrs. Reynolds, let me put a blanket across your shoulders to warm you," Miss Leary pleaded. "Please don't tear up the gown. The doctor will be here in a couple of minutes, and in the meantime, you can talk to Mr. Reynolds. He's right outside and he's been awfully worried about you."

"My husband is dead," Adrienne stated baldly.

The girl blushed crimson at her faux pas, her gaze skittering back to the medical chart. Adrienne looked at her closer, unwillingly feeling a twinge of sympathy. The poor girl couldn't be past twenty-one and was clearly inexperienced with pain-in-the-ass patients.

"I'm sorry, Miss Leary," Adrienne said in a milder tone. "I'm tired and worried and my head hurts like hell."

"It's just that there's this man in the hall. He brought you in and he seems very worried about you. I assumed he was your husband."

Drew, Adrienne thought. "The man in the hall was once a friend of mine. He found me after I'd been attacked on the street. His name is Drew Delaney. He's the editor of the newspaper."

"You don't say?" Miss Leary breathed in awe.

"That's right. And if you'll throw that threadbare excuse for a blanket over me, he can come in until the doctor arrives."

Miss Leary looked as if she were going to burst into tears of relief. The harridan on the examining table was obviously losing steam, and no one was going to write her up for not being able to keep her patient under control. "Of course you can have a blanket, Mrs. Reynolds. Why, even your hair is wet. You must be freezing." She whipped a blanket out of nowhere and, with hands moving so fast they seemed a blur, began spinning the cloth around Adrienne.

"You know, the rain stopped for a while, then it started up again about twenty minutes ago," she said in her professional "calming" voice as she wielded the blanket. "Just hearing rain, even in the summer, makes me feel cold, especially in the ER. I always wear a sweater myself."

"The one you have on is a lovely shade of blue," Adrienne said, trying to make up for her earlier sharpness.

"Oh, thank you. My mother knitted it for me." For a finishing touch, Miss Leary tucked the blanket under Adrienne's chin as if she were an enfeebled old lady. Adrienne cocked her head, the only part of her body she could still move, listening to a demand over the loudspeaker for Drs. Gorman and Price, STAT. Miss Leary looked troubled. "I heard out at the desk the EMS is bringing in a terribly burned man. I just *hate* burn cases."

"I've always thought death by fire would be a horrible way to go," Adrienne said. "Any idea who it is?"

"No. And I hope I don't have to help with this particular case. I'm always afraid I'll faint if the person looks too gruesome." She gave Adrienne a shaky smile. "I have to get over my squeamishness or I'll never be a good nurse, and I want to be the best." She stood back and looked at Adrienne. "There. You should be all nice and warm. I'll go get Mr. Reynolds. I mean, Delano. Whatever. He's very handsome. Oh, don't tell him I said that. It was inappropriate." Miss Leary blushed again and fled the emergency room.

In a moment, Drew sauntered in, took a long look at her, and said, "Greetings, Nanook of the North. Planning on going ice fishing?"

Adrienne unsuccessfully tried to loosen the blanket. "I made the mistake of saying I was cold, and that sweet nurse put me in this straitjacket."

"Want me to help you out of it?"

Adrienne thought of her thin gown hanging open in the back. "Never mind. At least I'm warmer than I was before."

"No wonder. You're in a cocoon." He frowned. "How on earth did she manage that arrangement, anyway?"

"I have no idea, but she meant well, Drew. And she thinks you're handsome, which I wasn't supposed to tell you. I *will* tell you to leave her alone. She looks like she's about Skye's age."

Drew grinned. "Contrary to popular belief, I do not chase every woman I see. But even after all these years and with your dripping hair, scraped forehead, bad temper, lack of gratitude, and abysmal fashion sense, I find you appealing. I've only made myself stay away from you since I came back to town because you're seeing the formidable Sheriff Flynn."

The same old Drew, Adrienne thought. Always joking to hide more serious feelings. She felt a jolt of surprise. He *was* feeling something more than ordinary concern about her. He smiled, but in his dark brown eyes she saw deep worry. "I'm okay, Drew. Really. I just want to get out of here and be with my daughter."

"Your daughter is fine."

"Is she with Vicky yet?"

"No. Philip and Vicky are at a party and Rachel is out with the great white hope of the Allard family—"

"Bruce."

"Yes, Bruce, one of my intrepid reporters. Anyway, everyone will be home within a couple of hours. In the meantime, Margaret will pick up you and Skye."

"Margaret?"

"Margaret Taylor, the pitt bull Philip calls a campaign manager. I don't think Vicky has been informed of your attack. We couldn't have it spoiling any of Philip's political socializing."

"I want to get out of here as soon as possible."

"Well, the pitt bull is here to rescue you," a female voice said pleasantly. Adrienne and Drew looked at the woman standing in the door of the emergency room. Her black hair was as always pulled into a glossy French twist, her makeup subtle and flattering to her olive complexion, her almond-shaped eyes as clear as a teenager's. She wore a sage-green linen pantsuit, perfectly tailored and without one wrinkle. "I was shocked to hear about what happened to you," she said. "Are you all right, Mrs. Reynolds?"

Adrienne was deeply embarrassed that the woman had heard Drew call her a pitt bull, but Drew looked unfazed.

"Yes, I'm just banged up a bit. I look a sight. And please call me Adrienne."

Drew smirked, recognizing Adrienne's friendly tone as a palliative for guilt. He probably knew how much Vicky resented Margaret, and that naturally her resentment would affect Adrienne's feelings. "I spoke with your doctor in the hall," Margaret went on affably. "He said you're determined to go home, and although he'd rather you stay, he can't force you. I'll help you dress, then drive you home. Or rather, to your sister's house. The doctor says you shouldn't be alone tonight." She turned to Drew and said coolly, "May we have a bit of privacy, Mr. Delaney?"

Drew smiled. "Adrienne, I'll leave you in capable hands."

"Thank you so much for everything," she said sincerely. "If you hadn't come along when you did—"

"But I did, so don't dwell on dark thoughts. Say hello to Skye for me." He turned to Margaret, his smile turning mechanical. "Ms. Taylor."

"Mr. Delaney." Her own smile was stiff, her dark eyes cold. "Although since I have you here, I must say I thought your editorial on Philip in last night's paper was rather unfair, don't you?"

"If I did, I wouldn't have printed it. But now isn't the time for a debate. Please take Mrs. Reynolds home and make her comfortable. She's had a hard evening."

As Drew left, Adrienne had a wild desire to call out, "Come back!" For some reason, she didn't want to be left alone with Margaret. The woman intimidated her, which Adrienne knew was ridiculous. They were both college educated, successful—at least Adrienne believed she was on the road to success—but there was something about Margaret that made Adrienne feel unpolished and bumbling. No more than five feet two, Margaret gave the impression of being much taller with her perfect posture, ever-present high heels, and hair always pulled back in a gleaming black twist, which gave her a look of dignity and maturity although she was only thirty-two. Then there was her body language, graceful yet assertive, and a quick, stunning smile that won over people even if it never seemed to reach her eyes. Her slightly sharp nose and thin lips kept her from being a natural beauty like Julianna or Rachel, but she was certainly striking and emanated a cool, controlled sex appeal.

She drew near Adrienne, a tiny worry line daring to mar her forehead. "Earlier Mr. Delaney filled me in on your attack, so please don't feel you have to explain it to me. For now I think trying to keep your mind off what happened would be best for you." She smiled. "I'll leave you alone so you can get dressed. Unless you need some help, that is."

Adrienne looked at Margaret's immaculate, expensive pantsuit and thought of her own old jeans, T-shirt, and worn denim jacket soaked with rain. "I can manage but thanks anyway."

"Fine," Margaret said in a way that made Adrienne feel she knew exactly why her help had been declined. "I'll get you out of here in a jiffy and then we'll pick up Skye. I'm sure seeing her will make you feel better."

"About a hundred percent better." Adrienne slid off the examining table. "I'm so glad she wasn't with me."

"The attack wouldn't have happened if she had been."

Adrienne looked at her. "What do you mean?"

"The attacker wouldn't have been eager to take on two women instead of one. And Skye seems like a strong, quick-witted girl to me. She would have fought."

And I do not seem strong, quick-witted, or able to fight, Adrienne flared mentally, but managed an imitation of a smile. "Of course, you're right. Two against one." But she couldn't resist adding, "But I can hold my own in a fight."

"Yes, I believe Philip has said you were always something of a scrapper." Margaret gave her a disparaging look as if she thought Adrienne had probably indulged in plenty of scraps, no doubt in back alleys and seedy bars. Adrienne couldn't win with this woman. Margaret was too adept at crushing a person's image with a look and a few masterfully chosen words. She probably did the same thing to Vicky, Adrienne thought.

"We couldn't locate Sheriff Flynn, so there's a deputy here waiting to take a statement from you," Margaret went on. "I'll give you about ten minutes to get dressed before I send him in. Don't put on your jacket—it's soaking wet. You'll catch cold. I have a dry raincoat in the back of my car you can use. And I certainly wish I'd thought to bring a blow-dryer for your hair. It's hanging in soggy ringlets all over your shoulders."

With that Margaret swished out of the door, marching smartly down the corridor to efficiently accomplish "springing" her from this prison, while Adrienne stood in the cold room with her cut forehead and soggy ringlets. She yanked the flimsy gown over her head and slipped into her damp jeans that had gotten filthy at the knees when she fell. She no longer felt like an attack victim deserving sympathy, but instead like a slovenly, tiresome creature purposely messing up everyone's evening. Honestly, she thought in annoyance, even when Margaret Taylor was being helpful, she still managed to be an absolute menace to one's self-esteem.

Before he left the hospital, Drew Delaney stopped at a vending machine. A can of Coke slammed out in return for his quarters and he opened it, drinking deeply as he realized how thirsty he was. It had been a long evening and he was tired. He leaned against the side of the machine, realizing his lower back had begun to hurt after all the hours he'd spent on his feet today. You're getting old, Delaney, he thought, although he'd never admit it to anyone except himself.

"I heard downtown that Adrienne Reynolds had been assaulted on the street. How is she?" he heard a man ask. The guy couldn't have been more than two feet away from Drew, who was hidden beside the vending machine, but the man's voice sounded familiar.

"Roughed up a bit," a woman answered. Margaret Taylor, Drew realized immediately. He'd know that clipped tone anywhere. "It could have been worse if Drew Delaney hadn't shown up to play the hero."

"You sound disappointed that it *wasn't* worse." Who the hell was that? Drew wondered. Deep, self-consciously polished voice. So familiar. "Did you want her to be killed?"

"Of course not. I'm not a monster, Gavin."

Gavin Kirkwood! Drew hadn't realized Gavin and Margaret had more than a polite acquaintance formed at the Hamilton parties, but they were sounding confidential with each other now. He shrank against the wall, hoping neither came nearer the vending machine and saw him.

"Does Kit know what's happened to Adrienne?" Margaret asked.

"No. She'd be here in a minute if she did. I didn't stop by The Iron Gate and tell her. I didn't want to upset her."

"Do you really care if she's upset or not?"

"Yes. You probably don't believe it, but I do."

"You're right. I *don't* believe it."

"I don't care what you think," Gavin said.

Margaret laughed softly. "Why, Gavin, you *should* care what I think. Don't forget—you have a lot to lose."

After a pause, he almost hissed, "You're a monster."

"Sticks and stones, darling."

"Listen, Margaret, I'm not going to let you push me around anymore."

"Is that so?"

"Yes. Our arrangement is *off*."

A beat of silence followed before Margaret said in a soft but somehow dangerous voice, "Our *arrangement,* as you so delicately put it, is off only when *I* say it's off."

"Or what?"

"Or I go to your rich wife and I tell her everything. Is that what you want, Gavin? Because you know I don't make empty threats. You also know you're nothing without Ellen to give you the kind of life you could never in a million years make for yourself!"

Drew waited for an angry response from Gavin, but nothing followed. He could almost picture the handsome but characterless Gavin Kirkwood standing in the hall with his mouth slightly open, searching madly in his mind for a scathing reply and coming up dry.

"I assume your silence indicates acquiescence," Margaret said briskly. "At least, it does if you know what's good for you. Good night, Gavin. Run home to Ellen where you're needed. At least expected. I have everything under control and I intend to keep it that way with no interference from you or anyone else."

Margaret marched past the vending machine with her gaze straight ahead. Drew was certain she hadn't seen him. But five minutes later, after he'd left the hospital and headed for his car in the parking lot, he saw Gavin Kirkwood sitting motionless behind the wheel of his Jaguar, his shoulders slumped, his face desolate.

2

"I'm sorry I've spoiled your evening," Adrienne said when they pulled away from the hospital in Margaret's car. "I'm sure you had better things to do than play chauffeur for me and Skye."

"Don't be silly." Margaret smiled. "I was doing nonessential paperwork, just trying to keep myself busy until Philip gets home to tell me how the evening went."

Not *Vicky* and Philip. Just Philip, Adrienne thought, bristling slightly. Vicky definitely didn't imagine Margaret's possessive air when it came to Philip, and Adrienne didn't blame her for resenting it.

The rain had slacked off to a slight drizzle, but as they glided along in Margaret's new Thunderbird, Adrienne felt chilled, even wrapped in Margaret's dry raincoat. Mist circled the streetlights, giving them a ghostly glow, and a cloud cover hid the moon and stars. The evening felt bleak and lonely.

"I don't know the address of the woman who took Skye home," Adrienne finally said to fill the silence. "It's Mrs. Granger. The daughter's name is Sherry."

"Drew Delaney got the address. I think he even called about an hour ago to tell Skye you'd be fine."

"That was thoughtful."

"Don't get carried away with his kindness. He's a reporter and this is the second big event you've been involved in today. Ingratiating himself to you is self-serving. He thinks you'll be more inclined to give him details about finding Julianna Brent."

Adrienne felt strangely annoyed by the comment because she knew Margaret could be right about Drew's motive. He wasn't above manipulating people to get what he wanted, even if it was just information. Still, she couldn't forget the look of genuine alarm and concern in his eyes when he'd tended to her on the rain-washed sidewalk.

"I've offended you," Margaret stated. "Sorry. I forgot you and Drew were once an item."

Damn Philip for giving Margaret *that* embarrassing tidbit, Adrienne thought. "We went out a few times when I was in high school. That's all. There is *nothing* between us." She paused, thinking of what Margaret would make of that overreaction. "I'm sorry I snapped. My head hurts."

"You'll feel better when you can take some aspirin get out of those damp clothes, and into a warm bed."

They remained quiet until they reached the Granger house. When they pulled in the driveway, Margaret said, "I'll get Skye. If you go to the door, there will be questions I'm sure you don't feel like answering."

"You're right. But if Mrs. Granger is like me, she won't let Skye leave with someone she doesn't know."

"Mrs. Granger doesn't know you either, Adrienne."

The woman had the infuriating habit of always being right, Adrienne thought, peeved. No wonder she drove Vicky crazy.

When they reached a cozy brick two-story home, Adrienne stayed in the car while Margaret went for Skye. The door opened and a bulb burning in a carriage light illuminated a plump woman, obviously Mrs. Granger, who nodded, clasped her hands as if in concern, smiled, leaned out the doorway and waved to Adrienne, then disappeared into the house. In a moment, Skye shot out the door, calling something over her shoulder to Mrs. Granger, and dashed to the car. Adrienne stepped out and the girl flung her arms around her mother.

"Oh Mom, are you all right? Mrs. Granger gave me some stupid story about you spraining your ankle, but I knew it wasn't true. What happened? Did you walk in on a robbery at Photo Finish? That's what I've been imagining. That you got shot trying to wrestle the gun away from the robber."

"Good heavens!" Adrienne laughed in amazement. "I never dreamed you thought I was so brave! Actually, I got mugged before I reached Photo Finish."

"Mugged?" Skye drew back and looked at her. "I thought that only happened in places like New York City."

"I guess the craze has finally reached even Point Pleasant, West Virginia."

Skye delicately touched the bandage on Adrienne's forehead. "What's under that? Something bad?"

"A cut. Minor. A couple of stitches." Four, to be accurate, but she wanted to minimize the situation. "I banged my head on the sidewalk when the mugger knocked me down. Other than that, I'm just a little sore and bruised."

Skye hugged her gently. "I'm so happy. But Mrs. Granger should have told me the truth. At least then I wouldn't have imagined something lots worse."

"Telling you I had a sprained ankle was my idea. Don't

blame Mrs. Granger. I keep forgetting you're not a little girl who has to be shielded from everything."

Margaret was already seated behind the steering wheel. "All right, ladies. Time to go to the Hamilton house."

"Aunt Vicky's?" Skye asked. "Why?"

"The mugger took my purse," Adrienne said. "He has keys to our house. It's safer for us to stay with Vicky until I get the locks changed."

"Brandon!" Skye cried. "He's there all alone!"

"I'm sure he'll be fine," Margaret said offhandedly. "You can check on him in the morning."

Skye was indignant. "In the *morning*! He hasn't had his dinner. He hasn't been let out since morning. Besides, he'll be scared in a dark house all by himself. We have to go get him."

"Skye, dogs are quite self-sufficient," Margaret said with authority. "He probably won't even miss you."

That did it. Skye flushed. Even if Adrienne had agreed with Margaret, which she didn't, she knew Skye would retrieve her dog if she had to walk the two miles to their house to get him. "If we're spending the night at Aunt Vicky's, then Brandon is coming, too." Skye sounded like a supremely self-confident twenty-five-year-old not about to take guff from anyone. "Ms. Taylor, please take us to pick up Brandon."

"Skye, really, you're being silly—"

"I have to agree with Skye," Adrienne said, earning an appreciative smile from her daughter. "Either we get the dog or we spend the night in our own house."

Margaret sighed gustily, stared straight ahead, and finally muttered, "Oh, all *right*." She was furious. Adrienne didn't care. She even enjoyed the woman's frustration a bit and she knew Vicky and Rachel would relish hearing about Margaret's iron will being overridden by Skye.

After they picked up Brandon, Margaret cringing as the big, long-haired black dog piled onto the immaculate pale upholstery of the backseat, they headed for Vicky's. As soon as Adrienne saw the house, her spirits sank even lower. Although Adrienne knew her own home was an interior designer's nightmare—a hodgepodge of clashing styles and colors and patterns—it seemed like a vibrant, living thing next to Vicky's stately white Colonial completely furnished in shades of pallid pink, chilly blue, and stark white. Nothing encouraged a guest to enter, kick off his shoes on an Aubusson rug, and curl up on a stiff-backed, brocade-covered sofa.

The house had belonged to Philip's wealthy Great-aunt Octavia, who had raised him after his parents died when he was young, and the old lady's rigid, chilly presence still permeated every room. Vicky had wanted to make changes in the décor, but Philip allowed only identical replacements of furnishings deemed too worn to remain. A noted interior designer had stated in his column that the home was a pristinely beautiful sanctuary. Adrienne thought it looked about as cozy and nurturing as an ice castle. A few carpet spots, live plants bearing a couple of dead leaves, a *TV Guide* lying open on an end table, and a mass-produced picture in a cheap frame would have been an improvement as far as Adrienne was concerned.

But she knew change was out of the question. Octavia Hamilton had never intended the house to look as if it belonged to ordinary people with ordinary lives, and her nephew seemed determined to carry on the tradition. The only change Philip had made since his great-aunt died was to set a towering pole bearing a huge American flag in front of the house. Seeing it always made Adrienne feel as if she were arriving at a government building instead of her sister's place.

Although lights burned throughout the house, none of the family had returned. Margaret unlocked a side door and they entered the large, stark white and stainless steel kitchen. She pointed to a small room to the left. "The dog can stay in the laundry room."

"The laundry room!" Skye was appalled. "He always sleeps by my bed."

Margaret gave her a tight smile. "In *your* house. Not in this house. Philip doesn't want animal hair all over the place. Rachel has never had a pet."

"And that's a shame!" Skye looked reproachfully at Margaret. "Rachel told me when she was little she *really* wanted a pet. I don't think she should have been denied having something to love because her dad was afraid of getting some animal hairs on the furniture."

"And urine and feces on the antique rugs," Margaret returned.

"Dogs can be house-trained. Brandon is," Skye asserted. "He would *never* make a mess in the house, would he, Mom?"

"No, he wouldn't," Adrienne said mildly. "He's really a well-behaved dog, Margaret. And, after all, this is my *sister's* house too, and I know she doesn't mind having dogs. If I break the rules, I'll confront Philip. I won't ask you to take the responsibility."

Anger flashed in Margaret's dark eyes for a moment. Then she said in a carefully expressionless voice, "As you point out, this is not *my* house, but I was hired to carry out Mr. Hamilton's instructions. So I must insist that you put the dog in the laundry room for now and take up the matter with Philip later."

Adrienne thought, What about Vicky? Doesn't she have any say around here? But she decided picking a fight with Margaret would only make the evening worse.

Adrienne nodded at Skye. The girl looked at both her and Margaret resentfully before leading the big black and white dog into the small room. Margaret sighed. "She's upset. It's better that I never had children. I don't have a way with them."

She sounded almost wistful and Adrienne felt a twinge of sympathy for her. Maybe after years of directing political campaigns, of giving orders to dozens of people, of feeling ultimate responsibility for the success or failure of a candidate, Margaret didn't realize she came off at all times like a general commanding the troops, a demeanor that didn't encourage warm relationships with teenage girls. Adrienne wondered if Margaret had always been so bossy and self-assured, or if her own teenage years been filled with normal teenage insecurities and sensibilities.

Skye came out of the laundry room, closing the door behind her and looking tragic. "Honey, a night in there won't kill Brandon," Adrienne said. "It's not like he's been cast out into an ice storm."

"But he's used to being with me. He doesn't understand."

"He'll be fine." Margaret's voice held a trace of kindness. She was trying. "I'll go upstairs and help you get settled into the guest rooms. Which ones would you like?"

"I want to stay with Mom, not in a separate room," Skye said promptly. "We want the room next to Rachel's. It has the biggest TV."

Margaret looked doubtful. "I don't think your mother is up for television . . ."

"I'm always up for TV," Adrienne lied, seeing Sky's incipient glower. The girl had already been pushed far enough today with the murder, the attack on her mother, and finally Brandon's incarceration in the wretched laundry room without his cushion or his toys or even his rawhide chewbone. "Really, Margaret, I can't sleep unless I watch some television first. And there's no sense in messing up two rooms."

Twenty minutes later Skye lay across the king-sized bed watching a police show as Adrienne walked back into the room wrapped in one of Vicky's terry-cloth robes. Her bath had felt wonderful, the hot water easing some of the tension from her neck and shoulders. She'd used lots of bath oil and placed several vanilla candles around the tub. Candles made by Lottie Brent. "Your sister is my mother's biggest customer," Julianna had told Adrienne a couple of years ago. "And she's gotten a lot of her friends to buy them by the dozen. I'm so grateful to Vicky. It's important to Mama to feel like she can earn her own living, with as little help from Gail and me as possible."

A wave of sadness hit Adrienne so hard she felt almost dizzy. She would never again see Julianna's beautiful face alight with joy or hear her girlish laughter. She was gone. All that remained of Julianna Brent in this world was a cold, pale corpse lying in a morgue. It seemed impossible. And awful.

"Mom, are you all right?" Skye had glanced away from the television and was looking at her in alarm. "Are you sick?"

Yes, I'm sick at the thought of my friend being dead, Adrienne thought. My friend being *murdered.* "I'm fine, honey. I feel much better after my bath."

"You smell good—like vanilla—but you're awful pale."

"I was generous with Vicky's vanilla bath oil. And I'll have my normal color back by morning."

"I hope so." Skye sighed. "Mom, except for when Daddy got killed, this has been the worst day of my life."

Adrienne went to the bed, sat down, and put her arm around her daughter. "I know, baby. It has for me, too. But it's over now. The whole awful nightmare is over."

Adrienne spoke with conviction, but she was lying. She had an inexplicable but certain feeling that the nightmare was just beginning.

3

"For God's sake, Adrienne, you look like someone beat you up!"

Philip Hamilton—tall and striking in a tuxedo, every light brown hair in place, each little wrinkle flatteringly placed on his patrician face to give him a look of youthful experience and wisdom—grimaced ferociously down at her as she leaned against pillows propped against the headboard. "What's *wrong* with you?" he continued angrily. "Why were you out prowling the streets alone at night?"

"Philip, I must finally admit to you that I've become a hooker." Adrienne couldn't help herself. She was enraged that he was clearly more offended by the "undignified" attack on her than concerned about her welfare. "In my new line of work the hours are bad, but the boost in income has been a godsend. Getting beaten up now and then is just a normal hazard of business."

Philip glared and Vicky stepped forward. "Oh, please don't tease him, Adrienne. He hates that." Vicky's forehead was creased, her cheeks flushed, and her blue eyes dark with worry. "Margaret gave us the gist of what happened. She said you're not badly hurt, but you don't look all right to me."

"I'm going to be fine. I just have some bruises and a cut on the forehead."

"Who did this to you and why?" Philip demanded.

"I didn't see who did it. I was attacked from behind. As to *why,* I suppose someone wanted the huge sum of cash I always carry in my purse."

She'd be damned if she'd mention her belief that someone had really been after her camera and give Philip another reason to blast her for playing amateur detective. Thank goodness Skye was with Rachel, who had returned from her date with Bruce about half an hour ago.

"Margaret says Drew Delaney was hanging around you at the hospital," Philip snapped.

"Drew Delaney *saved* me," she returned indignantly. "He scared off the mugger, then called for an ambulance, made arrangements for Skye to be taken care of, and stayed with me at the hospital until Margaret came for me."

"Delaney only stayed with you to get information," Philip stated emphatically. "I hope you didn't babble all about me."

"Actually, you're all I *ever* talk about, Philip. *You.* Night and day. You're in my every thought—"

"Please!" Vicky said shrilly, running a hand through her short ash-blond hair, exactly the color of Rachel's. "You two are like bickering six-year-olds. Philip, you're being completely insensitive. And Adrienne, you're being ridiculously defensive."

Adrienne couldn't believe she heard herself saying petulantly, "Well, *he* started it!" Philip looked like he was going to fire back, "Did not!" But their gazes met and a slow, unwilling grin appeared on Philip's handsome face before Adrienne burst into reluctant giggles. "She's right, Philip. We sound absurd. I'm embarrassed for both of us."

"I'm embarrassed for us, too," Philip said to her surprise. "But I'm the one who owes an apology. I'm sorry. It's been a very long day and I'm really on edge. I took out my bad mood on you." He sighed. "God, I need a drink."

"So do I," Vicky said.

"You've had enough." He sounded as if he were speaking to a child and Vicky's cheeks flamed. Philip gave Adrienne a tight smile. "I'll leave you to talk to your sister. And I'm truly sorry for what happened to you. I'm glad you weren't hurt more seriously."

After he left, Vicky sat down on the bed and took Adrienne's hand. Her own was damp and not too steady. "You really are all right, aren't you? You're not just covering up?"

"They wouldn't have let me leave the hospital if I weren't fine," Adrienne said, omitting that she'd left against medical advice. "But you look drained, Vicky. I'm sorry I caused a scene with Philip."

"You didn't cause it—he did. He's been in a foul mood most of the day, and the party tonight was just grueling. Dull host and hostess, even duller guests, and far too many crammed into the party room at the club, not to mention faulty air-conditioning. I've perspired all over this silk dress. My makeup is streaked and my hair's gone flat in spite of all the mousse I used. I'm a mess."

She sounded completely defeated and looked as though

she might burst into tears. Adrienne remembered when Vicky had enjoyed all the social life that went with being the wife of Philip Hamilton. But she hadn't seemed to enjoy it for the last couple of years. She looked perpetually harassed and tired.

"We both had awful evenings. I think all of us, including Philip, needs some sleep." Adrienne smiled at her sister. "Everything will be better in the morning."

"It has to be," Vicky said dully, her usually pretty eyes bloodshot. "It just has to be."

4

Adrienne wasn't sure what woke her up. She'd been having a wonderful dream of swimming in the huge pool at la Belle with Julianna and Kit. Then something jerked her from sleep and she was instantly alert and on guard, like an animal sensing danger. She sat up, pulling the blanket to her chest as if it could protect her. But protect her from what?

Music.

She heard familiar music. Loud. Pulsating. Annie Lennox's hauntingly zombielike voice singing "Sweet Dreams."

"Skye?" Adrienne whispered in spite of the music. Then louder, "Skye?"

She reached over but the other side of the bed was empty. Although she knew Skye wasn't there, she flipped on the bedside light and looked again. The sheets were barely rumpled, the fluffy pillow cool.

"Skye!" Adrienne leaped from the bed, tripping on the hem of her taller sister's satin pajamas. Music blared on. A song she'd once loved now only reminded her of a brutally murdered friend. "Skye, where are you?"

Her daughter certainly wasn't blasting a song from the nineteen-eighties in her aunt's house during the middle of the night. But who was? And where was Skye?

Adrienne didn't bother looking for the robe she'd worn earlier. She dashed into the hall and nearly collided with a startled-looking Rachel emerging from her room. "What's going on?" Rachel asked.

"Is Skye in your room?"

"No. I thought she was sleeping with you."

The door at the end of the hall flew open and Vicky dashed out, clumsily tying the belt of her robe. "Rachel, you're waking the whole household with that music!"

"*I'm* not playing music," Rachel flared back indignantly. "It's two in the morning."

Philip stomped into the hall, his hair on end, his pajamas rumpled. "What in God's name are you girls doing at this hour?" he thundered at Rachel. "I have to be at that damned Woman's Club luncheon tomorrow. I need my sleep!"

Rachel's face turned pink with rage. "Why are you blaming me? I'm not playing music. It's coming from downstairs. Maybe Skye's playing it." Her gaze narrowed. "Or maybe it's Margaret."

"Don't be a fool!" Philip said scathingly. Rachel flushed an even deeper red and lowered her head. "Margaret went home hours ago and she would never do such a stupid thing!"

Rachel looked up. "But *I* would?"

Adrienne headed for the stairs. "You three stand there and argue," she flung over her shoulder. "I'm going to find out what's going on. Skye is *not* playing that music but someone is. She could be in trouble, if anyone besides me cares."

She hiked up the long pajama bottoms and ran as fast as she could down the curving staircase. At least Brandon wasn't barking, she thought. Maybe that meant the house hadn't been broken into. Brandon would bark at an intruder.

Except the big dog was shut in a laundry room, unable to alert them to danger. Damn Philip and his rigid household rules, Adrienne fumed.

A delicate lamp with a crystal base burned in the living

room and an overhead light shone in the service hallway running between the kitchen and the dining room. Adrienne dashed into the dining room and ran through it to a small room fitted with an impossibly ornate desk, two tiny, brocade-covered chairs of the Louis XV period, and three walls of huge tapestries that overpowered the small room. Vicky had told her that Great-aunt Octavia called this her "morning room" where she went over household accounts, wrote thank-you notes, and sent out invitations. Vicky hated the room, particularly the supposedly priceless but ugly gray and beige rug where a CD player had been placed, blasting out the last notes of "Sweet Dreams." Beside the player sat two lighted, jasmine-scented candles just like the ones that had surrounded the bed at la Belle where Julianna's body had rested. In front of the candles lay pieces of shattered glass as red as blood.

SIX

I

A moment of silence spun out after "Sweet Dreams" finished before the next song began. Adrienne yelled "Skye? Where are you?"

She heard a dull thud above the sound of the music. Then another. They came from across the hall, in the kitchen. Vicky and Philip now stood motionless in the doorway of the morning room gaping at the CD player as if it were a poisonous snake. Adrienne pushed between them and ran into the kitchen, ignoring the chill of slick white vinyl beneath her bare feet. "Skye?"

"In here!" Two more thuds came from the laundry room at the far end of the kitchen. A metal-framed kitchen chair had been wedged beneath the doorknob, jamming it. Adrienne slid out the chair and threw open the door. Skye came toward her but Brandon made it first, flinging himself at Adrienne, jumping up and placing his big paws on her shoulders while licking her face amid a flurry of ecstatic whines.

"Mom, we were so scared!" Skye cried, moving closer to her mother. Brandon wouldn't budge, making little talky noises as if verifying the horror of their predicament. Adrienne gave him a hug, and took his paws, gently lowering him to the floor while uttering comforting sounds. When he was somewhat calmed, he moved so she could tend to her daughter, who hugged her with equal passion.

"I couldn't sleep knowing Brandon was down here all by himself, scared and lonely," Skye explained. "So I came down. We cuddled up and fell asleep. All of a sudden, Brandon barked a couple of times, jumped up and headed for the door. I knew by the way he was acting that something was wrong. I yelled 'Who is it?' but no one answered. I got really scared and then I heard a noise at the door. I guess that was someone putting the chair under the knob so we couldn't get out. I still grabbed Brandon and held his mouth shut, though, because I was afraid the person out there was the man who'd killed Julianna. I thought if Brandon stayed quiet and didn't make a big fuss, the man might not change his mind and come in and murder us, too. Then there was all that music! We didn't even try to get out until we heard you yelling."

"You did exactly the right thing," Adrienne said.

Skye managed a shaky smile. "So what happened. A robbery?"

"I don't know yet. Let's go to the others. They're in the morning room."

Adrienne made no attempt to shut Brandon up in the laundry room again. He was frightened and needed to be with Skye. To hell with Philip.

The elder Hamiltons had stepped into the room, but it was Rachel who stood by the CD player. She leaned down, punched the off button, then sank to her knees and blew out the candles. "I *hate* the scent of jasmine. Mom, did you buy these from Lottie Brent?"

"No," Vicky said faintly. "I only buy vanilla scent."

Rachel picked up a piece of red glass. "My wind chimes!" she cried. "I brought them in from the porch before I went out with Bruce because the wind was so strong."

The beautiful, hand-painted Venetian glass chimes, Adrienne thought. Philip had bought them for Rachel on a European trip when she was fifteen and she'd loved them dearly. Sometimes Adrienne saw her simply staring up at them, her face bathed in light shining through the ruby glass.

Rachel began gathering the pieces of glass and asked in a trembling voice, "Why would someone do this?"

"Finding out how someone got in this house would be a better question," Philip said. He turned to Vicky. "Did you turn on the security system?"

"Yes, of course." Vicky hesitated. "At least, I think I did."

"You *think* you did?" Philip's face stiffened. "Don't you remember doing something that important?"

"I was so tired and Margaret was telling us about Adrienne. I rushed upstairs to see her. I was upset and I just don't remember!"

"All it takes is punching a few buttons to keep us safe at night and you don't remember." Philip looked at his wife as if she were an idiot. "Honestly, Vicky, where is your mind lately?"

Vicky seemed to shrink inside her lovely kimono robe and Adrienne felt a surge of anger. "Vicky is not the only person in this house," she snapped at Philip. "Why couldn't *you* turn on the security system?"

Philip shot her a steely look. "It's Vicky's job. I assumed she'd done it."

"Oh, *stop* it!" Rachel shouted, tears running down her cheeks. "All you two do is argue. I'm sick of hearing it. And shouldn't we be checking the house to see if anything is missing? Or if anyone is still *here*?"

"We should call Sheriff Flynn," Skye said.

"He's the county sheriff and we're in the city limits," Adrienne said. "This is a matter for the city police."

"Still, Lucas would come if *you* asked, Mom," Skye argued.

Philip turned to glare at the girl and caught sight of Brandon. "Put that dog outside or back in the laundry room."

"No." Skye steadily met Philip's stare. "If somebody's still in the house, Brandon could be protection."

Adrienne knew very well Brandon's forte wasn't protection, but she was so proud of Skye for standing up to the formidable Philip, she didn't add a word.

Philip continued to look at the girl for a moment, clearly surprised and perhaps a bit daunted, then announced in an overloud voice, "I'm going to search the house."

Vicky clutched his arm. "No. If someone is still here, he could hurt you. We'll wait for the police. Where are they, anyway? Aren't they supposed to come when the security alarm goes off?"

"The alarm has to be turned *on* before it can go *off*." Philip was so angry he talked through clenched teeth. "I'll only look around a little. Vicky, you call the police. Skye, put the dog back—" He wavered. "Keep the dog out of my way. Rachel, go upstairs if you can't stop whining over your wind chimes."

"Do you have any orders for me, sir?" Adrienne asked tartly.

Philip threw her a narrow-eyed look. "I think you've caused quite enough trouble for one night. Go back to bed."

"Not with the police coming. I'll put on a pot of coffee."

"Fine. Bake some cookies, too. We'll make a party out of this whole damned mess."

Adrienne started to fire back a scathing reply when she suddenly realized how awful Philip looked—gray, drawn, ten years older than he had last week when she'd seen him. He was unnerved by the situation—maybe even frightened— but there was something else wrong, too. She could see a vein throbbing in his temple. Was he on the verge of a stroke? Did healthy men in their mid-forties have strokes? She felt an unaccustomed twinge of concern for him.

"Be careful, Philip." He threw a startled look at Adrienne. "Everyone is right. Someone could still be in the house. Take Brandon with you."

"Brandon!" Skye cried. "No! He could get hurt!"

Philip paused, then raised an eyebrow at Adrienne. "I guess some people consider it better to sacrifice me than the dog," he said dryly.

"Considering the way you're acting, it's no wonder," Adrienne returned.

Rachel dropped a piece of glass from her ruined wind chimes and headed upstairs. Skye started to follow, then stopped. "I think she wants to be alone," she whispered to Adrienne as Philip started down the hall. "Her dad hurt her feelings. I never heard him talk to her so mean before."

"He's upset."

"Mom, sometimes I don't get why Aunt Vicky married him. He's such a grouch when he's not in front of all the people he thinks are important and might vote for him."

"I know, honey. But he didn't use to be that way. When Vicky married him, he was charming and funny. A little bit arrogant, but still an agreeable person. He even liked *me*." Skye grinned. "I can't imagine what's happened to him over the years. But we're not going to worry about Philip now. You and Brandon stay and protect me and Vicky."

"I need a drink," Vicky said suddenly. "Want one, Adrienne?"

"No. They gave me some kind of painkiller at the hospital. And I don't think you should have one, either. The police might smell it on your breath."

"To hell with them." Resolutely, Adrienne and Skye trailed after Vicky into the kitchen and watched her mix two shots of vodka into a small glass of orange juice. As she took a large gulp, Adrienne wondered if alcohol was becoming a problem for her sister.

Fifteen minutes later, two deputies arrived. Every light was on, inside and outside, and Adrienne had caught sight of neighbors peering from their windows even though it was two-thirty in the morning. Vicky sipped a second drink and sat at the kitchen table, the earlier alarm in her blue eyes dulling to an indifferent glaze. Adrienne called Lucas and put on a pot of coffee while Skye hovered near the small kitchen television, ostensibly watching an old movie while keeping out of the way.

As the city deputies searched the house, Philip stalked after them, with loud, nonstop hectoring. Adrienne knew someone less influential than Philip Hamilton would have been told to sit down and stay out of the way while the deputies did their work. Which is exactly what Lucas Flynn did when he arrived. He took Philip aside and talked with him earnestly. After a couple of minutes, Adrienne could see some of the tension ease from Philip's rigid face and shoulders. For a man like him, she guessed, merely having the county's chief law enforcement officer present at his little drama would make Philip feel better.

Shortly afterward, Lucas had a moment alone with Adrienne. "I didn't find out until about eleven o'clock what happened to you on the street this evening. God, I'm sorry."

"I'll live. But I did come here to spend the night because I thought I'd be safer. So much for my infallible judgment."

Lucas shrugged. "You couldn't have guessed this would happen. The security system wasn't turned on and there's no sign of a break-in. Any idea what's going on here?"

"You mean it was an inside job?" Lucas's mouth quirked at her language. She ignored his amusement. "Do any of us strike you as likely suspects, Sheriff?"

"For breaking wind chimes and blasting a boom box in the middle of the night? Not really."

"Nothing was taken?"

"Not according to Philip."

"Lucas, this is even stranger than it seems. Those candles are the same scent as the ones that were in Julianna's room at the hotel. And the song playing on the boom box was 'Sweet Dreams' by the Eurythmics. That has been Julianna's favorite song for twenty years. She played tapes and CDs of it, and she sang it all the time." Suddenly Adrienne felt as if Julianna were running one of her long, cool fingers down her neck, filling her with a terrible feeling of dread.

"Lucas, someone knew I'd immediately connect the candles with finding Julianna's body. And they knew I'd associate 'Sweet Dreams' with Julianna," she said urgently. "The song wasn't a random selection."

He looked at her in concern. "Then why was it being played in *this* house?"

"Because somebody is watching me and knew I was here tonight." Unconsciously, she reached out and clutched his wrist. "Lucas, that song was meant as a threat to *me*."

2

Although the police left within the hour and everybody went back to bed, Adrienne doubted if anyone got any sleep. By six o'clock, everyone except Vicky was up, all in varying degrees of tired grouchiness except for the irrepressible Brandon, who seemed to have found the evening's uproar vastly entertaining. His mood improved even more when at six-thirty the housekeeper, Mrs. Pitt, arrived and, after fixing breakfast for the humans, gave him a big slice of ham with scrambled eggs and a freshly baked biscuit.

Just as Adrienne was popping a piece of warm, buttery biscuit into her own mouth, Margaret arrived, a well-dressed whirlwind, asking questions about the break-in, taking notes, firing orders to everyone present about what should and should not be said to reporters, whom she referred to as "vultures."

Rachel looked at her sourly. "It's so nice to know you think of me as a vulture, Margaret."

"I don't. You're just a summer intern on a local paper, not a real reporter," Margaret returned with cold dismissal.

Rachel clattered her fork on her plate and pushed her chair away from the table. "I've had enough." She glared at Margaret. "Of breakfast *and* you. As far as I'm concerned, you can—"

Adrienne interrupted loudly. "Mrs. Pitt, will you fix a pot of coffee for me to take up to Vicky?" Rachel stomped out of the kitchen, throwing a murderous look at Margaret. "And maybe a couple of those delicious biscuits, too."

Mrs. Pitt, a middle-aged woman cursed with a face that looked like she'd bitten into an unripe persimmon and blessed with the disposition of an angel, nodded and smiled. "Coming right up," she said as she retrieved a thermos and breakfast tray from a cabinet. "Mrs. Hamilton *is* partial to my biscuits."

"Where's Vicky?" Margaret demanded. "Is she sick?"

Adrienne bristled at her tone. "Vicky was tired after the party last night and the break-in certainly didn't help. She didn't sleep a wink." Adrienne had no idea whether or not Vicky had slept, but she felt protective of her sister in the face of Margaret's aggressiveness. "She needs to spend the morning in bed."

Margaret huffed with impatience at this frailty on Vicky's part, but before she had a chance to say anything, Philip intervened. "I'm not feeling on top of the world, either. Let's take this morning off, Margaret."

She looked at him as if he'd just ordered her to strip naked. Her eyes widened, her lips parted, and her whole body registered shock. "Take the morning off? The *entire* morning?" He nodded. "Philip, have you forgotten the Woman's Club luncheon? We need to go over your speech. And I want to bring you up to speed on that new sewer project in Baker County."

"If there's one thing I can't bear to talk about this morning, it's a sewer system," Philip groaned as he poured a third cup of coffee. "And I know my speech, although I'm cutting down on some of the statistics you added."

"Are you saying *women* are bored by statistics?" Margaret asked stiffly.

"I'm saying that at this kind of gathering, *everyone* is bored by a barrage of statistics. It's a luncheon, Margaret, not a corporate board meeting."

Margaret's carefully colored lips compressed in annoyance. A slim foot encased in an expensive taupe pump tapped on the vinyl kitchen floor. "Maybe you'll feel more like working in an hour or so."

"Maybe," Philip said offhandedly. "But I don't think so. After all, Margaret, we're leaving day after tomorrow for the northern part of the state. Even though I have this luncheon, I need the afternoon and evening to rest. We've had a hectic schedule for the past couple of months." Adrienne noticed that he looked deeply tired, as if all his natural dynamism had drained away during the night.

"Vicky *will* rouse herself to go on the trip north, won't she?" Margaret asked testily. "It's important for her to be by your side."

"She knows that and of course she'll go," Philip said. "Rachel will stay here since she has a job, so at least you won't have to put up with her since you two don't seem to get along."

Margaret looked offended. "I try to get along with Rachel. *She* is the problem."

"Whatever." Philip glanced at his gung-ho assistant. "Since you have so much energy this morning, Margaret, you can give Adrienne and Skye a ride home."

"Take them home?" Margaret couldn't hide the dismay in her voice. "All the way home?"

Philip looked exasperated. "No, Margaret, I thought you could drop them at the corner and maybe they could hitch a ride to their house. Yes, *all* the way home."

"I didn't mean it the way it sounded. It's just that I have so much to do." Margaret sighed. "All right. Since you don't want to work, I might as well put my time to good use." She paused, her gaze falling on Brandon who was scooting his bowl around the kitchen, trying to get the last morsels of food. "You want me to take the dog, too?"

"I don't think Skye is inclined to give him up." Philip managed a small smile for Skye. "So, yes, the dog will go, too. Soon. I can tell Adrienne and Skye are anxious to get home. We didn't offer them a very peaceful night."

"Fine," Margaret said shortly. She shot a glance somewhere just past Adrienne's head. "Ready to go?"

Adrienne hadn't considered leaving yet, but Philip was obviously in a hurry to clear his house of her and Skye. And especially Brandon. He couldn't hide his impatience. "I'm not even dressed, Margaret," Adrienne said. "Give us twenty minutes."

Exactly twenty-three minutes later Margaret hustled them into her car. The rain had stopped hours ago. The sky was cloudless and, in the morning sun, the grass and flowers looked bright and renewed. As they pulled out of the driveway, Adrienne exclaimed, "Isn't it a beautiful morning?"

"I suppose," Margaret said flatly.

"*I* think it's a beautiful morning, Mom," Skye said dutifully.

Adrienne looked at the stone-faced Margaret. "I'm sorry to put you out like this. I'll be glad to pay for having the inside of your car detailed if Brandon has gotten hair on the upholstery."

"That won't be necessary," Margaret said curtly. Her plans for the morning had gone haywire and she wasn't taking the change well. Flexibility wasn't one of her strong points, Adrienne thought, both amused and annoyed. "A long-haired dog is terribly messy, though," Margaret added. "If you must have a dog, a poodle is best. *They* don't shed."

"Well, now, isn't that just fabulous for them?" Adrienne shot back sharply. Margaret's jaw tightened, but there was nothing Adrienne could say to take the sting from her words. She decided to leave well enough alone.

Afterward, only the sound of Brandon's panting broke the silence on the uncomfortable three-mile drive home. Adrienne felt like whooping with joy when they turned onto her street until she saw two patrol cars parked in front of her house.

"Good God, *now* what?" Margaret burst out.

Adrienne leaned forward in her seat, as if a closer look could make the certain sign of trouble disappear. But the patrol cars remained. She saw Lucas standing on the front walk.

"Mom?" Skye said tentatively from the backseat.

"Lucas is here," Adrienne answered. "Everything will be all right."

Adrienne didn't know what was wrong, but having the sheriff on the scene lowered her fear level a notch. Margaret pulled into the driveway and sighed. "I'll wait to find out what's wrong."

"You don't have to, Margaret. I'm sure there's nothing you can do to help."

"Philip will need to be informed of the current problem."

"I see. You're not staying because of us, you're staying because of *Philip*," Adrienne returned sharply. "He's always your number one concern."

Margaret said coolly, "I get paid to make him my number one concern."

I just hope making him your priority is professional, not emotional, Adrienne thought, but kept her mouth shut. Now certainly wasn't the time to start an argument with Margaret.

Adrienne got out of the car as Lucas walked up to her. He looked tired and a bit rigid around the mouth, the way he always did when he was under strain. "What's happened?" she blurted before he had a chance to say anything.

"A city deputy cruised past this morning. He knew about your mugging and that you'd spent the night at your sister's, but the front door was wide open, so he stopped to take a look. He knows about our relationship so he called me as well as the other city cops. We haven't had time to do a thorough search, but your place has been tossed."

"Tossed?"

"Searched. There doesn't seem to be any real damage, so vandalism wasn't the cause, and theft appears to be out because your televisions, VCR, DVD player, and stereo haven't been touched."

"Searched," Adrienne repeated, then fell silent for a few seconds to process the information. Then it hit her. "The camera! Someone was looking for the camera with the pictures I took at the Belle!"

Lucas raised his eyebrows. "What pictures are you talking about?"

Adrienne went to Margaret's car, opened the back door, and withdrew her denim jacket. "This was soaked so Margaret gave me her raincoat and I threw my jacket in the backseat and forgot it." She plunged her hand into the inner pocket. "Here it is!" She held up the Olympus Zoom 170 and boomed triumphantly, "It's been in Margaret's car all night. Not at my house, not at Vicky's!"

Lucas stared quizzically at her, then said calmly, "Will you please slow down and explain to me what this camera has to do with anything?"

"You're too excited, Mom. I'll tell it." Skye sounded remarkably mature and composed. She stood by her mother, holding tightly to Brandon's leash. "When we were at the Belle yesterday morning, Brandon was running around in the woods and I was chasing him. Mom said she thought she saw someone—not me—hanging around in the woods. So she took photographs."

"Why?" Lucas asked.

"Because she believed the person might be a thief and she would have gotten a picture of him so you could identify him and catch him. I didn't really see anyone, but I felt like someone was in the woods, too."

Adrienne stepped in. "After we found Julianna, I thought I might have gotten a picture not of a vandal but of her murderer. I was taking the camera to Photo Finish when I was mugged. I think the mugger was after my camera."

"Because the mugger was the killer," Skye added unnecessarily.

"You believe that same person raided the Hamilton house last night when they didn't find the camera in your purse?" Lucas asked.

"Yes. And before or afterward, he searched my house. Since my house wasn't robbed, it makes perfect sense."

Lucas nodded slowly. "Yes, it does." He reached out. "I'll take that camera and get the film developed. It's not safe for you to have possession of this any longer."

Adrienne handed him the camera. "I'm sorry I didn't tell you about it yesterday. I was so rattled after we found Julianna."

"I didn't think you were trying to withhold evidence," Lucas said with a smile. "But you surely got yourself in trouble by not giving it to me yesterday morning."

"I doubt if whoever killed Julianna would have known if I *had* given you the camera unless he was still watching me. But I feel better having it out of my possession." Adrienne cast a gloomy look at her house. "I guess I'd better go in and see how much damage has been done."

The floribunda bushes on either side of her front door looked radiant in the morning sun. Adrienne drew in their strong, sweet scent as if it could fortify her. The thought of a stranger pawing through the contents of her home made her feel even more violated than the attack last night.

She stepped inside and found that entering her own home felt like an assault on her vision after spending time in Vicky's subdued house. The living room contained an explosion of yellow, rose, ripe peach, and blue furnishings—some modern, some antiques, some makeshift creations of her own like the coffee table with a huge block of amber glass for a top and faux books for sides. Cushions now lay on the floor. Drawers hung open, their contents spilled. Magazines and books lay in heaps and a potted plant had been turned over, leaving dirt on the carpet. The room was a mess, but nothing appeared to have been broken. The same was true of the kitchen and dining room, but it was only the contents of one room that brought panic to Adrienne's heart. Her studio.

She dashed down the hall to the mid-sized bedroom with corner windows she'd converted into her workroom. She expected to see a catastrophe. Instead, a studio easel stood near the windows holding a fresh canvas she'd just stretched and primed, intending to use for her painting of la Belle Rivière. The oil painting she planned to show at the French Art Colony Summer Gala sat on another easel beside the wall. It had been there for two weeks, drying, and to her great relief, it hadn't been defaced. On a long worktable, all her tubes of oil paint were still arranged in neat lines. There was no sign that someone besides herself had been in the room except the open worktable drawers and a sketch of Skye that lay on the floor undamaged.

"Someone could have had a heyday in here," Lucas remarked. "Apparently your intruder was an art lover."

"Thank goodness. I couldn't possibly replace the painting by the wall in time for the gala, and I had my heart set on using it." She peered at it more closely to make sure the uninvited guest hadn't been tempted to leave some little sign of his presence in oil paint. He hadn't.

Slightly comforted, Adrienne headed from the studio to her own bedroom. At the doorway she stopped, her heart sinking. This room had not been treated as gently as the studio.

A small chair nearly blocked the doorway. Lucas moved it out of the way and said, "I haven't checked this room yet. Better let me go in first."

"No one is hiding in there." Adrienne glanced at the sun-washed room and filmy curtains wafting in the breeze coming through an open window. "If someone was still around this morning, he would have gone out the window when the police arrived."

She stepped into the room and looked around. All the drawers of her oak dresser had been pulled out and the contents dumped. Underwear, nightgowns, panty hose, and socks lay everywhere. The bed had been stripped of the spread and sheets, and the mattress and box spring pushed off the frame. Shoes and boxes from her closet had been flung around the room almost as if the intruder had gone into a frenzy of frustration.

"I hope you didn't have anything valuable in here," Lucas said.

"Luckily, my extensive collections of jewels and furs are

stored in vaults," Adrienne murmured, trying to sound light although she was more disturbed by the chaos in front of her than she cared to admit.

She walked slowly to the dresser whose top was bare. Her small jewelry box and silver-backed brush and mirror set given to her by her mother had been swept off the top. The mirror was broken and beside the pieces of glass lay more glass from her shattered cologne bottle. A strong wave of tuberose scent hit her when she drew near.

"So much for the money I spent on a new cologne this week," she said drearily. "Money wasted, although I'm glad I didn't spring for actual perfume."

"The damage could have been much worse than a broken mirror and a bottle of cologne," Lucas reminded her.

"You're right. I should be grateful—"

At that moment, Adrienne looked up from the mess on the floor. Her expression froze and Lucas followed her gaze. On the big mirror above the dresser had been scrawled a message in red:

LEAVE OR DIE

SEVEN

I

"Oh, my God," Adrienne gasped. "Is that written in blood?"

Lucas walked toward it, then peered closely. She noticed he was careful not to touch the dresser top or the mirror. Finally, he said, "It's not blood. It's waxy."

Adrienne crept closer to him, never removing her gaze from the message. Then she recognized the color. "It's lipstick. Persian Red. I left it on the dresser."

Lucas backed away from the dresser and looked around. "I don't see the tube. Are you sure it's your lipstick?"

"Yes. The color was too bright for me in natural light, but the case was pretty so I left it standing on the dresser."

"The tube could be here in this mess."

Adrienne turned to him. "Lucas, you act like the only important thing is finding the lipstick. Hasn't the message sunk in yet?"

" 'Leave or Die.' Pretty melodramatic. I think it's meant to scare you, not actually warn you."

"I'm glad you can be so sanguine about it!"

"When you use words like *sanguine,* you're mad," Lucas said mildly. "I'm not taking the message lightly, Adrienne. I'm just not panicking over it. And neither should you."

"Of course not. It's par for the course to come home and find death threats scrawled on my mirror. What the hell am I getting so shook up about?"

Lucas put his hands on her shoulders and looked deeply into her eyes. "Do you have faith that I know what I'm doing as a cop?"

"You know I do. But—"

"No buts. This *could* be a threat. But my instincts tell me that if someone really wanted to harm you, they would have done a lot of damage to this house. Whoever searched the place was almost careful until they got to this room, where I figure they fell into a temper fit for not finding anything. And that message sounds like something a kid would write."

"So you think all of this is just nothing."

"I didn't say that." He glanced around, his eyes clearly focused inward, and finally said, "I think you and Skye should stay at Vicky's for a few days. Just in case."

"So we wouldn't be alone *just in case* we're in danger? Well, that won't work. Philip and Vicky are leaving tomorrow morning on a campaign trip. Only Rachel would be there, and if I'm a target, I don't think Vicky would appreciate my aiming danger her daughter's way. Besides, their house was broken into, as well."

"Because the alarm system wasn't on. You don't even have an alarm system."

"I'll have one installed today."

"Adrienne, you might not be able to get one today," Lucas said. "If you're determined to stay away from Rachel to keep her out of harm's way, then you should just leave Point Pleasant."

"Leave Point Pleasant? Where I have a teaching job? A job I *need*? A job I could lose for good if I just walk out?"

"You're only teaching two classes in summer school."

"Nevertheless, the classes have started. If it was just a matter of my being gone for a few days, missing each class even two times wouldn't be so bad. But you don't know when you'll find Julianna's killer. It could be weeks. I *can't* be gone that long, Lucas." He was still scowling, but she'd felt she had to dig in her heels on this issue. Her teaching position was absolutely necessary for the livelihood of her and her daughter. She took a deep breath and spoke with a pretense of confidence. "Besides, even if the murderer isn't in the photos I took, he can't go on thinking I saw him and have just decided not to tell on him."

"Why can't he?"

"Because he knows I'd be afraid of him. He'd know I'd want him locked up. After a few days of silence from me, he'll have to realize he has nothing to fear from me."

"And in the meantime?"

"In the meantime you'll use your considerable influence as sheriff to insist a security company install an alarm system today. Skye and I will be extra careful. I won't let her out of my sight, which will drive her nuts but make me feel better. Rachel will be safe in her house, Skye and I will be safe in our house, and all this trouble will die down."

"I'm not so sure about that, Adrienne," Lucas said slowly. "There's something I haven't told you."

She stiffened, wanting to clap her hands over her ears like a child but forcing herself to listen. "What is it?"

"Claude Duncan died in a fire last night. That's why I didn't come to the hospital when I heard about your attack. I was at his place. It was awful. The cottage went up like a torch, Adrienne, and I'd bet my life it was no accident."

2

The smell of charred wood hung over the rubble like a low-lying cloud, befouling the clean morning air. A shroud of ashes dulled the colors of the nearby shrubbery and flowers, and the remaining grass around the burn site lay flattened and drenched by the fire hoses that had unsuccessfully tried to quench the fire that had devoured the caretaker's cabin.

Drew Delaney couldn't hold his breath any longer. He drew in air that felt as if it were singeing the inside of his

nose and brought tears to his eyes. Even his meager breakfast of toast and coffee rolled in his stomach as he thought of
the man that had met his end in this inferno.

Claude Duncan.

One of the town's losers. One of the town's human jokes.

Drew remembered being seventeen and speeding away
from la Belle Rivière in his uncle's silver Corvette on a
steaming summer day. He'd felt hot, he'd felt cool, he'd felt
on top of the world because that night he had a date with
Adrienne, in his opinion the prettiest girl in town, and he
was taking her out in the Corvette. Yeah, it had been shaping
up to be one fine day.

Then he'd spotted a lanky boy with stringy hair trudging
down the road. Drew recognized him instantly. Claude Duncan, the manager's son. He was around eleven, thin, stringy,
and hunch-shouldered as if drained of every bit of joy and
confidence. Almost without realizing what he was doing,
Drew had stopped beside him. "Hey, Claude, where're you
going?"

Claude had jumped and said nervously, "I'm not up to
anything bad. Honest."

Drew had laughed. "I didn't say you were. I just asked
where you're going. You look like a guy in need of a ride."

"Oh. I do? I mean, I am. I'm goin' to the drugstore for my
mom. She's sick and Dad's too busy to pick up the refill of
her medicine."

Drew had stared at the boy. The drugstore was four miles
away. His father expected him to walk eight miles round trip
in this heat? Probably. Mr. Duncan was a first-class jerk in
Drew's opinion. "How about a ride?"

"A ride?" Claude had looked at the Corvette as if it were
some kind of fabulous space vehicle. "In *this*?"

"Sure. Hop in. I'll get you to the drugstore in no time."

Claude had gingerly gotten in the car and gazed around
him with wide eyes. "This is the coolest car I've ever seen,
Mr. Delaney," he'd said in awed tones. "Is it yours?"

"No, my uncle's. But I'll have one like it someday soon. And my name's Drew. I'm way too young to be called Mr. Delaney."

"Oh. Yes, sir. Drew. I'll remember that. But in front of my dad, I have to call you Mr. Delaney. It's one of his rules."

Screw his rules, Drew had almost said, but kept silent. Encouraging Claude to defy his father would only get the boy into trouble.

Drew had waited in the Corvette outside the drugstore for Claude, drawing the admiring looks of several fine-looking girls, in which he'd basked. When Claude had emerged from the store, his shoulders no longer drooped and his step was almost jaunty. To his amazement, Drew realized he couldn't stand to whisk Claude right back to the hotel and his father. Instead, he'd taken him to the Dairy Queen, where they'd each had a chocolate sundae, then he'd roared around town a couple of times, radio booming, to show off the car. Claude had actually laughed, and Drew realized that in all the years he'd had been allowed to hang around the pool at la Belle because he was Kit Kirkwood's friend, he'd never seen Claude even smile.

They'd returned to the hotel in a little over an hour, much quicker than Claude could have made the trip on foot. The boy had climbed from the Corvette, looking enraptured, and beamed at Drew. "Thanks, Mr. Delaney. I mean Drew." He'd blushed. "Honest, this has been the best day of my whole life!" Then he'd bolted toward the little cottage, smiling and clutching the bag of medicine for his mother who Drew had heard was slowly dying of cancer.

When Drew had returned to Point Pleasant less than two years ago, he couldn't believe the change in the once wide-eyed boy with so much joy bottled up inside. Clearly, his spirit had been broken, no doubt by the formidable Mr. Duncan, whom Kit Kirkwood's mother had always tolerated because he ran la Belle so smoothly. A few times over the last couple of years, Drew had bought Claude a drink in a local bar and chatted with him for a while, but the encounters were depressing. Claude never had much to say when he wasn't drunk, his wits dulled by emotional abuse and alcoholism. When he'd been drinking, he was alternately a depressed whiner or a ridiculous braggadocio. Drew had felt immensely sorry for the man Claude had become.

And now the poor guy was dead before he'd reached the age of thirty.

Drew had still been at the hospital with Adrienne when Claude had been brought in last night, horribly burned. A nurse Drew had once dated had told him confidentially that Claude had second- and third-degree burns over eighty percent of his body. Even if he'd been alive when he reached the hospital, he would never have stood a chance. But she'd also heard a doctor observe that the pupils of Claude's eyes were completely constricted, indicating ingestion of drugs. She said she hoped Claude had been "out of it" before the fire got to him.

Claude's death could have been accidental, Drew thought. After all, la Belle had suffered more than its share of deaths over the years. But two in less than twenty-four hours? Even for la Belle that would be hard to imagine. Unless the deaths were connected. But Drew wondered what possible relation Julianna Brent could have had to Claude Duncan. Certainly not romantic. Certainly not business. Something they both knew? But what? The identity of Julianna's lover? Hell, Claude couldn't keep any information to himself for more than a day. If he'd known who was her lover, he would have blabbed the name all over town, swearing everyone he told to secrecy. Drew was convinced Claude hadn't known the name of Julianna's lover. So, what could have been the link in their deaths?

Drew closed his dark eyes and shook his head. Sometimes his reporter's curiosity wore him out. His mother had called it plain old nosiness and warned that it would get him in trouble someday. But that hadn't happened yet, nor had he learned to turn off the inquisitiveness of his mind.

Yellow police tape surrounded the remains of the cottage. A middle-aged, dumpy deputy with a perpetually red face Drew knew as Sonny Keller strode toward him. "I don't know how you got past the roadblock on Rivière Lane, Delaney, but you're not supposed to go near the cottage."

"I simply walked around the roadblock through the woods, and I'm nowhere near the cottage," Drew answered pleasantly.

"Sheriff Flynn doesn't want a bunch of souvenir-seekers up here."

"I didn't intend to raid the place. Besides, it doesn't look like there's much left to take."

Keller shook his head. "It was a hell of a mess. There wouldn't be anything at all left if somebody hadn't spotted the fire from the highway and called it in right before that second cloudburst hit. All that rain's the only thing saved Claude."

"For a short, agonizing time at least." Drew shuddered inwardly. "Any idea what caused the fire?"

Keller looked at him cagily. "I know your game. You'll run right back to your newspaper and print every word I say. Flynn said for us to keep quiet about what we know."

"Then you *do* know what caused the fire."

"I didn't say that."

"Oh," Drew said in mock disappointment. "I figured with all your experience, Keller, you of all people would probably know something."

"Well, actually, *I* do." Drew had known Sonny Keller couldn't keep his mouth shut if someone hinted the lawman didn't have all the answers, no matter what Lucas Flynn had ordered. "Flynn's having an arson expert come to look at the place this afternoon," Keller almost whispered, looking over his shoulder although no one was near. "Can you believe that? We don't need some smart-aleck so-called expert up here messing around. It's plain as day that idiot Claude got drunk, turned over his bottle of whiskey, passed out, and dropped a lighted cigarette in the alcohol. *Voilà!*" he ended triumphantly, pronouncing the word *vi-o-lay*.

"Hmmm." Drew nodded solemnly as if he were thinking this over. Then he said, "But Claude could hold a lot of liquor. If he'd drunk so much he'd passed out, there couldn't have been enough alcohol left in his bottle for a cigarette dropped into it to cause a fire big enough to wipe out this place, Keller. How do you explain that?" he asked in polite perplexity.

Sonny Keller hesitated, clearly troubled by the complication Drew had thrown into his simple explanation. Finally he drew a deep breath and said with bravado, "Well, I say a cigarette in a little alcohol could have caused it. Dozens of ways the cigarette could have ignited the liquor to cause a big fire. Yes indeed, that's the answer."

"Maybe so," Drew said casually, "but I knew Claude a little bit and I see two problems with that scenario. One, Claude didn't smoke. His mother died of lung cancer and he swore never to touch a cigarette. And he kept that promise. Never had a pack on him and never accepted one if someone offered. And two, the doctor who examined him before he died said his eyes showed he was pumped full of some drug. Now I happen to know that Claude was *terrified* of drugs. Liquor he couldn't get enough of, but he would never have voluntarily taken anything except an aspirin or an antibiotic." Drew looked at the increasingly glowering deputy. "And Keller, all of that says to me that someone must have helped Claude Duncan on his way last night."

3

A shrine. That's what this place was—a damned shrine to Julianna Brent.

Gail Brent stood in her mother Lottie's cabin. She hated the place. Lottie had lived in it all of her life and called it "humble." Gail called it a dump, which hurt Lottie and made Juli angry. But it *was* a dump, Gail thought defiantly. It was small, primitive, full of furniture bought at yard sales and some crude pieces built by her grandfather, with faded rag rugs on the cheap wooden floor no amount of varnish could make presentable. And to make matters worse for Gail, over the last sixteen years, the walls had become almost covered with photos of Julianna in fashion layouts and on magazine covers with names like *Vogue, Glamour,* and *Cosmopolitan.* None of Gail's school papers bearing As and glowing comments earned places. They were just smiled at, vaguely commented on, then tucked away in a cheap folder. Meanwhile, every time Lottie prominently displayed another picture of Julianna, Gail had felt like a voodoo doll being stabbed with a needle.

Gail's watch showed that it was ten till eight in the morning, but Lottie wasn't home. Gail was certain her mother hadn't been home for at least twenty-four hours. There were no cooking smells, no open windows, and the cat on the front porch was mewing hungrily. Why had Lottie been gone so long? Was she just out wandering? Or in light of Juli's murder, was Lottie's absence more significant?

Gail's gaze fell on a particularly striking photo of her sister in a forest-green sequined gown with her auburn hair pulled high, and her golden-brown eyes innocent and coquettish at the same time. Gail hated to admit she thought her sister was beautiful, and she couldn't stop comparing herself to Julianna. There was no contest, she thought glumly, walking over to a small mirror for a self-study.

Her hair was shoulder-length, a glossy natural dark blond. My hair is great, Gail thought. Her boyfriend, Deputy Sonny Keller, seemed half in love with her hair, which he once compared to honey-colored satin when he was drunk. He loved her hair and her big breasts, even though she thought they were too big and were beginning to sag although she was only thirty-two and had never nursed a child.

And although her teeth were perfectly straight and white, looking at her round face with what everyone called "chipmunk cheeks," her small and murky blue eyes, her snub nose, and her too-thick neck sent Gail into the habitual fit of depression.

When she was growing up, Lottie had continually told her she was cute, even pretty when she smiled, but Gail had been certain Lottie was lying. She knew Lottie hated her because Gail looked like her father Butch, who'd been short and squat, an uneducated but smart man whom Lottie had driven away with her craziness. Gail had seen a goodness in her father no one else ever seemed to notice, and she knew her father had loved her, even though Juli had always captured all of his attention and his kisses. Julianna and Lottie had been *happy* when Butch left, Gail seethed inwardly after all these years. *Happy!* She'd been devastated.

Gail unconsciously clenched her teeth at the thought, then quickly relaxed her jaw. She didn't want to chip a beautiful tooth by reverting back to the clenching and grinding that had plagued her as a child. But she couldn't seem to help herself lately. She despised Julianna's latest romantic involvement. She found it filthy, almost unholy if she had been religious, which she was not in the least. But most of all, Gail viewed it as sickeningly unfair. Once again, Juli had gotten what she wanted, just like *everything* was for her!

I should have done something about the situation years ago, Gail chided herself. Julianna had caused a man who loved her too much pain. Instead, Gail had let things drift while she worked out a plan. But as usual, she'd vacillated, afraid to take action until she'd poked every possible hole into every scenario she'd concocted. In the meantime, the situation had reached critical mass and gotten completely out of control. And to top it off, now Julianna had probably become a saint to the man Gail loved more than life.

Feeling hot tears of grief and frustration beginning to run from her murky blue eyes down her chipmunk cheeks, she pushed aside a heavy trunk and looked at a piece of scuffed wood beneath it. Gail got one of her mother's kitchen knives and began gently running it around the edges of a barely visible square crack in the wood. Around and around, careful not to damage the already worn varnish. After nearly three minutes, she was able to pry the blade into a crack and lift up an eight-by-ten-inch piece of wood. She laid the piece aside, reached inside and clutched a velvet sack that had covered a particularly fabulous bottle of Crown Royal given to her father by a Christmas-generous boss. Neither the boss's mood nor the Crown Royal blended whiskey had lasted long, but Gail had cherished the bag, worked on a secret hiding place for it every time she found herself alone in the cabin, and used it for safely squirreling away keepsakes for years.

Gail knew Lottie was nowhere near the cabin—she could almost feel the absence of Lottie's "aura"—but she still glanced over each shoulder before she dumped out the contents of the velvet bag. She smiled when she saw the hair ornament her mother had made—there had been two—one for her, one for Juli. Two barrettes almost two inches long, made in the shape of a butterfly with tiny chips of blue, green, and pink Austrian crystals sprinkled on the gossamer wings.

She picked up one diamond stud earring. The man Julianna had cared about for a while and Gail had adored wore it almost constantly until it disappeared from his dresser one day. The last item in the velvet bag was her love's picture, a small sketch she'd done, not very good, but recognizable. That was why she'd obliterated the face, just in case her hidey-hole were ever discovered. Besides, she didn't need to look at a picture to remember his face. It was burned into her brain.

Gail wanted to take her treasures home, but she didn't dare. She didn't think she was under suspicion for her sister's murder, but you could never be too safe. She wiped off each item and slipped it back into its velvet bag and down into the hole. She carefully put the trunk back in place, and walked out of the cottage.

On the porch, she glanced around. A fierce morning sun had washed the sky and the air clean. Beside Gail, her mother's small cat Calypso let out a tiny, pitiful mewl of hunger. Gail looked at the cat for a moment, gave it a slightly lopsided smile, said, "Things are tough all over, cat," and walked purposefully to her small white car, the cat looking pathetically after her.

4

"Good heavens, did a tornado blow through here?" Kit Kirkwood surveyed the shambles of Adrienne's living room. "It'll take forever to get this place back in shape."

"Not really." Adrienne slid a heavy seat cushion back onto the couch. "Only a couple of little things were broken. The rest was just *tossed,* as Lucas says."

"Let me help you clean up."

"I can manage. Skye is helping."

"And with me helping, things will go even faster."

Kit had dark brown hair that an incredibly expensive haircut gave a casually tousled look. She wore Capri pants, sandals, a T-shirt, and only a slash of pale lip gloss and a bit of mascara. Without the dark lipstick, the blush, and the eyeliner she applied to her hazel eyes when she was at the restaurant, she appeared at least five years younger. Usually Kit had a wide, lovely smile, but not today.

"I'm wondering just what the hell is going on in this town," Kit said, picking up a lamp. "It's beginning to feel like we're in an episode of *The Twilight Zone.*"

"It always has. Don't forget, Point Pleasant is supposed to be suffering under an old Indian curse."

"Now you sound like my mother."

"I'm beginning to think her belief in the supernatural has been undeservedly dismissed." Adrienne shoved the last cushion onto the couch and stood back, hands on hips. "Here we are making light of the situation when Julianna has been *murdered*. What's wrong with us?"

"Shock." Kit set down the lamp on a table and came to Adrienne, wrapping an arm around her shoulders and pulling her close. "Back when we were teenagers, I thought I was ordinary, you were special, and Julianna was bigger than life. She was so beautiful, so energetic, so joyful that she seemed . . . I don't know . . . *eternal*. That sounds stupid, but even when she was having trouble with drugs, I knew she'd come through it. And she never forgot us. Even at the height of her career, I don't think I ever went more than a month without talking to her."

"I know," Adrienne said sadly. "Her attention meant so much to me when Trey and I were in Las Vegas. I was miserable and worried about money, especially after I had Skye and I was still trying to get my master's degree. I wrote to Juli, but I couldn't afford to make a lot of long-distance calls. She understood without my having to explain. She'd call me and talk forever. Her phone bills must have been huge. But I always felt better after I'd talked to her. Well, when I talked to you, too. It's just that Julianna—"

"Had a more exciting life than I did. We could both live it vicariously."

By now, Adrienne's eyes had filled with tears. "I'm going to miss her so much."

"Me, too. Nothing will ever be the same for us."

"Or Lottie." Adrienne sighed. "How's Gail taking it?"

Kit dropped her arm from Adrienne's shoulders and shrugged. "She's the same old Gail. A cipher. You'd never guess her sister had just been killed. Yesterday she came in for the evening shift as if nothing had happened. I told her to take the night off. She said that wouldn't be necessary. Can you believe it? But I insisted she go home. I was so angry that she was unfazed by her sister's death, I just felt like slapping her."

"No wonder. Certainly she felt *something*. Julianna was her only sister."

"Of whom she was wildly jealous. She has none of Juli's beauty, her charm, her ambition. Gail is okay looking, pleasant when she feels like it, and efficient. That's it. I tried to befriend her for Julianna's sake—I even gave her a job—but I can't make myself like her. I believe she's one of the coldest people I've ever met."

Adrienne began shoving the heavy coffee table back into place. "Gail was devastated when her father deserted the family. She was also ashamed of their poverty. Juli didn't give a damn."

Kit pushed on the other end of the coffee table. "I love the slab of glass on this thing, but it weighs a ton," she gasped. "What does Lucas have to say about all of this?"

"The break-ins, Claude's death, or Julianna's murder?"

"Any of it."

"I don't think he knows much about Julianna yet. Her body is still at the medical examiner's office in Charleston. They'll determine the cause of death. Same with Claude."

"Claude? He burned to death."

"There was something else wrong with him. Lucas wasn't specific, but he doesn't think his death was an accident."

"Another murder?" Kit exclaimed. "Jeez, I never gave that a thought." She sat down hard on a hassock. "Do we have some kind of maniac running around town?"

"Apparently."

"My God."

They both stiffened when the doorbell rang. Their gazes met as they stood perfectly still, frozen with anxiety. Then a man yelled, "Adrienne? I mean, Mrs. Reynolds? It's Rod from Rod's Lock and Key. Sheriff told me to come myself instead of sendin' one of my employees 'cause you know me. I'm here to install your new locks and your security system."

Adrienne let out her breath and went to the door. She opened it a crack and looked out at Rod, whom she'd known since childhood. He grinned and she smiled back. "Rod, it's good to see you."

"You, too, Mrs. Reynolds."

"Rod, when did I become Mrs. Reynolds to you?" She swung the door open. "We went all through school together."

Rod's oversized teeth shone in his lean, weathered face that spoke of all the time he toiled outdoors when he wasn't laboring at his business. His father had owned a small farm and worked Rod shamefully hard when he was young. After he inherited the place, Rod continued to handle it by himself, refusing to make his young sons near-slaves as he had been. "Well, Adrienne, aren't you lookin' pretty these days?"

"Yes, I think the bandage on my forehead does wonders for me." She smiled. "The same for dark circles under my eyes from no sleep."

"It'd take more than a bandage and dark circles to ruin that face, although I'm awful sorry about what you've been through. Lord Almighty, I heard you found Julianna Brent's body." Adrienne nodded, hoping he wouldn't ask for any details. "And then you got mugged and now your house's been broke into." He shook his head dolefully, deep creases forming between his heavy, sun-bleached eyebrows. "Sure glad you were at your sister's, although I heard her place got broke into, as well. And the Hamiltons with that fine alarm system I put in. The most expensive one we've got. I don't get it."

"The alarm system wasn't turned on, Rod."

He looked relieved and annoyed at the same time. "Well, I'm glad there wasn't nothing wrong with the system, but confound it, why pay a fortune for a fancy system like that and then not turn it on?"

"It was an oversight. When Philip and Vicky got home from a party, they found Skye and me and our dog as unexpected houseguests and I'd just come from the hospital after getting bashed on the head." She tried to smile lightly. "Everyone was a little off center last night. I'm fairly certain that was the first time the alarm had been left off."

"Phew. That makes me feel a whole lot better," Rod said. "Wouldn't want to think I've been chargin' a lot of money for an alarm system that's not what it's cracked up to be."

"Aren't you even going to speak to me, Lightning Rod?"

Rod turned to face Kit and broke into an even bigger grin, showing more teeth. Adrienne was certain the man must have more teeth than the standard thirty-two. "Kit Kirkwood, no one's called me Lightnin' Rod for nearly twenty years!"

Skye had come into the room. "Hello. Why do they call you Lightning Rod?"

Rod's eyes lit up. He'd always loved to tell this story. "When I was three years old, I took off running in a field during a storm. My mother spotted me just as a big lightning bolt hit the ground about five feet from me. She fainted."

Skye gasped. "No wonder! Were you hurt?"

"Not a bit. They said I thought it was funny. I didn't think it was so funny, though, when I was thirteen and ridin' my bike home to beat a storm and lightning hit a telephone pole that crashed right down in front of me. Wires were flyin' everywhere, thrashing around like snakes and throwing out some pretty mean sparks."

"My goodness, you're a walking disaster," Skye said in an awed tone.

"Skye!" Adrienne burst out.

Rod laughed. "That's okay, Adrienne. She's right. Close calls with lightnin' are my claim to fame. But God seems to be lookin' over me, honey." He looked at Adrienne and Kit. "Well now, isn't this a pleasure? Of course, the circumstances are bad, but I get to see two of the prettiest girls in my graduating class. Don't tell the wife, but I had crushes on both of you."

"You had crushes on at least *twenty* girls," Kit said dryly. "But you ended up with the right one. I always thought Carrie was sweet *and* pretty. Just terribly shy."

"She's not nearly so shy now. And she's gotten even prettier with age. She's a fine mother, too."

At that moment, Brandon wandered in and immediately approached Rod's offered hand. "Dogs always know when a person's partial to them," Rod declared. "My two boys each got a dog. Brown and White."

"What are their names?" Skye asked.

"Brown and White." Rod seemed puzzled by her question since he thought he'd already given their names. "And what's this big fella's name? Blackie?"

"Brandon," Skye said promptly.

Rod looked slightly bemused. "Well, Brandon's a fine name. Fancy, but . . . fancy." He glanced at Skye. "Think Brandon would like to help me change the locks?"

"I bet he'd love it! And can I watch, too? I never saw a lock get changed."

"I don't want you and Brandon to be in Rod's way," Adrienne said.

Rod shook his head, the cowlick in his thick, sun-streaked hair waving as if it had a life of its own. "Kids are never a bother to me, Adrienne. Just a pure pleasure. I'd have a dozen of them if the wife hadn't told me in no uncertain terms there'd be no more than four. Number three's on the way—be here in a couple of months. I'll have to get that one a dog, too." He looked at Skye. "Maybe you can help us pick out a name for it, something fancy like Brandon."

"What did you have in mind, Mr. . . ."

"Just Rod, honey. I was thinkin' of gettin' a beagle and calling him Flop Ear."

"Flop Ear!" Skye burst out in horror before she remembered her manners. "Well, Flop Ear's nice, but maybe we can think of some names you'd like even better while you work on the locks."

Adrienne looked at Kit. "Seems it's time for us to take a break. Want some iced tea or coffee? You look pale."

"I need coffee. Strong."

"Rod?"

"Coffee would be great. I don't know what my two assistants here drink."

"I'll see that they're both taken care of," Adrienne said. "Don't work them too hard."

Rod immediately began chattering to Skye and the noise followed Adrienne and Kit to the kitchen. "Do you suppose he really had crushes on us?" Kit murmured. Adrienne whispered back, "I think he did, but back then, we were all too afraid to get near him for fear of immediately being struck down by lightning."

They struggled to suppress laughter until they got into the kitchen and closed the door. There they collapsed, giggling like girls Skye's age over something really not all that funny, although the laughter was a good release from the tension and dark thoughts that had gripped them earlier.

A minute after Adrienne had pulled two tissues from her pocket and they each wiped away tears of laughter, she said, "You can have coffee but I don't own one of those fancy bean grinders like you have. I can't give you the quality you're used to."

"Frankly, I never go to all that trouble for myself. Anything is fine."

While the coffee brewed, Kit ran her hands through her thick dark hair, tucked it behind her ears, then pulled it forward again. Fiddling with her hair was a sure sign of nerves with Kit. "Do you know who Julianna was involved with? Who she could have been with at la Belle?" she asked abruptly.

"No. But Skye thinks it was your stepfather."

Kit gaped. "*Skye* thinks it was *Gavin*? Why?"

Adrienne took down two mugs from the cabinet. "She goes to Vicky's parties for Philip to keep Rachel company because Rachel hates them. Anyway, the two of them have noticed that when both Gavin and Juli are present, Gavin constantly touches Julianna."

"Gavin constantly touches *all* young women," Kit said in disgust. "Did Skye have anything else to go on?"

"Just that Gavin would have keys to la Belle, making easy access for secret assignations." Adrienne poured coffee into the mugs and set one in front of Kit. "I'm only telling you this because I *don't* think Julianna was involved with Gavin. I thought she just put up with him out of consideration for Ellen. But your mother is bound to hear the rumor and she might believe it."

"You bet she'll believe it." Kit sighed. "Honestly, how she could have stayed with that jerk all these years given his affairs is beyond me. I know she was crazy about him when she married him, but she doesn't love him anymore. She told me she stayed with him when she first found out he was a philanderer because I needed a father after mine jumped ship." Kit scoffed. "Gavin was *never* like a father to me. Or to Jamie. Then he let Jamie die—"

Kit broke off. She had adored her adopted little brother who had drowned one night last summer at la Belle. Finally, she said, "I think Jamie's death sent Mother over the edge. As for Gavin, he can't leave her if he wants to end up with a penny of her money, and she won't let him go voluntarily with a nice settlement. He's too greedy and too much of a weakling to just walk away empty-handed. So, her retribution for Jamie is to hang on to Gavin and make his life miserable. And she does. Sometimes I could almost feel sorry for Gavin." Kit paused. "Almost."

"If Lucas is focusing on Gavin as a suspect, he hasn't said anything to me." Adrienne took a sip of her coffee. "Of course he wouldn't. No one could ever accuse Lucas Flynn of having loose lips. I do know he's worried about Lottie, though. Before he left here this morning, he told me they still haven't found her. She might not even know Julianna is dead."

"She does."

Adrienne looked at Kit in surprise. "You've seen her?"

"Last night at the restaurant." Kit had brought her purse into the kitchen with her and fished inside for a pack of cigarettes and her gold, engraved lighter. Adrienne tapped her fingers on the kitchen table impatiently while Kit lighted her cigarette and drew on it, slowly blowing out smoke. Finally Adrienne said, "Well, are you going to tell me about Lottie or not?"

"If you're going to take that tone with me, I won't tell you anything at all."

They had been friends for too many years to get angry with each other over a flare-up of annoyance, particularly in a nerve-wracking situation like Julianna's murder. Besides, Adrienne noticed how Kit's fingers trembled as she brought the cigarette to her mouth a second time.

"Lottie came to the restaurant last night," Kit finally said again. "She sat outside in the gazebo looking at the lights on the trees. She said she felt better in my 'magical garden.'" Kit took a sip of coffee and another drag on her cigarette. "She said she'd known when she woke up yesterday morning something had happened to Juli. There was something about an owl hooting and one of her *bad feelings*. She went on about la Belle being a place of doom just like Mother does, and she mentioned Juli being involved with someone. She didn't say who, but apparently she knew they met at la Belle."

Kit drew a deep breath and looked over at the pot of vibrant red begonias hanging in front of the window as if she couldn't meet Adrienne's eyes. "She was rambling more than usual, but what really frightened me is that she had some blood on her dress and she smelled of l' Heure Bleue."

"Julianna's perfume," Adrienne murmured.

Kit nodded. "And you know how spotless Lottie keeps those old dresses of hers. If she'd gotten blood on a dress from a cut on herself, she would have scrubbed it out. Unless it was Juli's and she picked it up at the same time as the perfume scent." Kit looked over at Adrienne, her eyes anguished. "Adrienne, she was at la Belle yesterday morning. She *touched* Juli's body. And for some reason, she didn't call the police."

Adrienne was appalled that Lottie had seen her beautiful daughter dead. Then the significance of Kit's words hit her. "Lottie knew Julianna had been murdered but she didn't call the police? What are you implying? That *she* killed Juli?"

"I don't know," Kit said miserably. "She said what Julianna was doing was *wrong*. And you know how strange Lottie is."

Adrienne had always cared about Lottie and everything in her fought what Kit seemed to be saying. "Kit, Lottie is eccentric. So is *your* mother." Kit gave her a reproachful look. "Don't get mad. You know it. They're both odd, but they were two impressionable girls who grew up together and influenced each other. And they've both had bad—well, *terrible*—experiences at la Belle. They both hate it. But being unusual is a far cry from being a killer. You can't believe Lottie killed her own daughter!"

"Oh, I don't." Kit stubbed out her cigarette. "But why didn't she call the police? And last night, when I went in the restaurant to get her some tea, she disappeared. This morning I went to her cabin. She wasn't there and I don't think she'd even been there since yesterday morning because her cat Calypso was sitting on the porch meowing to beat the band. She was hungry, and you know Lottie would never let Calypso go hungry if she were around."

"Lucas said they were still looking for Lottie yesterday afternoon. Honestly, with the shock of the break-ins, I forgot to ask him about her this morning." Adrienne frowned. "Of course she's gone wandering for a day or two before, but these circumstances are different." She paused. "I should go feed Calypso."

"I took her back to my apartment."

"You're keeping Calypso?"

"Because she means so much to Lottie." Kit had always tried to play tough girl. She hated for people to think she had a soft heart. "I dropped her off at the apartment with a can of tuna and a bowl of milk. After I leave here, I'm going to Wal-Mart for a litter box and some more cat food."

"And catnip and a scratch pad."

"Good idea. And maybe some treats."

Adrienne grinned. "You've never had a pet, Kit. Are you sure you want to take in Calypso? You could just stop at the cabin each day and feed her until Lottie comes home."

Kit looked at her gravely. "That's the problem, Adrienne. I have this sickening feeling that Lottie will never come home again."

4

That night Adrienne lay sleepless, mentally ticking off the points in favor of her staying in Point Pleasant. First, there was her job. She'd been teaching part-time for three years and she had a good chance of being hired full-time at the end of this summer. Unless she abandoned her summer classes in mid-semester when no one else was available to take over. Such unreliability would put an end to any hopes of a full-time job that would solve her money worries, and perhaps even knock her out of the part-time position. No, she couldn't take that risk. She had a daughter to support.

As for continuing to live in the house, she couldn't afford a motel room for an indefinite stay for her and Skye as well as kennel fees for Brandon. Kit lived in an elegant but small one-bedroom apartment above her restaurant. She didn't have room for them, although Adrienne knew she would gladly have taken them in. And finally, Adrienne could not risk Rachel's safety by moving into the Hamilton home.

No, staying in her own home was her only option. And she'd taken precautions. All doors and windows had new locks and the house now sported a new security system installed this afternoon, its cost taken care of by a loan from Vicky. Adrienne had decided she would never leave Skye here by herself, especially at night. And although Lucas said that at this time he didn't have the manpower to provide full-time surveillance, a patrol car would come by three or four times a night.

All of her reasons for remaining in her home in Point Pleasant made perfect sense—the only sense considering her circumstances—until she remembered the words scrawled on her mirror: *LEAVE OR DIE.* Threatening words written in lipstick that looked like blood.

Adrienne glanced at the bedside clock. One-fifteen. She'd been trying to sleep since eleven. She got up, went to the kitchen, poured milk into a mug, and put it in the microwave. When it was warm, she added a dash of brandy and carried her drink to the big rose-colored studio chair in the living room. The only illumination came from a small dusk-to-dawn fixture set near her front door whose light seeped in the picture window across from her chair but faded to pathetic weakness by the time it reached the street. And naturally, she thought, the giant, strong streetlight placed near her house on Hawthorne Way had flickered out earlier this evening and wouldn't be fixed by the electric company until later in the week.

More lights, Adrienne thought as she curled up in the chair, tucking her bare feet beneath her. That's a precaution she hadn't thought of in the daylight. She would call tomorrow and have two stronger dusk-to-dawn lights placed in her yard, one in front, one in back. Maybe even three lights. The glare of lights would elicit complaints from the neighbors, but safety was her main concern, not fussy neighbors.

Her thoughts stopped as she saw the gleam of headlights piercing the darkness. Then came a car—a car that slowed as it passed her house. She held her breath, squinting although she had near-perfect vision. Then she saw almost neon-yellow stripes on the car's silver body. A police cruiser checking the house, just like Lucas had promised.

Adrienne relaxed, slightly comforted. She took another

sip of her cooling milk and brandy. She would go back to bed as soon as she finished her drink, she promised herself. She would go back to bed and *sleep* because she had to go to the art gallery tomorrow to deliver one of her paintings that would be entered in the contest held during the summer gala next week, and she had to teach a class in the evening. Just Art Appreciation 101, which she'd taught so many times she could do it without thinking, but she still needed to work up enthusiasm. If she acted bored by her subject, the students quickly picked up on her vibes and also lost interest.

Another set of headlights lanced the night. The patrol car had passed just ten minutes ago, so this car must belong to someone who lived on the barely traveled street, Adrienne thought. Few of her neighbors were night owls, though, so she looked with curiosity at the car creeping by her house. She didn't recognize it. It was smaller than most of the cars that belonged to neighbors. And it was going so *slowly*.

Apprehension tingled along Adrienne's spine. She didn't know a lot about car models, but this one looked to be a two-door with a long hood and short trunk area. People in this neighborhood favored the huge, gas-guzzling sport utility vehicles she hated but had bought to accommodate her art supplies and a frequent passenger, Brandon. Adrienne leaned forward and looked more closely at the unfamiliar car. Because of the bad light, she couldn't tell if it was dark green, blue, or black. It didn't stop in front of her house or do anything suspicious. Still, she didn't like the idea of an unfamiliar car inching past her house at 1:40 in the morning.

"Two nights ago I wouldn't have thought a thing about it," she murmured as her hand reached for the phone to call Lucas. Then she paused. He had looked exhausted this morning. He needed an undisturbed night's sleep. Besides, it was one thing to be cautious, and another to be paranoid.

Still, she continued to sit in her chair, her milk going tepid and forming a skin on top, the only sound in the room the ticking of a regulator clock on the mantel. Her eyelids grew heavier as the minutes rolled by. Then she jerked in her chair, glanced at the clock, and saw that she'd slept for twenty minutes. Almost half an hour had gone by since she'd seen the dark car.

With a groan she uncurled her stiff legs and shook them. The pins and needles of returning circulation had begun to stab at her calves when she saw the glow of approaching headlights. She held still, ignoring the discomfort in her legs, as once again the dark two-door car drifted by.

And this time Adrienne caught the blur of a face behind the wheel looking directly into her picture window.

EIGHT

I

"I just got back from Photo Finish with the pictures you took at the Belle," Lucas said. Adrienne's hand tightened on the phone receiver. "There's nothing in them we can use."

"Nothing in them!" she burst out. "Lucas, I *saw* someone through the viewfinder!"

"I didn't say there was nothing in them. I said there's nothing we can *use*. There's definitely a blurry form partially hidden by trees. But you can't even tell if it's a man or a woman."

"Then use computer enhancement. I've seen it done on television."

"And it always works on television, but this is real life. We'll give it a try, of course, but I'm not optimistic."

"Oh damn." Adrienne stood at the kitchen window looking out at the bed of pansies beside the patio. "Lucas, I know the figure in those photos is Julianna's killer."

"No, you don't *know* that," Lucas said patiently. "I haven't gotten Julianna's autopsy report yet. We don't know the time of death. If it was even just a half hour before you arrived, though, why would the murderer hang around in the woods?"

"I don't know." She paused. "Unless it had something to do with the wreck on the highway. With all that commotion and the police at the scene the killer couldn't get down the hill and away from the Belle."

"Then why didn't he go on *up* the hill? Why keep lurking around the hotel when you and Skye came along with a dog, no less?"

"Well . . ."

"Well, what?"

"Give me time. I'll come up with a reason."

Lucas chuckled. "When you do, call me immediately. Let's forget about the photos for now. Did you sleep well last night?"

"No. And because I couldn't sleep, I sat in the living room and saw something that bothered me." She told him about the dark car with the long hood and short trunk.

"Short trunk? That's called a short *hatch*."

"What do you call the piece on the trunk that's like a narrow shelf?"

"A spoiler. I don't suppose you saw the license plate."

"I would have given you the number before I blundered through that description."

"You did fine with your description. But I can think of a number of car models that have a similar frame. You couldn't tell anything about the driver?"

"No, just a blur. Just like the figure in the photos. My world is filled with blurs."

"Frankly, I'm almost glad you didn't get a good photo of the person up at the Belle. That kind of knowledge could be dangerous to you. That's why after I took a look at them, I told Hal at Photo Finish where and when you'd taken the pictures but that they didn't show us anything. Hal tells everything he knows. I'm also repeating that information to every other blabbermouth in town. If the killer is someone around here picking up information, I want him to know you didn't see much and got nothing identifiable in the pictures." He paused. "But I don't like the idea of a car cruising by your house so slowly more than once last night. It did only go by twice, right?"

Adrienne felt ashamed to admit she'd fallen asleep in her

chair around three o'clock. "I should have stayed awake and watched."

"You were exhausted."

"I'm still exhausted. And I have a stiff neck from a night in the chair."

"Then get some rest today."

"I can't. I have to take my painting to the French Art Colony for the gala. I also need to go to the grocery store, and I teach a class tonight. It's strange to think that life goes on in spite of at least one horrible murder."

"Life goes on, but not in the same way." Lucas's subdued voice sounded worried. "Now more than ever you have to be careful. I mean it, Adrienne. Take absolutely no chances, both for your sake and for your daughter's."

2

"Are there any scary stories about this place?" Skye asked. "I mean, is it supposed to be haunted or anything?"

"Goodness, no." Adrienne looked at the dignified brick front of the French Art Colony with its thick white pillars. "I don't know of one ghost that is rumored to make its home here."

"Phooey," Skye muttered in disappointment. "Point Pleasant has lots of haunted places. The Art Colony is right across the river in Gallipolis. How did we manage to get all the spooky beings? Hey, maybe after the Belle is torn down, its ghosts will come over here!"

"Since when did you start believing in ghosts?" Adrienne carefully began removing the canvas-covered oil painting from the back of her car. "Even when you were little, you didn't believe in ghosts and monsters. You were the bravest child I ever knew."

"I'm still brave," Skye said reassuringly. "It's just fun to pretend places can be haunted. Is the French Art Colony as old as the Belle?"

"It's older."

"Well, there you go. In movies and books, ghosts always like old places. No ghost with any pride would hang out in our house. It's too new and only has one floor. But *this* place would be a ghost's dream house."

"Skye, you should write stories about the paranormal. Maybe you'll be the next Stephen King and I won't have to worry about money anymore." Adrienne banged her head on a window as she struggled to lug her painting from the car. Her lack of sleep and the heat of mid-morning added to her frustration. "Honey, please stop ruminating about ghosts and help me."

"Skye to the rescue." In two minutes, they'd safely removed the painting. "Success! What would you do without me?"

"I don't ever want to find out." Adrienne pushed her long hair behind her ears, wishing she had pulled it back in a braid and conscious of the bandage decorating her forehead. "But keep your opinions about ghosts to yourself when we get inside. I think Miss Snow is here today and she's paranoid about anything that might tarnish the reputation of the Art Colony."

"I think having an Art Colony ghost would be cool."

"She wouldn't. She doesn't think anything that's not in an etiquette book is cool."

The French Art Colony had been a huge brick home in its younger days. A black wrought-iron fence surrounded the well-kept grounds. Adrienne and Skye strode toward the building on the brick sidewalk and climbed the steps of the big porch. As Adrienne had feared, the most active member of the Art Colony board, Miss Snow, was in attendance today. She opened one of the double front doors and stood waiting for them to enter, a tiny, stiff smile causing crinkles on her parchment-skinned face. The woman was tall, white-haired, cadaverously thin, had a dark flat-eyed stare, and habitually dressed in navy blue, brown, or deep purple. She'd always reminded Adrienne of the ominous housekeeper Mrs. Danvers in the novel *Rebecca*.

"Good morning, Mrs. Reynolds." Miss Snow's voice was as cold as her last name. She looked at Skye with distaste. "You've brought your child."

Adrienne forced a smile. "I wish you'd call me Adrienne. And Skye is fourteen now. Hardly a child. She's been a big help to me today."

"Yes, well . . ." Miss Snow trailed off doubtfully.

Adrienne could feel Skye bristling behind her and said in a loud, overbright voice, "I've brought my painting for the competition before the gala!"

"So I see." And you don't need to state the obvious, Miss Snow's tone said. Adrienne liked every one of the other board members, all of whom were extremely friendly, unpretentious, and insisted on being called by their first names. Adrienne realized she didn't even know Miss Snow's first name. She suspected the woman had been christened "Miss Snow." For heaven's sake, why did *she* have to be manning the helm, Adrienne thought ruefully, on a day when she certainly didn't feel like indulging the woman's superiority complex?

They all still stood awkwardly in the doorway. Miss Snow finally said, "The painting must be heavy. You might as well come in with it. Is it oil or watercolor?"

Adrienne had not worked in watercolors for ten years. "Oil."

"Oh dear. Another oil. We have so many." She sighed. "Well, I believe the chairman has chosen a nice place for it on the second floor anyway." Miss Snow turned to a small table and riffled through papers. "Yes, second floor, the room on the right. Your painting will hang just left of the fireplace. What's the name of it?"

"*Autumn Exodus.*"

Miss Snow checked her papers again. "Yes, that's what

it says here." It's official, Adrienne thought sourly. The title is verified. "Autumn . . . whatever will hang left of the fireplace."

"*Autumn Exodus.*" Adrienne couldn't keep the sharp edge from her voice. "To the left, as you said. I think I can remember."

"Mom, can I stay down here and look at the other paintings?" Skye asked.

"Sure," Adrienne said. Miss Snow looked distressed as if envisioning Skye placing sticky fingers on every piece of art. Skye veered left into the sunny Music Room. "I think I'll start here."

"Don't touch the grand piano," Miss Snow warned harshly, trotting anxiously after Skye. "It's an antique. And so is the chandelier!"

"Gosh, Miss Snow, I can't very well touch the chandelier unless you're planning to get me a ladder." Skye laughed.

Two points for Skye, Adrienne thought with a smile. Miss Snow was the only person Adrienne knew of whom the girl purposely tried to annoy.

Adrienne got a firm grip on her painting and headed toward her favorite feature of the French Art Colony—the floating stairway. Although strongly anchored to the wall on one side, the railing side of the staircase bore no structural support, giving it the appearance of swirling through thin air all the way up to the fourth floor. Adrienne always pictured a beautiful woman in an evening gown gracefully descending the lovely stairs.

Sometimes wedding receptions were held at the Art Colony, and Adrienne had imagined someday seeing Skye posed in a glorious white dress on the staircase. But not for at least ten years, she told herself. Maybe longer. She didn't want her little girl to grow up and throw herself into the responsibilities of marriage too soon, the way she had when she'd married Trey Reynolds at twenty-one, before either of them was really ready.

Adrienne hung her painting on the assigned spot and stood back for a look. The card the chairman had already put in place beside where the painting would hang read "Adrienne Reynolds, *Autumn Exodus,* oil on canvas, 22" x 26"." It was one of the largest pieces she had ever done and also one of the best. She'd chosen the scene late last November, when she'd seen about twenty Canadian geese floating on a large pond in an open field bordered by a line of giant blue spruce trees. As she'd watched, ten of the big geese, who mated for life, lifted gracefully from the water, wings spread, their brown feathers and the white streaks on the sides of their black heads showing clearly against the mellow gold glow of a fading autumn afternoon. In the painting, she'd used a bit of yellow for luminosity on the snow-tipped tree limbs and grayish blue in the background to indicate evening creeping onto the landscape. She thought she'd captured the agile, flowing movement of the birds along with the intricate play of light and shadow. She smiled, proud of the painting and allowing herself a small hope of placing in the competition.

Adrienne started back down the stairs, then stopped. Something waited for her on the third floor, something that seemed to call out irresistibly. Slowly she ascended the floating staircase, running her left hand over the cool, polished wood of the railing. This is a mistake, she thought. This is going to upset me. This is going to hurt. But she couldn't help herself.

When she reached the third floor, Adrienne turned right, paused, then stepped through a doorway. She drew in her breath. The room had an official name, but for the last four years, most people had called it "the Julianna Room" because of the life-sized portrait at the far end—a portrait of Julianna painted by the extraordinarily talented man who had been her husband, Miles Shaw.

Adrienne didn't turn on the lights in the room. She didn't need to. A shaft of sunlight streamed through one of the big windows and fell directly on the portrait as if nature had staged the lighting to best effect. Miles had donated the paint-ing to the French Art Colony, never to be sold. During the last four years, it had become one of the establishment's biggest attractions. And with good reason, Adrienne thought.

In the portrait, Julianna stood in a three-quarter turn with her face full forward. She wore a black satin dress with a black lace overlay. With masterful touches of brown, Miles had accented every filigree of the intricate ebony lace over the midnight satin. The neckline dipped low, partially expos-ing the curve of Juli's breasts. Her hands were clasped loosely just below her waist, a large black Tahitian pearl ring set in platinum on her left middle finger. Her long auburn hair touched by copper highlights fell in soft waves over her left shoulder beneath a magnificent black lace-covered leghorn hat.

But the highlight of the portrait was Julianna's face. The cool Grace Kelly perfection was tempered by the hint of an arch smile and the promise of amour in the sherry-colored eyes that seemed to follow the viewer around the room. No doubt about it, Adrienne thought. Miles Shaw had created a masterpiece. And more important, he had captured an in-credible image of Julianna Brent that could last for centuries.

Miss Snow must have turned on the sound system to dis-courage Skye from playing the antique piano the girl had no desire to play. As Adrienne stood mesmerized by the por-trait, a classic song rendered beautifully by the group Black-more's Night flowed around her:

> *Alas my love, ye do me wrong to cast me out dis-*
> *   courteously,*
> *And I have loved you for so long delighting in*
> *   your company . . .*
> *Greensleeves was all my joy,*
> *Greensleeves was my delight,*
> *Greensleeves was my heart of gold*
> *And who but Lady Greensleeves . . .*

"Do you think I should have called the portrait *Greensleeves* instead of *Julianna*?"

Adrienne started, then turned to see Miles Shaw standing less than three feet behind her. From the day Julianna had introduced Miles to Adrienne, she had thought he was not the handsomest but certainly the most striking man she had ever met. His mother was Shawnee, and he had inherited her shining black hair, which he wore pulled back in a ponytail that hung halfway to his waist, beautiful light bronze skin, and high cheekbones. He was around six feet four with an aquiline nose that was slightly crooked from an old break, lips with a sensuous curve, and the only truly raven-black eyes Adrienne had ever seen. He had the broad shoulders of a bodybuilder tapering to a slender waist and long legs that moved as gracefully as a dancer's. He wore tight jeans, and a long-sleeved black shirt. Around his neck hung a leather cord bearing a large nugget of turquoise set in oxidized silver, a gift from Julianna for his thirty-seventh birthday.

Adrienne thought he looked older than he had when she'd seen him a year ago, a new network of lines surrounding the startling eyes, and the hollows sinking deeper under his cheekbones. One expected him to have a booming voice to match his size. Instead his words were always soft, almost sonorous and insinuating, as if his listener were the only person in the world. Julianna had told Adrienne she'd first been attracted to Miles because of his voice.

"I've always thought 'Greensleeves' was about a woman who was deliberately hurtful," Adrienne said, finally finding her own voice. "Julianna wasn't like that."

"It's possible for a person to have two sides."

"Yes, but I knew Julianna for almost thirty years—"

"Much longer than I did. Maybe much better than I did." Miles quirked an eyebrow. "But maybe not."

Adrienne took an uncomfortable step backward away from Miles, then turned to the portrait to hide her retreat. "It really is a beautiful painting," she said lamely.

"Julianna was my inspiration. For a while."

"I was always sorry things didn't work out for the two of you."

"They were working out for me. Apparently they weren't working for her," Miles said sardonically.

His closeness and the theme of his conversation made Adrienne increasingly nervous. She couldn't just run from the room. She had to say something in response to Miles's remarks. "Julianna was a restless soul, Miles. I don't think she was cut out for marriage."

"Really? Not to *anyone*?"

It wasn't actually a question. It was a challenge. "No, I don't think to anyone. Honestly." The song had changed but the room seemed to be getting smaller and hotter. And Miles seemed to be getting closer, although Adrienne hadn't seen him take a step.

Miles glanced at the portrait. "When I painted that, I thought I'd captured her soul."

"You did."

"I captured what she projected at that time. Sauciness, yes. But also innocence. That wasn't necessarily the true Julianna."

"You captured the image of a beautiful woman. She wasn't perfect, Miles, but then no one is. She did have warmth, compassion, and joy, though. I see all of that in the portrait."

"You're perspiring." Miles reached out and gently touched the bandage on her forehead. "And you've hurt yourself. Or more precisely, someone hurt you. A mugger. That's what I heard."

"Yes. Night before last. He got away with my purse, some cheap lipstick, an old comb, and all of ten dollars." Her attempt at a lighthearted laugh came out more like a bleat of fear. "Philip is furious with me. Bad publicity and all."

Miles's face turned hard. "Philip Hamilton is a pompous fool who cares only about himself."

"Oh!" Adrienne was startled by the pure hatred of his tone. "Well, I'd like to think he loves my sister and niece. I mean, I'm sure he does. He just has such a huge ego. Maybe that goes with being a politician. You'd have to have a lot of confidence to run for governor, after all, with all those speeches and people looking at you constantly and, well, everything . . ."

She ran out of words and breath at the same time. Miles's fingers still touched her bandage. His intense eyes still probed hers. He leaned closer and for a wild moment she thought he was going to kiss her. A surprisingly strong swell of panic surged through her, but she stood frozen, her heart thumping like a small, trapped animal's.

"Sorry to interrupt, but you know how pushy we newspeople are."

Miles's hand dropped away from her forehead. As he stepped aside and turned, Adrienne saw Drew Delaney. He almost lounged against the doorframe, but his face was taut, his dark eyes slightly narrowed. "I'd like to get a quote from each of you on the upcoming gala."

Adrienne fought an impulse to run to Drew and let him fold her in loving arms as he'd done when they were teenagers. But that had been a long time ago. He probably hadn't loved her then, and he certainly didn't now. Still, she was overjoyed to see him. Her knees felt weak from her apprehension of Miles and she walked to his side.

"Sometimes I like being a reporter better than an editor." Drew took the damp hand she'd thrust at him, shaking it as if they were meeting for the first time. It was an unnatural gesture after their long acquaintance, and Adrienne knew Drew recognized it as her way of masking uneasiness.

Miles seemed to vibrate with hostility. "I would think our little gala would be beneath your interest, considering the murders."

"Murders?" Drew repeated innocently. "I thought Julianna Brent was the only murder victim."

Miles flushed. "I meant Claude Duncan. Someone told me he'd probably been murdered. I don't remember who."

"I wish you did. I'd like to quote this source who seems to know more than the cops do."

Adrienne knew the police suspected Claude's death was not an accident, but Lucas had not stated so publicly. Did Miles really have a source? Or, worse, did he know firsthand that Claude had been murdered?

"Unfortunately, I don't know any more about the death of Julianna than anyone else," Miles said as he crossed the room and passed by Drew, heading for the floating stairs. "I'd sure as hell like to get my hands on the son of a bitch who killed my ex-wife, though. I'd kill him slowly and painfully, just like he deserves."

Miles's words were vicious, but his tone lacked depth. Adrienne knew that he'd once loved Julianna passionately, but none of that love resonated in his voice or his face.

"Well, sensational murders certainly boost circulation, but we don't want the *Register* to became known as a tabloid," Drew said blandly. "That's why we want to give plenty of space to the Art Colony Gala. Lend the newspaper a little class, you know?"

"Even though the Art Colony is in Ohio, not West Virginia?" Miles asked tartly.

Drew ignored the sarcasm. "We cover more than West Virginia news."

"But working on the *Register* must still seem disappointing compared to your days on the *New York Times*," Miles said innocently.

"I like the slower pace."

"Slow is right." Miles wasn't going to back off. "I suppose even though you left under a cloud, you still have a few connections at the *Times*. If you'd wanted to do her a favor, they could have gotten Julianna's name into the gossip columns, sparked a little interest in her, maybe gotten her back into modeling."

Drew's jaw tightened. "I'm not sure where that idea came from, Miles. I also don't know what makes you think Julianna would have wanted to return to modeling."

"Julianna was Julianna. She loved attention but she hadn't gotten much for a few years. I'm sure she was missing the hoopla that used to surround her." Miles shrugged. "And she *never* turned down help from men when she could get it."

"If I had the influence you seem to think I have, Miles, I'd get a gig for myself and you'd see me on the cover of *Vanity Fair*," Drew said lightly. "Maybe your spy network needs tuning up. Try keeping surveillance on Gavin Kirkwood. He might prove more interesting."

By now, Miss Snow had arrived at the third-floor landing with Skye in tow. Skye's eyes were wide, Miss Snow's narrow lips pressed nearly into invisibility although brilliant pink flared along the tops of her cheekbones. "I didn't realize everyone was gathering up here," she snapped. "I thought interviews would be conducted downstairs in the drawing room where we could have tea. Better yet, in the kitchen, so we won't get anything dirty."

"Will people at the gala get to drink tea in the drawing room?" Skye asked with feigned innocence. "Or do they have to stand in the kitchen?"

"*Formal* guests may eat wherever they like," Miss Snow announced.

Drew grinned. "I sure hope you serve pigs in a blanket. I just *love* pigs in a blanket."

"And sardines!" Skye jumped in. "With horseradish sauce and beer!"

Miss Snow looked appalled. "You don't drink beer at your age, do you?"

"No more than two or three bottles a day," Skye returned blamelessly. "Mom says it gets your creative genes perking."

Even Miles couldn't hide a smile although Drew had long since given up trying. Adrienne was half aghast, half admiring of her daughter's audacity, but Miss Snow's reaction was un-mitigated insult. She glared at Skye, then turned on Drew. "I thought you had an interview to do, Mr. Delaney."

"I really just needed a few short quotes from participants."

"That leaves me out," Miles said. "I'm not offering a picture for competition this year, but Adrienne is. You should get a quote from her."

"*I* am on the board of directors," Miss Snow reminded Drew. "I can tell you anything you want to know about the collection."

"I know, Miss Snow," Drew said smoothly. "I'll be back for your comments. Right now I'd like to walk Adrienne and Skye to their car."

"I don't think Ms. Reynolds is ready to leave," Miles stated, clearly more upset by Drew's domination of the action than by the thought of Adrienne leaving.

"Yes I am," Adrienne intervened. "I have a busy day."

As they strolled down the brick walkway leading from the French Art Colony, Adrienne drew a deep breath. Drew threw her a sideways glance and asked, "Mind telling me what was going on back there with you and Miles Shaw?"

"I'm not sure, but he was weird. I wouldn't say Miles and I were ever friends, but certainly not enemies. Today he was giving me the creeps, though."

"He always gives me the creeps," Drew said. "I wouldn't be surprised at anything he did."

Adrienne looked at him. His dark eyes were as intense as Miles's, but without the threat and innuendo. Sunlight emphasized his deep laugh lines and the tiny, humorous quirk at the edge of his mouth. Suddenly, warmth for him flooded over Adrienne. Embarrassment at her reaction didn't stop her from reaching out to take his arm as they strode down the brick walk away from the French Art Colony. Then she spotted an automobile parked at the curb.

"What kind of car is that?" she asked sharply.

Drew looked surprised at her tone. "It's a Camaro."

Adrienne scrutinized the dark blue, two-door car with its long hood, short hatch, and spoiler. It looked just like the car she'd seen cruising stealthily past her house several times last night.

"Do you like it?" Drew asked. "It's mine."

4

Lucas Flynn wanted a cigarette. He'd given them up six weeks ago and had been making do with the nicotine patches, but today they weren't working. He felt jittery and irritable as hell, and he decided he couldn't stand the craving anymore. As soon as he finished reading the autopsy reports that had just come in, he'd break down, sneak outside, and have a Marlboro. Maybe two. Probably three.

One of the tasks Lucas liked least about his job was wading through autopsy reports. Cold, scientific analyses of gaping wounds, blood loaded with toxins, and corpses nearly decapitated by strangulation with wires turned human beings into soulless pieces of meat, little more than hapless frogs dissected by bored high school biology students. But the reports were essential and Lucas knew the faster he read them, the quicker he could reenter the world of the living and of simple pleasures like smoking. And having a good lunch. He decided to treat himself to a midday meal at the Iron Gate Grill.

He pulled a sheaf of papers toward him, put on the reading glasses that last month the optometrist had deemed necessary and that Lucas hated passionately, and began to read about Julianna Brent, age thirty-six. She had never borne a child and appeared to have been in excellent health, except for a blow to the skull caused by a blunt object and a deep puncture wound to the carotid artery on the left side of her neck.

Lucas knew the blow to her head had come from the heavy ceramic lamp base whose pieces he'd found lying beside the hotel bed. Bruising on Julianna's scalp had been scant both because the skin tightly stretched across bone bruised less easily than loose skin, and because death had occurred shortly after the blow. The puncture wound was not so easily analyzed. Something sharp had been thrust into the neck with tremendous force, but the edges of the wound bore no tearing, indicating the weapon had been round with a sharp point. No weapon capable of inflicting such a wound had been found at the crime scene, but judging by the depth of penetration, it must have been approximately three inches long. Possibly it could have been a bit shorter, the force behind the weapon driving it deeper into the soft tissue of the neck and leaving a longer cavity.

The massive blood loss indicated that Julianna had still been alive when the carotid was punctured. The fact that she lacked defensive wounds suggested that she'd been knocked unconscious by the lamp base, then attacked with a sharp object and allowed to bleed to death.

Lucas stopped reading and looked at the tan wall lined with file cabinets across from him. Only he didn't see the cabinets. He saw Julianna lying on that bed, her beautiful face peaceful if almost supernaturally white, her hair spread over the deep and bloody wound in her neck, the butterfly clip sparkling with pink and blue Austrian crystals against her right temple. Someone had brutally murdered her and then posed her, even pulling the sheet and blanket over her naked body.

According to forensic psychologists, covering the body after a murder indicated the killer felt conflicted, and while his desire for someone's death drove him to personally slaughter the person, he then felt compelled to bestow a bit of dignity by covering his victim.

But Julianna's murderer had not felt conflicted. Lucas somehow felt sure of it. He just hoped no one else did. The fact that she'd been carefully covered to her neck with a satin sheet, and her hair had been combed, had not been released to the press. But Rachel Hamilton was a reporter.

She was also related to the people who had found Julianna and could describe the loving state in which she'd been left. He trusted Adrienne to keep her mouth shut about those details. He was afraid a girl of Skye's age would not be able to keep such knowledge from her cousin Rachel, whom she idolized.

Lucas realized he'd been staring at his file cabinets, lost in thought, for nearly five minutes. Mentally groaning, he picked up the autopsy report on Claude Duncan.

He stared at the typed page for a moment, not seeing the print, only the puffy, bleary-eyed face of Claude as he'd looked the morning he stood outside the room at la Belle Rivière, holding his ax in a ridiculous attempt to guard the room where Julianna lay dead. *Ridiculous.* That was a word most people would have applied to Claude. Ridiculous. Absurd. Dumb. Pitiful. A waste. And they would have been right, Lucas thought. In the great scheme of things, Claude Duncan hadn't counted for much. But Claude was also the kind of person no one disliked enough to bother murdering. Unless he knew something. With Claude's luck, he'd merely been in the right place at the wrong time.

The first part of the report told Lucas little that he hadn't already guessed from viewing the remains. Over fifty percent of Claude's body had been covered by third-degree burns, which destroy the skin and leave underlying structures exposed. Second-degree burns took care of another thirty percent. The high temperature of the fire had caused the tissues to rupture, resulting in the splitting of skin all over Claude's body.

His skull had been fractured, but the medical examiner did not believe Claude had received a blow to the head, which would have caused the bone fragments to be localized and shoved *into* the skull. Instead, intracranial pressure had produced brain lesions, and the bone fragments from the skull were displaced *outward*. Both injuries were common phenomena resulting from intense heat and did not necessarily point to Claude being killed before the fire was set. It looked more as if the fire, not a physical assault to the head, had caused Claude's death. Supporting this conclusion was the fact that he had a carbon monoxide level in his blood of around five percent and carbon particles had been found in his air passages, indicating that Claude had still been breathing while the fire raged.

The puzzling thing was that in most deaths by fire, the carbon monoxide blood concentration exceeded ten percent, and more carbon particles were located in the air passages than had been found in Claude's. Therefore, it appeared that while he had been alive during the fire, he had not been breathing normally.

Lucas frowned in thought. He was certain Claude had been drunk at the time of the fire, but drunkenness doesn't usually cut down on air intake. So, Claude's condition had to have another explanation.

Results of the toxicology tests provided it. Aside from a high alcohol content, Claude's blood had contained a large amount of oxymorphone hydrochloride, a semisynthetic opioid substitute for morphine.

Lucas already knew the principal effects of opioids, such as respiratory depression. They also repressed the cough reflex, which would explain why Claude had a much lower carbon monoxide blood concentration and fewer carbon particles in the air passages than would be expected. He wasn't breathing normally and he'd had little capacity to cough up the small amount of carbon he *had* been able to inhale.

Lucas also knew opioids resulted in sedation.

"Sedation," he said aloud. "Must be very convenient to have your victim sedated, unable to run or even crawl, but still breathing if you want his murder to look like an accidental burn fatality."

"Something you need, Sheriff?"

Lucas looked up at Naomi, his perky new secretary and a part-time dispatcher, who had the bad habit of constantly interrupting his thoughts. "Nothing, thanks."

"Well, it's just that you were talking. I thought maybe you were talking to me. Wanting something. Coffee, maybe."

"No, thanks."

"Okay." Naomi had inched into the room as she chattered and now nearly stood on tiptoe trying to peer over the top of the papers in his hand. "Is that an autopsy report?"

"Yes," Lucas said in irritation.

"Anything interesting in it?" she asked, blue eyes snapping with curiosity.

"A couple of very interesting things," he returned sharply. He'd had enough of cigarette abstinence and also of her badly concealed curiosity. He rose from his chair.

"Interesting things about Julianna Brent?" Naomi continued, undaunted.

"About her *and* Claude Duncan."

"Oh, *him,*" she said with indifference. "Nothing juicy about *her,* the model?"

Lucas gave her a withering look, deciding that she didn't just annoy him. He definitely disliked her. "Sorry, nothing juicy enough to satisfy you, I'm sure." Naomi looked bland, totally missing the insult. "If I'm needed, I'll be outside for the next ten minutes or so." He saw her eyes on the autopsy reports and picked them up. "I think I'll take these with me and look at them in the light of day."

"Oh, okay. But I could file them for you."

"No, thanks."

"Well, if you're sure."

"I am." And I'm also sure this will definitely be a three-cigarette break, Lucas thought as he strode past the unnerving innocent-faced girl with the rapacious eyes. Just as sure as I am that you will never get a chance to even *glance* at these reports if I have to lock them in a safe.

Naomi wore a sharp-edged cologne that made Lucas's nose tingle, and she'd frozen her silver-frosted mouse-brown hair into immobility with some kind of hair spray that seemed to contain Super Glue. She did not step aside and he had to press himself against the doorframe in order not to rub against her body as he passed by. "You enjoy your smokes, Sheriff. You work *so* hard, you really deserve a break, even if smoking isn't a healthy habit." She smiled insinuatingly and nearly cooed, "Maybe someday I'll get the chance to make you stop. Smoking, that is."

By sheer force of will, Lucas did not shudder. He did decide, however, that Naomi would not be working here this time next week.

5

"Henri Toulouse-Lautrec is probably most famous for two things," Adrienne said to her art appreciation class. "First, for being a dwarf, or to use the more politically correct term, a little person. Second, for leading what many consider a dissolute or wild life in the nightclubs and brothels of Paris."

"He sounds like my kind of guy," a grinning, blunt-featured boy in the back row said loudly. "The part about the nightclubs and whorehouses, not the dwarf part."

A prim-faced young man near the front muttered, "She said *brothels,* not whorehouses. Also, Toulouse-Lautrec was a great artist. That's what you should remember him for, cretin."

"What was that, dork weed?" the brash one challenged loudly.

"He just pointed out that Toulouse-Lautrec was a great artist," Adrienne said quickly. The two guys had been at war since the class had begun and, in her mind, acted like they belonged in the seventh grade, not college. "Toulouse-Lautrec was greatly influenced by Degas and Gauguin, but he developed his own style——that of a graphic artist. This is what makes his paintings so suited to lithography, or posters. Let's look at a few."

"Fantastic. Can't wait, can you, dork weed?" came loudly from the back of the room.

Dork weed sighed in martyrdom. Adrienne gritted her teeth, dimmed the lights, and placed a slide of *At the Moulin Rouge* into the projector. "This really isn't a scene of gaiety as it appears at first glance. The characters in the painting don't look truly happy. Another interesting aspect of this piece is the figure of the short, bearded man standing next to the tall man at the back of the room. The short man is Toulouse-Lautrec. He put himself into his own painting!"

Adrienne looked around. What had she expected? Gasps of awe? Yelps of delight? The class was silent. Dork weed stared at the slide in grim concentration while cretin yawned hugely. Ignoring the lack of verbal reaction as she plowed on with what she'd thought was a fascinating slide show, Adrienne glanced at her daughter.

Adrienne slumped at the back of the room. The girl had been of two minds about coming. Attending a college class had made her feel grown-up and sophisticated. But she'd been embarrassed about being dragged to a class taught by her mother. During the first half hour, she'd looked alert and even took notes. Now, in the second hour, she had abandoned her notebook as well as her scrutiny of the other students and looked positively glassy-eyed with ennui. After all, no notes were being passed, no one was chewing the gum forbidden in secondary school, and there were no cute boys under the age of eighteen who might be interested in a fourteen-year-old girl.

To top off her misery, Skye's favorite television show was on right now. Adrienne had set the VCR to time-tape the program, although Skye had complained that taped shows lost their "immediacy," a term she'd picked up from Rachel. But in light of the break-in along with every other horrible thing that had happened in the last couple of days, Adrienne wasn't going to let her daughter stay by herself this evening, even though the class ended at nine o'clock, before Skye's bedtime. In fact, she wondered if she'd ever feel safe leaving her precious Skye unattended ever again.

• • •

"That was *really* a good class, Mom," Skye said as they walked through the lighted parking lot to their car.

"Thanks, honey." Although a few times you looked like you were going to lapse into unconsciousness from boredom, Adrienne thought. "You know, those two guys calling each other names aren't typical college students."

"I figured. They seemed like guys in *my* school. I didn't pay any attention to them. Just you."

"Maybe you'd like experimenting with painting soon."

"Uh . . . I think I take after Daddy more than you. I want to be a writer."

"Your dad wasn't a writer."

"When he was in Las Vegas, he wrote his comedy routines. He told me."

Adrienne didn't want to think about those mildly amusing routines Trey had created and thought were hilarious. "I thought you were more interested in writing murder mysteries."

"Oh, I am," Skye assured her. "I hope your feelings aren't hurt because I don't want to be an artist. I just don't think I have any talent for painting."

Adrienne put her arm around Skye's shoulders. "My feelings aren't hurt. My father wanted me to be a doctor, but I didn't *want* to be a doctor. So, I followed my own desires. That's always the best way to go."

"It wasn't for Daddy. Being a hit in Las Vegas was his big dream, but it turned out to be a disaster for him. I think it broke his heart." Adrienne was surprised by her daughter's mature observation. For a moment, she didn't know what to say. Then she began slowly. "Your dad didn't have the talent for a musical comedy act, but he had great charisma. After we came back to Point Pleasant, he was a fabulous salesman at your grandfather's furniture store."

"I'm glad. But I'm still sorry Daddy didn't get to do what

he really wanted to." Skye paused. "And I'm sorry I don't remember him as well as I used to."

Adrienne wondered what was the correct response to that remark. She couldn't very well say that Trey wasn't as real to his own wife as he used to be, either. Or that she sometimes wondered if she'd loved him as much as she'd told herself she did because she thought marriage to a good-looking, charming young man would make her forget a silly teenaged infatuation with Drew Delaney, an infatuation she couldn't let flare to life again, especially after seeing his car today had raised questions about his actions toward her.

"I didn't mean to make you sad about Daddy," Skye said.

"You didn't." Adrienne gave Skye a squeeze. "Daddy died four years ago. It's natural for our memory of him to dim a little bit so we *don't* get sad all the time. But you loved your daddy very much, and he knew it. That's what's important." Skye gave her a small, relieved smile.

"Here's the car at last," Adrienne said. "Next time we'll come earlier. I don't like having to park at the back of the lot even if it's well lighted."

The college was only about ten minutes away from their home and Adrienne was glad. She felt unusually tired after what had been a fairly easy class to teach. But when they neared the house, she was surprised to see a small, red car sitting beneath the new dusk-to-dawn light the electric company had installed near the street that afternoon.

"That's Rachel's car!" Skye said excitedly.

They found the young woman sitting on the front porch steps, her chin propped on a cupped hand. "I didn't think you two would *ever* get home."

"Is something wrong?" Adrienne asked anxiously. "Are Vicky and Philip all right?"

"Sure. Off on another campaign trip. I talked to them on the phone about three hours ago. Dad was practicing his speech. Honestly, I think he's forgotten how to talk normally. He just booms out sentences along with all these sweeping gestures. It's weird." Skye giggled. "Anyway, I felt kind of lonely in that big house by myself and I thought I'd come by to visit two of my favorite people. I forgot that you had a class tonight, Aunt Adrienne."

Adrienne caught the forlorn note in Rachel's usually animated voice. "We're delighted to see you, Rachel, but you shouldn't be sitting out here by yourself after our break-in."

"We had one, too. Besides, you've got this place lit up like a parking lot."

"Yes, it's a bit bright, but better safe than sorry." Adrienne looked at the picture window to see Brandon peering out, his tongue lolling. He adored Rachel. "Let's go in and get comfortable. I don't know what possessed me to wear high heels tonight."

"I'm so glad you're here!" Skye took Rachel's hand as Adrienne opened the front door and began punching numbers on the alarm system she decided she'd never get used to. "So many exciting things have happened the last few days and we didn't get a chance to talk about them! But I thought you'd be with Bruce tonight."

"He wanted to go to a movie, but I wasn't in the mood. Bruce is okay, but I don't want to spend as much time with him as he wants to spend with me." Rachel grinned and tapped Skye's nose. "You are *much* more fun than Bruce Allard." She stooped and hugged an elated Brandon. "And you're much more handsome!"

After Rachel double-checked Adrienne's handiwork with the alarm system and Adrienne kicked off the hated spike heels, they all trailed into the kitchen. It was then she knew exactly how downbeat Rachel was feeling when she asked for hot chocolate. Hot chocolate had always been her greatest source of comfort. Skye promptly said she was also dying for hot chocolate, even though she'd announced on the way home she wanted lemonade because of the unusually hot June night. Adrienne was always amused by Skye's desire to be like her beautiful, older cousin. Amused and glad. Rachel set a good example.

"How is your job going?" Adrienne asked Rachel as she poured herself a cup of chocolate she didn't really want.

"All right, although I'm not getting to do as much with the Brent murder as I'd like."

"I don't have any more information from Sheriff Flynn," Adrienne warned.

Rachel's face reddened. "This time I didn't come to pump you for information. I promise. The murder is just on my mind a lot."

Adrienne sat down at the kitchen table with the girls. "Rachel, the murder of Julianna Brent is the most sensational story the *Register* has handled for years, and as bright and promising a reporter as you are, you haven't even graduated from college yet. Drew probably feels you don't have enough experience to take over the story, not to mention the resentment his giving it to you would cause among the other reporters who've been at the paper for years instead of a couple of months."

Rachel took a sip of hot chocolate and, ignoring her small marshmallow mustache, said gravely, "I guess you're right, Aunt Adrienne."

Skye nodded. "Sometimes Mom has real good ideas."

"Thank you, dear," Adrienne said dryly.

"But there's Claude Duncan's death, too," Rachel said. "Maybe someone deliberately set that fire."

"Where did you hear that?" Adrienne asked sharply.

"Well, I heard that Sheriff Flynn had an arson expert look over the site. And murder makes sense if Claude saw something the morning Julianna was killed."

"If he did, why wouldn't he tell the police?"

"I don't know. He wasn't very smart. Maybe he didn't realize the importance of what he'd seen, but the killer didn't know that, or he thought Claude might realize it later."

"Wow, that's a great idea, too!" Skye looked at her mother.

"I have to start taking notes if I'm gonna write murder mysteries someday. Although I'd rather not write one about Julianna's murder."

"I'd rather you didn't too, honey. If you're sure you want to write murder mysteries, I'd like for you to stick to entirely fictional characters, not one of my best friends."

The doorbell rang. Brandon barked and all three females jumped, then stiffened. Finally Rachel quirked a smile and said, "I don't think murderers or thieves ring the bell. It's probably Sheriff Flynn, Aunt Adrienne."

Of course, Adrienne thought. If she was going to stay in this house, she couldn't fall apart every time someone came to the door or called. And she hadn't talked to Lucas since morning. He was probably dropping by to check on them.

But it wasn't Lucas at the door. It was Bruce Allard—tall, handsome, blond, tan, and smiling winningly. "Hello, Mrs. Reynolds. I saw Rachel's car parked out front and I'd like to speak to her, if I'm not interrupting."

Rachel appeared beside Adrienne. "What is it, Bruce?" she asked before Adrienne had a chance to say anything.

"You said you weren't in the mood to go *out* to a movie, but you didn't say anything about not wanting to stay *in* to see one, so I rented a DVD." He held it up. "*Chicago*. One of your favorites."

Rachel stared at him for a few moments before saying expressionlessly, "I've seen it five times."

"I thought maybe you had, so I also got *Mulholland Drive*."

"Then why don't we watch it here?" Adrienne suggested. Rachel clearly didn't want to spend an evening alone with Bruce or she wouldn't have declined his earlier invitation.

Bruce's charm-you-to-death smile wavered and Adrienne caught a flash of anger in his blue eyes, anger that vanished so fast she thought she might have imagined it until Rachel said quickly, "I don't think that movie is really suitable for Skye."

Skye looked stricken and burst out indignantly, "I'm *not* a little girl!"

Rachel gave her a sly wink and she subsided, realizing Rachel had only been using her as an excuse not to burden them with Bruce for the evening. "Okay, Mr. Allard, you win." Rachel's voice sounded tired. "We'll go back to my house to watch the movie."

"Rachel, if you'd rather spend the evening with us and not see *any* movie, I'm sure Bruce would understand," Adrienne said, her annoyance with Bruce growing.

"Rachel and I have a standing date, Mrs. Reynolds." Bruce's expression was pleasant, but his voice was firm. Adrienne's annoyance flared into strong irritation. She'd always known the indulged son of one of the town's most affluent families was self-assured, but tonight he struck her as downright arrogant. Rachel had already broken off their "standing date," then gently tried to rebuff him at Adrienne's door. But Bruce showed a bold determination to get his own way. It wasn't an attractive trait.

Rachel had picked up her purse and was starting out the front door when Adrienne caught sight of Bruce's car parked behind Rachel's.

"I like your car, Bruce," she said. "What kind is it?"

He nearly preened at the compliment. "It's a GTO. They just started making them again after twenty years. It's got 350 horsepower. I can go from zero to sixty miles an hour in five seconds."

"Oh, stop bragging and let's get going," Rachel said with a forced laugh. She bent slightly and gave Adrienne a quick kiss on the cheek.

But Adrienne hardly noticed the uncustomary physical affection from her niece. All of her attention was fixed on Bruce's GTO—black, two doors, with a long hood, a short trunk, and a spoiler. Another car like the one that had kept up surveillance on her house throughout the long hours of the previous night.

NINE

I

"Why in heaven's name are you holding that cat? You're allergic to cats!"

Kit Kirkwood looked up to see her mother Ellen in blue linen slacks and a white silk blouse that last summer had fit her perfectly and now looked at least one size too big. Ellen's complexion was pasty in spite of a careful makeup job, and her frosty gray eyes were slightly sunken and surrounded by shadows concealer couldn't hide. My God, how she's aged this last year since Jamie died, Kit thought. She looks ten years older.

"I outgrew my allergy to cats about twenty years ago," Kit said calmly, stroking the cat that had tensed at the shrillness of Ellen's voice. "And this isn't just any cat. It's Lottie's Calypso. Don't you recognize her?"

"Calypso?" Ellen squinted. Kit was certain her mother needed glasses but refused to wear them because she thought they made her look older. Ellen never forgot how she looked beside her handsome husband, Gavin, who was fourteen years her junior. "Why do you have Lottie's cat?"

Kit sat in the gazebo near the outside bar at the Iron Gate Grill. They would not open for lunch for two hours and she was taking advantage of the clear, gently warm morning to relax. "Mother, why don't you come into the gazebo and have a seat instead of yelling at me from out on the sidewalk?"

"I don't want to get my slacks dirty."

"The chairs have been wiped clean this morning. Join me for a mimosa."

"At this hour?" Ellen tried to look surprised at the invitation, but Kit knew her mother hadn't just happened by. A lifetime had alerted Kit to her mother's oblique approach to topics she thought would incite arguments. "Well, maybe I can spare a few minutes," Ellen said. "And I guess a mimosa wouldn't kill me."

Ellen entered the gazebo and sat down carefully as if the chair might blow up beneath her. Kit motioned to a waiter wiping off the tiki bar and asked him to bring two mimosas.

Ellen gazed balefully at the bar with its torches and South Pacific look. "I do wish you'd get rid of that thing, Kit."

"Why? People love it."

"It's disrespectful. After all, your restaurant is next to the approach of the old Silver Bridge."

The Silver Bridge again, Kit thought with a groan. She hadn't been born when the bridge connecting West Virginia and Ohio crumbled. Ellen had told the story so many times, though, Kit felt as if she instead of her mother had been sitting helplessly in a car on the approach that dreadful night of December 15, 1967, when the bridge collapsed, dumping Christmas traffic into the frigid water of the Ohio River. Forty-six people had died, including two of Ellen's close friends. Ellen was almost as obsessed with the disaster of the bridge as she was with the unfortunate history of la Belle Rivière.

The waiter delivered the mimosas and dashed away. Ellen gazed after him. "Why does his hair stick straight up like that?"

"Hair gel."

"You should make him stop wearing it. He looks like he stuck his finger in an electric socket." Ellen touched her own hair—short, carefully styled, and dyed the exact deep brown of Kit's—then took a sip of her drink. With one of her habitual quick changes of subject, she asked, "Why did Lottie give you Calypso?"

"She didn't. I brought the cat home because Lottie is missing."

Ellen's gaze jerked to Kit's. "*Missing?* Why didn't someone tell me?"

"You weren't in great shape yesterday, Mother."

"I certainly wasn't too far gone to hear that my best friend is missing!" Although Ellen and Lottie traveled in entirely different social circles, Ellen had remained close to her childhood companion. "Maybe I shouldn't get upset, though," Ellen said hopefully. "Lottie goes on her little walking tours every year."

"This time is different. Her daughter has been murdered. I don't think she'd be in the mood for one of her casual strolls to look at the countryside after Julianna's death." Kit paused, stroking the tiny Calypso under the chin and sending her into an ecstasy of purring. "Lottie was here last night. She wouldn't come inside the restaurant. We sat out back on a bench. She seemed extremely calm—too calm, considering how she adored Juli. She also seemed a little scared. I went inside to get her some tea and she was gone when I came back. I've been to her cabin and it looks like she never returned. Calypso was obviously starving so I brought her home with me."

Ellen looked genuinely alarmed. "You know Lottie would never neglect an animal. Something is wrong aside from Juli's death. Someone should be searching for Lottie!"

"The police are, Mother."

Ellen scoffed. "They aren't working overtime, I'm sure. They're too carried away with Julianna's murder to worry about poor Lottie. How's Gail?"

"She acts like she couldn't care less about Lottie *or* Julianna."

Ellen scowled. "That awful girl! She's like her father Butch. You barely knew him, but he was odious. Surprisingly smart in a conniving way, but odious. Completely unprincipled. Lottie only married him because Butch was her father's boss and Butch wanted Lottie." Ellen sighed. "Lottie used to be so pretty. Beautiful, really, like Juli. She always wanted to please her father. Besides, he told her she was lucky to get Butch because no one else would want her after what had happened to her at la Belle."

"Lottie's life has been tragic," Kit said softly.

"But she emerged from everything bad that happened to her with such a placid outlook. And two daughters she remained proud of, no matter what. She always believed Julianna could break back into the modeling world if she wanted to, and that Gail could do anything she pleased if she would just apply herself. Gail could have gotten a college scholarship, but she would never leave here. It was as if something held her. Maybe the hope that Butch would come back."

"That doesn't sound like an enticing hope," Kit said dryly.

"It wouldn't be to us, but it might to Gail. There's no accounting for the human heart." Ellen grimaced then said with determination, "I'm going to look for Lottie as soon as I leave here."

Kit knew it was useless to point out that her mother would begin to tire in an hour. Ellen cherished Lottie and had always wanted to improve the woman's lifestyle, but during their friendship of over half a century, Lottie had never accepted even a loan. As if reading her mind, Ellen said, "Lottie can't have gone far. She has no money." Ellen watched Kit stroking the cat then said emphatically, "Miles Shaw killed Julianna."

Kit's gaze sliced toward her mother. "He was out of town."

"So he says."

"The police confirmed it. Besides, you're talking about *murder,* Mother. Miles couldn't do something like that!"

"I think he could."

"And you know him *so* well," Kit returned scathingly.

"I know him as well as I need to. Besides, *you* are still in love with him."

"I am not, Mother. I never dated Miles. We were friends. I introduced him to Julianna."

"You were just friends because *he* wanted a platonic relationship, not you."

"That was a long time ago, Mother. I'm seeing J.C. now."

"That handsome blue-eyed man who's in your restaurant all the time? I've no doubt you're attracted to him, but you're not in love with him like you were with Miles." Kit's lips tightened. "If you'd talk about it, Kit—just admit it—you'd feel better."

"You will not give up, Mother," Kit said through clenched teeth. "You keep nipping at peoples' heels like some damned little terrier until they say what you want just to get you to *shut up*! It's one of the things that drives Gavin crazy about you."

Ellen's pale eyes hardened. "Let's leave Gavin out of this."

"Yes, let's. He doesn't stand up well to close scrutiny."

Ellen set down her mimosa glass with a bang. "You are in one foul mood today, daughter, and I don't feel like subjecting myself to it any longer." She stood up. "I'm going to look for Lottie."

"Do you want me to go with you?"

"No! I will find Lottie on my own."

"Try your best," Kit murmured as she watched Ellen march stiff-backed toward her Mercedes. "But you won't find her."

2

Adrienne had set up her easel and determinedly began her painting of la Belle Rivière an hour ago. Kit still wanted it and Adrienne wouldn't disappoint her. She also wanted to do the painting for herself, not just for Kit, because the Belle was a landmark that shouldn't be forgotten just because of Ellen Kirkwood's belief that it was haunted. The woman was downright irrational when it came to some matters, the hotel being one of them, and her intention to destroy the place made Adrienne angry, in spite of what had happened to Julianna here.

But Adrienne found that trying to forget Julianna's fate, even long enough to accomplish a couple of hours of painting, was beyond difficult. Although the police had sealed the doors, from the outside the hotel looked as pristine and majestic as always. The last year of neglect had not seemed to touch it, as if it had been protected from time by some kind of supernatural protective shield. The atmosphere was different, though. Adrienne felt the air of ruin, of desolation, even of malevolence emanating from the beautiful, deserted hotel. It seemed alive. And corrupt.

For a moment she felt like packing up her equipment and leaving, in spite of the patrol Lucas had come by every hour or so to make sure she was all right. Then she drew a deep breath and closed her eyes. Adrienne, you're being absurd, she told herself sternly. You're as fanciful and easily spooked as a kid. It's just a building. And you're not alone out here. People know where you are, and the cops check on you fairly regularly. Besides, the murderer isn't hanging around so he can kill you out in the open in broad daylight.

She opened her eyes. She released her breath. She even made herself smile.

She did not feel one bit better.

Adrienne always painted to music at home but rarely when she painted outside. Today, though, she knew the dark atmosphere of a murder scene that would bother her might be lightened by music. Rock. Loud rock. So she'd brought her boom box and was listening to "Save Me." She was just turning up the music a notch higher when Ellen Kirkwood came to a screeching halt in her Mercedes and nearly leaped from the car.

"Adrienne!"

Oh God, Adrienne groaned inwardly. Ellen was going to throw a fit about her doing the painting. But the woman surprised her. "Hard at work so early in the morning?"

"It's ten-fifteen, Ellen. Hardly early."

"You young people are so full of energy. I used to be the same way." You used to be a whirling dervish one day and in bed the next, Adrienne silently recalled. Ellen's erratic behavior had always set Kit on edge and with good reason. It didn't allow for a peaceful home environment. Ellen looked around. "Where's your little girl, Moon?"

"It's Skye. She was invited to her friend Sherry Granger's house along with a couple of other girls for sunbathing around the pool. Mrs. Granger is a vigilant mother and I knew Skye would have more fun frolicking in the Granger pool than stuck with me all day."

"I'm sure she will." Ellen shot an icy look at the boom box. "*What* is that music?"

"It's a song by a group called Remy Zero."

"Good Lord. It's terrible."

"That's a matter of opinion."

"No, it's terrible. I don't know how you can paint with that racket going on." Ellen's gaze darted around the grounds. "Have you seen Lottie?"

"No, Ellen. No one has seen Lottie except for Kit."

"She told me about Lottie coming to the restaurant." Ellen let out a huge sigh. "I'm worried sick and *I'm* going to look for Lottie since the police aren't doing anything."

"They are, Ellen."

"She's still missing, isn't she?" Ellen challenged. "They can't be doing much. I'm sure I can find her. She's around here somewhere. I can feel it. Perhaps she's in the woods."

"You're going to search the woods for her?"

"Yes, of course. I grew up here at the hotel. I know these woods like the back of my hand."

The woman looked frail, hectic color burned high on her cheeks, and her rate of speech was faster than normal. She had no business tramping around the woods by herself.

Resolutely, Adrienne wiped her brush clean. She was annoyed by the interruption, but she'd never forgive herself if she let the woman go off on her own and get hurt. And the sunlight could not last at this perfect slant for more than another ten minutes, anyway. At least she told herself these were the reasons she was abandoning her work. Deep down, she wasn't sure Ellen wasn't just providing her with a convenient excuse.

"I'm ready for a break, Ellen. Mind if I go with you?"

"I'd love for you to go with me as long as it's to help me look for Lottie, not to look after me. I don't need to be looked after. I'm much stronger than anyone has *ever* given me credit for."

Which was probably true, Adrienne thought. Ellen Kirkwood had been through enough shock and sadness in her life to break most people, but she soldiered on, acquiring a quirk here, a superstition there, but still prevailing.

After making a quick call on her cell phone to police headquarters to tell them she was taking a walk up the hill with Ellen Kirkwood so the patrolman wouldn't be alarmed when he made his usual half-hour check on her and found her gone, Adrienne tramped along beside Ellen as they started toward the hill beyond the hotel. "Did you know that the first time my mother walked me around these grounds," Ellen said, gesturing at the graceful lawns of la Belle, "I screamed my head off and couldn't be quieted? Even at three weeks old, I sensed something wrong about this place."

"Lots of babies cry steadily, Ellen. Skye did."

"*I* didn't. Mama said I was a very good baby—quiet and docile when I was away from la Belle. For the first six months of my life, we lived with Mama's parents. Then Father had a falling-out with Mama's father, and my father had an apartment fixed for us on the third floor of la Belle." Ellen shook her head. "Afterward, Father wouldn't let Mama and me spend much time with her parents."

"I'm sure your father wanted you and your mother with him as much as possible," Adrienne said carefully, sensing Ellen's growing ire over an old problem.

Ellen snorted. "Possessions. That's all we were to Father. He wanted us here because he wanted people to believe Mama couldn't bear to be away from him. She was quite the beauty, you know, and from a much higher social stratum than he was, although he had more money. But him being happy and satisfied with his wife was a myth. Father had a mistress."

Ellen's stride picked up speed with her anger. Adrienne looked at the woods looming ahead. She wasn't in the mood for a vigorous hike. She was also growing uncomfortable with Ellen's personal disclosures. "She was beautiful if you like that bursting-with-health, flashy look," Ellen spat out. "She was married to the family's *doctor*. The man who'd delivered me. Apparently, the respectable life with a husband years older than she was bored her, though. She soon started hunting for entertainment and ended up breaking her husband's heart and ruining my mother's life."

The sun dimmed as they walked into a stand of maple and elm trees toward the south of the hotel, leading in the direction of Lottie's cabin. A trio of sparrows bustled through the glossy maple leaves, chirping exuberantly. Ellen paid no attention to them. "But I suppose Kit has told you all about *that* scandal," Ellen said almost accusingly.

"No, she didn't." Adrienne sidestepped a cluster of poison ivy.

"Well, since you're being kind enough to help me look for Lottie, I'll tell you the story."

"You don't have to, Ellen, especially if it's painful for you."

Ellen ignored her. "The affair had gone on for a couple of years before my father tired of her and wanted to end it.

Everything came to a head during a New Year's Eve party at la Belle. I was twelve. I'd sneaked into the party in the ballroom and saw Father talking to her. She began to make an awful scene and threw champagne in Father's face. Father struggled to get her out of the ballroom quickly. My poor mother slunk out in embarrassment. My father put the woman in one of the rooms on the fourth floor. She was drunk and must have had a cache of pills with her—maybe morphine.

"A couple of hours later, she jumped from the fourth-floor porch. She screamed all the way down, landed on the terrace, and split her skull on a stone urn." Ellen paused, then added tonelessly, "I'll never forget the sight of all that bright red blood on the snow while the music was still playing merrily away in the ballroom."

"My God, how awful!" Adrienne burst out, truly horrified. "You actually saw her?"

"Oh yes. No one was paying much attention to me. Unfortunately, someone was watching my mother. Or claimed to be. A maid said she saw Mama coming out of that woman's room just minutes after she jumped. Naturally, speculation followed. People said Mama had pushed her. There was a police investigation. It was terrible. Mama wasn't strong to begin with and the investigation, the suspicion, and the scandal crushed her although she never stood trial. Still, she wasn't the same afterward and just wasted away over the next three years. It was all Father's fault. I never forgave him."

Part of Adrienne was intrigued by the story of Ellen's past. Another part was repelled by the sordidness and tragedy. She didn't want to hear more and decided to change the subject.

"You know Lottie better than anyone, Ellen. If she's not hurt, why would she vanish at a time like this? She's not even here to help plan Juli's funeral."

Ellen looked troubled. "Of course she *could* be hurt,

lying out in the woods, helpless." Then she brightened. "But I don't feel that's what has happened. I think she's hiding."

"Hiding? Why? Because she knows who killed Julianna and is afraid of being murdered to keep her silent?"

"Lottie is far too brave for that kind of behavior. If she knew who killed Julianna, she'd immediately go to the police, consequences be damned. Lottie seems frail, but she's incredibly strong. Always has been." Ellen paused, her breath quickening. "Even as a young girl. What she went through here at la Belle . . ."

They'd gone deeper into the woods now. Cicadas whirred in the trees, and sunlight stabbed only intermittently through a heavy canopy of leaves onto pads of moss on the ground. A squirrel darted in front of them and ran up a tree. Adrienne jumped, but Ellen seemed oblivious.

"You *do* know what la Belle did to Lottie, don't you?" Ellen asked.

"I know something happened to her on the grounds when she was young. I don't think even Juli knew the details."

"No, Lottie wouldn't have dwelled on it. She rarely spoke of it even to me." Ellen drew a deep breath as if she were already feeling winded by the climb up the hill in the growing midday heat. "I'd grown even closer to Lottie since my mother's decline. Mama barely spoke and spent most of her time in bed, and my father traveled even more than usual."

"That's sad," Adrienne said, thinking how inadequate the words sounded.

"Lottie's mother had died years earlier, so we turned to each other for company. It was summer and she was almost always here. One night there was a dance. La Belle was full of people. Lottie and I didn't have escorts—we were only fourteen—and after the dance she set off for the cabin alone. I should have sent someone with her to make sure she got home safely, but I was young and silly and thoughtless."

Ellen went silent, carefully stepping over a cluster of vines in her beige canvas wedgies that were already hopelessly stained with grass and dirt. The trees grew closer together here, and the sun seemed to have completely disappeared above the leaves. Even the air had cooled in the shadows.

"When I went to the cabin around noon the next day, Lottie's father said she'd never come home the night before. He said he thought she'd stayed at la Belle, not that he was the type to give her much thought at all. We began a search. She wasn't found until evening."

Ellen swallowed hard and her voice quivered. "A man had grabbed her before she'd even gotten off the la Belle grounds. He'd knocked her out and dragged her into an old toolshed where he'd tied her up with rope and proceeded to rape and beat her all night. I know you've seen the scars on her temples. You should see the rest of her body. Even her wrists and ankles are scarred from the ropes he used to truss her up like a pig. And the repeated rapes were so brutal—" Ellen choked back a sob. "She was nearly dead."

Adrienne shivered. "I had no idea," she barely whispered, her throat closing against tears. "Was the man caught?"

"No. Lottie said she didn't see his face. Everyone decided it must have been a vagrant. My father was particularly adamant about the theory of a vagrant." Ellen paused, then said harshly, "Father was *too* adamant. There was a man staying at la Belle. A rich, prominent man I later learned was trailed by rumors of deviant behavior. The day after Lottie was found, I heard my father arguing with him. The man promptly left for Europe and never returned to la Belle. I'm sure he was the monster who brutalized Lottie and that my father shielded him. After all, Father couldn't let it be known that a patron of la Belle was capable of such hideousness. Father ordered the toolshed razed, as if that showed how much he cared for Lottie's plight. And that was the end of it. Not even the police bothered to continue their investigation for more than a couple of days—as if poor Lottie didn't matter."

Adrienne felt vaguely nauseated, partly by the thought of

young Lottie bound and repeatedly raped, partly by the seemingly endless trek through the woods accompanied by Ellen's tales of horror. Adrienne also found Ellen's growing shortness of breath unsettling. She was glad she'd come along, even though she was certain the search was fruitless, but she was also worried. Ellen definitely didn't look well. Adrienne unobtrusively tapped her pocket to make sure she had her cell phone to call 911 if Ellen actually collapsed.

Lottie's cabin finally came into view and Adrienne felt relief rush over her. "Thank goodness. I hope she's inside," she said.

Ellen shook her head. "I wouldn't count on it. The windows are closed and there are no clothes hanging on the line to dry. This is Lottie's laundry day."

"But under the circumstances—"

"If Lottie were home, she would have done her laundry. I know her better than you do, Adrienne."

"I can't argue that point." Ellen looked tired enough to drop and Adrienne said casually, "Do you want to look in the cabin even though you think Lottie isn't there? We might find some sort of clue."

"You mean like the convenient note stating where she's gone?" Ellen made a face. "Sorry to be sarcastic, dear. I'm a bit frayed at the seams these days. Yes, let's go in. Maybe at least we'll find some sign that she's been in the cabin during the last couple of days."

But they didn't. As they climbed the porch steps, an impressive collection of colored glass, delicate wood, and slender metal wind chimes tinkled in the slight breeze, but otherwise all was silent. Inside, the shabby cabin remained spotless, as if it had just been cleaned that morning, but it still had a feeling of having been unoccupied for perhaps days. "Doesn't Lottie believe in locks?" Adrienne asked as the front door squeaked open on rusty hinges and they walked in. Ellen made a beeline for a cane-backed chair and plopped down, trying to hide her heavy breathing.

"No, believe it or not after what happened to her when she was young. She's been lucky, though. The place has never been robbed."

"I wish I could say the same." Adrienne remained standing, looking at all the pictures of Julianna. "I wasn't burglarized, but my house was invaded. So was my sister's."

"I heard. I cannot believe someone would break into Philip Hamilton's house with the whole family home. What was the point?"

To terrorize me, Adrienne thought. To play Julianna's favorite song on a boom box to let me know I'm in danger because of some photographs I took—photographs that showed nothing.

"You have the oddest look on your face," Ellen said. "Do you know something about the break-ins you're not saying?"

"Of course not."

"You and Kit lie equally badly."

"I wasn't sure Lottie had a phone," Adrienne said, ignoring the jibe as she touched the bulky, old-fashioned black telephone sitting on a table near the door.

"She hates it and only has it because Juli insisted and paid for it."

"Are you sure it's still working?"

Ellen lifted the receiver, then held it out so Adrienne could hear the dial tone. "Alive and kicking." Ellen stood up slowly, putting a hand on her lower back that must have begun to ache. "Which is more than I will be able to say for myself if I don't get moving before I stiffen up." She took a deep breath. "We aren't going to find Lottie by sitting around here gabbing. I have a particular place in mind I want to check. It's near the top of the hill. Are you up for a climb?"

"*I* am, but I'm afraid you're pushing yourself, Ellen. You aren't used to this much exercise."

"Nonsense." Ellen bristled. "I'm much stronger than I look."

I hope so, Adrienne thought, because you look like you

could break as easily as a dry twig. "Onward and upward, then. But let's take it slow." Ellen shot her a simmering look. "Maybe the climb isn't getting to you, but it is to me. My thighs are beginning to feel the strain." Which wasn't true, but Ellen looked slightly mollified.

Ellen carefully shut the cabin door behind them although no locks protected the place from intruders. Adrienne tied back her shoulder-length hair with a piece of string she'd found at Lottie's and enjoyed the touch of cool air on her neck. She glanced at Ellen, whose carefully set curls had begun to wilt. Thorns from a multiflora rose cluster had snagged her expensive silk blouse, and she was missing a clip-on earring. Still, she looked determined as she marched slightly ahead of Adrienne, physically proclaiming herself as leader of this expedition.

"I wish you would stop looking at me like I'm going to fall into a dead heap any minute," Ellen snapped. "It's getting on my nerves."

"I didn't mean to annoy you."

"I know. You've always been a very polite girl, Adrienne. Far less turbulent and headstrong than Kit." Adrienne had no intention of responding to that comment. "I don't look like it now, but I used to be quite athletic," Ellen stated. "And I was a first-rate dancer."

"Really? Ballet?"

Ellen laughed. "Good heavens, no! I danced to rock and roll. *Real* rock and roll, not that nonsense you were listening to earlier." Her smile faded. "Jamie and I danced."

Adrienne thought of Ellen's adopted four-year-old son who'd drowned in the pool at la Belle last summer. "Your little boy enjoyed dancing?"

Ellen looked confused for a moment, then shook her head. "My cousin Jamie. We were cousins by marriage. He was three years older than I and the love of my life. He was unbelievably handsome. He had a smile that could stop your heart and more charm than anyone has a right to."

"No wonder you loved him."

"He was a senior at Princeton University but he came back home to celebrate his twenty-first birthday," Ellen went on, seeming to speak more to herself than to Adrienne. "Father had arranged an elaborate party in la Belle's ballroom. I wore a blue satin cocktail dress that Father said was too low cut, but Jamie said I was the most beautiful girl he'd ever seen. I knew he was going to propose at the end of the evening. I've never been so happy in my life. Then, around midnight, we were dancing to "Love Me Tender" by Elvis Presley and Jamie froze. He got the strangest look in his eyes, grabbed his head with both of his hands, and fell down. People screamed and scattered. A doctor ran to us and kneeled over him. I just looked at Jamie, my darling, his body limp, his eyes empty, his smile gone forever."

Ellen swallowed and her voice turned hard. "They later determined he had a brain aneurysm that burst. They claimed he'd been doomed from birth, but I don't believe it. La Belle destroyed him, just like it did my little boy, my second Jamie."

Adrienne knew an *I'm sorry* would sound hollow, and Ellen seemed removed, as if she wouldn't hear a thing Adrienne said anyway. No wonder the woman hated la Belle, Adrienne thought. She didn't believe the hotel was responsible for Ellen's tragedies. It was nothing more than a building. Still, the losses and the horror the woman had suffered at the hotel were staggering and certainly enough to make an impressionable nature like Ellen's believe there *was* something evil about the place.

"I went around in a daze for a year after Jamie's death," Ellen continued. "Then I married Kit's father. He was a total rotter. Father bought him off after he'd gotten drunk and given me a beating when I was pregnant with Kit." Ellen blinked rapidly as if warding off tears. "Then Father died and I devoted myself to my child and the hotel until I met

Gavin." She sighed. "Gavin reminded me of Jamie. Sometimes he still does."

Adrienne looked up at a hawk gliding serenely above them. Ellen had just explained so much. Her relationship with Kit, no doubt troubled because Kit was the child of a man Ellen probably hated. Why Ellen had married the seemingly aimless Gavin and allowed him to adopt Kit, thereby stripping the child of her brutal father's name.

By the time they reached the top of the hill, Adrienne was breathing hard but Ellen seemed to have gotten her second wind. Her stride quickened as they passed two cherry trees whose trunks supported mounds of honeysuckle vines. A sweet, almost overpowering scent hung in the hot, humid air. Then Adrienne heard a familiar sound. A caw. She looked up to see a crow sitting on a tree branch staring down at her with its beady, conscienceless eyes. The old rhyme, the one she'd thought of the day she'd found Julianna's body, came back to her:

"One's unlucky . . ."

"What's that?" Ellen asked, turning her head to look at Adrienne, who hadn't realized she was speaking aloud. Adrienne's mind rushed on. One crow was unlucky. But *six* was death. Could five more be lurking around?

"Ellen, let's go!" Adrienne said shrilly with sudden, irrational panic. "There's nothing here."

"That's what most people think." Showing far more stamina than Adrienne would have believed, Ellen began vigorously tugging at a thick tangle of honeysuckle vines.

"Please, Ellen, we should go!"

"Nonsense." Ellen continued tearing at the vines. "What's wrong with you? You sound like a scared little girl."

Adrienne rushed forward, meaning to stop Ellen, but she was too late. Ellen had torn away the vines with surprising ease to reveal the weathered wood of a rectangular lid. With a considerable strength that astounded Adrienne, Ellen lifted the heavy wooden lid and let it drop back onto the ground with a thud. Then she leaned down and yelled into the hole, "Lottie, it's Ellen. Don't be afraid. Adrienne and I have come to see if you're all right."

"You think she's down *there*?" Adrienne asked incredulously.

"Maybe." Adrienne watched as Ellen kneeled down and began speaking sweetly into the unknown depths. "Lottie, dear? You don't have to hide anymore. I'm here."

Adrienne couldn't believe anyone would take much comfort from the presence of frail Ellen. But then Ellen had proved she wasn't as frail as she appeared to be. Or pretended to be.

But what Adrienne really found hard to accept was that Lottie could be living in this vine-blanketed underground shelter. The silence following Ellen's comforting, echoing words seemed to prove her right.

Ellen lowered herself farther and landed on the floor. "Be careful," Adrienne said. "It's dark. There might be snakes or rats."

"I'm watching my step," Ellen returned absently, her gaze darting everywhere except the floor. "Do you have a flashlight?"

"Just a penlight."

"Then bring it down here."

Adrienne reluctantly followed Ellen inside. Cold, dank air wrapped around her like a shroud and she stopped. "What is this place, Ellen?"

"One of the early head caretakers of la Belle was a bit odd." Naturally he was, Adrienne thought wryly. "He believed la Belle was his own little kingdom. When he got too old to work, my grandfather replaced him, but he refused to leave. So, Grandfather allowed him to build an unobtrusive place on the grounds. That was the stipulation. The man was a veteran of World War One and he built a bunker—you can't be much more unobtrusive than that—and he lived here pretending he was still overseeing the care of la Belle while the war raged on around him. He died in here in the 1930s. My father didn't find him for several days. That must have been disagreeable."

"No doubt," Adrienne echoed hollowly, appalled.

"Lottie and I found the bunker nearly forty years ago. She actually tripped and fell right onto the lid, where the vines were thinnest, and we investigated. We didn't tell anyone we'd found it. We cleaned it up inside but left the vines as camouflage and christened it the Hideaway. We made a vow to always keep the place a secret. I never even told Kit about it. She would think it was strange and always be nagging me to destroy it."

"That might not be a bad idea, Ellen," Adrienne said carefully. "It could be a danger if a child found it, crawled in, and couldn't get out."

Ellen ignored her, peering around in the semidarkness. Finally she kneeled and picked up a blanket. "Lottie's quilt. She made this last year. I recognize the pattern. And here's a pillow."

As Adrienne moved forward for a closer look, she kicked over a glass jar. She picked it up and sniffed. "A candle. Jasmine scent."

"And another one here." Ellen dropped the quilt. In the dim light seeping through the open door into the gloom of the building, Adrienne saw Ellen place her hands on her hips. "The poor thing has been staying here."

Something squeaked in the corner. Adrienne jumped, hoping it was a mouse, not a rat. "Ellen, this place is awful!"

Ellen shrugged. "When you fear for your life, I guess you can put up with a lot to feel safe."

"Are you certain Lottie thinks someone will try to kill her?"

"I'm not *certain,* but I know Lottie and it's the only answer that makes sense." Ellen paused. "Adrienne, I said that I'd never told Kit about this place. I would appreciate your not telling her about it, either."

Adrienne felt a jolt of surprise. "If you don't want your own daughter to know about it, why did you allow me to see it?"

Ellen started slowly for the door and said over her shoulder, "Because I know you would never hurt Lottie."

Adrienne stared after her. What was she implying? That Kit *would* hurt Lottie? Why?

There would be no sensible reason unless Ellen believed Kit had killed Julianna and Lottie knew about it.

TEN

I

"I'm sorry, Lottie. So sorry. My fault. All my fault."

Gavin Kirkwood lay beside his wife in bed, his head propped on his hand as he looked down at her troubled, dreaming face. She'd greased her skin with a cream he knew cost over a hundred dollars a jar—cream that promised a decrease in wrinkles and an increase in firmness. The cream was a rip-off. In spite of faithful use for six months, Ellen's complexion still bore the inevitable traces of age and gravity. Gavin knew that within a year, she would resort to plastic surgery.

He really didn't care if she looked thirty. The sexual attraction he'd felt for her when they first met had vanished long ago, and he was frankly relieved that not much was expected of him in the lovemaking department anymore. Ellen was too depressed since the death of young Jamie last year to care about sex. That was the only good thing that had come from Jamie's death. Gavin had loved him too, and although Ellen had sucked up all the sympathy offered by friends and relatives, Gavin had often wished he'd drowned instead of the intelligent, charming little boy. For a long time, Gavin's world had turned gray and cold without the child. But no one seemed to notice *his* pain, or to care.

Ellen had arrived home at five o'clock today claiming she'd been out looking for Lottie. She was sweating, shaking, scratched by thorns, and so weak she could barely stand.

Gavin wasn't sure some of her maladies weren't just attention-seeking acts, but to be safe he had promptly called her doctor, who'd given Ellen a mild lecture on overexertion, then to Gavin delivered a downright harsh lecture on his lapse in looking after Ellen. As if anyone could ever make Ellen cooperate, Gavin had thought in fury. He'd felt like punching the guy, but that would have brought on a fit of hysterics from Ellen and probably a lawsuit from the doctor. So, as he did so often, Gavin had seethed in silence while Ellen's emotional state took dominion over his life, and he endured being belittled by yet another person contemptuous of a man they believed had married only for money.

Now, five hours after the doctor had given Ellen a tranquilizer and sent her to bed, Gavin lay miserably beside her, suffering through her slurred rambling and maddening restless leg movements. He had a brief but almost overwhelming desire to lay a pillow over her perspiring face and hold it in place until the woman finally stopped talking. And breathing. The urge became so strong, Gavin was frightened and promptly threw back the covers, abandoning the bedroom without even bothering to put on a robe. The pretentious silk pajamas Ellen made him wear covered enough of his well-toned body so the maid wouldn't be shocked if she happened to hear him rattling around the house and emerged from her room to investigate.

He ambled into the room Ellen had decorated and called *his* study, a room he found dark and depressing and inconvenient. But as much as he hated the study, one of his pleasures lay buried under a pile of folders in a desk drawer—sour mash Kentucky bourbon. Sour mash, he thought fondly, considered the finest of whiskies, requiring ninety-six hours of fermentation and at least four years of aging before it is thought fit to drink. Ellen thought the drink was crass and protested having it even brought into the house. But sometimes Gavin felt as though he couldn't get enough of it. Tonight was one of those times.

He poured a couple of shots into the simple drinking glass he also kept hidden beneath the folders in the drawer. Then he turned on the dim, green-shaded desk light and sat down on his heavily padded desk chair, leaning back and staring up at the beamed ceiling. He was so tired. Exhausted. But sleep wouldn't come. In fact, it had been eluding him since the death of Julianna. With her, for the first time in many years, he'd felt like a man. And now the feeling was gone, probably forever.

When Kit was an adolescent and he'd just married Ellen, he'd paid no attention to Kit's friend Julianna. She was just a tall, skinny girl with a mass of auburn hair who talked too much for his taste. Of course, her talking was better than Kit's sulking. But of the three friends, he'd preferred Adrienne. Not sexually. At that time Ellen was still good-looking and, although he knew everyone thought he'd married the woman fourteen years his elder for her money, he'd been genuinely attracted to her looks, her sophistication, her charm. He'd actually loved her. And she'd been crazy about him. *Besotted* was the word his mother had used. "She's besotted with your handsome face and your smooth line," she'd said venomously. "Just like I was with your father. But give it time, Gavin my boy. She'll find out what a loser you are. I know from experience."

When he was young, Gavin had had the confidence to almost ignore his mother and approach any woman. His good looks and glib tongue surprised even him, but they were assets he'd first realized he possessed when he was sixteen, when his twenty-four-year-old, uncommonly glamorous history teacher had come on to him. Between her and Ellen had come a slew of women, of all ages and all degrees of attractiveness and intelligence. But not until Ellen had a woman possessing looks, smarts, *and* money pursued him.

Gavin had been flattered by and truly infatuated with Ellen. He'd happily married her and blessed his lucky stars. What he hadn't counted on was her passive-aggressive dominance, her neuroses, her knack for the finely crafted, subtle art of emasculation that was far more powerful than his mother's clumsy, overt attempts.

Between the controlling wife, the contemptuous stepdaughter, and the drowning death of his young adopted son—a death wrongly attributed to Gavin's negligence—Gavin Kirkwood had been almost completely demoralized when he met Julianna again at a party being held in Philip Hamilton's house.

As far as Gavin knew, Julianna was not a particular friend of Philip's or Vicky's. Vicky's younger sister Adrienne had been part of the triumvirate of best friends including Kit and Julianna. He surmised that Julianna, a former world-famous model, had been invited as a star attraction. And it had worked. People flocked to the parties and hovered around her like groupies. Including Gavin.

Over the course of the next three months, Gavin realized he was falling deeply in love for the first time in his life. He'd tried to hide his feelings from everyone except Julianna. Tried damned hard.

But he hadn't been successful. Margaret Taylor had seen right through him and threatened to tell his wife if he didn't pay for her silence. And to make matters worse, Julianna didn't have romantic feelings for him, which she'd told him in an almost heart-wrenchingly kind and ego-protecting way. He'd been crushed. He'd felt cold and dry and old and hopeless.

And then one night, to his complete astonishment, Julianna had called him. She'd been upset. She said she felt she could trust him and needed to speak with him *alone*. She'd asked him to come to her apartment. He'd made it to Julianna's apartment house in record time, bounded up the stairs, started to rap on the door, then froze. He'd heard voices inside. Loud voices. Angry voices. Of course, he knew Julianna's. But he was fairly sure he recognized the other one too and something being said about an affair.

He'd tucked himself away in a chair placed in an alcove and waited. And waited. After two hours, no one had emerged from the apartment. Things had gotten quiet. But Julianna had said she needed to speak with him alone, and she most definitely wasn't alone, so he hadn't gone to the door.

Instead, in defeat he'd dragged himself home, trying to ward off depression by telling himself he'd talk with her tomorrow. Surely, she'd want to talk to him then as much as she had tonight.

But the next day, Kit had called and announced that Julianna was dead. She had been murdered at la Belle.

Turning the phone over to Ellen, Gavin had walked straight into the bathroom and thrown up. Then he'd had a drink *and* one of Ellen's tranquilizers, driven his wife up to that damned hotel as she'd insisted he do, and stood weakly behind her, unable to look at his beautiful love lying pale and cold as stone beneath satin sheets.

He would never get over it, he thought now as he poured another double shot of bourbon. Losing Jamie had been devastating, but at least his death had been an accident. Julianna's death was no accident. It was deliberate and obscene. It would be the end of Gavin Kirkwood.

But he wasn't quite done in yet, he thought. Someone should pay for what they had done to Julianna, he resolved, draining the glass, his expression hardening into vicious determination.

And someone would.

2

"We're home!"

Adrienne stood silently for a moment, holding the phone, before she realized the shrill, falsely cheerful voice she'd heard was her sister Vicky's. "Welcome back, Vicky. How was the trip?"

"Typical campaign stuff. Smiling. Shaking hands. Me not remembering any of the damned names of possible campaign contributors. Awful meals. I'm dying to have a good meal and a drink with someone I actually *like*!" High, brittle giggle. "Can I treat you to lunch at The Iron Gate?"

"That sounds wonderful, Vicky, if it's all right for Skye to join us."

"Oh." Vicky sounded as if she'd just thumped back to earth from a high altitude. "Well . . . sure."

Skye, who'd been looking disconsolately into the open refrigerator for something interesting to eat for lunch, turned and made frantic hand motions. "Just a minute," Adrienne said to her sister, then to Skye, "What's wrong?"

"If Aunt Vicky wants you to go someplace with her, let me go to Sherry's. I *was* invited, but you said I'd wear out my welcome. I wouldn't, though. Patty will be there. And Joel, I think."

"Who's Joel?"

"Oh, he's just Patty's brother. Nobody important." Skye's speech grew faster and her face turned redder. She has a crush on Joel, Adrienne thought, making a mental note to ask Sherry's mother about him. "Anyway, I can go to Sherry's and you can go with Aunt Vicky and we can both have fun instead of us just sitting here looking at each other."

"And not having fun."

"Well, it's not that. It's just . . ."

"That you're getting tired of being watched over like an eight-year-old." Adrienne pretended to think about the matter. "Okay. Get your bathing suit—not the two-piece sexy one I didn't want you to buy—and you can spend the afternoon with Sherry and Joel Who's Nobody Important. I'll meet Vicky, and we'll both be in better moods tonight."

An hour later, Skye had been deposited at Sherry Granger's with reassurances from Mrs. Granger that Skye was a lovely girl who could never wear out her welcome. Adrienne noted with amusement that Skye and Sherry elaborately ignored Patty's brother Joel, who had the confidence of a boy aware of his own good looks, not to mention the superiority of being one year older than the girls. Skye would have a challenge on her hands winning the affection of this teenage Romeo, she thought.

Adrienne drove downtown and found the last parking space in a crowded noonday lot at The Iron Gate's lunchtime Grill. She walked in and immediately spotted Vicky, who was already sipping a drink and waving enthusiastically to catch Adrienne's attention. As soon as Adrienne sat down, Vicky gushed, "You look *wonderful*! Did you get some sun yesterday?"

"A little more than I meant to." Adrienne touched the bridge of her sunburned nose. "I took a long walk. I'm sure it was good for me, but my muscles are telling me I need to exercise more often."

"A drink will fix that. I'm having a piña colada. Very festive. Want one?"

"It's a little early, Vicky."

"Nonsense." Vicky motioned to a dark-haired waitress. "She'll have a piña colada. And I'll have another."

"Another?" Vicky threw her a frosty look, and Adrienne knew she was asking for trouble if she commented on Vicky's alcohol intake. Philip no doubt had chastised her about it while they'd been away. "Aren't you worried about calories?" she amended in a light tone.

"Not today. I put on a good show on the trip. I was the perfect campaign wife. Now it's time to enjoy myself." Vicky looked pale and a sheen of perspiration covered her upper lip. She reached quickly for her drink, her hand trembling so much she almost ran the paper umbrella up her nose before her mouth located the straw, and she sucked up half of the piña colada.

"What's wrong, Vicky?" Adrienne asked. "Did something happen on the trip to upset you?"

Misery glimmered in Vicky's blue eyes. "It was just the usual. Tasteless food, endless smiling, Philip being charming in public and a bear in private. And all the while, Margaret bossing around everyone and acting as if *she* were Philip's wife!"

"It seems Philip would speak to her about that kind of behavior. It can't make a good impression on all the people they both want to vote for him."

"Oh, Margaret's smart enough not to do it in public," Vicky said bitterly. "In front of an audience, she keeps herself in the background. When it's just family, she treats me like I'm invisible and Rachel like crap. Margaret and Rachel had a terrible argument right before we left on the trip."

"About what?"

Vicky looked down at her drink again. "I don't know. It's always something. Then Philip walked in and reprimanded *Rachel*. Not a word to Margaret about showing a little respect for his own daughter. And he allows Margaret to treat me like I'm a nonentity. I've spoken to him about it, and he says, 'She's *supposed* to be more concerned with me than you, Vicky. Why do you want all the attention?' He makes me sound like a spoiled brat. I *don't* want all the attention. But he doesn't even listen to me." Her eyes filled with tears. "He's having an affair with her," she announced sharply.

"Oh, surely not." Adrienne heard the lack of conviction in her own voice. She hoped Vicky didn't notice, but she'd had her own doubts about Philip and Margaret. "Philip wouldn't cheat on you."

"I didn't used to think so. Not because he loves me. Because of his public image. He'd be too afraid people would find out." The waitress delivered the drinks—the first one Adrienne didn't want and the second one Vicky didn't need—and left menus. "Before, I've never had the feeling that he'd risk being unfaithful. But Margaret *is* damned attractive. Physically, that is. Her personality leaves much to be desired, although she's usually sweet as pie to Philip.

Flatters him until it's sickening, and he just eats it up. You know how *stupid* men are when it comes to their egos!"

"I don't remember Dad being that way."

Vicky dismissed him with a sweeping wave of her hand. "Oh, *he* doesn't count."

As a man? Adrienne smiled inwardly. She wondered how her father would have reacted to that comment. "Listen, Vicky, do you actually have *proof* that Philip is having an affair with Margaret?"

"He hardly ever touches me."

"He's under a lot of stress."

"Stress never bothers any man!" Adrienne wondered if it were the rum in the piña coladas that was suddenly making Vicky such an expert on men. "And I don't know of anyone Margaret's involved with," Vicky went on angrily, her voice too loud. "I don't think she's dated for ages, and I'm sure she's not the kind of woman who can go for long without *sex!*"

"Well . . ." Adrienne went blank. She felt a little hot with embarrassment when she noticed the men at the table behind Vicky had gone silent, listening to the tirade of the wife of a gubernatorial candidate, a tirade that gave every indication of picking up piña-colada-fueled steam. With relief, she looked up to see Kit drawing near. "Here's Kit!" she burst out. "I'll bet you haven't seen her for a while!"

"Gee, it's been at least a week," Vicky said dourly, clearly not wanting to cut short the topic of Margaret and Philip. But years of practice in the political venue allowed Vicky to quickly assume a look of forced pleasantness for Kit. "Hello there, Ms. Kirkwood. Looks like business is good."

"Almost too good," Kit said. "Sometimes I wish we'd have a few bad days so I could get some rest."

"Some people take vacations," Adrienne said, motioning for Kit to sit down.

Kit scooted next to Adrienne but focused on Vicky. "So how is the campaign trail?"

"Tiring but exciting." Vicky slipped into the role of enthusiastic, supportive wife. She and Kit had never been anything but casually friendly. "I really think Philip is going to be our next governor, although he claims if I say that too much, I'll jinx him."

Kit smiled blandly. "I didn't know Philip was superstitious."

"He's joking." Vicky's false, professional smile faded and she abruptly asked, "Have there been any new developments in Julianna's murder?"

"Not that I know of," Kit said. "Adrienne's the one with the inside source."

Adrienne shook her head. "Lucas isn't big on talking about cases with me."

"Even if the case involves one of your best friends?" Vicky asked, dipping her head toward her straw again.

"That would make him even less likely to let me in on details. He wouldn't want to upset me."

Kit grimaced. "As if anything could make Juli's murder sound worse than what you saw."

The waitress came to take orders. Kit declined. Adrienne and Vicky ordered, Vicky freezing Adrienne's objection to a third drink with an icy glare. Then she did a quick shift and looked pleasantly at Kit. "I'd weigh two hundred pounds if I worked here around this delicious food all the time."

Kit grinned. "*All the time* being the operative words. Sometimes I get sick of just the smell of food, no matter how good it is." Kit turned to Adrienne. "I hear you and Mother had quite an adventure yesterday."

Was there an edge to her voice? Adrienne wasn't certain. But Kit's hazel eyes showed no anger. Only curiosity. "I was painting at the Belle when your mother came by, determined to walk up the hill to Lottie's cabin and look for her along the way. Unfortunately, we didn't find her."

"Lottie is still missing?" Vicky asked in surprise. "I

thought she would have been found or just come home while we were gone."

Adrienne shook her head. "No. Anyway, Ellen and I saw nothing of her. But the jaunt just about did in Ellen." She felt guilty about not mentioning that they had gone farther up the hill to the vine-covered bunker Ellen called the Hide-away, but on their way back to the hotel, Ellen had made Adrienne give her sacred promise that she wouldn't mention it. Like a child, Ellen had insisted the promise be repeated three times. "Is Ellen all right?" she asked Kit.

"Not really. Last night she was a mess. The problem was more emotional than physical, as usual with Mother, but Gavin had to call her doctor. Then he called me. He can't handle anything on his own. Or maybe he just doesn't want to take responsibility for Mother. Whatever. But that's how I know about your walking tour."

"I'm sorry," Adrienne said sincerely. "I should have stopped her."

Kit smiled ruefully. "You *couldn't* have stopped her short of tying her to a tree. She has a will of iron, and she's a lot stronger than she looks or acts. Physically, that is. I'm grateful you went with her. She wouldn't let *me*."

Adrienne thought of how Ellen had said she hadn't minded Adrienne going with her because she knew Adrienne wouldn't hurt Lottie. Did she fear Kit would?

No. The idea was nonsensical, Adrienne thought. After all, it was Kit to whom Lottie had gone after Julianna's murder, not Ellen. Kit that Lottie had turned to, not her best friend, Ellen. *Not Ellen.*

"Adrienne, are you all right?"

Adrienne glanced up as she felt blood drain from her cheeks. Her sister was looking at her somewhat blearily, but Kit's eyes seemed to have narrowed slightly. Kit knew her too well not to realize something disturbing had crossed Adrienne's mind. "I'm fine, Kit," she said brightly. "Just hungry."

But she still felt uncomfortable as Kit abruptly said she'd leave them to their lunch and swept away from the table. Kit *did* suspect something, Adrienne realized. And whatever she suspected was making Kit feel extremely uneasy.

Feeling wretched and confused, Adrienne forced down what should have been a delicious lunch while her sister harangued endlessly about Margaret Taylor, the woman Vicky hated.

3

"I get so tired of skulking around like a pair of teenagers. I wish we could bring our relationship out into the open."

Margaret Taylor gave Miles Shaw the long, slow blink she knew he found enticing, and ran her foot up his bare leg to the top of his thigh. "But darling, you know I can't pull the focus away from Philip onto myself, and that's just what I'd be doing by announcing that I'm seeing a world-famous artist."

Miles laughed softly. "World famous. Now that *is* funny."

"You *are* famous."

"Maybe in a tristate area. Big fish in a little pond. That's all I am."

"A fabulously talented fish who will soon be well-known in a much bigger pond. As soon as I get Philip elected, give me two or three years to work on you. Your name will be known all over the United States and Europe."

Miles reached out, touching the silky length of Margaret's gleaming black hair. "Not lacking in confidence, are you, Ms. Taylor?"

"There's no room for insecurity in my business."

"And you do know your business. You're an expert at disseminating *and* concealing information. But are you certain Philip doesn't at least have an inkling about us?"

Margaret turned slightly and picked up her glass of red

wine from the bedside table. "I'm quite certain. I've taken great pains to keep us a secret."

As she sipped, Miles looked at her closely. "Then why do you lower your eyes when you talk about our secret? Is it to hide a little flicker of doubt in your eyes?"

Margaret's forehead wrinkled slightly. "Maybe there's just a *little* doubt." She took another sip of wine, her voice hardening. "It's that damned Rachel. I think *she* suspects us. And if she does, she'll tell her mother."

"And you don't want Vicky to know about us because she thinks you're having an affair with Philip, which thrills you." Margaret tried to look insulted and failed. The corner of Miles's lips crooked. "You really can't stand Vicky, can you?"

"She frustrates me." Margaret replaced the wineglass on the table, turned, and began tracing tiny circles on Miles's chest. "From what I've heard, Philip made a good choice when he married her. She was attractive, charming, self-possessed, even fairly savvy about political affairs. She was quite satisfactory as a politician's wife. She even had some backbone, like her sister, although I don't care much for Adrienne, either. She watches me, like she's waiting for me to screw up. Of course, that's because Vicky has told her all kinds of unflattering things about me."

"Imagine that," Miles said dryly.

"I don't know what happened to Vicky over the years, but now she's so damned *weak*," Margaret went on heatedly as if Miles hadn't spoken. "And whiny. And not nearly so physically presentable. Do you know that half the time she doesn't put on her makeup properly?"

"Good God! I had no idea!"

"You think it's funny, but it's *not*. It's a sign. Vicky isn't careful about her looks because she's fast on her way to becoming an alcoholic. I think she has her first drink by ten in the morning. Certainly by noon. An alcoholic wife! She could ruin everything for Philip!"

"All right. I see the trouble with Vicky. I hardly know her, but she doesn't appeal to me, either. So let's move on to Rachel. What's your problem with her?"

Margaret's expression turned rancorous. "I have lots of problems with Rachel, not the least of which is she doesn't appreciate that a great life has been handed to her on a silver platter. She takes it for granted, like it's her due. If she'd had to scramble to pull herself out of the dirt like I did, she might value a thing or two. Instead, she looks down on me."

"Are you sure she looks down on you? Or is that your imagination? You can be a little paranoid about how people view you."

"That is *not* true!" Margaret drew away from him, her face turning pink.

"Uh-oh. Hit a nerve."

"No, you did not hit a nerve. You accused me falsely. I don't like it."

"What you don't like is being criticized." Miles smiled and drew her close again, cupping her firm, bare breast. "But most people don't like being criticized unless they're masochists. I'm sorry, lover. I've had too much wine. My mouth is running away with me."

"Your mouth is just fine." Margaret kissed him deeply, then licked his earlobe. "No earring tonight?"

"You nearly tore it out last time." He chuckled. "Besides, I seem to have misplaced it. Hey, speaking of tearing, how about tearing ourselves out of this bed for a while, going to see a friend of mine who's having a little party, then returning for more fun and games?"

Margaret tensed as she pulled back and looked him full in the face. "Those friends who indulge in drugs?"

"Only moderately, for mind-expanding purposes."

She shook her head. "No, thanks, darling. Too risky. Whenever we're there, I feel like the cops will be sweeping down any minute. Besides, Philip has an important meeting tomorrow."

"*Philip* has a meeting, not you."

"When Philip has a meeting, so do I. You know I have to be on my toes so I can brief him."

Miles sighed in disgust. "Good God. If only people knew they were electing you instead of him."

"What do you mean?"

"I mean *you* seem to do all the work. Philip is like an actor, reciting for the public the lines you've given him. He's just a puppet, a conventionally good-looking guy in an expensive suit who can memorize."

"That is not true, Miles. Philip Hamilton is a brilliant man." Miles snorted. "He *is*. But no political figure does all his research. Not even the president."

"Now *that* I can believe."

Margaret sat up in bed, not bothering to hold the sheet in front of her breasts, her hair hanging long and tangled over her shoulders. "Are you jealous of Philip?"

"I'm jealous of the time you devote to him. He always comes first. You can't go here with me. You can't go there with me. Being seen in public with me might cause gossip that could detract from Philip. God, Margaret, you make me feel like a whore." Miles's ebony eyes blazed. "Maybe that's all I am to you. A whore."

"That's absurd."

"Then prove it. Devote one whole night to me instead of to Philip."

"I've devoted *many* nights to you. It's just that I'll have to cut this particular night a bit short. I have notes to go over, then I need a full night's rest. Alone."

"And you forgot to mention all of that when you invited me to dinner." Miles flung off the sheet and stood up, his imposing six-foot-four frame leaning over the petite, small-boned Margaret. "I don't like being taken advantage of, Maggie."

"Taken advantage of!" Margaret scrambled from the bed and stood across from him. "I didn't know fixing you an excellent dinner and having sex with you was taking advantage of you!"

"Why? If I'd fixed dinner for you, had sex with you, then told you to leave, you'd be mad as hell. But because you're doing it to a *man,* it's a whole different story. That's the trouble with you feminists. You don't change things. You just turn old conduct on its ear, treat men like crap instead of vice versa, then feel justified!"

"That is preposterous, Philip!"

His eyes narrowed and he said in a low, angry voice, "My name is *Miles,* Margaret."

She flushed. "I *meant* Miles. I say Philip a hundred times a day. It just comes out sometimes."

"Yeah, like when you're in the presence of a naked man." Miles bent and picked up his jeans. "You've just been playing with me, haven't you? Using me as a smokescreen for your real love interest—Philip Hamilton."

"Oh please," Margaret nearly spat. "Don't compare my morals to those of someone like your beloved Julianna. She's the one who slept with so many men she no doubt got them confused. She would have stooped to anything. But you didn't care, did you? You were blind to what she was. Absolutely, totally blind. A *fool!*"

As soon as the words were out of her mouth, Margaret knew she'd made a grave mistake. Miles stopped fastening his jeans and looked at her, fury growing in his eyes, fury deep and strong and dangerous. Margaret had never been afraid of a man before. Not really. But to her intense surprise, she was now.

And the odd thing was, she didn't quite know how this fight had started. The last few minutes seemed like a blur with the argument spinning out of control, stunning her with its speed and bitterness. But Margaret was an old hand at retrieving unpleasant situations. All it took was some charm and finesse.

She rallied her forces and smiled sweetly. "Darling, we were having such a lovely evening and now we've turned it into something silly. We sound like kids, and I'm sorry for contributing to it. It's been a grueling day. Can't we just bury the hostility and go back to our earlier peace and comfort?"

Miles gave her a hard look and reached for his shirt. "I think it's time for me to get out of here."

"You're going to leave? Now? It's not even ten o'clock!"

"You have your important meeting in the morning, remember? You'd better be in bed within half an hour or you'll have circles under your eyes and then God knows what will happen. Maybe it will cause Hamilton to lose the election."

Margaret forced a laugh. "No one pays attention to me at these events, and even if they did, I don't think I'd be jeopardizing Philip if I looked a little tired."

"I wouldn't be so sure. You're the brain behind the puppet. If you look tired, people will think the campaign is falling apart."

She sighed. "Listen, darling, sometimes I get carried away. I'm a perfectionist."

"No kidding," Miles said wryly as he finished buttoning his shirt and yanked back his hair in its long ponytail. "Well, I'm a perfectionist, too. I have a painting to work on tonight. *Now.* Sorry, I forgot to mention it earlier. Hate to eat, screw, and run, but you of all people know that duty comes first."

Margaret dashed to his side, placing her hand on the back of his head and trying to pull his face toward hers for a passionate kiss. But she couldn't bend his head. Suddenly his neck seemed as rigid as iron. And the look in his eyes turned her cold to the bone.

"Don't, Margaret," he said barely above a whisper. "Don't try to kiss me, don't clutch at me, don't even touch me." She drew back, stunned by the venom in his voice. "And one more thing, Maggie. Don't you *ever* say a bad thing about Julianna again, or I swear to God, I'll make you regret it."

In fifteen minutes, Miles climbed into his car while Margaret hovered near the half-open front door, her silk robe tied loosely around her. Anger, confusion, and a little fright churned behind her dark eyes. She felt stunned. And hurt. But never one to let another person get the upper hand, she slammed the door, locked it, and flipped the dead bolt. The gesture was futile—after all, Miles wasn't coming back—but she knew he'd heard the noise of the slamming door, which somehow made her feel better.

The big grandfather clock in her living room chimed ten times. How she'd loved that cherrywood clock when she was a teenager, and how surprised she'd been when the elderly man who'd been her mentor and her lover had given it to her when she got her master's degree in public relations. "I'm an old man. I no longer need it," he'd said. "But when you look at it, you'll remember me. And don't say you're not leaving me, because I know you are. You've outgrown me, and I won't be greedy and pitiful by trying to hold on to you. But I can't forget how when you came to me at sixteen, you seemed like a magical gift. And a magical female needs a magnificent, chiming clock to let her know when it's the witching hour—the hour of midnight on a full moon when a witch's powers are at their strongest."

"I wish you were still here," Margaret said wistfully to the lover who'd died a year after their parting. "You would know how to handle Miles. You would know whether or not he really loves me, or if I'm just a poor substitute for his lost Julianna. The bitch! If I told what I knew about her death, I could change quite a few things that need changing, and not just because of Miles."

By eleven-thirty, Margaret had put the dishes in the dishwasher, gone over her notes for tomorrow, watched the news, and written a rare letter to her mother, but none of these activities had settled her nerves. Margaret finally slipped into an old sleep shirt and went into the bathroom to begin her nighttime beauty ritual, all the while still smoldering over the woman who'd caused her so much trouble in life, and who still managed to cause her trouble in death.

Julianna Brent. Margaret could easily strip away any

illusions people had about that piece of work. Yes, Julianna was beautiful. She was also a self-seeking, heedless, idiotic woman of thirty-six who had the sense of a twelve-year-old. Even *less* sense, Margaret fumed as she slathered cleansing cream over her face. Yes, she could shake up quite a few things if she revealed the name of Julianna's killer and the reason for her death. And at the moment, she almost felt like doing it, to hell with the consequences.

Margaret rubbed a washcloth over her face, wiping hard at the cleansing cream, then winced as the stuff ran into the corner of her eye. It was guaranteed not to sting. The guarantee was false. She felt as if she'd poured vinegar directly on her right eyeball. "Dammit," she muttered, bending down and leaning sideways to let water from the spigot run into her eye. "Dammit, dammit, *dammit!*"

Margaret splashed water, letting it run into her hair, into her nose, splashing it onto the mirror above the sink. Finally, it began to trickle down the side of the new mahogany vanity she'd just had installed. Salt from the water softener would cause the water to leave spots and mar the shining varnish of the vanity. She fumbled for a hand towel and stooped to wipe dry the wood. Then, even with one eye clenched against pain and the other blurry from the water dousing, she saw it.

A foot.

A foot in a terry-cloth house slipper.

Margaret raised up. "What on earth?" she got out before something slammed against the back of her skull.

She dropped to the floor as if her bones had dissolved. Her forehead raked the sharp edge of the vanity and her knees folded, trapping her lower legs beneath her thighs.

In a flash, someone was at her, delivering a crushing blow to her upper face, smashing the orbital bones around her eyes. Her vision vanished, as if a shade had been dropped, but she remained conscious, able to hear more facial bones snapping, nasal cartilage crunching, teeth shattering.

At first, Margaret felt nothing. She lay crumpled—blind,

silent, stunned to near-insensibility, and stupefied. Then pain lashed at her, searing through every limb, taking away her breath. Her left arm flailed aimlessly, unconsciously, and was promptly pinned against the floor. Another explosion of pain ripped through her as something cold and heavy smashed her elbow.

Margaret finally drew enough breath to scream and choked on fragments of broken teeth. Her teeth had been perfect, she thought in the tiny corner of her mind that remained sensible. They'd looked like porcelain veneers. Now they mixed with blood and clogged her throat. She emitted a gurgling sound. "Not so good with the words now, are you, Margaret?" a voice asked. "Not so sure of yourself anymore." Something smashed down on her chest and she heard a rib snap before she experienced the pain of a jagged edge puncturing a lung. "But you know what the Bible says: 'Pride goeth before destruction and a haughty spirit before the fall.' So you see, you had it coming. No, I guess you don't see. You won't see anything again. So sad. You'll just have to take my word for it."

Margaret thought in agony, Why can't I pass out? The blows to her body had stopped. The taunting voice had stopped. But she could still hear. And worst of all, she could still feel. Some deep instinct kept nagging her to get help, to drag herself from the bathroom to the bedroom phone. But another instinct, stronger and more powerful, wanted to avoid pain.

She lay perfectly still, sensing someone watching her, waiting for a jerk, even a twitch, before raining blows on her again. She barely let herself breathe. She felt consciousness shrink into a tiny spark within her body. Or what was left of her body.

If I live, she thought with a strange cool certainty, no one can fix me. No one can even make me halfway presentable. I will be pathetic. Repulsive. A freak.

And that, for Margaret Taylor, who had worked so hard to make herself perfect, would be worse than death.

It's over, she thought bleakly. In ten minutes, her intelligence, beauty, ambition, and potential had been shattered like the fragile bones of her face. How invincible she'd felt just this afternoon. How annihilated she felt now.

Blood streamed down the ruin of Margaret's face and soaked into the cream-colored bathroom carpet. After what seemed hours she felt the sharp edge of pain dull and the rapid pace of her heart begin to slow. It's ending, she thought in relief, knowing someone still hovered and watched. It's finally ending.

As Margaret drew her last breath, she heard the grandfather clock in the living room chime twelve times, cheerfully announcing the arrival of the witching hour.

ELEVEN

I

Once a week Margaret Taylor's cleaning lady, Ruby, arrived at seven A.M. sharp so the smells of the disinfectants she used would have dissipated by the time Margaret arrived home eleven hours later. Margaret claimed to be allergic to cleaning solutions. Even their scents made her eyes swell and caused her to sneeze, she said.

Ruby thought "Miss Perfect" simply found something repellent about even seeing scrubbing and scouring, much less doing it herself. Ruby wondered if Margaret's mother had cleaned houses for a living and Margaret had been ashamed of her. Or better yet, if at one time the prissy Margaret was forced to clean houses herself for a living! That made even more sense to Ruby, who considered herself quite astute at analyzing people. She often wondered if she shouldn't throw over her cleaning career and become a psychologist so she could earn hundreds of thousands of dollars a year just sitting in some fancy office listening to people babble about their boring selves all day.

But thoughts of a career change deserted Ruby on the morning she walked slowly through the Taylor home, noting the telltale signs of the supposedly secret lover's visit, and found the body of Margaret on the bathroom floor. At least she thought it was Margaret. As Ruby screamed her way out of the house and into the quiet, early-morning neighborhood, all she'd really registered was a crushed, bloody, hideous thing resembling a human female lying on the impractical cream-colored carpet in front of the bathroom vanity.

Ruby had shrieked halfway down the residential lane when dignified Dr. Hawkins, who was always up with the birds, ran out in his plaid robe and literally wrestled the stocky, flailing Ruby to the street. She continued to screech and howl and jabber uncontrollably until, wincing, gentle Dr. Hawkins delivered a sharp little slap to her plump cheek. Ruby's eyes flew wide and she slapped him back. Hard. But at least she shut up.

"My God, woman, what's wrong?" Dr. Hawkins asked, trying to blink back stinging tears brought on by the blow from Ruby's work-hardened hand.

But it was too late. She'd seen the tears and was heartsick at what she'd done to the poor man, and him being from England and a college professor of literature, no less. "Oh, Dr. Hawkins, I am *so* sorry." Ruby, who was forty-five, considered Dr. Hawkins remarkably handsome for a man in his late fifties. He was also a widower and well off. "It's just . . . you wouldn't believe . . . It's so *horrible* . . ." An image of the shattered body rose up in her mind again and she let out another chilling wail.

"Madam . . . I'm sorry, I don't know your name—"

"Fincher," Ruby sobbed. "*Miss* Ruby Fincher."

"Yes, well, Miss Fincher, please try to calm down and tell me what's wrong. It can't be all that bad."

"She's *dead*!" Ruby bellowed. "At least I think it's her. The Taylor woman."

Dr. Hawkins drew back. "Dead? Oh no. That can't be. She's a very young woman. Perhaps she's just sick."

"Sick! I don't think so! She's layin' on the bathroom floor beaten to a pulp, head all smashed in, teeth knocked out, blood *everywhere*." Ruby didn't seem to notice Dr. Hawkins's look of nausea as another thought struck her. "Lordy, I'll never get that carpet clean!"

"My heavens," Dr. Hawkins said weakly. "We must do something—"

"I am *not* going back to that house!"

"No, no, certainly not. We'll call someone. Yes, that's what we'll do. We'll go into my house and call 911." He gently tried to loosen Ruby's boa constrictor grip on his neck. "Are you able to walk, Miss Fincher?"

"Yes, I think so." Ruby hoisted herself up to her tennis-shoe-encased feet, stepped back from Dr. Hawkins, tottered slightly, then took his arm as if to steady herself. "Yes, I can make it as far as your house as long as I lean on you."

"That's just fine. Lean on me as much as you need to, Miss Fincher." They started slowly to his large, slate-blue Cape Cod. "My goodness, this is just unbelievable. I still haven't quite taken it in. And *you*, you poor dear. To have seen such a sight!" Dr. Hawkins shivered slightly. "I'll place the call and then fix you some tea. Good hot tea. That will set you right up."

Ruby shot him her most fetching smile, thinking that under the circumstances she'd rather have a double shot of scotch even if it was seven in the morning, but tea with Dr. Hawkins was better than nothing. Yes sir, maybe Miss Too-Good-to-Wipe-My-Shoes-on-You Margaret Taylor had done Ruby a favor. Because of her, Ruby had finally gotten to say more than "hello" to Dr. Hawkins.

Then Ruby pictured the crushed mass that was now Margaret and touched the tiny gold cross she always wore. She wouldn't allow herself to think bad thoughts about that woman, no matter how high-and-mighty she'd been. Ruby would go to church tonight, light a candle, and say a prayer for her. Yes, that would clear her conscience. She'd say a Catholic Hail Mary, and add a nice Protestant off-the-cuff prayer asking that Margaret find peace in the Hereafter. That should do the trick.

And she'd hope no one would expect her to clean up that carpet.

2

"Adrienne? Did I wake you?"

Rarely did her niece call her simply "Adrienne." "No, Rachel. I've been up about twenty minutes." Adrienne glanced at the kitchen wall clock and saw that it was shortly after eight. "Is something wrong?"

"Yes. Big time." Rachel drew a deep breath and said with labored calm, "Margaret has been killed."

"Killed?" Adrienne repeated blankly. "In a car wreck?"

"No." Rachel's voice wavered. "She was murdered. In her house. The cleaning lady found her this morning."

The word *murdered* stunned Adrienne into silence. All she could picture was the annoying, elegantly groomed, fast-talking, dominating whirlwind that was Margaret Taylor lying quietly dead in her house.

"Aunt Adrienne?"

"Yes, honey, I'm here."

"The press has already gotten wind of it. There are a few reporters here and no doubt more on the way. Dad is shouting like a crazy man at Mom and me like it's our fault. I'm forbidden to go in to work today and Mom is on her way to falling apart." Rachel's tone turned hesitantly pleading. "Could you come over? I think Mom really needs you."

"I'll be there as fast as I can." An odd calm born of shock filled Adrienne. She felt strong and capable and business-like. "Don't go out and talk to those reporters, even if some of them are your friends. That will only make your father mad at you. And try to keep him away from your mother. Tell him if he thinks shouting will help the situation, then go down and do it in the basement."

Adrienne sensed a smile in Rachel's tone. "Thanks, Aunt Adrienne. You're a lifesaver."

Adrienne set down her morning mug of coffee and walked into Skye's room. She usually didn't sleep this late, but they'd both been restless last night and stayed up until past midnight eating popcorn and watching the eerie movie *The Others*. Brandon now lay on his giant cushion beside Skye's bed, snoring, his upper lip flapping every time he exhaled. Adrienne had to lean over him to gently shake the girl awake.

Skye muttered, scowled, then looked at her mother with huge, alert eyes. "Wha's goin' on?"

"Something has happened. Margaret Taylor is dead. Rachel called and asked that we come over to their house for moral support. The press is already there."

"Dead! Wow." Skye threw back the covers and stepped over Brandon, now wallowing in a valiant attempt to get sleep-stiffened muscles moving. "What did Margaret die of?"

"Well, it seems she was . . . murdered."

"Murdered!" Skye froze. "*How?*"

Adrienne stared at her, realizing she hadn't asked Rachel. "I don't know."

"You don't *know!*" Skye looked at her in disbelief. "Gosh, Mom, how can you not know? Didn't you even *ask?*"

"No. I was so surprised and Rachel sounded rushed and worried." Skye almost fell over Brandon, who'd managed to rise on his front paws although his rear was still firmly planted on the cushion. "We'll find out how Margaret died when we get to Vicky's," Adrienne said briskly to stem further questions. "Dress quickly. Rachel says her parents are really upset."

"No doubt! Mom, how can you act so calm? It's *another* murder, for Pete's sake. And even scarier, it's another murder of someone we knew!"

Adrienne went cold inside. Maybe that's why she hadn't asked Rachel for the details of Margaret's murder. Skye was right—another person they knew had been murdered, and the implications were so frightening she didn't want to think about them.

She and Skye had a brief skirmish over taking Brandon

along. When they pulled into the Hamilton driveway and a small but aggressive gaggle of reporters descended on them, Adrienne was glad Skye had won. A one-hundred-pound dog growling ferociously backed away most of them, none of whom knew that Brandon had never bitten anyone in his life. The growling was a trick Skye had taught him and as soon as they reached the house unscathed, he looked at his mistress with his tongue lolling happily, expecting the praise he always got for turning in an Oscar-worthy performance.

Mrs. Pitt greeted them, her face even homelier than usual. "Isn't this just the worst thing? Those awful people out there banging on the door, even trying to look in the windows! Ms. Taylor always handled them with no fuss and I thought getting rid of them must be easy. I can see that it isn't, but I'll never get to tell her I know what a good job she did."

"I don't think Margaret needed compliments to bolster her confidence." Adrienne realized how harsh she'd sounded and ended lamely, "She loved her job."

"That she did." Mrs. Pitt shook her head dolefully. "No one wanted a regular breakfast this morning so I just made cinnamon rolls. Can I interest either of you?"

"I'm kind of hungry," Skye said.

Mrs. Pitt finally smiled. "Good. Rachel is in the kitchen drinking coffee. Maybe you can talk her into eating something, too."

"I'll skip food and go to my sister. Is she in her bedroom?" Adrienne asked, already knowing the answer. Ever since Vicky was a teenager, she'd retreated to her bedroom when she was upset.

"Yes. She only came down twice this morning and each time she and Mr. Hamilton . . . well . . . this is hard on everyone."

Which meant Vicky had collided with Philip's wrath and fled. Adrienne wondered angrily how the hell Philip thought causing an uproar in his own home could do anything except make matters worse.

"You go on up to your sister, Ms. Reynolds," Mrs. Pitt said. "I'll bring some coffee and rolls in a little while."

Mrs. Pitt had been with the Hamiltons for ten years and Adrienne sometimes felt the efficient, solicitous widow was all that held the family together. She patted the woman's arm. "Thanks. And don't let Brandon eat too many cinnamon rolls."

Upstairs she tapped lightly on the bedroom door and entered without waiting for a response. Vicky lay propped up in bed, her complexion pasty, her lips colorless, and her blond bangs pushed back, revealing a hairline damp with perspiration. She lifted a cigarette to her mouth with trembling fingers, inhaled deeply, then said, "Thank God you're here. I feel like I'm going to have a nervous breakdown."

Adrienne had expected her sister to be agitated over the situation. She hadn't expected her to be devastated. After all, Vicky didn't even like Margaret. But she couldn't have looked more ravaged if the murder victim had been Rachel.

Adrienne walked across the room and sat down on the bed beside Vicky, who promptly said, "Don't say a word about me smoking. I haven't had a cigarette for a year, but I think I deserve one now."

"I wasn't going to say anything."

"How's Rachel?"

"Okay, I guess. She's in the kitchen with Mrs. Pitt. Skye was going to join her. You know Rachel likes Skye's company."

Vicky nodded vaguely. Adrienne looked at the wreck of her sister and asked, "What happened to Margaret?"

"She walked out of here at six yesterday, still giving orders, went home, and got herself murdered."

"You mean someone was waiting at her house? She walked in on a burglary?"

Vicky shrugged. "I don't know much. Only that she was found by her cleaning lady this morning." She paused, as if deciding whether or not to divulge more information. "She was in the bathroom. She'd been savagely beaten. One reporter told Philip she was almost unrecognizable."

"My God," Adrienne breathed. "If she'd been attacked after just entering the house, she wouldn't be in the bathroom."

"I've told you all I know. All that matters."

"All that matters?"

"Yes. She's gone. For good. Out of our lives. To me, that's all that matters."

"Vicky, I know you didn't like her. Neither did I, but she didn't deserve to be beaten to death."

"Didn't she?" Vicky blew out a thin, swift stream of smoke. "We really didn't know her that well. Not really. At least I didn't. For all I know, she did do something awful and got *exactly* what she deserved."

Adrienne sat silently, stunned by the virulence of her sister's words. She realized that Vicky's feelings about Margaret went much deeper than dislike or even jealousy. She had despised the woman and was glad she was dead, even if her death had been brutal. Adrienne felt a cold tingle run down her back as the knowledge of her sister's pure hatred of the murdered woman sank in.

As shaken as Adrienne was, she concentrated on keeping her facial expression and voice neutral. "I wonder if they have any leads, as they say on TV?"

"I don't *know*." Vicky stubbed out her cigarette and immediately shook another one out of the pack. "You're the one romantically involved with the local lawman. You have a much better source of information than I have. Hasn't he been on the horn to you already?"

"No, Vicky, he hasn't," Adrienne said quietly. "Lucas has been a bit elusive lately."

Vicky clicked her lighter and raised her eyebrows. "Is the romance cooling?"

"I wouldn't say it was ever red-hot."

"No, I never thought so," Vicky said slowly. "He used to

work for Philip, you know. I got to know him fairly well. He's a good man, Adrienne."

"I know."

"Much more dependable than Drew Delaney."

"What does Drew have to do with anything?" Adrienne heard her voice rise defensively. "I'm not seeing Drew."

"I didn't say anything about your actions. Just your feelings." Vicky took another deep drag on her cigarette. "I think Rachel has a crush on him."

Adrienne gratefully latched onto Rachel for a change of subject. "Drew is handsome and extremely charming. And she's clearly not head over heels for Bruce Allard. I can't say I blame her. He's far too impressed with himself."

"His whole life his parents have told him how wonderful he is. You should hear them. It's sickening. No wonder he's arrogant. But he's harmless and close to Rachel's age. I don't mind him. But getting involved with Drew Delaney is quite another matter."

"Who's involved with Drew Delaney?" Philip demanded, striding aggressively into the bedroom as if ready for imminent battle. "Are you seeing Delaney, Adrienne?" Before she had a chance to answer, he rolled his eyes and sneered. "That would be par for the course. First Trey Reynolds, a Las Vegas lounge lizard, then the local middle-aged Lothario."

Rage rushed through Adrienne. "How dare you speak that way about my dead husband?"

"It's true!"

"Trey was a performer. So are you. And for your information, Philip, a lot of people have more respect for Las Vegas performers than political performers!"

Philip's face turned crimson. "Don't you ever compare me to him again!"

"Oh, I won't. I just realized I'm doing Trey a great disservice." Philip's fists clenched but Adrienne couldn't hold her tongue. "And I'm *not* seeing Drew, although if I were, it wouldn't be any of your business!"

"Everything that reflects on my career is my business."

Adrienne jumped up, glaring into Philip's face. "I have *nothing* to do with your career!"

"You are my wife's sister. What you do reflects on me. I wouldn't expect you to consider that, though. You've always thought only of yourself with absolutely *no* regard for Vicky and me, not to mention Rachel."

"You're the one who shows no regard for Vicky and Rachel, not *me*!" Adrienne's heart raced along with her rage. "Look, Philip, I know you're shocked by what's happened to Margaret, but that doesn't give you the right to ride roughshod over everyone. Particularly not your wife, your daughter, *or* me!"

"He's more than shocked by Margaret's death," Vicky suddenly said in a cold, metallic voice. "He's crushed because he was in love with her."

"Oh, good God!" Philip exploded, his furious gaze shifting from Adrienne to his wife. "Not this jealousy refrain again!"

"Yes, again." Tears stood in Vicky's reddened eyes. "I know Margaret had a lover, and that lover was you, Philip."

Philip seemed to tighten and coil like a snake. Adrienne drew back from him slightly, wary of what was to come. At last he spoke to Vicky with cool contempt. "You *are* right about one thing, my dear. Margaret did have a lover. I just got a call from a contact I have on the police force. It seems Margaret's cleaning lady knew her better than we did. According to her, Margaret had a hot and heavy thing going with Miles Shaw."

"Julianna's Miles?" Adrienne blurted in surprise.

"The one and only." Philip continued to look at his wife. "So what do you make of that, Vicky?"

Vicky seemed to shrink into the bed pillows, looking stricken. Adrienne thought of how much Vicky had hated Margaret, how sure she'd been Philip was having an affair with her, and how terrible she looked, as if she'd been through some powerful, savage experience.

And Adrienne wondered where her sister had been at the time of Margaret's murder.

3

A bead of sweat rolled down from Miles Shaw's hairline, through the web of shallow crows' feet shooting from his eyes, over his high cheekbone, and dropped off his jaw onto his black shirt. Sheriff Lucas Flynn stared at him across the table in the interrogation room at police headquarters. Lucas noted that Shaw was making a supreme effort to return an unflinching gaze and not quite achieving it. About every ten seconds Shaw's green eyes skittered right, left, or downward at the slender artist's hands he fought to keep serenely motionless.

"You know Margaret Taylor has been murdered," Lucas began abruptly.

"I knew it when you came banging on the door of my studio this morning."

"But not earlier."

Shaw shook his head. "I'd just gotten up."

"And you didn't see it on the news."

"I don't watch the morning news."

"And you didn't see the body when you were in Ms. Taylor's house this morning."

"I wasn't in her house this morning."

"But you were last night."

Shaw hesitated. His gaze shifted. Lucas watched closely as a number of thoughts flashed behind Shaw's eyes. Finally he came out with, "Yeah, okay. I have no reason to lie. I *was* in her house last night."

"Until what time?"

"Ten o'clock."

"Ten exactly?"

"Yes."

"My goodness, you're precise about times," Lucas said affably. "Most people aren't so exact."

"Margaret has a grandfather clock. It was chiming when I went out the door."

"Convenient."

"I'd say coincidental."

"And Margaret was alive when you left?"

"Of course she was alive," Shaw snapped.

"Because later she suffered a hell of a beating. Somebody took something like a two-inch hammer to your girlfriend, Shaw. Her face was crushed. She must have been in terrible pain, but she didn't die immediately."

Shaw's hands clenched and his jaw tightened. "Margaret was perfectly fine at ten o'clock when I left."

Lucas smiled. "Want something to drink, Mr. Shaw? Coffee? A soft drink?"

Miles looked nonplussed at the change in tone. "I want a cigarette."

"Sorry. No smoking in this building."

"Figures."

"You'll live longer."

"By skipping one cigarette?" Miles scoffed. "I doubt it."

"You smoked a different brand than Margaret, didn't you?"

Miles glanced at him with a mixture of incredulity and humor. "What does that have to do with anything?"

"It's one of the ways Ms. Taylor's cleaning lady, Ruby Fincher, knew you'd been around last night. You left cigarette butts in the ashtray that weren't Margaret's brand."

"And I'm the only person in town who smokes Camels?"

"These cigarette butts were found in an ashtray on Margaret's nightstand next to the rumpled bed on which we've found semen stains."

"Which means I'm the man Margaret was involved with, right?"

Lucas shrugged. "According to Ruby Fincher."

"She's a regular Sherlock Holmes, isn't she? Tell me,

what were her brilliant insights that nailed me as Margaret's lover?"

"Well, a few weeks ago Ruby found a clipping about you on Margaret's desk. She noticed a new painting in Margaret's house, one of yours, which Margaret gushed over to Ruby when she rarely bothered to bestow *any* conversation on the woman. And one time you left that chunk of turquoise you wear around your neck on Margaret's nightstand along with an empty pack of Camels. Ruby recognized the necklace from the photo that accompanied the article clipped from the newspaper. You see, Mr. Shaw, it's always the little things that trip you up."

"Those and nosy domestic help." Miles leaned back in the wooden chair and crossed his hands behind his neck. Lucas's gaze was drawn to Shaw's long, gleaming braid. No man in this area wore a braid woven through with a strip of leather like Shaw's. Lucas had never paid much attention to it before, but suddenly it got on his nerves. It seemed pretentious and precious and self-consciously artsy. Shaw had the air of a damned peacock, Lucas fumed, showing off like he was really something, above all the rest of the unimaginative, untalented fray with which he must deal on a daily basis. "Is something wrong, Sheriff?" Miles finally asked, his voice faintly insinuating as if he already had an inkling his mere presence was pissing off Lucas.

"Not beyond the obvious." Let Shaw make of *obvious* what he cared to, Lucas thought. "Why didn't anyone ever see you with Ms. Taylor? Why didn't the two of you ever talk about your relationship or go out in public?"

Miles shifted in his chair, his hands dropping from his neck. His fingers twitched with the habitual smoker's urge to hold the stick of tobacco like a prop. "Keeping things quiet was Margaret's idea. She said news of a romance might detract from Philip Hamilton's campaign. I always thought it was more likely she was afraid he'd get jealous."

"Do you think Philip Hamilton had romantic feelings for Margaret?"

Miles paused, absently running his ring finger over a black eyebrow. "I think the man is possessive of every woman who enters his sphere. He starts thinking of them as his property. They have to live up to his standards, behave in ways he finds suitable. And never pull attention away from *him*." Miles looked directly at Lucas. "He even feels that way about Adrienne. You can't tell me you haven't noticed it."

"Actually, I haven't." Lucas kept his voice calm although Shaw had ruffled his composure by dragging Adrienne into the interrogation. And the man was right about Hamilton. Lucas remembered Adrienne telling him how selfishly Philip had behaved when she was attacked, worrying only about the bad impression she might have made as his sister-in-law. Still, Lucas wasn't going to give an inch to Miles Shaw. "Adrienne is extremely strong-willed. She wouldn't let Philip Hamilton boss her around."

Miles threw back his head and laughed, jarring Lucas although he tried not to show it. "Strong-willed is one way to describe Adrienne. I can think of more apt terms."

Lucas stared hard at Miles, knowing the man was trying to bait him by implying he knew Adrienne more intimately than Lucas thought. But the sheriff wasn't about to give Miles the satisfaction of appearing fazed by innuendo. "We need to establish your alibi, Shaw, if you have one," he said coldly. "Where did you go after you left Margaret?"

"Heaven's Door. That place out on Route 2."

"What time did you arrive?"

"I don't know. Between ten and ten-thirty."

"No grandfather clock chiming to announce the exact hour?"

"No," Miles said coolly. "But I went there directly after I left Margaret's."

"Why didn't you go home?"

"I didn't feel like it. Too much energy to burn."

"And you like to dance."

"No, I don't like to dance, but I do like to listen to music. They have a good band."

"Several bands play at Heaven's Door. Which band was playing there last night?"

"Nepenthe. The word is Native American for *peace*."

"Thank you for the vocabulary lesson, Mr. Shaw. Have you ever gone to Heaven's Door before?" Lucas asked.

"Several times."

"Alone?"

A slight hesitation. A slight waver of the eyes. "I've always gone alone, yes. But sometimes I meet someone there."

"Anyone in particular?"

A pause. "Well, yes. There's a girl. Her name is Nikki. That's all I know about her. And before you ask, I've left with her."

"Care to give me more information so I can check your alibi with her?"

"She's about five six or five seven, dark-haired, attractive, young. I don't know her last name. I don't know where she lives. We never go back to her place. Relatives live with her. And she wasn't there last night, so you couldn't check anything with her anyway."

"Really? Nikki with no last name, no known address, and missing last night just when she could provide an alibi for you. Once again, very convenient, Mr. Shaw."

Miles fell silent, clearly trying to control anger. And maybe a growing sense of fear. Finally, he lifted his hands in a gesture of helplessness. "Look, I can't help it. I've only been with Nikki a couple of times, and believe me, if I could use her for an alibi, I sure as hell wouldn't hold out on you. But I can't be the only person who's seen her at Heaven's Door. And I'm sure people must have seen *me* at Heaven's Door last night."

"You? Oh sure. What was I thinking? Fans must be all

over a famous artist like you. Sort of the local Andy Warhol, aren't you? Do they drive you nuts for autographs, that kind of thing?"

"I'm not a thing like Andy Warhol, although we share something in the looks department. *Distinctiveness,* Sheriff Flynn," Shaw said in a maddeningly self-satisfied voice. "I am six feet four inches tall. I have black hair that is almost waist length. I have definite Native American looks. *Good* looks. In other words, I stand out in a local crowd."

Shaw smirked at Lucas, then lounged back in his chair like some smart-ass juvenile delinquent. Lucas felt like kicking the leg out from under Shaw's chair.

"Well, Mr. Shaw, you'd better *hope* you stand out in a crowd," Lucas said with quiet force, "because otherwise you have no alibi. Without an alibi, the prosecuting attorney and I are going to think you savagely murdered and mutilated a young, respected, innocent woman who just happens to be the campaign manager for a gubernatorial candidate. And if we arrest you for that murder, don't expect a groundswell of support, because people aren't going to have much sympathy for you, Miles my boy. Not much sympathy at all."

TWELVE

I

At six o'clock, Adrienne and Skye sat down to watch the evening news. Raptly, they listened to the opening jingle, which ended to show the face of a twenty-something anchorwoman with the orthodox, polished good looks of a thousand other anchorwomen. She beamed at her audience. "Good evening, everybody! Thanks for joining us!"

Immediately her sparkling expression turned solemn. "First tonight, police tell us thirty-two-year-old Margaret Taylor was beaten to death in her home in Point Pleasant some time around midnight. Ms. Taylor was the campaign manager for gubernatorial candidate Philip Hamilton."

The image of the anchorwoman vanished to be replaced by a still picture of Margaret alone, her olive-skinned face touched by a gentle smile, her almond eyes lovely and vulnerable, her black hair uncharacteristically falling in shining waves over her shoulders. Next flashed a photo of a trim and smartly dressed Margaret smiling radiantly up at Philip with Vicky pushed slightly into the background looking careworn, narrow-eyed, grim, and a bit hostile. "Oh no," Adrienne moaned.

Back to the solemn-faced anchorwoman. "Ms. Taylor was found in her home at seven o'clock this morning by her cleaning lady, Ruby Fincher." On came a video. A woman's eyes darted nervously sideways as someone obviously motioned her to "go." She then looked bug-eyed at the camera and drew a deep breath. "I've never seen anything so terrible in all my thirty-five years!" Ruby began with gusto. "I was *horrified*! *Terrified!* Sick to my *stomach*! Why, I had to go take a *nerve* pill!"

Ruby Fincher paused but continued to stare straight into the camera, her moon face reddened by excitement, her blue eyes bright and avid. Clearly, she was having a difficult time not smiling for her audience. She did not look the thirty-five she claimed to be, but she did look like she was having the time of her life. The woman who had found the grotesquely battered body of Margaret Taylor was a media star and enjoying every moment of it.

Ruby vanished. On came the lovely news anchor still looking grave. "Officers say Ms. Taylor's house did not appear to have been broken into, nor were there signs of burglary. Police are conducting an intensive investigation. Although they have several suspects, no arrests have been made."

Skye continued to stare quietly at the television while Adrienne sat with her mouth open for a few seconds. Finally, she recovered, closed her mouth, swallowed, and said, "That Fincher woman was a disaster."

"No kidding," Skye agreed. "And did you see that picture of Margaret with Uncle Philip? They looked like they were in love. Now it won't just be Aunt Vicky who thinks Uncle Philip and Margaret were having an affair."

"How do you know what Vicky thinks?" Adrienne asked, surprised.

"Rachel told me. But I knew anyway. Aunt Vicky always watches Uncle Philip really close and she gets all jumpy and weird when Margaret is—*was*—around." The anchorwoman was now babbling happily about a cookout being held for charity. While she talked, the station showed some truly awful video footage of people lumbering slowly around a picnic table heaping food on paper plates, then stuffing their mouths. Adrienne thought that newspeople always seemed to pick out the biggest eaters for such shots, giving the impression the town was populated by gluttons.

"I bet Miles Shaw killed Margaret," Skye said abruptly. "He's so strange. He totally creeps me out."

"Did you ever see Margaret with Miles?" Adrienne asked, because Skye had spent much more time at the Hamilton household in the last few months than she had. "Did he come to any of the parties?"

Skye shook her head. "None that I went to. Rachel said her dad doesn't like Miles. She thinks that's probably why Margaret didn't want Uncle Philip to know she was dating him."

"Oh." Adrienne made a decision. "Don't tell Sherry and all your friends. Don't tell a soul, but I talked to Lucas this afternoon. He said he questioned Miles, and he has an alibi. He was at this place called Heaven's Gate—"

"Door, Mom. Heaven's Door."

"How do you know?"

"Gosh, Mom, everyone's heard about it. It's *the* place to be if you're older and cool. But go on."

"Anyway, Miles was at Heaven's *Door* at the time of Margaret's murder. He was there for a couple of hours. A lot of people saw him. He's kind of hard to miss with his height and his hair."

"Yeah, I guess he is." Skye thought this over. Then she looked at Adrienne earnestly. "I promise not to tell *anyone*, Mom, but I still think he did it. Somehow, he killed Margaret and he's gonna get away with it."

After the evening news ended, Adrienne had a feeling of expectancy. It lasted through the huge pizza they had delivered from Fox's Pizza Den and devoured with their usual record speed. It lasted while Adrienne watched an unfunny situation comedy and Skye had an extended conversation with Sherry, whom she had not seen for an almost unbearable twenty-four hours. It lasted through Adrienne's attempt to burn off nervous energy by rearranging contents of the kitchen cabinets and forcing an offended Skye to go to bed to make up for her postmidnight bedtime the previous night.

At eleven o'clock, as Adrienne sat on the patio soaking up the cool night breeze, the phone rang. Adrienne knew the bad thing she'd tensed for all evening had finally arrived with the summoning of a telephone.

She ran into the house, not bothering to close the patio doors, and picked up the phone receiver. After she said hello, a short pause followed. Then a scratchy, thin voice asked, "Adrienne?"

"This is Adrienne Reynolds." The voice sounded vaguely familiar, but she couldn't quite place it. "To whom am I speaking?"

A small, rusty laugh. "Adrienne, dear, it's Lottie. Julianna's mother."

"Lottie!" Adrienne burst out. "Lottie, we've all been worried sick about you."

"I'm quite all right. I told Kit I would be. You shouldn't have been worried."

"Where are you?"

Another pause. "I'd rather not say."

"But Lottie—"

"Please, dear, let's not waste time worrying about me. I have someone else's safety on my mind, and something I feel I must tell you. The time has finally come."

"Lottie, let me bring you to my house. Then you can tell me what you need to."

"No, Adrienne. You must let me do this my way, or I won't do it at all. I don't mean to be difficult, but I have my reasons."

Adrienne sighed, feeling helpless, but Lottie was in control now. There was nothing Adrienne could do except to go along with her. "Okay, Lottie. You have my full attention."

"You've always been such a good girl, Adrienne. Skye is fortunate to have you for a mother."

"I think she might disagree with you on that matter right now. I'm enforcing a bedtime."

Lottie chuckled, then coughed. Adrienne started to ask again if she could pick up Lottie, but she'd already been given her orders, and she knew Lottie could be inflexible when her mind was made up. She didn't want to annoy the woman and have her hang up. "I'm sure Skye will forgive you by morning," Lottie finally said when the cough subsided. "And now for the reason I called. I heard today that Margaret Taylor was murdered. I met her once when I was at your sister's house and Vicky was buying candles from me. More candles than she needed, I'm sure, but Vicky is a generous soul. I can't say the same for Miss Taylor. I didn't care for her. Nevertheless, I'm sorry she came to such a tragic end. But I also learned that Miles Shaw is, as I believe they say, the prime suspect in her murder." Lottie paused, then said emotionally, "Adrienne, Miles did not murder *anyone*."

"We don't know that, Lottie."

"*I* know it."

Adrienne knew Lottie had always been fond of Miles. She'd been heartbroken when Julianna left him, and Adrienne had understood Lottie's disappointment. Although Miles was eccentric and off-putting to many people, Adrienne never doubted he'd genuinely loved Julianna, and he'd been a stabilizing influence on her tempestuous, impulsive, often reckless nature. But Adrienne's opinion of Miles had changed over the last four years. His manner had grown biting since the breakup, his behavior changing from eccentric to erratic. Adrienne didn't trust Miles anymore. She no longer felt she knew what he might be capable of doing.

"Lottie, the sheriff told me Miles admitted to having an affair with Margaret," Adrienne said gently. "He even admitted to being with her the night she was murdered."

"He did not kill her, Adrienne. Miles doesn't have murder in him."

"Lottie, how can you be sure?" Adrienne braced herself

for a harsh question. "For that matter, how can you be sure he didn't murder Julianna out of jealousy because she had a lover?"

"I *am* sure," Lottie said emphatically. "Miles loved Julianna. He hated the man she was involved with at the time of her death, but he didn't hate *her*."

"Miles *knew* who Julianna's lover was?" Adrienne burst out. "Do you?"

Silence seemed to vibrate over the phone line for a few moments. Then Lottie said reluctantly, "Yes, dear, I know who it was."

"Are you going to tell me?"

"Only because the situation has escalated to the point where I think you *need* to know." Lottie drew a deep, slightly raspy breath. "I'm sorry to tell you that Julianna was having an affair with your brother-in-law. Philip Hamilton."

2

Adrienne carried the cordless phone receiver into the living room and sat down in the studio chair across from the picture window, far away from Skye's room, where she could talk without being overheard.

"Lottie, if Philip was having an affair, it was probably with Margaret. He barely knew Julianna."

"That's what most people think, Adrienne. That's what Julianna and Philip wanted them to think. But the truth is quite different. Julianna met Philip when you girls were young and he was engaged to Vicky. Julianna and Philip fell in love then, dear. They've been in love ever since."

Adrienne was astounded. She remembered how she, Kit, and Julianna had hovered around Vicky, enraptured by the idea of her marrying a handsome, wealthy young man in a beautiful ceremony followed by a lavish reception at la Belle. They'd gotten on Vicky's nerves, but she'd been so happy, she'd endured their constant presence, endless questions, and squeals of delight. And Adrienne remembered Philip drifting in and out of the frantic preparations, seeming not to notice anyone in particular. Not even Vicky, now that she thought of it.

"But Julianna was so young," Adrienne said desperately, trying to cling to the hope that Philip's love for her friend was only the product of Lottie's imagination, yet realizing in retrospect that something had been wrong. Philip had not acted as a loving fiancé should. And dredging her memory, Adrienne recalled that his gaze had seemed locked on Julianna more than a few times. Still, Adrienne did not want to believe what she was hearing. "Lottie, if Philip was in love with Julianna, why did he marry Vicky? Was it because Julianna was too young for marriage?"

"The problem wasn't age," Lottie said sadly. "It was background. Lineage. Julianna was the daughter of Butch and Lottie Brent. We were hardly members of the Social Register set. Philip had had political aspirations since he was a boy. That Tartar of a great-aunt—Octavia, I believe her name was—began his indoctrination early. Vicky came from a fine family. She was lovely, intelligent, and low-key with infallible manners. I don't believe she ever made a social misstep in her life."

"She didn't," Adrienne said flatly. "I believe she had the same aspirations as Philip. At least she did at the time they married. I don't think the life she dreamed of turned out to be as golden as she'd hoped."

"Life often has a tendency to disappoint us. Or rather, most of us. Julianna could have turned out like her sister Gail—bitter that she didn't have better parents, more money, more respect in this town—but she didn't. Julianna had a wonderful gift for making the best of things and doing it joyfully. It's no wonder to me that Philip loved her." She paused, then said quickly, "I meant no offense to Vicky. She's a lovely person."

"She *can* be a lovely person, but she's not exciting and ebullient like Julianna was. And certainly not as glamorous." Adrienne paused. "When did Julianna's affair with Philip begin?"

"It really was nothing more than sweet encounters and love letters until Julianna returned from New York. That's when things became . . . physical," Lottie said uncomfortably before emitting another rattling cough. "Juli felt guilty about it and ended things for a while. That's when she married Miles. But Miles couldn't make her happy. So she left him and resumed the affair with Philip."

"Did Miles know about Philip?"

"I'm not sure. If he did, he never said anything to Julianna. She would have confided in me."

"Lottie, why are you telling me all of this now?"

"Because I'm worried about Miles. The sheriff loves you. You have influence with him. You can talk him into leaving Miles alone." Lottie clearly overestimated Adrienne's power over Lucas, especially because Adrienne wasn't convinced of Miles's innocence, but she didn't have a chance to argue before Lottie went on in a weak, breathy voice. "Adrienne, I want you to know that Julianna did not like betraying your sister. She suffered over her duplicity. But she loved Philip so much she couldn't seem to help herself. He claimed to love her just as much. He told Julianna that after he became governor, he would leave Vicky and marry her."

"Leave Vicky and marry Juli?" Adrienne repeated in disbelief. "Lottie, I don't know what Philip told Julianna, but he would *never* have done that. His aspirations don't end with being governor. He intends to someday run for president. Dumping his wife for a woman he'd been having an affair with for years would be political suicide!"

"I know. And Juli knew, too. She just wanted to be with him, even if it had to be in the shadows. But she pretended to believe him."

Adrienne's hands went cold. What if Philip *hadn't* known

she was pretending? What if he'd believed Julianna was in-
tent on having him no matter what she had to do to get him?
If so, she would have been a liability, perhaps a liability
from whom he might have done anything to free himself.
Maybe even murder.

Adrienne suddenly felt uneasy about Lottie. More than
uneasy. Downright apprehensive.

"Lottie, you've been playing hide-and-seek long enough,"
she said strongly. "I want to come and get you. You don't
sound well."

"I have a little cold, nothing serious."

"It could be pneumonia."

"Heavens, no!" Lottie's voice had grown thinner and
rougher. "I'm just fine. You don't need to worry about me."

"But I *am* worried, Lottie. Please tell me where you are."

Lottie hesitated. "No. Absolutely not. I only called to
help Miles. I can take care of myself." She seemed to choke,
then broke into a violent fit of coughing. Finally gasping,
she tried to catch her breath.

"Lottie, I *mean* it. You're sick."

"Nooo."

"Lottie, where are you?"

"Maybe I'll see you tomorrow. After I do my laundry."
Lottie had begun to sound vague the way people did when
they were feverish. "I haven't done laundry this week. There's
no excuse for bad housekeeping . . ."

"Lottie, are you there?" Nothing. "Lottie?"

Lottie did not speak. Adrienne strained to hear if the
woman was breathing, meaning she was still holding the
phone, but all she heard was a familiar tinkling sound. Gentle. Melodic. Wood and metal. Glass.

Wind chimes! Suddenly Adrienne remembered the collection of wind chimes hanging from the porch of Lottie's
cabin. She must have stopped at home to make her call to
Adrienne and left the door open although a wind was blowing up.

Adrienne said the woman's name loudly into the phone three more times and finally heard a rasp of breath, but no words. She feared Lottie had collapsed. She'd spent several nights outside, one in that awful storm that had hit the night of Julianna's death. Her only shelter had been the terrible bunker Ellen called the Hideaway. Now Lottie was probably seriously ill. And alone.

"Skye!" Adrienne called loudly. "Skye, come here!"

The girl arrived in an instant. Clearly she hadn't been asleep and now sensed distress in her mother's voice. "What's happened?"

"It's Lottie." Adrienne held up the phone receiver. "She called me. She sounded really sick. Then she just stopped talking but she didn't hang up. I'm fairly sure she's at her cabin."

"Let's call 911!"

"We can't. Lottie has been hiding because she's scared. A call to 911 would go out over the police scanners. Half the town has them. Whoever Lottie is hiding from could hear and get to her before the paramedics do." Adrienne paused. "I don't want to hang up this phone and break the connection with Lottie, so get your cell phone. We'll call Lucas on his private line, not at headquarters. Those calls go out on the scanners, too. I'll tell Lucas to go to Lottie's."

In less than a minute Skye was back with the cell phone in hand and Brandon at her heels. "Do you know Lucas's number?" she asked anxiously.

"After a year of dating? I think so," Adrienne said dryly. She punched buttons, hoping desperately Lucas was at home. Relief rushed through her when he said hello. "Lucas? I think we have an emergency that I need for you to keep to yourself. No notification through official channels. It's important."

"Good God, Adrienne, what is it?" he asked tensely. "Are you and Skye all right?"

"Yes, but I'm not sure Lottie is. She called and I think

she's at her cabin, but she sounded extremely sick, then she stopped talking. She could be unconscious. I don't want to call 911 because I don't want her to be frightened."

"So you want me to go to her."

"Well, yes, but I want to get to her first. She's afraid of just about everyone, Lucas. Including you. If I go to the cabin, I can calm her, or at least hold her hostage, until you get there and help me take her to the hospital. Would you be willing to help me do that?"

"I'd be willing to help you do just about anything, Adrienne, but I'm not sure it's safe for *you* to be up on that hill in the dark after all that's happened lately."

"I'll be fine. I don't intend on spending the night. I just need a twenty-minute head start, and your promise that you won't call the paramedics."

"She might *need* the paramedics."

"She doesn't need her location broadcast over police scanners just in case she's right and someone is out to kill her. She's not crazy or paranoid, Lucas. I have a feeling she knows who killed Julianna, and the murderer *knows* she knows."

Lucas hesitated, then said, "All right. I'm not leaving you alone for long, though. I'm starting out for Lottie's in twenty minutes."

"Thank you, Lucas," she said sincerely. "You're a wonderful man."

"Yeah, so they say." He paused. "I love you."

"See you soon," Adrienne said quickly and clicked off, feeling guilty to the depths of her soul.

After Adrienne said good-bye to Lucas, she turned to Skye. "I'm not going to risk taking you with me up on that hill. It could be dangerous."

"You can't go alone, Mom! I'm not a little kid. I won't get in the way or get hurt."

"I can't take that chance." She briefly thought of taking

Skye to Vicky's, then immediately rejected the idea. After all, Philip might be the person Lottie had been hiding from for days. He could be Julianna's killer. And so could Vicky, her mind said reluctantly. If Vicky knew about Philip and Julianna, she might have done the unthinkable to her rival. "I'm going to leave you here alone. I want you to turn on the security system as soon as I leave. Don't go to the door for *anyone* besides Lucas and me. Not even Aunt Vicky. And if someone calls, don't tell them you're alone. Say I'm in the shower or something. Promise."

"Okay, I promise. But you shouldn't go out alone either, Mom."

"It can't be helped." Adrienne rummaged through her purse for the car keys that always found their way to a bottom corner.

"You can take Brandon." Adrienne looked up in surprise. Skye was more careful about Brandon's safety than her own. She would be devastated if anything happened to the dog, but she was offering him to her mother for protection.

"Brandon should stay here to look out for you, honey. I'll be okay without him."

"Maybe. But you'd be safer *with* him." Skye gave her a look shadowed with the unselfish devotion Adrienne knew she would display as a woman. "Please do it for me, Mom. I'll feel better if I know he's with you."

Adrienne felt an embarrassing pressure of tears behind her eyes, and clutched Skye to her. "You're a generous girl. I'm very proud of you. And grateful."

Skye pushed back, gave her a wavering smile, then said enthusiastically, "C'mon, Brandon. You're going on an adventure with Mom. Let's get your leash!"

The dog immediately started prancing and snorting, sensing fun on its way. Adrienne hoped that in half an hour he would still be having fun and that she wasn't leading the two of them into danger.

Wind tossed cobalt-colored clouds across the silvery stars

and moon, giving the warm night a restless look. After eleven P.M., traffic slowed dramatically in Point Pleasant. Adrienne felt almost alone on the road leading north of town to la Belle Rivière, definitely a confidence-draining experience. She turned on the radio, as always taking comfort from music, and glanced at Brandon, whose tongue hung out in drippy anticipation. At least *he* seemed to be enjoying the ride, she thought.

Until the charming Butch Brent, Julianna's father, had deserted the family over twenty years ago, a gravel road had led from the highway all the way up to the cabin on the side of the hill opposite la Belle. The distance was greater than on the hotel side, but the going had been easier. Lashing rainstorms and heavy snows had gradually washed away the old gravel, though, and tree limbs had grown untrimmed until they constricted the road to a narrow lane.

Ellen and Julianna had argued with Lottie, insisting she allow them to pay for road improvement, but Lottie had held firm on the issue. In fact, she grew extremely agitated whenever her daughter and her friend pushed the matter. Julianna had once told Adrienne she thought the ruined road gave Lottie a feeling of safe isolation. At the time, Adrienne hadn't understood Lottie's preference for inaccessibility over comfort. After hearing the story of the atrocity Lottie had endured in the garden shed on the open lawns of la Belle, though, she could now empathize with Lottie's desire to be nearly unapproachable.

Tonight, Adrienne opted to use the secluded ruin of a road rather than walk across the lawns of la Belle where she would be exposed. She turned off the highway and began climbing what seemed like barely more than a path topped by a thin layer of gravel. Before long she reached the giant evergreen trees that stood like sentinels on either side of the road. Before she'd gone half a mile, the gravel began to peter out.

The car jolted over small potholes and grooves caused by

water draining down the hill. This was one of the few times she was glad she'd bought the bulky SUV with four-wheel drive when she preferred sleeker, sportier cars. Brandon had fallen into a trancelike study of the scenery, not that there was much to see. The farther up the hill they went, the closer the evergreen limbs crowded. Needles brushed the roof of the car. Adrienne had the sensation that actually the car was not moving but that the trees were, creeping in and crouching down like threatening creatures closing in on their prey. How ridiculous, she chastised herself. This was what came of staying up late to watch *The Others* last night. The movie had sent her imagination into overdrive. Shortly, though, she'd be in Lottie's cabin and Lucas would stride in, strong and capable, to save them.

But save them from whom? Probably no one, Adrienne mused. Lottie seemed convinced someone meaning her harm was pursuing her, and the power of her fancy was so strong she'd instilled her fear into Adrienne. Adrienne paused, thinking. Had it actually been Lottie who'd instilled the fear? Had Lottie *ever* said she was hiding from Julianna's killer? No, Adrienne realized, startled. It had been Ellen who'd declared Lottie was running because she knew who'd killed Julianna, not Lottie herself. Was Ellen right about Lottie's motives? And if so, could Ellen know from whom she was hiding? After all, it had crossed Adrienne's mind that perhaps Lottie was avoiding Ellen. But why?

The headlights picked up deep ruts in the road ahead. Adrienne turned the wheel slightly left, keeping one set of tires on the hump between the ruts, the other set on the tiny bit of ground between a rut and the wall of trees. The speedometer read that they were going five miles an hour, but it felt like two. This road is a disgrace, she thought. Something would have to be done about it come spring whether Lottie liked it or not.

Brandon suddenly barked and Adrienne jumped, shifting

the wheel, and sending the tires directly into the ruts. The car hit with a thud and moved only another foot or so before she heard the sound of metal abrading on gravel and dirt. She pushed gently on the accelerator. The abrasion grew more intense and the car moved slower. Finally, the sound amplified into downright grating. Shuddering, the car slowed, then stopped. When she tried to move forward again, the tires spun uselessly.

"Oh no," she groaned. "We're hung on the frame. That means no traction, Brandon, and that in turn means we're stuck." He looked at her with expectation. "Looks like you and I get to go for a walk."

Brandon knew the word *walk* and promptly began shifting in his seat and whining with joy. Adrienne attached his leash and as she climbed out the driver's side, he scrambled over the console to follow her.

Out on the road, she glowered with pure hatred at the useless car. The night seemed extremely dark. The wind had picked up. She was tired. She was scared. Abruptly her cell phone rang and she almost screamed. Brandon was too busy snorting heady and mysterious smells in dirt under the trees to pay any attention to her. "Hello," she said tightly into the phone.

"It's just me," Skye said. "I had a bad feeling. Is everything all right?"

"I got the car stuck in ruts on the road."

"Gosh, Mom, you should be more careful."

"I *am* careful," Adrienne said with sudden, sharp defensiveness. "Besides, it's really Brandon's fault."

"I know. He's a terrible driver," Skye giggled. Adrienne grew more annoyed. "Is he okay?"

"Your *dog* is having a ball. Your *mother* is another matter, not that I seem to be your first priority." Adrienne paused and took a deep breath, forcing down the nerves making her querulous. "Skye, you haven't gone out or called anyone, have you?"

"No. You said not to. Is Lottie okay?"

"We haven't reached the cabin yet so I don't know. We'll have to walk the rest of the way. It's not far, though."

"Good. I'm glad Brandon's with you."

"Yes, he's been a tremendous help so far. I don't know what I would have done without him."

"Give him a chance, Mom. He might surprise you."

"I'll believe it when I see it." She took another deep, supposedly calming breath that didn't help at all. "I'll call you when we get to Lottie's. Lucas should be here soon."

"Good."

"Don't go out."

"I won't."

"And don't open the door for *anyone*."

"*Okay,* Mom. Jeez." Skye hung up. So did Adrienne, feeling frazzled and mean. She'd make up to Skye for her last few days of grouchiness and overprotection. They'd do something fun together, like shop for new fall school clothes. She'd even let Skye pick out a couple of outfits Adrienne thought looked too sophisticated for a fourteen-year-old. "Come on, Brandon," she called, cheering up slightly. He looked at her, then ambled over, letting her take his leash in her hand. "Onward and upward."

Brandon seemed much more prepared for a trip onward and upward than Adrienne did. Of course, he'd slept most of the day while she'd paced and wrung her hands and fretted. There was a lot to be said for fretting, she thought. It kept your mind active. It kept the old central nervous system on its toes.

It also made you cranky and exhausted.

She decided she should have taken a nap this afternoon, but she'd been too restless. And she'd had no idea she'd be trekking up an overgrown trail to Lottie's house at eleven-thirty at night.

The stiffening wind sent the evergreen limbs swaying and their needles whispering as if they had a dark secret. Brandon, excited by the unusual night outing, pulled ahead, sending her stumbling over the road's bumps and snaky rivulets. Snaky? Snakes, she thought. Did snakes come out at night? Adrienne wished she had on knee-high boots instead of canvas tennis shoes. Why on earth hadn't she taken time to change shoes? Or to bring the giant five-cell Mag-Lite flashlight that had belonged to her West Virginia state policeman grandfather? She could also have used it as a weapon.

Right, she mused. It would be just like her to have the presence of mind, not to mention the bravery, to successfully beat the crap out of an attacker with a flashlight.

Adrienne trudged on, feeling as if she'd walked half a mile instead of about a hundred feet. A mist slowly lowered from the infinite night sky, twining around the treetops, twisting in the wind. The phrase *forest primeval* echoed maddeningly in her mind. She had to remember she was not in some uncharted wilderness. She was on the remains of a road Lottie traveled on foot almost every day.

Suddenly she heard a rustling in the woods to her right. She stopped dead. So did Brandon, his ears perking up. She clenched her hands, wishing again for the giant flashlight. Or a gun she didn't know how to use. Even Mace. Anything.

More rustling. The wind, she thought. Just the wind. But Brandon's ears were still standing straight up and a growl rumbled in his throat. He didn't growl at the wind.

And then she saw it. A young deer with giant ears and huge, gentle eyes, looking back at her with as much fear as she regarded it. She said a silent prayer that Brandon would not go charging after it, dragging her along. Or dragging it down for a bloody kill. Not that he'd ever shown the slightest interest in pursuing a deer before.

The three of them stood paralyzed for what seemed an endless time. Then the deer turned its head and bounded away in great, graceful leaps. Adrienne realized she'd been holding her breath, and she let it out, feeling as if her chest were ready to explode. "I am not cut out for a life of mystery and danger," she murmured to Brandon. "I wish we were home in front of the television." But she'd made it this far, and she was determined not to run away before she had at least done her best to find Lottie. She owed that much to Julianna, no matter how nervous she felt out here in the dark.

In spite of the wind, Adrienne had begun to perspire from trotting to keep up with Brandon by the time they neared Lottie's cabin. First, she heard the wind chimes jingling and clinking from the porch roof. Then she saw light turned vaporous by the mist seeping from the windows. And what appeared to be an open door. Why would Lottie, apparently so frightened she'd been on the run for days, sit in her cabin with the door wide open? Adrienne felt as if her heart were contracting as she and Brandon picked up speed, rushing toward what could only be a portentous signal.

"Lottie?" she called before they reached the porch. "Lottie?"

But the only answer was the sound of the wind chimes jangling. As she climbed the porch steps, Adrienne looked closer at them in the light. Then she saw them. Red, hand-painted Venetian glass chimes just like the ones Philip had brought to Rachel from Europe. The girl had cherished them as a special gift picked just for her. But apparently Philip had bought two sets, one for his lover, Julianna, which she had hung on her mother's porch where few people except herself would see them. Adrienne had looked right at them the day she was here with Ellen, and neither their similarity nor their significance had registered in her mind.

"Lottie?" she called again, not expecting an answer as they crossed the porch and stood in the open doorway. Several hurricane lamps of frosted glass burned softly inside, bathing the cabin's shabby furnishings in a creamy glow in the lonely night. "Lottie?"

Adrienne and Brandon had just stepped over the threshold when something whistled past Adrienne's head and shattered one of the lamps. Immediately, Adrienne dropped to the floor, instinctively pulling down Brandon with her as if he were a child. She cowered next to him as another shot whizzed into the cabin, then another, and another.

And then came silence.

THIRTEEN

I

Time seemed to stop as Adrienne lay beside Brandon, her face buried in his shining black hair. He hadn't moved. She was afraid he was dead. She was afraid to raise her head to see.

She inched her hand around to his chest and felt the heart beating strong and regular. "Brandon," she whispered in relief. "God, I'm glad you're alive." He whined and shifted in a slow effort to rise. "Don't stand up," she said as if he could understand her. "Someone might still be out there with a gun and this time they won't miss."

If they *had* missed. Her own body felt strangely anesthetized. She wondered if she was injured and going into shock, or merely scared into numbness. And she wasn't sure Brandon hadn't been shot. Skye will be heartbroken if I've let something happen to him, Adrienne thought. She'll be crushed.

She felt hot tears running into her eyes, tears of fear and regret for having been foolhardy enough to come out here after Lottie. Yes, she had been concerned. Yes, she had been afraid Lottie might run away from anyone except her. But she hadn't thought of the danger to herself, or the fact that she might make her daughter an orphan. She'd been a reckless fool.

Adrienne and Brandon still lay on the wooden floor, pressed together, her tears pouring into his hair, when someone directly above her said, "Good God, Adrienne, are you all right?"

She froze. Playing dead. After all, it worked for animals. Just go away, she thought. Assume you've been successful in killing me and go away.

She heard the front door shutting firmly. Then hands gently touched her back. Brandon raised his head and growled. "It's all right, boy," a man said soothingly. "I'm here to help. Just settle down."

Drew. Drew Delaney was bending over her. Right after someone had been shooting at her.

"Adrienne, are you hurt?" he asked. "Answer me if you can. I'm afraid to turn you over."

Finally, she said, "I'm not in pain. I don't think I've been shot." She made a feeble attempt to roll over. Drew placed his hand firmly across her neck to stabilize it and helped turn her. His dark gaze ran up and down her body. "I didn't see any wounds in your back. There's no blood on the front of you, either. I think you're okay."

"I do seem to be damned near indestructible, don't I?" she asked with a feeble smile. "First I'm beaten. Then I'm shot at." She paused. "I lead the life of a superhero."

Drew grinned. "How do you like it?"

"It sucks. I'm resigning." She turned her head and looked at Brandon. "Do you think he's hurt?"

"No. Just scared." He paused and she heard him moving across the wooden floor. Then, one by one, the lamps went out. "Now we're not such easy targets," he said.

"Did you find Lottie?" Adrienne asked fearfully, picturing the woman lying dead in her tiny cabin.

"No. Apparently, she's escaped again." She heard him walking slowly back to her, kicking a chair leg in the darkness. Then, beside her ear, he said, "You can stand up now. Just stay away from the windows."

Adrienne rose slowly and unsteadily, like someone who has been in bed a long time and hasn't regained sure footing.

Drew came to her side and took her arm. "All right?" he asked.

"Yes. I just have a weird dizzy feeling."

"That always happens to women when they stand next to me."

"Oh yeah? Well, it's gone now, and you're still here."

"I didn't say it lasted for hours."

She couldn't believe he'd made her smile, even in this awful situation, and she was glad he couldn't see her face. She looked down at Brandon. In the faint glow of moonlight coming through the front window, she watched him clamber up even more slowly than she had. Adrienne kneeled and ran her hands over his body, then rubbed her dry palms together. "No blood, thank goodness," she said brightly. "Looks like we both made it through unscathed."

Then her legs gave out and she plopped down hard on the wooden floor. "Good God, Drew, someone tried to *kill* me!"

He squatted down beside her. "The reality just hit you, didn't it?"

"Like a lightning bolt." Adrienne felt tears running down her face and was surprisingly embarrassed. She brushed at them impatiently, but not before Drew had touched her cheeks and felt them for himself. "Now I'm going to have a weeping fit on top of everything else. What next?"

"Weep all you want if it makes you feel better," he said comfortingly. "I'd weep too if I didn't have this macho image to maintain."

Before she quite knew what she was doing, Adrienne had buried her head on Drew's shoulder while tears flowed and her body shook. "I was so s-scared," she murmured. "I just stepped in and then there were explosions, or what sounded like explosions, and they seemed to go on and on, and I was sure I was going to d-die."

Drew gently gathered her long hair, draped it over her shoulder, and began stroking her neck. "I know you were scared, baby. Anyone would have been. But you're safe now."

"Yes. I'm s-safe. But I'm not your baby."

"Sorry. The drama of the moment made me revert to high school. That's what I called you then, remember?"

"It was a lifetime ago."

"Oh, not *that* long." He stopped stroking her neck and began a less intimate patting on her back. "And you're not all that different than you were then."

"I am, too. I've changed a lot more than you know."

"Probably not as much as I have. I'm not *quite* the cad I used to be."

"You were worse than a cad. You broke my heart." Adrienne could have bitten her tongue for that last candid statement. She snuffled and, with an effort, pulled away from him. She was enjoying his warmth, his scent, his deep and lulling voice far too much. She quelled a deep, absurd desire to throw her arms around his neck and kiss him. Instead, she demanded loudly, "Did you see anyone outside? Do you *know* who tried to shoot me?"

Drew blinked at the sudden change in her mood and volume. "No, I didn't see anyone. Whoever was shooting must have been standing just inside the tree line, out of eyesight."

"And *what* are you doing here?" she snapped.

"What are *you* doing here?"

"I asked first."

"I was following you." She pulled farther away from him, furious and afraid. "Following me? *Why?*"

"Because if you're foolish enough to come up here by yourself at night, you *need* to be followed by someone to look out for you!"

"You couldn't possibly have known where I was going when I left the house." She paused, her fear growing. "It's *your* car I've seen cruising past my house at night, isn't it? And this isn't the first time you've followed me, either."

"Is it a criminal offense to try to protect you?"

"That's what Lucas is for!"

Drew's voice hardened. "Oh yes, the sheriff who put

surveillance on your house for *one* night after the break-in, then pulled it. Is that the loving and protective Lucas to whom you're referring?"

Adrienne tried to hide her surprise and said staunchly, "The surveillance was on our house for more than one night."

"No, it was *not*. I ought to know. I've lost enough sleep to kill me this week trying to provide the surveillance our esteemed sheriff apparently didn't think you deserved. And by the way, where is Sheriff Flynn tonight? Shouldn't your great love be with you here on this dark, tree-covered hilltop as you look for a feeble old lady? After all, it's not as if this town hasn't had *three* murders already. Was he going to just sit by and let you be the fourth?"

"He's on his way," she nearly hissed through clenched teeth. "I called his private number and asked him to meet me here. Lottie had called me from the cabin, but I thought if anyone else approached her first, she might take off. It was *my* idea to come alone—"

"And he *agreed* to that idiotic plan?"

"It was not idiotic," she said icily. "And you didn't let me finish. He agreed to let me come first and to arrive shortly afterward."

"Well, it *is* shortly afterward. So, where the hell is he?"

Yes, where the hell was he? Adrienne wondered. He should have been here by now, especially in light of the fact that her own arrival had been delayed by getting the car stuck and having to walk part of the way. "He'll *be* here," she said stubbornly. "Soon."

"So what are we supposed to do? Stay in this cabin like sitting ducks until he decides to amble by?"

"We're not sitting ducks. The lights are off. The door is closed."

"The door with no lock. And we're in a cabin that's about as stalwart as a house made of sticks. A high-powered rifle could probably pierce right through the walls. Yeah, we're safe, Adrienne. I feel completely secure."

Rage born of fear rushed over her and she reached out, hitting him hard on the chest with the palms of both hands. Then she hit him again. "Well, if I'm such a dummy, why don't *you* come up with something useful besides criticism? *You* figure a way out of this mess!"

Drew grabbed her wrists and held them firm. "You're right. I'm sorry. I'm being a jerk. Just don't hit me anymore."

She fought off a fresh wave of tears and swallowed. "I didn't mean to hurt your chest."

"You didn't. Only my feelings."

"Oh, Drew, *please* don't start joking."

"You know I always do it when I don't know what else to say. Or do. But I'll stop for now. And don't you dare cry again."

"I wasn't going to."

"That's debatable. Anyway, here's the plan. We're going to forget about the sheriff for now. I'm going to call 911 on my cell phone and get the police up here as fast as possible. Then, while we've got a crowd of officials around us, we're getting off this godforsaken hillside and going back home. Hopefully, our sniper won't decide to pursue us."

"Pursue us?" Adrienne repeated. "You mean pursue *me*. I'm the one he shot at." Suddenly, she felt as if her heart had stopped. "Skye. She's at home alone. If whoever tried to shoot me *does* follow me home, or has already gone there . . ."

She couldn't finish. She'd told Skye not to open the door or to go out. She had never thought to tell her to stay away from windows.

"We don't know how long it will take the cops to get here," Drew said in a calm but urgent voice. "We could be stuck up here for at least an hour. You need to get Skye out of that house. Call Vicky and have her pick up Skye."

"No, not Vicky." Drew said nothing, but she could feel his curiosity. She couldn't tell him about the ugly doubts that had begun to form in her mind about her sister's or brother-in-law's possible involvement in the murders of Julianna and Margaret. "Skye has a friend named Sherry Granger. Sherry's mother is great. I'll see if she'll pick up Skye. You call the police, I'll call Mrs. Granger, and if she agrees to babysit, I'll call Skye and tell her I want her to go to the Granger house for the night. I think she'll be safe there."

"Sounds good," Drew said. Then he added thoughtfully, "I just wonder what's made you doubt your sister so much you don't trust her to look after your daughter."

2

"Are you *sure* Brandon is all right?"

"Yes, Skye, your dog is in tip-top form." Adrienne had told Skye only that there had been some trouble at Lottie's, she could possibly be held up for hours, and she wanted Skye to go to the Granger house for the night. "Throw some stuff together and be waiting for them."

Earlier, Mrs. Granger, who had insisted Adrienne call her Louise, had mercifully asked few questions about what quandary Adrienne had gotten herself into now and assured her that she and her husband would immediately pick up Skye. "I don't know about you, but I always feel safer with a man along," Louise said confidentially. "Especially one like my Russ. He's six two and two hundred and twenty pounds. No one messes with him!" Louise giggled. "Don't worry about picking up Skye when you get home. You'll probably be tired after what you've been through?"

A slight prod for information, which Adrienne answered with a simple and disappointing *yes*. "Well, the girls can sleep in late tomorrow," Louise said. "You just call when you're ready for me to bring Skye home. We think the world of her. I'll be glad to help you out any way I can. Well, Russ says I'm chattering on worse than my mother. Don't worry about Skye, Adrienne. And you be careful, too. *Real* careful.

I don't know what in the world has happened to this town lately. It must be that old Indian curse everyone talks about—Chief Cornstalk's curse—kicking in. I think half the population's gone crazy. Well, 'bye, dear. God bless and keep you."

"You, too," Adrienne had ended awkwardly. She was used to simple good-byes. She looked at Drew. Her eyes had adjusted to the near darkness, and she could see moonlight touching his. "Well, that gets Skye taken care of. I won't have to worry about her."

"I'm surprised you went off and left her alone."

No reproach edged Drew's voice, but Adrienne bristled anyway. "I have a first-rate security system. The place was shut tight as a drum. I told her not to go out, and not to answer the door. I thought I'd only be gone about half an hour. And she's not a baby!"

"Whoa, girl." Drew laughed gently. "I've been put in my place. It was a stupid remark."

"No it wasn't," Adrienne said, suddenly feeling deflated. "It *was* stupid of me to leave her alone. Fourteen-year-olds can be heedless, no matter how many warnings you've given them."

"People of any age can be heedless. And you do have a pretty snazzy alarm system. Lightning Rod told me all about it right after he installed it. He always had a crush on you, do you know that? And besides the alarm system, you've got all those dusk-to-dawn lights in your yard. The place is even better lit than Heaven's Door."

"I don't have flashing neon," Adrienne said, giggling in spite of herself.

"I'm sure Lightning Rod could arrange for you to get some. The guy's got connections, Adrienne." Drew pointed skyward. "*Big* connections, when you figure how many times he's been nearly hit by lightning and escaped harm."

They sat close together, cross-legged on the floor, chatting about nothing important while they waited. They waited for the police to arrive. They waited for Lucas, although neither of them mentioned him again. They waited for another possible attack. They waited for the end of this eerie, frightening seclusion. Finally, Brandon whined, pawed Adrienne, then laid his head on Drew's lap.

"He likes you," Adrienne said.

"I like him. Dogs in general, but especially big dogs. Rachel tells me he's nearly the center of Skye's life."

"He is. Her father rescued him from the pound and gave him to Skye for her tenth birthday. She was thrilled." Adrienne paused, then said quietly, "Trey died that night."

"I know. The motorcycle wreck."

"He'd never even been on a motorcycle before. But he'd had too much to drink, decided he was indestructible, and went roaring off on a friend's Harley. He lost control and swerved in front of a semitrailer, for God's sake. Not even a little pickup. Trey Reynolds always had to do things *big*. He wouldn't wear a helmet. Every time I think about it, I get so mad I think if he were still alive, I'd kill him. And then I feel so guilty I can't even look at Skye."

"It's natural to feel anger when someone you love dies," Drew said. "Especially when they kill themselves doing something asinine. And what he did *was* asinine, Adrienne. You can't get mad at yourself for realizing how irresponsible he was being when he climbed onto that motorcycle."

"He did a lot of reckless things after we came home from Las Vegas. I think he was trying to make up for his failure out there by showing how adept he was at everything else he tried. And brave. But he wasn't brave. He was just foolhardy." Adrienne sighed. "You don't have to comfort me anymore. I think I'm through whining."

"You're not whining."

"Yes I am, and I told you to stop comforting me." Her back was beginning to ache from tension, and she stretched out on the floor. "Don't worry. I'm not fainting. I'm just trying to stretch the kinks out of my back."

"I could walk on it for you."

"No, thanks. Then Brandon would think he should join

you, and I don't think my poor lumbar region could handle the weight of both of you." Adrienne closed her eyes for a moment, and in the complete silence of the cabin, picked up on a distant sound. "A siren!" She jerked up. "I hear a siren. The police are *finally* coming!"

The siren wails grew louder for nearly a minute, then stopped. "Your car has them blocked," Drew said. "It blocked me, too. They can't get their cruisers up here, but they'll come the rest of the way on foot."

"That road," Adrienne said vaguely. "It has to be fixed. Lottie can't go on living in this kind of isolation." She stopped, her throat tightening. "If she's still alive. She could be lying out in the woods dead."

"Lottie knows these woods like the back of her hand. And all that walking she's done over the years has kept her fairly spry." Drew reached over in the semidarkness and patted her hand. "I'm not giving up on her yet, and neither should you. It would be bad luck."

Adrienne forced a smile. "I guess Lottie is worth suspending my disbelief in luck for the time being. I promise to keep the faith."

In minutes, the beams from flashlights—the big flashlights Adrienne had wished for earlier in the evening—cut through the darkness in front of Lottie's cabin. They heard voices as policemen talked to each other, then someone yelled, "Anyone in there? If so, come out with your hands up and *no* funny business!"

Drew groaned. "Only our valiant Deputy Sonny Keller would actually come out with such a corny line." Drew stood up and went to the door, opening it a fraction. "This is Drew Delaney. Adrienne Reynolds and I are the only ones here. We're unarmed, Keller."

"Are you sure?"

"Am I sure?" Drew muttered at Adrienne, rolling his eyes. "Yes, Keller," he yelled back. "May we come out without being greeted by a hail of bullets?"

"Okay. But walk out *slow*. With your hands *up*."

"Did you get that?" Drew asked her. "He's a tough one. You mess this up, woman, and he'll drop us dead in our tracks."

Adrienne burst into giggles resulting from nerves and bemused disbelief. She'd prayed for rescue from the little cabin where she'd almost been killed, but she hadn't expected the rescuer to consider *her* the danger. Ludicrous as she felt, though, she stepped slowly onto the porch with her hands raised above her head. Deputy Keller marched closer and gave her a hard look. "What's so funny? Is this some kind of prank? Because if it is . . ."

He let the horror of possible consequences hang in the air as Drew followed Adrienne and mercifully took over for her. "She's only smiling because she's happy you saved her, Deputy. This certainly wasn't a prank. Someone shot at her with what sounded to me like a high-powered rifle. It's a miracle she wasn't killed."

"And didn't nobody shoot at you?" Sonny Keller asked.

"I arrived a couple of minutes after Adrienne. A couple of crucial minutes. I found her on the floor of the cabin, but she hadn't been hit. She was pretty scared, though. We both were. I'm telling you, Deputy Keller, we're sure happy you're here to take over. I feel safer already, don't you, Adrienne?"

She nodded. Keller looked at Drew suspiciously, not quite sure whether or not he was being made fun of, then decided *no* one in their right minds could be ridiculing him for his heroic rescue, and relaxed his posture slightly.

"You folks come on down off that porch. Could still be someone in these woods. Will that dog bite? Better get him on a leash."

"He *is* on a leash," Adrienne said. "But he doesn't bite anyway."

"Hmmm. He looks like a biter to me," Keller pronounced. Then he turned to the other policemen. "Men, fan out!"

he thundered to the small cluster of patrolmen standing right beside him. "You know the drill. Use utmost caution because our perp is armed and dangerous. I repeat, *dangerous*! Is that clear?"

A general disgruntled murmur and a few smirks appeared behind Keller's back before his troops marched off into the woods with Keller's dire warnings still echoing in their heads. Adrienne knew the guy drove Lucas wild. Now she saw why.

"Where is Sheriff Flynn?" she asked.

"Off duty," Keller replied.

"I know that, but he was supposed to meet me up here," Adrienne said.

Keller looked cagey. "A little rendezvous?"

Adrienne started to snap back a sarcastic remark, then thought better of it. "Lottie Brent called me. She was here at the cabin. I called Lucas and told him I'd meet with her first so she wouldn't be afraid and run away again, then he could come just a little while later and we'd take her to the hospital. I didn't think I could manage her alone. I also knew I should notify someone in authority that I'd located her. But he never showed up."

The leer faded from Keller's paunchy face. "You sure he was comin' up here to meet you?" She nodded. "You sure he's had plenty of time to get up here?"

"More than enough." Adrienne knew better than to suggest that she take control of the situation. "Deputy Keller, would you please call him on his cell phone and find out where he is? Maybe he's had car trouble."

Sonny Keller frowned, his expression showing the first signs of intelligence it had since he arrived. "Or maybe he met up with that sniper before you did."

FOURTEEN

I

"Just get in the car, Adrienne," Drew said impatiently. "It's getting chilly up here and you're exhausted."

"I don't think I should leave until they've located Lucas."

"There are a dozen cops looking for him."

"Not a dozen."

"A lot. And cops looking for Lottie. Cops with *guns,* which we don't have, while there happens to be someone with a semi-automatic rifle roaming around. I, for one, think we should get the hell out of Dodge before we get ourselves killed. You have a daughter to think of, Adrienne."

"Oh, that's good, use the ultimate guilt card," she nearly snarled at him, furious because he was right. She was accomplishing nothing by standing around outside of Lottie's cabin making a possible target of herself. "I can't just leave my car up here."

"Why not? What's going to happen to it? And may I point out that it's stuck? It will have to be pulled out of those ruts. My car, on the other hand, had an excellent driver behind the wheel and is still functional. In peak condition. So get in and stop bitching."

"You are *so* gallant. How could I possibly resist such an offer?"

Adrienne climbed into the dark Camaro that had cruised past her place several times one night, frightening her. Drew said he'd been looking out for her. And maybe he had, she thought. It would be like him to do something on a whim. He probably thought he was being terribly valiant. But she would still rather it was him cruising past her house than Rachel's boyfriend, Bruce Allard. Vicky said he was okay, just a little arrogant, but Adrienne liked to make her own assessments of people, and the night he'd stopped at her house and nearly insisted Rachel leave with him, he'd made a less than favorable impression.

"I thought that last yawn was going to unhinge your jaw," Drew said as they pulled off the hill and started south on the highway toward town. "Will you be able to stay awake all the way home?"

"It should only take ten minutes. I'll make it. What about you? You look fresh as a daisy."

Drew burst into laughter. "Well, now, I can't remember the last time a woman said that to me. I think it was my mother when I was two. But I've always been a night person. Sometimes it's not so great. Lends itself to insomnia."

They drove in silence through the outskirts of town, then turned onto Adrienne's street. Most of the houses had tasteful, glowing lamps standing beside their front walks. The grounds around Adrienne's house glared like an amusement park.

"Oh God," she said. "No wonder none of the neighbors are speaking to me since I had the lights installed."

"They probably can't get any sleep. It's like being in those countries where it's light half the year."

"The Land of the Midnight Sun. My mother would be so embarrassed."

Drew smiled. "Your mother would be glad you had sense enough to put up enough lights to scare away any intruder, unless he's absolutely nuts."

They pulled up in front of Adrienne's house. Drew got out and rushed to open her door, startling her. She couldn't remember the last time a man had opened a car door for her. She mumbled "Thanks" and could think of nothing else to say as he walked her to the front door, then stood looking at her. "I'm home now," Adrienne said uncomfortably. "Good night."

"You're not brushing me off. I'm staying."

"I beg your pardon?"

"No need. It's my pleasure."

"Drew, you are not spending the night with me."

"I'm not leaving you alone. You can't call Kit and ask her to stay with you. She'll be busy at the restaurant until after midnight and then she's always tired enough to drop dead. Or so I've heard."

"I *know* you have no direct knowledge of *her* sleeping habits," Adrienne said. "She's probably the only woman in town who's missed out on your charms at night."

"Oh, Adrienne, you make me blush. Of course, since Kit's not available, you could call up Ellen and have a slumber party. She could tell you about all the spooky things that have happened at la Belle."

"I think she already has," Adrienne said morosely.

"Or there's Miss Snow from the French Art Colony. Now she's a live wire. She'll keep you drinking and dancing and trying out new hairstyles till morning."

Adrienne sighed. "I guess you're invited for the night."

"Why, thank you kindly, my lady."

"Any port in a storm."

"I was hoping for a more gracious acceptance of my offer, but at least I'm getting in the door."

"And that's all you're getting, buster," Adrienne said firmly. "If I weren't scared witless tonight, you wouldn't be staying here. This is *not* a romantic evening. *No* hanky-panky. Not even any flirting."

"This is sounding like more and more fun. Am I allowed to take off my jacket, or must I keep it zipped up to my neck?"

"Zip it. I'm going to call and check on Skye. You and Brandon go sit in the living room. I'll fix you something to drink later."

"Thanks. We'll each have a margarita. With salt."

Louise Granger assured Adrienne that Skye and Sherry had gone to bed before eleven and were now pretending to be asleep, although she could hear them murmuring behind Sherry's closed door. "Can you remember being that young and having so much to say?" Louise laughed. "Of course, when every little thing from hairstyles to movie stars are of utmost importance, I guess you do have quite a bit more to say than us middle-aged women. Oh, not that you're middle-aged, Adrienne. You look a good ten years younger than me."

"No I don't," Adrienne said truthfully. "Listen, Louise, I can't tell you a whole lot about what went on tonight, but I don't want to leave you completely in the dark. The woman who was murdered at la Belle, Julianna Brent, had been a friend of mine for a long time. I was close to her mother Lottie, too. Lottie has been missing. She lives in a primitive little cabin near la Belle, and she finally called me this evening. I went up there to find her, but she wasn't home." Adrienne decided to completely omit any mention of her being the target of a rifle. "The police decided to come up and look for her. Lottie isn't well and she could be out in those woods, hurt. They wanted me to stay around for a while in case they found her so I could calm her if she was frightened by all the unfamiliar men in uniforms."

"Well, that poor thing," Louise said sympathetically. "I've heard of her. She sells candles, doesn't she? We bought some at the Women's Club. Quite a few of them, really. We do such good work at the Women's Club. You aren't a member, are you, Adrienne? You should become one. I'm sure you'd enjoy it *so* much!"

Adrienne nearly let out a groan. Since she was an adolescent, she'd hated club work. "Well, I'm pretty busy now, but we'll see. So, I just wanted to check on Skye and give you a heads-up on what kept me away from home. Thanks so much for coming to get her and letting her spend the night." Sensing that Louise was drawing breath for more conversation,

Adrienne let out a noisy, fake yawn. "Oh, my goodness, I'm nearly asleep on my feet. Can hardly hold my eyes open. Thanks again, Louise. 'Bye."

Louise was saying something about talking more about the Women's Club in the morning as Adrienne hung up. Please don't let me be a spineless wimp who gets guilt-tripped into joining, Adrienne asked whoever controlled such matters. She wasn't a joiner. That forte had always been Vicky's.

Adrienne called from the kitchen, "Are you hungry?"

"I could eat a bear," Drew yelled back.

"How about blueberry muffins instead? I got Vicky's housekeeper, Mrs. Pitt's, recipe and actually baked a successful batch this afternoon. I could heat them in the microwave and put on a pot of coffee."

"Sounds good. But what happened to the margaritas?"

"We're standing vigil tonight, Drew, *not* having a party. Besides, after one margarita Brandon always has the lampshade on his head and wants to salsa-dance."

"Sounds like fun to me."

"*Vigil,* Drew. Keep the word in mind."

Ten minutes later, Adrienne clattered back into the living room carrying an overloaded serving tray while she talked fast and furious, laughing shrilly as she slopped too much milk into coffee cups and dropped a pat of butter on her best rug.

Finally, Drew reached out and placed two fingers on her lips. "Hush, Adrienne," he said gently. "Just hush, take a deep breath, and relax."

Her false gaiety popped like a balloon. "I don't think I can. I was trying not to be a wreck, to act brave and resilient, but when I was in the kitchen, everything that's happened tonight hit me. I could be dead—"

"But you're not."

She ignored the interruption. "And here you and I sit, talking and laughing like nothing's wrong while both Lottie and Lucas are missing and someone's going around *shooting* people, for God's sake!"

"We don't know that anyone has actually been shot. You were only shot *at*—"

"Oh, that's fine. Shot *at*. I feel so much better now!"

Drew sighed. "Before you get mad at me *again* tonight, would you let me finish a thought?" Adrienne shut her mouth. "First, someone shot at you—not once but three times—and you weren't touched. Now, either that someone is a bad shot, or he didn't mean to kill you. Second, Lottie wasn't in the cabin. There was no blood, not even any sign of a struggle. Think of how easy it would for her to hide in the woods she's lived in all of her life. She probably knows of hiding places no one else has ever seen."

Adrienne thought of the Hideaway. Ellen knew about it. Would Lottie have gone there? Should *she* have told the police about the place? She hadn't. Now that seemed silly. Still, she didn't know who might be in the woods, overhearing every word she said. "Third," Drew continued, "Lucas Flynn didn't show up. That's odd, but not necessarily a disaster. A dozen things could have happened to him."

"Like what?"

"He got a flat tire."

"He doesn't answer his cell phone."

"The battery is dead."

"You have an answer for everything."

"No I don't. I'm just saying answers exist that aren't catastrophic. C'mon, Adrienne, it isn't like you to be a neurotic pessimist."

"How do you know?"

"Because I've known you since we were six. I had you completely analyzed by the time we turned seven."

Adrienne gave him a hard look. "Life is just one big joke to you, isn't it?"

To her surprise, Drew recoiled. Adrienne hadn't thought anything she could say would really touch him, much less sting. "No, Adrienne, I don't think life is a joke," he said solemnly. "I think life is hard and hurtful and very often wantonly cruel. That's why you have to look for the good things, try to be positive and not always expect the worst. If you don't, the dark side of life will overwhelm you. You probably find that philosophy as unbearably shallow and banal as you find me, but that's how I feel."

He turned his attention to his coffee, taking a deep sip and wincing slightly at its heat, then looking over at Brandon. The dog stared back at him mournfully.

"I don't think you're shallow or banal," Adrienne finally said. "It's just that in the past you were so cavalier about life. About *me*." She glanced down at her hands. "I was in love with you years ago. Really in love. And you knew it. If you didn't feel the same, you could have talked to me, let me down gently, *something* that showed an ounce of consideration for my feelings. Instead, you took off for New York after graduation, called a few times, sent some letters, then some postcards, then got married! I had to hear about your marriage from someone else. Do you have any idea how that felt? I deserved better from you, Drew Delaney. I deserved *better*!"

Drew stood up, walked to the front window, and stared out at her front lawn blazing under dusk-to-dawn lights. "Don't stand in front of the window," Adrienne said. "You're making yourself a perfect target if the shooter decided to follow us home."

"Thanks for caring," he said absently and stepped back without haste. He didn't seem at all concerned that someone might be aiming a rifle at him. Adrienne walked over, pulled the draperies shut, then returned to her chair. She couldn't think of a thing to say.

"Adrienne, I wish I had a good excuse for what I did back then," Drew finally began, his voice low and hesitant. "All I can say is that I was young and ambitious and extremely self-centered. *And* inexperienced. I'd lived all my life in this little town and then I went to New York City." He looked at her and smiled regretfully. "It was like being on a different planet. So much was going on all the time. I was awestruck, and I dived into the action like I used to dive into the pool at la Belle. It wasn't long before this town and everyone in it began to seem far away, not just physically but emotionally. I met new people I thought were bigger, better, more exciting than anyone I'd ever known. It took a few years for me to learn the simple lesson that people are basically the same underneath no matter where they live. It's only the façade that sometimes glitters more brightly. And that's when I decided to come home and try to start over."

"Start what over? Your career?"

"Partly. Mostly my personal life. I've been married twice, Adrienne, and I didn't really know either of those women."

"What are you saying? That the divorces happened because they disappointed you? They weren't good women?"

"They were probably fine women. Honestly, I didn't get to know either of them well, not the way you should know a wife. I didn't bother to because I quickly realized they weren't what I'd once had, what I wanted more than anything." He looked at her. "They weren't you."

Adrienne fell silent, stunned. Drew went back to looking out the window. She stared at the floor. The phone went off like a bomb and Adrienne nearly leaped out of her chair.

"Good grief!" she yelled accusingly at no one, then ran to answer. It was Lucas.

"Are you all right?" he asked.

"Yes. Yes, I'm fine, considering. Lucas, where *were* you?"

"In a ditch. Unconscious. Someone shot out one of my tires. I went careening off the highway into the woods. Then they shot me in the shoulder. It took a little while for Sonny Keller and the troops to find me."

"My God," she breathed. "How badly are you hurt?"

"The doctor says I'll live. The shot went straight through and there's no bone damage. I could in good conscience take a day off, but I don't want to. I couldn't stand to. I have to find out what's going on in this area." He paused. "Keller filled me in on what happened to you."

"No doubt it was the same shooter, but how did he know to get both of us? No one knew you were coming to Lottie's."

"I don't know," Lucas said vaguely. He sounded as if he were in pain. "I must have been followed. And so were you."

She knew Drew had followed her. He openly admitted it. But she was certain he hadn't shot at her. That meant there was another player in the game, someone still out there, still waiting for another shot.

2

After Lucas's call, Adrienne told Drew the sheriff was wounded but not seriously, the trouble seemed to have died down for the night, and he could leave.

"I don't think so," he returned equably after a moment of thought. "Lottie hasn't been found. Neither has the shooter. That doesn't make me feel any better about your safety than I did a half hour ago. So I'm staying until morning whether or not I'm welcome."

Adrienne worked hard at looking resigned to hide her vast relief. She was still deeply shaken by the shooting at Lottie's cabin, and the fear she'd carried around with her for the past few days remained settled like a cold rock in her stomach. She was jittery. She was cold. She was wide awake, every nerve tingling. She couldn't imagine calming down for weeks, much less tonight, and she was glad she didn't have to wait alone through the long dark hours until morning.

Both she and Drew agreed they were too wired to sleep, but they still switched from caffeine-infused coffee to wine in an effort to wind down a notch. Adrienne put on some music, and they sat down a few inches apart on the couch. Brandon fell into a comfortable, snoring stupor at their feet.

Finally Drew asked, "Does Lucas have any idea who might have shot him?"

"No. But he said they haven't been able to locate Miles Shaw since he was questioned before noon yesterday about Margaret's murder. Miles seems to be purposely making himself scarce."

"Shaw has no reason to be frightened. He has an alibi. At least ten people have already sworn they saw him in Heaven's Door at the time of Margaret's murder."

"Ten people? How do you know that?"

Drew looked at her cannily. "I have sources in the police department, my dear. I know every word Shaw said in his interrogation and every step that's been taken in the ensuing investigation."

"Well, aren't you the deep one," Adrienne said, only half joking. "But I shouldn't be surprised. Even back in high school you had a gift for keeping your finger on the pulse of things."

"It is a rare and fine gift," Drew agreed solemnly. "It's called being nosy."

"Lots of people are nosy but they aren't good at finding out what they want to know. You are a master at it. No wonder you went into journalism. But back in high school, you claimed your goal was to write the Great American Novel."

"About five hundred thousand other people and I want to write it and end up working at newspapers instead." He drained his wine and reached for the bottle that sat on the huge stained-glass-topped table in front of them. "Good wine."

"Nothing expensive. I'm hardly a connoisseur like my brother-in-law."

"Philip probably doesn't even like wine. He just collects expensive vintages because he considers it the correct thing to do for someone in his social position. Philip always does the correct thing."

"*Almost* always," Adrienne said sourly, instantly regretting her words when Drew gave her a quick, curious look.

Still, in this moment of closeness, Adrienne wanted desperately to ask Drew if he'd known about Philip and Julianna. She couldn't, though. She had to remember that Drew was a newspaperman. Philip was family. Technically, at least. Philip had never felt like family to her, and she knew his feelings toward her were less than kind. They'd always barely tolerated each other. Julianna's passion for him baffled her. So did her ability to keep it a secret for so long. Adrienne never had a clue. Had Kit known? Drew tilted his head, his dark eyes twinkling at her. "What's on your mind?"

"The strange ways of romance." He raised his eyebrows and she went on, knowing drinking too much wine too fast was making her dangerously talkative but unable to stop herself. "I mean, the way people are attracted to each other. Or not. There can be a man and woman you'd think would ignite all kinds of sparks between each other, but *phttt*. Nothing. Then there are some people you would never expect to look twice at each other and they fall madly in love. *Really* in love for years. Maybe forever, if love actually goes on forever, even beyond death." She looked at him. "I'm babbling."

"No you're not. You have something definite on your mind. I *know* your talk of love lasting forever wasn't inspired by Margaret and Miles. I *hope* it wasn't inspired by you and Lucas Flynn." She dropped her gaze. "You're thinking about Philip and Julianna, aren't you?"

She gaped. "You *knew*?" He nodded. "How? For how long?"

"How did I know? By watching. Closely, I admit, but neither one of them is an outstanding actor. For how long? For years. Since Julianna was a teenager. The first time I saw them together when I came back from New York, I could see that their feelings had only gotten stronger."

"I'm astonished," Adrienne said faintly. "I didn't see anything."

"I don't believe that. You're too perceptive to have missed

it. You just shut out what you saw because Julianna was one of your best friends and Philip is married to your sister."

"You really saw it twenty years ago?"

"I really did. At la Belle, where all weird things flourish. Ellen Kirkwood isn't completely off her rocker for thinking there's something definitely not right about that place. It seems to be a breeding ground for bad situations—violent situations, tragic situations, potentially destructive romantic situations."

"She told me the hotel's history one day, and I felt the same way you do about her not being as crazy as she sounds when she talks about the place." Adrienne took another sip of wine she knew she didn't need. "Do you think the relationship between Philip and Julianna led to Juli's murder?"

Drew nodded. "Yes, Adrienne, I do. I'm not saying I think Philip killed her, although I'm not ruling that out because he could have snapped if she got too demanding or threatened to go public. I think Philip is capable of killing in the heat of the moment." He paused. "Or, Julianna's murder could have been the product of Philip's or someone else's careful planning, of someone waiting to get her in a secluded place where the killer had plenty of time to get away. Less time because you and Skye showed up unexpectedly. But whatever the circumstances, I think Julianna was murdered because she loved Philip Hamilton."

"And the other murders?"

"By-products of the first. A terrible chain reaction to Julianna's murder."

"Oh, my God," Adrienne moaned.

"You're too smart not to have thought of this before."

"I *had* thought of it," Adrienne admitted, "but haphazardly, not as coolly and logically as you. And I didn't know until tonight that Julianna was involved with Philip. I was like Vicky. I thought he was probably dallying with Margaret."

"Or maybe that's what Vicky wanted *you* to believe that's what she thought."

"That *is* what Vicky thought, Drew. What are you trying to do? Get me to say I believed Vicky was capable of killing her rival, Julianna?"

"Instead of saying you thought she was capable of killing her rival, Margaret?"

"I did *not* think—" she began heatedly, then broke off. Yes, when she'd seen how ravaged Vicky had looked the morning after Margaret's body had been found, Adrienne had feared deep in her bones that Vicky, maybe having consumed far too much alcohol and too many pills, had done the unthinkable. Adrienne drew a deep breath, all of her defensiveness crumbling under the weight of exhaustion, and let her head drop onto Drew's shoulder. "I don't know what I think anymore and I'm getting a helluva headache."

"No wonder." Drew's right hand came up and he began massaging her neck. "This is where your tension headaches start. They always have."

"I give up. You *do* know me well. And what you're doing feels wonderful."

Adrienne sipped more wine. Drew rubbed her tight neck muscles with exactly the right amount of pressure. From the CD player, Don Henley sang "Taking You Home," about the love he'd found that was like nothing he'd ever known before. Adrienne lost herself in the lyrics, drifting along with Don's words and Drew's gentle and familiar touch. With a start, she realized that for the first time in days—maybe even years—she felt warm and secure and, incredibly, *loved*.

Her head jerked up. "What's wrong?" Drew asked huskily, his breath warm on her cheek, his depthless dark eyes probing hers. She couldn't answer. She didn't trust her own voice. As if understanding what she wouldn't make herself say, he gave her the old, intimate smile she knew so well and gently placed his hands on either side of her face and drew it closer to his own. "Don't worry, Adrienne," he murmured.

"We're together and everything is going to be all right. I'm going to make it all right. You'll see. So just relax for tonight, my darling. Pretend we're the only two people in the world."

And with a sigh, she did.

3

"Adrienne? Adrienne! Are you all right in there? Adrienne, I swear, if you're dead—"

Adrienne's consciousness rose, broke water, then slid into the dark, quiet depths again until the strident voice refused to let it float in peace and summoned her back to the bright colors, harsh lights, and sharp edges of the waking world. Adrienne blinked, stretched, coughed, then finally realized that Kit was pounding for all she was worth on Adrienne's big picture window right behind the couch.

"If you're asleep, wake *up*," Kit shouted. "Dear God, *please* just be asleep. Don't be dead, Adrienne. Don't you *dare* be dead!"

Adrienne opened her eyes wide, looked over at Drew, whose head moved although his eyes were still closed, then she lifted her head and glanced down at the afghan covering their naked bodies. Out of reflex, she pulled it higher, although nothing but their shoulders were exposed.

The draperies had caught on the back of the couch, leaving them open at least an inch. Squinting, she could see Kit outside trampling a marigold bed as she bent and stooped and knelt, trying to peer through the crack in the draperies. When Kit saw Adrienne move, she let out a whoop of joy and smacked her hands against the glass. Adrienne groaned. Then slowly, every muscle and joint rebelling, she rolled off the couch and began scrambling for her clothes. She finally made it to the front door, fumbled with the lock and dead bolt, then opened it to a dazzling blaze of morning light.

Adrienne immediately shut her eyes against the brightness as Kit pulled her forward and closed strong arms around her. "God, Adrienne, why didn't you answer your phone? You just go around getting shot at, run home, and unplug the phone!"

"I didn't unplug the phone." Adrienne's tongue felt too big for her mouth. "Besides, I have a cell phone."

"Two phones, no answer." Kit stepped inside and closed the door behind her, mercifully shutting out the blinding morning light. Adrienne glanced at her through slitted eyes. Kit's short, dark hair looked as if she'd run a damp comb through it, not put it through the ritual washing and curling-iron routine, and her eyes were bloodshot from sleep deprivation. She wore sweatpants and a wrinkled T-shirt, her pale skin had a grayish cast, and a narrow scratch snaked its way across her forehead. "I have been worried *sick* about you."

"I'm sorry. You have no idea—"

"You're right." Kit suddenly sounded angry. "I have no idea because you wouldn't bother to let me or anyone else know you were all right." She glanced over at Drew, floundering on the couch like some dazed creature on unfamiliar territory. "Well, no wonder you didn't want to bother answering the phone."

"Kit, I was not avoiding the phone," Adrienne returned irritably. Then she had a horrible thought. What if Drew stood up. He wore nothing under the afghan. "Coffee!" she nearly shouted. "I must have coffee! Come into the kitchen with me."

Kit had begun to grin. She turned to the living room and called, "Drew, stop struggling with that afghan. You look like you're in pain. Coffee is coming up."

"Thank God," he groaned as the two women disappeared into the kitchen.

Adrienne reached for the coffee bin and Kit sat down at the kitchen table. "Before you start firing more questions at me," Adrienne said, "tell me to what I owe this frantic morning visit, flatteringly loud joy over discovering that I'm not dead, and fury that I didn't answer a phone that never rang."

"Gail Brent. She called me this morning. You know she dates Sonny Keller, the cop. He told her all about you going to Lottie's cabin, someone shooting at you, you getting away but Lucas being shot. When I couldn't reach you, I was afraid whoever shot at you at the cabin got to you later." Kit paused. "I don't think Keller knew Drew Delaney was keeping you company while Lucas is in the hospital. If so, he'd be spreading the news all over town. Of course, *I'm* surprised—no, *stunned*—myself, although I've never thought Lucas was right for you. He's too serious."

"This is not a big deal, Kit. Drew was protecting me."

Kit exploded into laughter. "Stop cackling," Adrienne snapped, although her facial expression wasn't as stern as her voice. "We had quite an evening."

"I'm *sure*," Kit guffawed.

"Will you quit it? You sound like you're fifteen."

"And the two of you *look* like you're fifteen, all tousled hair, guilty glances, and flaming cheeks."

"Flaming cheeks? You're imagining that. Drew has never blushed in his life. Besides, neither of us has anything to blush about."

"Come on, Adrienne, I'm your best friend. I deserve to get the details about everything. You can start with the shooting."

"Thank you. I thought you found the shooting part boring, just a prelude leading up to the *big moment* with Drew."

"I want to hear about the whole evening. And you're dumping way too many grounds in the coffeemaker basket."

"No I'm not. Drew and I need something to wake us up. We drank quite a bit of wine. Just to relax."

"While he was protecting you. All good bodyguards drink while doing their jobs."

"Do you have an extra toothbrush?" Drew yelled from the bathroom.

Kit bent double with laughter. "This gets better and better."

"Oh, be quiet," Adrienne snarled, unable to stop herself from grinning. "There's an unopened one in the medicine cabinet," she called back to Drew.

"If he asks for bubble bath, I won't be able to bear it," Kit choked out.

"If he asks for the bubble bath, I'm throwing both of you out." Adrienne flipped on the coffeemaker. "About my almost being killed last night."

"Oh yes." Kit wiped tears from her eyes and made an effort to look properly horrified. "What happened?"

"I'm sure you got the basic story from Gail." Adrienne sat down at the table as the coffeemaker kicked into action. "Lottie called me. She sounded really sick, but she refused to come into town. She wouldn't even tell me where she was, but I guessed she was at the cabin, so I decided I'd go to her without letting her know I was coming. I called Lucas and asked him to meet me there. I went, and as I was walking into the cabin, someone shot at me. With a *rifle*, I might add, not a handgun. Obviously, they missed. I hit the floor and was absolutely frozen and then Drew came along. Apparently, he'd been following me. Lottie wasn't in the cabin. Lucas never showed up. So, Drew called 911. Then he brought me home and stayed with me in case whoever tried to kill me the first time decided to try it again. He didn't want me to be alone. That's all there is to our being together."

"Try that last part on someone who didn't look through the slit between the draperies at the front window and see the two of you all wrapped up together on the couch."

"We *weren't* wrapped up together."

"You didn't see yourselves. Where's Skye?"

"At Sherry Grangers's. I sent her there as soon as trouble started at the cabin. I just hope she hasn't heard anything about the shooting." Adrienne paused. "You said Gail called you with the news. Why?"

"Because you're my friend."

"But Gail isn't *our* friend. I didn't think she'd care less what happened to either one of us."

Kit shot her a troubled glance. "You know, I was so upset over what she told me about you, I didn't even think about how odd it was for her to call me all full of concern for you. And you know something else? I asked her about her mother, and she said in this offhand tone that Lottie hadn't been found but that she'd turn up. Considering the shooting, that's cold, even for Gail."

"I agree." Adrienne got up to pour coffee. "How did you scratch your forehead?"

"What? Oh, that. I came tearing down the rear stairs from my apartment this morning and just missed smacking into a limb on the dogwood tree. I guess a twig got me. Is it bleeding?"

"There was a little bit of blood, but it's dried. You need to put some antiseptic on it, though. I have some in the bathroom."

"Which is occupied."

"Not for long." Adrienne set a mug of coffee in front of Kit, then headed out of the kitchen with another in her hand.

"Coffee in the bathroom?" Kit teased. "Not quite as good as breakfast in bed."

"It's as good as it gets around here."

Adrienne met Drew coming out of the bathroom. His face was flushed from vigorous splashing with cold water, his dark eyes were as bloodshot as Kit's, his hair stood on end, and Adrienne's heart caught at how gorgeous he looked in spite of it all. "Here," she said abruptly, thrusting the coffee mug at him and feeling like a girl of Skye's age with a crush.

Drew took it gratefully. "I'll have time to run home and take a shower and shave, but no time for breakfast. Eggs and toast I can manage without. Caffeine is a different matter." He slurped coffee. "Good and strong. Hey, is Kit giving you a hard time about me being here?"

"Just relentless teasing."

"Well, if it gets too bad, ask her where Miles Shaw spent the night."

"What do you mean?"

"I saw him going up the back stairs to her apartment last night."

"Before you followed me to Lottie's? Really, Drew, do you ever spend an evening at home minding your own business?"

"Not if I can help it."

"Miles Shaw?" Adrienne asked softly. "Are you sure?"

"It's kind of hard to mistake him for someone else. The guy's a giant and his hair is three feet long."

"Probably longer. I wonder what he was doing there?"

"I don't know, but he was carrying a knapsack *and* a small suitcase." Drew emptied his coffee mug and handed it back to her. "Thanks for this. I have to run." He hesitated, then leaned forward and gave her a glancing kiss on the cheek. "Take care of yourself today."

Adrienne stood in the hall, thoughts churning, until she heard the front door close. Drew Delaney had spent the night with her. Drew Delaney had kissed her good-bye. She thought she might be falling in love with Drew Delaney again. Good God.

"Adrienne, are you okay?"

Kit stood in front of her looking exhausted and worried. "Sure." Adrienne realized she didn't sound sure at all. "I'm just distracted. It was a long night. I'm worried about Lucas and Lottie. I need to pick up Skye and tell her about the shooting before she hears the news from someone else."

"I really don't think you should go out today considering

the attack on you last night," Kit said. "If you give me directions to the Granger house, I'll pick up Skye."

"Thanks, but the Grangers don't know you."

"Then call ahead and tell them I'll be picking up Skye. You aren't even dressed yet, Adrienne. I can have her back here before you're out of the shower."

Adrienne thought of how good hot water would feel on her sore neck and back muscles, and how much more cheerful she could look for Skye with shampooed hair and a touch of lipstick and blush. She didn't want her daughter to be any more worried than her banishment from the house last night must have made her feel already.

"All right. I'll call the Grangers. It's not far and I'm sure Skye is awake. Be sure to tell her that I'm fine."

After she'd given Kit directions, Adrienne opened the front door. Bright morning sun streamed in. "At least it's a nice day," she said. "I was afraid it would rain, which would make searching for Lottie even harder."

"Not to mention her being out in the rain making her even sicker." Kit stepped onto the porch. "Be back in a flash with your daughter." Adrienne was closing the door when Kit leaned toward the lilac bush and asked, "What's this?"

Adrienne opened the door again and stepped outside as Kit leaned down and picked up a manila envelope tucked under the lower branches of the bush. She held it out to Adrienne, who peered at the large, printed words on the front:

To Adrienne
Memories

"Memories?" Kit asked blankly. "Memories of what?"

But Adrienne didn't hear her as she opened the envelope and withdrew a photograph. Then her world shifted as she looked at a picture of her husband, Trey, lying beside a mangled motorcycle, his body contorted like a broken doll's, his right cheekbone sticking through what was left of the shredded skin on his face, and his left arm torn loose and resting nearly a foot away from his body.

"Dear God," Adrienne mumbled as she dropped the photo and sank slowly into an unconscious heap on the porch.

FIFTEEN

I

Miles Shaw stepped out of the shower half-blinded by steam from the nearly scalding water he loved, and began vigorously toweling himself. When he finished, he wrapped the towel around his long, black hair and walked barefooted into the bedroom. To his embarrassment, he nearly let out a girlish scream when he saw Gail Brent sitting on the bed. Her blue gaze traveled up and down his naked body before she slowly smiled and said, "Good morning, Miles. Did Kit take out room and board for last night in money or in trade?"

Miles whipped the towel off his head and held it in front of his crotch. Gail laughed delightedly. "Oh, Miles, really! Believe me, it isn't *that* special."

"How did you get in here?" he snarled, his face flushing under her scrutiny.

"Do you think I've worked at the restaurant all these years without managing to get a key to the apartment right upstairs?"

"*Kit's* apartment. She'd fire you if she knew you had a key."

"Yes, she would," Gail said nonchalantly.

"How often do you sneak into this place?"

"Only when I think there might be something intriguing going on. And you spending the night at this stage of the game certainly falls under the heading of intriguing. You see, I thought you were pining away in celibacy for my sister these past two years. Then I found out you've been having a hot affair with Margaret Taylor." Gail assumed a look of anxiety. "Gosh, Miles, isn't it a shame all your lady loves turn up murdered? It's so damned tragic, not to mention scary. And now you're all alone. Is that why you came running back to Kit? Because there's no one left? Or did you come back so you could kill her, too?"

Miles's fists clenched and his voice turned into a dangerously controlled whisper. "I didn't kill anyone and you know it."

Gail's eyes widened. "Why would I know that, Miles? Do you think I believe in the purity of your soul, your intrinsic goodness?" She smiled derisively. "*Intrinsic*. I'll bet Julianna didn't even know what that word meant. But then no one cares how good your vocabulary is when you're beautiful. Hell, they don't care if you can talk."

Miles glowered at her. His breath came fast and hard. Then, almost instantly, he appeared to grow calm. He walked to the chair by the bed, picked up his black jeans, and slipped them on, slowly pulling up the zipper as if he were alone.

"No underwear?" Gail asked coyly. "Good heavens, you really are a heathen."

Miles looked at her through narrowed eyes. "What-do-you-want?"

"I want to know why you're in Kit's apartment."

"That's none of your business."

"I'm making it my business. After all, you used to be my brother-in-law."

"As if family relationships mean *anything* to you."

"Even if they did, you're not family anymore." Gail tilted her head, smiling triumphantly. "I've got it! You're hiding, aren't you? But from whom? Not the police. You came up with an alibi for the time of Julianna's murder. You even managed one for the time of Margaret's murder. The cops are satisfied for now. You're not dodging arrest. So what's the deal, Miles?"

"Maybe I just wanted to be with Kit."

"That's a laugh. Not that I think she wouldn't just die to have you." She made a comic face. "Oh, pardon me for mentioning *die* in reference to one of your girlfriends."

"Kit has no reason to fear me. She knows that. Besides, she wasn't even here last night."

For the first time, Gail's round face lost every trace of humor. "She wasn't here?"

"She went out for a while." Miles hastily turned away from her and reached for his shirt.

"When did she go out? For how long?"

"I wasn't keeping tabs on her." Miles's voice became extremely casual. "What's your interest, anyway?"

"I heard there was some trouble up at la Belle last night."

"What kind of trouble?"

"You're getting really good at that innocent look, Miles." He didn't answer. "I don't know all the details. Something to do with Adrienne Reynolds. And my mother."

"Trouble with your mother? And you don't know the details?"

Gail shrugged. "My mother is always in some kind of mess. I don't pay much attention anymore."

"You never paid attention to her."

"Don't get sanctimonious on me, Miles."

He turned on her, his face livid. "What the hell do you want, Gail? Are you tracking down me or Kit?"

Gail bit her lip for a moment, suddenly appearing young and unsure. Then confidence seemed to seep back into her. She stood up in her too-tight jeans and low-cut top, pushed her thick hair behind one ear to display a dangling star-shaped earring, and threw him a cool look. "Maybe I'm checking up on you *and* Kit, Miles. After all, both of you have things to hide, especially about Julianna."

"Oh. You're investigating your sister's murder. That's touching, Gail. Really touching, since I know how much you loved her."

All the taunting drained from her face and her voice. "No, I did *not* love Julianna. And I won't pretend to be sorry that she's dead, but I don't intend to let *anyone* drag me into the fallout created by her murder. Or into any of the other bad stuff that's been going on in this town. No one's going to put the blame on me for anything. Not you, not Kit, not my mother, *no one.*"

"Your mother? What does your mother have to do with anything?"

"More than you know, Miles," Gail said solemnly. "More than you could even guess."

2

"If you don't open your eyes, I'm going to throw cold water on your face," Kit said. "*Ice* cold water. Now wake up!"

Adrienne grimaced, slowly opened her eyes a fraction, then closed them again. "My head hurts."

"No wonder. You banged it on the porch floor. Honestly, Adrienne, your brain is going to be mush if you don't stop bashing it on concrete."

"Thanks for the comforting words." Memory of the horrible photograph of Trey rushed back and she groaned. "Oh God, Kit. That picture. Trey's face, his arm—"

"Don't think about it," Kit said briskly. "You never saw it. It doesn't exist."

"What are you talking about? I held it in my hand. It was lying in an envelope under the lilac bush."

"You're going to *imagine* you didn't see it. I just read a book on how we can push ugly memories right out of our frontal lobes, or rearview lobes, or wherever memories are stored, if we just *try.* Go with me on this, Adrienne."

"You should get your money back for that stupid book." Adrienne sat up and touched the back of her head. "Ouch."

"It's a good thing you have plenty of hair." Kit began

parting Adrienne's hair and looking closely at her scalp. Adrienne thought they must look like monkeys in the zoo, one inspecting the other for lice. "I don't see any blood. I don't think you're cut."

"That's one blessing. The French Art Colony gala is tomorrow. I wouldn't want to go with a section of my head shaved where they had to stitch me up." She blinked against the morning sun, then forced her eyes open wide. "Help me up, please. My legs feel really weak."

Kit hoisted her up and led her on shaky legs to a chair in the living room. "I'm going to get you a cup of coffee," Kit said after Adrienne had leaned back in the chair and closed her eyes. "Or would you rather have a drink? Maybe some wine?"

"Kit, it's seven-thirty in the morning. Besides, after all the wine I drank last night, the very sight of more would make me throw up."

"Coffee it is, then. You sit still."

"I can't do anything else."

Although Adrienne's body felt paralyzed by shock, her thoughts dashed, plunged, scrambled, and raced. She opened her eyes and looked down at the photo she still clutched in her hand.

Trey Reynolds had wrecked a friend's new Harley-Davidson Electra Glide at ten-twenty on a mild May night. Adrienne remembered standing in the driveway, begging him not to go after he'd consumed numerous beers. He'd totally ignored her pleas not to go while he fumbled trying to find the starter button. After he'd fired the motorcycle into roaring life and blasted down the quiet street, she'd looked up at the sky. The moon had been full and creamy, the stars had tossed down spears of pure white light, fireflies had flashed brilliant pinpoints of color in the darkness, and Adrienne had thought it was one of the most beautiful nights she'd ever seen.

It had followed a happy afternoon—Skye's tenth-birthday

party, held on Vicky's big, lovely back lawn. Trey had presented Skye with Brandon, fresh from a trip to Happy Tracks Grooming Salon, shiny and smelling like a rose and wearing a red bow. Skye had been ecstatic, and Brandon had been one hundred pounds of immediate love for his new mistress and joy at being freed from the dog pound. After Skye went to bed, full of cake and ice cream, her new dog lying beside her, Trey had begun drinking, an all-too-common habit he'd fallen into over the last two years.

And on this particular day, the habit had caused his death.

Now, looking down at the photo, Adrienne was seeing Trey after his collision with a semi, his broken body harshly illuminated by the flash from police cameras. He looked so small lying on the road by the mangled Harley, his legs twisted beneath him, his arm lying a foot away from his body, his open eyes blank above the rest of his torn and ravaged face.

Kit returned with the coffee, set it down beside Adrienne, then took the photo out of her hand. "You've tortured yourself enough," she said, sliding the photo back into the envelope.

"I didn't go to the scene of the wreck," Adrienne said in a weak voice. "I identified Trey at the morgue. He was lying on a table with a sheet over him, his eyes closed, a bandage covering that exposed cheekbone. I knew how badly he'd been hurt, but I didn't *see* the damage." Her eyes filled with tears. "God, Kit, *look* at him."

"I don't want to look again. And you're not going to, either. The photo stays in the envelope. That's final."

Adrienne pulled her legs up into the chair and tucked them under her robe. Her hands trembled as she raised the cup of steaming coffee to her lips and she didn't even feel its heat as it went down her throat. She felt as if she'd never be warm again. Nor would she ever forget the grotesque image of her young husband, Skye's father, in that awful photograph.

"Who would send that thing to me?" she asked faintly.

"Whoever knocked you down outside of Photo Finish and took your purse. Whoever broke into your house and wrote 'leave or die' on your mirror. Whoever shot at you last night."

"But I can tell that this is a police photograph, Kit. It came from police files. Who could have gotten it in the first place?"

Kit had sunk down on the floor beside her and now sat cross-legged, sipping her own cup of coffee. She was quiet for a moment, then shook her head. "I don't know, Adrienne. Not Lucas."

"Good Lord, no!" Adrienne was appalled by the thought. "He would never do something so cruel."

"You're right. Even if he knew about Drew being here last night, I can't imagine him wanting to scare you. He's always tried to give you courage. Even after your house was vandalized, he encouraged you to stay, not run for the hills." She frowned. "He couldn't be jealous of Trey, could he?"

Adrienne almost choked on her coffee. "Jealous of Trey! That's ridiculous. Trey has been dead for four years, and I don't dwell on him. At least to other people. I tell Skye stories about him—good stories—so she'll always remember her father. But I don't think I've mentioned him more than five or six times to Lucas in the whole year we've been seeing each other. Besides, having me look at this picture would hardly be the best way to make me put Trey out of my mind."

"You're right." Kit went silent, then said with a note of restraint in her voice, "Adrienne, Drew is the editor of the newspaper. Wouldn't it be possible for him to get hold of police photos?"

"Drew? How?"

"I don't know. He could give some excuse."

"To whom? A deputy? And he'd just hand over the file?"

"Maybe not a *male* deputy." Kit ran the tip of her tongue

over her upper lip as she always did when she was nervous. "Drew *does* have a way with the ladies, as my mother would put it. He can charm the birds out of the trees—"

"Quit hiding behind your mother's clichés," Adrienne said sharply. "You mean Drew might have been underhanded enough to dazzle some bubble-headed female at police headquarters into giving him the file. Well, I don't think they employ bubbleheads and Drew wouldn't do something like that. He might be guilty of sometimes using less than honorable means to get a story, but there's no story in Trey's death. Not after all these years. And how could you believe Drew wants to hurt me? For heaven's sake, he *saved* me last night."

"*And* the night you were mugged. Haven't you noticed that he always just happens to be in the right place at the right time? Like being here last night to unplug your phone so no one could reach you, come over to keep you company, and send him home?"

"Kit, the phones weren't unplugged. The one in the living room was plugged in when I called Skye this morning. Have you forgotten how many times you reversed the last two numerals of my phone number? Did it occur to you that you were upset and dialed the wrong number?"

Kit looked slightly embarrassed for a moment and mumbled, "Well, maybe I did." Then she swallowed and came back loudly, refusing to give in on the point. "But your cell phone was in Drew's car."

"*I* left it there."

"And *he* didn't bring it in until this morning."

"We'd had a hell of an evening. He had more on his mind than collecting the stuff I forgot to bring inside. And what about this photo? You think he got it from police files. Well, even if he did, what was it doing under my lilac bush?"

"He put it there. Last night. Or this morning. I don't know when. He had the opportunity, Adrienne. You can't deny *that*."

Adrienne stared at Kit, wanting desperately to say something that would absolutely demolish every point Kit had made about Drew.

But, to Adrienne's total dismay, she couldn't.

3

"I got here as soon as I could," Adrienne said. "How are you feeling?"

Lucas Flynn's heavily muscled frame looked too big for the narrow hospital bed. His right arm was heavily bandaged at the shoulder, and a glorious bruise decorated the left side of his forehead. "I feel better than I look."

"I hope so because you're extremely pale."

"The blessings of painkillers are responsible for my physical comfort. And I look washed out, not *pale*. Pale is for sissies." He grinned at her. "Stop hovering in the doorway and come sit beside me. Getting a close look at that beautiful face will do more for me than any medicine they have in this place."

Adrienne edged closer to the bed and sat down in a vinyl-covered chair. Drew Delaney had spent the night with her. She'd entertained the thought that she might be in love with him. Again. Now she felt as if her expression reflected every ounce of guilt she felt, but Lucas didn't seem to notice. She started to burst out with apologies and explanations for her behavior, then decided that relieving her conscience would be selfish. Lucas had been shot last night. He could have been killed because she'd insisted he meet her at Lottie's. She felt even guiltier and knew she had to concentrate on making him feel better, not saying anything to hurt him.

She hid behind an obvious question. "Do you have any idea who did this, Lucas?"

"Not yet."

"I don't mean to be morbid, but I don't have any details about how this happened to you."

Lucas reached out and took her hand. "I was coming to meet you and suddenly I had a blowout. At least I thought it was a blowout. I now know someone shot the tire. The road is lined with trees, and I nearly went into one getting the car under control. I got out to look at the tire and I heard the second shot." He grimaced. "In the movies, the cop always says 'it's just a flesh wound' and goes on like he's only been stung by a bee. I can tell you that even flesh wounds don't feel like bee stings. It felt like my shoulder had exploded and I went down like a rock, not to mention that I hit my forehead on one and knocked myself out. It'll be a long time before I live that one down at headquarters."

"The only important thing is that you're all right," Adrienne said sincerely. "You *are* all right, aren't you?"

"I'm fine. I should be out of here by noon."

"Lucas, I called you on your cell phone. I told you it was important for your destination not to go out over the scanners. But it must have, for the shooter to know our destination."

"It didn't."

"Then how?"

"Don't you think I've racked my brain over that question? Someone could have been following me. Or you. But both of us?"

"No, that doesn't make sense. Unless two people are involved."

"Maybe, but unlikely." He looked at her closely. "But enough about me and my unfortunate mishap. You were almost shot, too. And although you're always beautiful, you don't look like you're feeling too well today. They told me you weren't hurt."

"Not at all."

"But you couldn't sleep after being shot at with a rifle, right?"

"You're sure it was a rifle?"

"Keller found some shell casings and bullets. Ballistics will tell us more about the rifle later today. But you didn't answer my question. Do you look so shaken up because of last night?"

Although Adrienne didn't want to upset him, she knew she had to tell him the events of the morning. At least part of them. "Something bad happened earlier today. Kit came over and we found a manila envelope beside the lilac bush at the edge of the porch." She took a deep breath. "Inside the envelope was a photo taken of Trey at the scene of his motorcycle wreck. It was horrible. It was also a police photo, Lucas. It must have been taken from Trey's file."

Lucas looked dubious, but his hand tightened on hers. "Seeing a picture like that must have been awful. But Adrienne, you know accidents attract all kinds of weirdos, some of them with cameras. It couldn't have been a police photo. The police files are closely watched."

Without a word, Adrienne picked up her tote bag, withdrew the manila envelope, and handed it to Lucas. He pulled out the photo and stared at it for a full ten seconds. "Dammit," he finally said. "This *is* a crime scene photo."

"Then how did it make its way to my front door?" Adrienne asked without accusation.

"If I'd had enough manpower to provide twenty-four-hour surveillance for you, this couldn't have happened."

"Oh, I'm not so sure. Where's there's a will, there's a way. Obviously someone was clever enough to get into locked files. The question is, who is both that clever and that determined to frighten me?" Adrienne paused. "Deputy Keller?"

"Sonny Keller? I have no respect for the guy, but why would he take out this photo?"

"Because Gail Brent asked him to?" Lucas looked at her quizzically. "Lucas, Gail dates Sonny. Gail also hates me. And I think she has something to do with why her mother is hiding like a fugitive. Gail doesn't seem to want her mother found, but I won't stop looking. Maybe this is her way of trying to scare me off, if the shooting didn't do the trick."

She thought Lucas would tell her in a kind and patient voice that her imagination was running away with her. Instead, his expression turned grim and he rang for a nurse. One appeared almost instantly. "Get a doctor in here to release me," he said without his usual courteous tone.

She gave him an automatic, placating smile. "The doctor will be here soon, Sheriff, but he's seeing a few other people first. I could get you some coffee or juice to sip on while you wait."

"I don't want coffee or juice. I want to be released. *Now.* Do I make myself clear?" With a mumbled, "Yes, sir," she scuttled away and Lucas turned to Adrienne, his face angry and determined. "I'm going to get to the bottom of this photo business, Adrienne, and when I find out who did this to you, I promise you that they are going to be *extremely* sorry."

SIXTEEN

I

"I want to assure you that all the board members here at the French Art Colony understand that you won't be able to attend the gala tomorrow night," Miss Snow said with unconvincing sweetness. "It's a shame, of course, but life has a way of taking unfortunate turns."

"But I have every intention of attending the gala," Adrienne said into the phone receiver. "I wouldn't miss it for the world."

"Oh . . . really." Miss Snow sounded so dismayed Adrienne almost burst out laughing. "Well, my dear, I don't listen to gossip but I'm afraid I have heard some of the dreadful things that have happened to you lately. I . . . *we* all realize how anxiety-ridden you must be and that attending the gala would just add more strain to an already troubled period in your life."

And you're terrified the "dreadful things" will follow me like little ghouls to the Art Colony and turn your gala into a disaster, Adrienne thought. "The last couple of weeks have been rather vexing," she said, imitating Miss Snow's archaic manner of speech, "but I'm sure the gala will provide a wonderful diversion for me. *And* my daughter."

"Oh!" Miss Snow's disposition clearly dropped yet another notch. "You are planning to bring her, too?"

"Certainly. She has a new dress. She's very excited."

"Yes, well, it *will* be an exciting event. Not one I'm certain is quite suited to *children,* but . . ." Adrienne could almost hear the woman casting around in her stuffy mind for ways to dissuade Adrienne from attending. "There will be a great many people here. Perhaps one of the people who has been giving you so much trouble. God forbid, of course," she added as an afterthought.

"Oh, I don't think anyone would try to create trouble for me in such a crowded arena," Adrienne returned. "Besides, my sister and her husband were planning to come with me. Vicky and Philip Hamilton? Do you know them?"

"Philip Hamilton? The gubernatorial candidate is planning to come to the gala?"

"Yes. If *I* do. If I don't come, he might skip it. But perhaps that would be best if you're afraid my presence might cause an embarrassing scene of some sort. Yes, you definitely might have a point."

"Well, my dear, let's not jump to conclusions," Miss Snow said hastily. "I do tend to worry too much—all of my relatives say so—and perhaps I have been creating problems where none exist. You're probably quite right—no one would threaten you or draw attention to themselves in an unseemly way in front of so many people. And it would be so disappointing if Mr. Hamilton did not attend. Oh, you too, of course. You do have a painting entered in the contest."

A painting you don't give a damn about, Adrienne thought. All you care about is the wealthy and prestigious Philip Hamilton attending your event. But she felt no rancor. Miss Snow couldn't help being a snob. She'd been reared to be one and had maintained the tradition all of her eighty-plus years of life.

"Who was that?" Skye asked, walking into the room.

"Just Miss Snow making sure we were still coming to the gala."

"She thought we'd skip it?" Skye looked stunned. "We've been looking forward to it for weeks. Your painting is in the contest. Aunt Vicky and Uncle Philip and *Rachel* are coming!" Rachel's attendance clinched it for Skye. Wild animals couldn't have kept her away.

Adrienne smiled at her daughter. "Do you want to try on your dress one more time for me so we're sure we have the hem just right?"

"Yeah!" Skye said excitedly. "And I'm not sure which necklace to wear. I'll let you decide which looks the most grown-up."

Adrienne leaned back in her chair, exhausted from the night, still reeling from the attempt on her life at Lottie's cabin and the photo of Trey someone had left for her this morning. She hadn't heard from Lucas since his hurried flight from the hospital, but that had only been a couple of hours ago. He hadn't had time to find out much. He hadn't been in condition to do anything, really. He should have been at home, resting. Instead, he was working, trying to protect her.

She only hoped that when she had to tell him soon that as much as she cared for him, she was not in love with him, he wouldn't hate her and regret all he'd done for her in this situation. She wished her feelings were different. But the heart couldn't or wouldn't be deterred, she thought ruefully. And her heart, foolish as it was, belonged to Drew Delaney.

2

"Do you mind if I sit here beside you for a little while, Mr. Kirkwood?"

Gavin Kirkwood, seated at the dimly lit, cozy elegance of the Iron Gate bar, looked at tall, blond, attractive Bruce Allard. The Allard family had been friends of Ellen's for ages. The Kirkwoods had frequently dined with them until the death of little Jamie last year, but Gavin had never cared for Bruce. Kit's latest boyfriend, J.C., had been sitting at the bar as long as Gavin, but J.C. respected someone obviously in the grip of melancholy and only made the occasional comradely comment. Bruce was another matter.

No, Gavin did not feel like being sociable tonight, especially for this bright-eyed kid who struck him as almost quivering with youth and enthusiasm. This evening Gavin felt at least ninety and completely worn out with life, but Gavin always tried to be gracious in public.

"Pull up a stool, Bruce," he said. "Haven't seen you for a while."

"I've been very busy, sir. *Very* busy."

Gavin hated being called "sir." It made him feel even older. The bartender meandered down the bar, smiling blandly, and raised his eyebrows at Bruce, waiting for his order.

"I'll have a strawberry daiquiri," Bruce announced with bravado.

The bartender stared at him. J.C.'s mouth quirked with ill-concealed mirth. Even Gavin couldn't help a sideways glance. Bruce's face turned pink. "On second thought, I'll have what Mr. Kirkwood's having."

"Single malt whisky, no rocks?" the bartender asked.

Bruce looked dubious for a moment, then regained his nerve. "Yes. And make it a *double*."

J.C. rolled his eyes at Gavin, making him almost smile for the first time that evening. "So, Bruce, has Drew Delaney been working you fairly hard at the newspaper?" Gavin asked.

"Like a dog, sir."

"You really don't have to call me 'sir.' 'Gavin' will do."

"All right, sir. Gavin. Sorry, but my father is very strict about me being respectful to my elders."

"Pretend I'm your age tonight. Exactly how old are you? Twenty-five?"

"Twenty-four, sir. Gavin. Twenty-five in September. Got a big party planned. Are you and Mrs. Kirkwood coming?"

"Don't know. We haven't been invited."

"Oh, you will be. My parents will want all the best people there." The bartender set down his drink. Bruce took a big slug. His throat muscles worked as he tried to stifle a gag, and tears rose in his eyes. In a moment, he managed in a gravelly voice, "Tastes damn good after a hard day."

The bartender quickly turned his back. J.C. looked down, hiding laughter. Gavin wondered what awful thing he'd done today to deserve the company of this clown. "Are you bringing Rachel as your date to the party?" Gavin deliberately asked before the boy had fully recovered.

Bruce nodded, swallowed, and cleared his throat. "Yes," he ground out. Another swallow. "Yes, sure. She *is* my girl. I plan on marrying her someday."

"Really? Does she know that?"

"I haven't formally proposed. Don't want to get her hopes up. Actually, truth be known, I don't want to spend money on some hunk of a diamond before I have to." Bruce laughed uproariously at this witticism. "But when the time comes, she'll say yes. She realizes, like I do, that we're made for each other."

God I hope not, Gavin thought. I always rather liked Rachel. "And when the time comes, you'll buy her that hunk of a diamond," he said instead.

"I sure will."

"With that grand salary you make as a reporter for the *Register*?"

"Not a chance of that. Thank God for trust funds. I'll get her something around three carats. Hell, four. I'll want everyone to know she's *mine*." He gulped more whiskey. "This stuff gets better with every sip."

"Better take it easy. It slips up on you faster than those strawberry daiquiris."

"Oh, I was just joking," Bruce lied. "I don't drink that crap."

Gavin pretended to be amused. "I didn't think so. You're too much of a man for a girly drink."

"Darn tootin'." Bruce looked surprised at the country expression that had just escaped his Princeton-educated mouth. "How's Mrs. Kirkwood these days?"

"Not so well. Her friend Lottie is missing. But I'm sure you know about that."

"Sure I do." Bruce looked meaningfully at the bartender who asked, "Another double?" Bruce nodded yes. He intended to be one hell of a man tonight. "I know about Lottie Brent. I've heard about her all my life. She's sort of a town character, isn't she? Tell me, Mr., uh . . . Gavin, has she always been crazy?"

Gavin stiffened at the young man's snickering tone. "She's been a friend of my wife's since childhood. I don't think Ellen would appreciate hearing Lottie called *crazy*."

"Yeah, I get it. But between you and me, Gavin, just how nuts is she?"

Gavin had come into contact with Lottie maybe five times in his life. She'd never said much to him, and what she had said didn't sound in any way like the conversation of an average person. But she was Julianna's mother, for God's sake, and he couldn't bear to hear this snide little twerp making fun of her. Still, Gavin needed to watch himself. He couldn't act too incensed about matters concerning Julianna without arousing suspicions.

"I think Lottie Brent is what you'd call eccentric," he said, forcing himself to sound offhand. "She doesn't look at the world quite like the rest of us do. And she had some bad experiences when she was young."

"Oh yeah? Like what?"

"I don't know exactly," Gavin said, although he did. The shed. The beating. The rape. "Something pretty upsetting a long time ago. And her mother died when she was young and she was left in the hands of an unsuitable father."

"Did he abuse her? Sexually, I mean?"

"I don't know," Gavin returned irritably. What was going on with this jerk, anyhow? "I never heard anything about abuse." He nodded to the bartender and, to his dismay, so did Bruce. "Are you sure you're up to another one of those?"

"At least one more. It's good stuff."

"Yes, it is." Gavin tried to sound pleasant, although he wished he hadn't just ordered another drink. Otherwise, he could leave the bar without appearing rude. Not that he cared what Bruce Allard thought of him, but if Bruce were insulted, he'd tell his daddy who would report to Ellen who would then give Gavin hell for a number of hours. He groaned inwardly and searched his mind for further conversation. "Bruce, I don't believe I've ever seen you in here before."

"I've been in the restaurant dozens of times and always had my drinks with my dinner. Along with a bottle of the finest wine they have on the list, of course."

"Of course."

"But once in a while, I get an urge to just sit with the guys, do some *real* drinking, shoot the breeze, you know."

"Oh yes."

"And frankly, you've always struck me as a really interesting guy, Gavin, but I've never gotten a chance to talk to you without our mothers around." Gavin gave him a hard look and Bruce turned crimson. "I mean *my* mother and your *wife*. Whew, this whiskey does a number on your tongue." He glared at his empty glass as if his faux pas were its fault.

"I told you to take it easy."

Bruce laughed heartily. Gavin stared. "Anyway, about Julianna. How much do you know about *her*?"

Gavin became aware that Kit had slid onto a stool beside J.C. She was putting on a good act of devoting her attention to her boyfriend, but Gavin knew she was really listening to him and Bruce.

"I know very little about Julianna," Gavin said stiffly.

Their drinks arrived and Bruce bolstered himself with a hearty gulp. "C'mon, Gavin, you must have known her since you married Ellen when Julianna was a teenager and friends with Kit."

"I met her. We didn't exactly hang out together."

Bruce laughed. "Good one! But I guess she hung out with just about every other guy in town."

"And what would make you think that?"

"Talk. Just talk around town."

"I thought journalists were taught not to automatically accept 'just talk' as fact. The journalists with integrity, that is."

"Well, sure. We are. We do. That's why I'm double-checking here, not just printing gossip. See, Delaney put me in charge of covering Julianna's murder investigation."

"Oh." Apparently, Bruce didn't think Gavin read the newspaper and saw that every big article about Julianna Brent's murder had been written by Drew Delaney, not Bruce Allard. Gavin asked, "What do Julianna's teenage years have to do with anything?"

"Why, they could be the key to her murder!"

"How?"

Bruce looked at Gavin as if he were stupid. "Because someone who had a grudge on her back then is her killer."

"I see. This person got mad at her when she was a teenager and then waited . . . what? Fifteen, sixteen years to do her in?"

"Maybe."

"A very patient person."

Bruce's eyes narrowed. "A lot of killers are patient, Gavin."

"Really? I didn't know that, but I guess in your line of work, you've come in contact with many more dangerous people than I have."

"You betcha. I've met some real badasses." Bruce stared into his drink, clearly ruminating on all the badasses he'd known in his spectacularly pampered life. The memories drove him to gulp more whiskey. Gavin decided the kid's head was probably beginning to spin. He would be leaving soon, thank God.

Then, suddenly, Bruce turned and pinned Gavin with his clear, laser-blue eyes. "So, Gavin my man, why haven't you come forward with what you know about Julianna's death?" he asked loudly. "Because I believe you *know* who killed her."

Gavin felt as if he were plunging through icy water, unable to breathe, to see, to move. He felt his mouth open slightly, then close again. Was it his imagination, or had the bar gone entirely silent, every ear trained on what words would next come out of his dry mouth? At last, he was able to draw a shallow breath, enough to utter a weak, "What makes you believe I know who killed Julianna?"

"Studying people. Watching people. *Knowing* people." Bruce no longer sounded even slightly drunk. "I'm very good at that because I'm also good at playing the fool, so people don't take me seriously and they let their guard down around me. I've been watching you all summer, Gavin. Watching you at those parties at Philip Hamilton's house. Watching you drool over Julianna. Watching you *follow* her around town. You had to know exactly what was going on in her life, and that means that you probably also know who killed her. If you didn't do it yourself out of jealousy, that is."

Gavin sat blinking at the arrogant, good-looking young man sneering into his face. Bruce Allard couldn't have been more proud of himself than if he'd just forced Gavin to confess to every murder and act of violence committed during the past few hideous days. And Bruce had done it because he thought he could get away with it, because everyone believed Gavin Kirkwood had no backbone, no spirit, no manhood left in him.

Slowly, a white-hot anger built within Gavin. It started in the pit of his stomach, worked its way into his chest, making him feel as if his lungs were going to explode, and finally it reached his eyes. Bruce still stared at him intently, triumphantly. And then, as the fury began to show in Gavin's gaze, Bruce's wavered. So did his smile. He pulled back fractionally, unwilling to retreat, but somehow realizing the impossible—that he'd miscalculated, he'd gone too far, he might be in trouble.

A wave of victory surged through Gavin as he saw the kid's uncertainty. Gavin had not experienced anything like victory for a very long time, and he felt wonderful. Exhilarated. Invincible.

Holding fiercely to his fury, to the sharp-edged look he knew lingered in his eyes, his slid off the barstool and leaned close to Bruce.

"If you were as smart as you think you are, young man, you would have kept your mouth shut," he said in a low, dangerously affable voice. "After all, if you think I've murdered once, even twice or three times to protect myself if you count Claude Duncan and Margaret Taylor, then what's to stop me from doing it a fourth time?"

Gavin couldn't believe it. His damned car wouldn't start. He sat in the parking lot of The Iron Gate in his one-year-old $70,000 Jaguar XK, turning the key again and again only to hear *click, click, click*. The battery was dead. Or maybe the alternator was shot. He opened the hood, but he really didn't know what he was looking at. He got back in the car and thought. All the local garages were closed at night. He could probably get Ralph from R & R Auto Repair to help him out but he didn't have his cell phone with him, and he wasn't about to slink back into the restaurant after his dramatic departure to make a call. Finally, he decided the car would be safe in the parking lot until tomorrow, and he would walk back to the house only four blocks away.

Although Ellen had retreated to her bed at seven o'clock with a migraine, Gavin had intended to be home by nine. Instead, he'd lingered at the bar until quarter to ten. Now he'd be even later because of the car trouble and the walk. He wasn't sure if Ellen would still be awake and angry that he'd deserted her, although when she had one of her headaches, she claimed just talking made her feel worse, and she banished him to a guest room for the night. Still, she usually wanted to know that he was in the house, fretting over her. Yes, if she were awake, she would be furious with him. But for once, he didn't care if she was furious, didn't dread a scene, had no intention of even checking up on her when he got in.

The night had a dark velvety feel, soft and warm and caressing. A light breeze occasionally sent gauzy clouds skittering across the moon and whispered in the leaves of large, old trees lining the sidewalk. Normally, an evening like this would have stirred a romantic nostalgia in Gavin, a memory of his youth when he still hoped that someday the love of a glorious woman would turn him into a glorious man. Julianna had revived that wonderful hope, but it had ended too soon and too horribly for him to even think about without feeling like a blade had pierced his stomach.

But now he wasn't thinking about the beauty of the night. He wasn't thinking about when he was young and there'd been a lovely dark-haired girl he'd thought might be the One. He wasn't even thinking about the hassle of getting his car out of the restaurant parking lot and finding someone to fix it as soon as possible. He was only thinking of that little ferret, Bruce Allard.

Gavin was astonished by how he had let that spoiled nitwit lead him, fool him, *bait* him. He couldn't have helped having Bruce sit down beside him, but he could have quickly finished his own drink and left, not sat there allowing himself to be manipulated by an arrogant young jerk who thought he was smart and cagey, but who didn't know a damned thing.

Except how to adroitly lure me right into that outburst, Gavin thought glumly. By tomorrow, half the town would have heard an exaggerated version of the scene that had

Gavin Kirkwood clearly, undeniably, viciously *threatening* Bruce Allard's life! A little groan escaped Gavin. What would be the repercussions of that rumor? What would be the repercussions of there having been an altercation at all? Exactly how sick was he of always worrying about *any* repercussions?

Around one hundred feet ahead and across the street, Gavin saw with relief the carriage lamps glowing atop brick columns that marked the entrance to his driveway. The four drinks he'd had at the bar had finally kicked in, slowing his walk, causing him to take the overly careful steps of an old man. And he felt dizzy. Only a bit, but enough to be a nuisance like a mosquito buzzing in his ear. He should have eaten dinner. Instead, he'd drunk all that whiskey on an empty stomach. Maybe having a sandwich when he got home would help. A hearty sandwich, two aspirins, and a B complex vitamin. Hadn't he read that B complex helped with hangovers? And a big glass of water. Water with lots of ice . . .

He stepped off the curb and began meandering across the quiet residential street, his thoughts consumed with the makeshift meal he'd soon fix for himself, his gaze focused on his feet that he couldn't seem to stop lifting too high.

Headlights snapped on, sending beams down the street, catching him directly in their glare. Gavin blinked and turned away his face. Dammit, didn't the driver realize he had on his high beams? Gavin picked up speed to get out of the idiot's way, then suddenly realized the idiot was picking up speed, too. An engine throbbed louder with growing momentum, and tires spun relentlessly over smooth concrete.

Gavin looked back just in time to see a dark form behind the wheel—almost leaning *over* the wheel as if in anticipation—before the front bumper hit his lower legs, and the grill crashed into his thighs. For a moment he felt as if he were flying then careening downward, his left hip striking the car's hood, his shoulder smashing against the windshield.

The car never slowed and Gavin lay splayed across the front of it for nearly forty feet before a piece of his shirt that had tangled on a windshield wiper tore loose, allowing him to roll off and have his right ankle snapped by a steel-belted radial tire.

The car sped on, leaving Gavin lying limp in the street as the velvety, romantic night closed around him.

SEVENTEEN

I

"My God, Kit, that's terrible!" Adrienne exclaimed. "How badly is Gavin hurt?"

"Broken hip, broken ribs, broken collarbone, shattered ankle. He had a concussion and the vision in his right eye is blurry. At least the doctor expects that to clear up fairly quickly. The rest of the stuff . . ." She sighed. "He's in bad shape."

Kit sounded almost, no, definitely upset. And the circles around her eyes said she'd been up all night. Adrienne was astounded not only that Gavin Kirkwood had been nearly killed by a hit-and-run driver, but also that his longtime nemesis Kit seemed to care so much. She'd arrived at Adrienne's ten minutes ago dressed hurriedly in jeans and a blue satin blouse, and requested a quick chat and a cup of "real" coffee before she had to go back to the hospital.

"How is Ellen taking it?" Adrienne asked as she poured Kit's second cup of coffee and also handed her a blueberry muffin, which Adrienne was starting to consider her pièce de résistance in the kitchen. "Mother was home with a headache when it happened," Kit said through a mouth full of muffin. "Adrienne, this is delicious! I might start having you make some for the restaurant. Anyway, Mother had taken her migraine medicine and no one could rouse her. I used my house key to get in. She was too groggy to understand at first." She paused. "I'll need another muffin."

"I thought you weren't hungry."

"My stomach thinks different. Anyway, Mother seemed okay at first, then fainted when we got to the hospital. Her breathing was bad, her color was awful, so now there are two patients in the family. Mother is in the room next to Gavin's. The only physical problem with her is strain put on her weak heart, but Gavin's physical state has certainly knocked the emotional stuffing out of her. I don't think she's issued an order all day. She just stares at the television and says 'It's my fault.'"

"Does she mean Gavin's accident?"

"It wasn't an accident."

"Okay, the attempt on his life. Why would someone trying to kill Gavin by running him down in the middle of town be *her* fault?"

Kit shrugged. "I don't know. Anyway, I'm sorry, but I won't be able to come to the gala tonight."

"I wouldn't expect you to. And you didn't have to come here to explain. You look like you've been up all night."

"I have, but I couldn't sleep even if I had the time. After finding that photo of Trey yesterday morning, though, I wanted to check on you in person so I could really *see* if you're all right."

"I am, considering all that's been happening. So far, Lucas hasn't been able to come up with any answers about the picture, though."

"No one at police headquarters jumped up and confessed to raiding the files?"

"Not a soul, even though Lucas said he has an idea who might be responsible. He won't tell me whom he suspects. Of course, he's not in peak form with his injury. I know he's in pain, although he won't admit it." Adrienne closed her eyes briefly. "In the last two weeks, the world has turned bizarre, Kit. I think I'm becoming almost numb to the shocks."

"You're far from numb, sweetie," Kit said. "Where's Skye, by the way?"

"At her friend Sherry Granger's. I have to be at the French Art Colony in about an hour to help with preparations, and she didn't want to spend the whole afternoon there. Since the Grangers are attending the gala tonight, Louise Granger suggested Skye spend the afternoon there and come with them. Considering all that's been happening around me lately, I think my daughter is safer in other people's company. And that's a terrible thing to have to admit."

Kit reached out and touched Adrienne's hand in an uncharacteristic gesture of affection. "I know it is. Listen, Adrienne, I don't want to spook you on your big night, but you're right. You're not out of danger and neither is your daughter. That's why I think that after tonight, you should leave town. I know you're worried about your job, but Mother has lots of influence. So does your brother-in-law, if just once he'd ever do anything for you instead of for himself."

Adrienne glanced down. "You think I've been irresponsible for staying here so long."

"You could have been killed at Lottie's cabin," Kit said softly. "Where would that have left Skye? Adrienne, you're the best mother in the world. But you've gotten yourself into a panic over your job, over not having enough money to support your daughter, and that's caused you to take risks. I'm partially to blame for not offering you the money to leave town, but I didn't think you'd take it."

"I wouldn't have."

"You're like Lottie and I respect your principles, but you have to accept help from someone—if not me, then Vicky—and stop being brave."

"You mean being an ass."

"Well . . . yes. What happened to Gavin wasn't a random hit-and-run, which only proves this mess is far from over." Kit's grip tightened almost painfully on Adrienne's hand. "So be careful, tonight, Adrienne, and then leave. Take your daughter and get out of this town for as long as it takes. If you don't, you're risking both your lives."

2

"Thank heavens, I finally I got things under control in the restaurant," Kit exclaimed as she rushed into her apartment, slamming the door behind her. "Now it's back to the hospital for afternoon visiting hours. I'll make my visit short, though. Then we can spend some time together." She stopped. "What's going on?"

Miles Shaw stood in front of her in the living room, a leather suitcase sitting beside him, a canvas tote slung over his shoulder. "I'm leaving tonight, Kit."

"Leaving?" she repeated slowly, then smiled in relief. "Oh, going back to your apartment. That's not necessary. You're not crowding me."

"I'm not going back to my apartment. I'm leaving town."

"Leaving town?" She blinked at him. "Where are you going? Why?"

"I can't answer either one of those questions. You'll just have to take my word for it that I have to go." He smiled. "Kit, I really appreciate you giving me sanctuary after Margaret got killed and the police were breathing down my neck, but—"

"Giving you sanctuary? Is that what this was about?"

"Ummm . . . mostly. I told you that when I asked if I could stay with you. Maybe I didn't use those exact words . . ."

"*Maybe* you didn't? You sure as hell did *not* use those exact words." Kit's voice rose along with her color. "You didn't use words even *close* to those. You used words like 'You're the only person I trust' and 'I need you more than I ever realized.' "

"Enough," Miles said, wincing as he raised his hands in a

gesture for silence. "I was pretty out of control. Maybe I implied things I shouldn't have."

"Like telling me Margaret had been one of many stupid dalliances after Julianna left you and now you realized that you wanted to be with someone you *really* cared about? Someone like *me*?"

Miles was beginning to look cornered. "Kit, you know you mean the world to me. You always have. It's just that I have to get out of town."

"Why? You have an alibi for the time of Margaret's death."

"Yes, but there's another reason. One I can't tell you."

"You always play the mystery man, Miles." Her voice began to tremble. "You've been divorced from Juli for years. Now she's . . . gone. And I know you didn't love Margaret. I thought finally we had a chance."

"Maybe we do. Just not now, Kit. Please let me go without the memory of you clinging and begging and haranguing."

"Clinging, begging, and haranguing? Is that how you see me?"

"Well, yeah. It's what you're doing now. Have a little faith in me, Kit."

"Faith in you? Why should I have faith in you?"

"Because you love me?" She stared at him. "Because you *do* love me, Kit. I know it. And because you're a strong woman with a lot of pride."

"I thought I was clinging."

Miles briefly closed his incredible green eyes. "I can't have this argument with you, Kit. I'm *not* going to have it. I'm leaving. I'll get in touch with you later. I promise."

He leaned forward to give her an obligatory kiss, but she pulled away. He saw tears in her eyes—tears shimmering over intense fury. He strode past her and out the door.

As Miles dashed down the back steps from her apartment, he could feel her at the window, still watching him. He thought about turning and giving her a wave, but he didn't know if she'd find it encouraging or insulting. He really didn't want to make her even angrier. Or to hurt her, but he had to leave. Tonight.

There was only one thing he had to do first.

3

"Don't drink all the refreshments, Adrienne," Miss Snow ordered. "After all, we are expecting quite a few guests tonight. We want to provide a wide variety of beverages and plenty of each kind. It would be *so* embarrassing to run out."

"I'm sipping a bottle of Coke I brought from home, not sucking the punch bowl dry," Adrienne returned irritably. She'd been working at the French Art Colony for three hours under the direction of Miss Snow, and the strain was getting to both of them. Two other people had arrived to help prepare for the gala, but Miss Snow made it obvious she found them below snuff. And Miles Shaw had neither shown up nor called, which caused Miss Snow tremendous distress she tried to hide by making excuses for him. Adrienne had often wondered if Miss Snow's pristine mind had made room for one object of erotic fantasy—Miles. She clearly adored the man. Adrienne was certain Miles knew. Miles *always* knew which women he had power over, and he used it shamelessly.

Miss Snow looked at the locket watch hanging over her flat chest. "The gala will start in less than two hours. The display rooms are now closed while the judges make their decisions."

"I know," Adrienne returned. "That's why I retreated to the kitchen."

"I would suggest you retreat to your home and change clothes. You're certainly not wearing *that,* are you?"

Adrienne looked down at her jeans, T-shirt, and scuffed white running shoes. "Why, yes. I picked out this outfit especially for tonight." Miss Snow scowled. "I'm not going all the way home to change," Adrienne said patiently. "I told you that I have my clothes in my car. I'll freshen up in the bathroom."

"You're going to take a *bath* in there?"

"A quick shower. That's what the shower is for. I promise to clean the bathroom thoroughly before the guests arrive. I just don't want to go home, then get caught in the evening traffic trying to get back here."

"Oh." Miss Snow brightened. "That means your daughter won't be attending."

"Yes, she will." Miss Snow looked so crestfallen that Adrienne took pity on her. "Of course, my brother-in-law, Philip Hamilton, and his family will be attending, too," she reminded the woman.

Miss Snow had obviously forgotten about Philip in her dismay over Miles Shaw's absence, but the mention of his name brightened her right up. "Oh, yes, Mr. Hamilton. How lovely it will be to have him here." Along with his money and the press coverage his attendance would bring, Adrienne thought sourly. "You know, I was great friends with his Great-aunt Octavia."

"That doesn't surprise me." Miss Snow looked at her sharply, not sure whether or not she was being insulted. She was, but Adrienne didn't want to completely alienate the woman even before the evening began. "From what I've heard, Octavia was a lady of taste and refinement."

"Oh my, yes," Miss Snow tittered. Her eyes took on a glow of remembered bliss. "Once we went to the opera together. It was one of the most stimulating evenings of my life."

What a humdinger of a life you must have had if opera with that disdainful, dry stick of a woman Octavia Hamilton was a highlight, Adrienne thought sadly, but managed a smile. "I think I'll give my daughter a call."

"Why don't you call the Hamiltons too and make sure they know what time the gala is starting. I'm thrilled that they are attending. I wonder if any of the paintings will appeal to Mr. Hamilton?" she mumbled, dashing off to make sure the gallery was in tip-top shape for the arrival of what she obviously considered royalty.

Adrienne called Skye and was surprised when Vicky answered Skye's cell phone. "Skye's here with us," Vicky said cheerfully. "She and Rachel are playing tennis. Skye left her phone on the kitchen counter so I just picked it up when it rang."

"She's supposed to be at the Granger house," Adrienne said sharply.

"It seems Mr. Granger is having heart pains. Or what he thinks are heart pains. His wife is beside herself and she brought Skye here so she and her daughter could hover by the dying husband's bedside throughout the afternoon and night. The girl seemed really bummed out, as Rachel would say."

"Maybe he *is* sick," Adrienne said in alarm.

"He looked amazingly healthy for a man who's having a heart attack," Vicky said. "He even turned down an ambulance. I think he just didn't want to get dressed up and come to the gala. But don't you worry, honey. We'll be there!"

Vicky sounded as if she were not only in a good mood, but also sober. At least Adrienne felt relief on that account. "How's Skye?"

"Fine. She brought the outfit she'd taken to the Grangers to wear tonight and it's lovely. Anyway," Vicky went on, "even Philip seems kind of excited about tonight. A little of the hoopla over Margaret has died down. I guess it will flare up again when her body is released for the funeral, but I'll deal with that when the time comes. For now I'm just enjoying having some normal family life without Margaret bossing everyone around." Vicky's voice tightened when she spoke of Margaret, her hatred of the woman still vibrating in her tone, and Adrienne's old, unsettled doubts about her sister playing a part in Margaret's murder began a slow and sickening rise. She forced them down, feeling treacherous for having *any* doubts, and changed the subject.

"I know Philip will refuse to be on time," Adrienne said. "He'll want to make an entrance. But please don't be *too* late, Vicky. I don't want half the gala to be over before all of you arrive."

"I promise we won't be late. By much," Vicky giggled again. "And good luck tonight. I hope your painting wins."

"Me too, but I'm not counting on it. By the way, one of the ladies on the board, Miss Snow, used to be a friend of Great-aunt Octavia's. It will thrill her senseless if Philip makes a big deal over her. She's tall, usually dressed in dark colors, has white hair drawn straight back, and she's about a hundred and twenty years old."

Vicky laughed. "I'll warn Philip. Even if she's from Ohio and can't vote for him, he'll still want to charm her."

"Especially because she has friends who live in West Virginia who *can* vote for him. Thanks for taking care of Skye today."

"No problem. See you later."

Adrienne hung up, trying to feel confident about the evening. But the suspicions she'd formed about Vicky and Philip lately had already ingrained themselves far too deeply for her to relax knowing Skye was in their care.

She was worried, and the feeling wouldn't go away.

4

Miles turned off the highway and drove slowly up the road to la Belle Rivière. He stopped in front, looking up at the grand old hotel. The evening sun had only begun to dim, turning from saffron to burnished gold against the sky. Venus, often called the evening star, glittered directly over la Belle, like a beacon signaling him, the north point in the compass of his grief.

He was relieved to find the place deserted. Not even thrill-seekers had turned out to stare at the murder site. They were probably having dinner, Miles thought. If television was dull tonight, they'd wander over, half excited, half scared that there would be more action at what most people had come to consider the "cursed" hotel. Ellen Kirkwood would be pleased, he thought. Local residents no longer thought she was crazy. They thought she'd been right all along about the resort being evil.

Miles pulled around to the back of the hotel and off to the side, where his car would be hidden by massive bushes. He got out and stood facing the hotel, studying every long porch, every balustrade, every door, and every window. And every shadow, because for early evening, the place seemed too full of shadows. It must have something to do with the architecture, he thought, a little ashamed of the pause those shadows gave him. He wouldn't let them scare him. Hell, Adrienne Reynolds had come up here to paint at least once after Julianna's murder. She hadn't been afraid, so he *certainly* wasn't going to get spooked. When he caught himself saying this aloud, he promptly shut his mouth and blushed, grateful there was no one to either hear him or see him.

Miles grabbed his knapsack out of his trunk and walked toward the back of the hotel. Security on the place had tightened since the day Claude died. Police had sealed the doors with yellow tape. Miles decided it would be easiest to break a window. Vandalism wasn't his style, but in less than a month wrecking balls would attack la Belle, so what would one broken window matter?

Miles took a hammer out of his knapsack and struck a pane in a French door. It didn't tinkle like crystal. The glass made a sharp cracking noise, then tumbled to the floor. He reached in and unlocked the door, not worrying about a security system. Kit had told him Ellen had turned off the system months ago, almost hoping someone would break in and burn down the place so she wouldn't have to bother with demolition.

Miles picked up his knapsack and walked slowly into the hotel. He'd broken the window of an office. Out of curiosity, he opened a couple of the file drawers, but they were empty. Maybe Ellen had stored files on the people who once stayed in the hotel. Or maybe she'd had them destroyed. He sat down behind a fine mahogany desk that must have been used by the manager and would be sold at auction before the hotel was demolished. Idly, he opened a drawer, and near the back he found a bent and faded photo of a teenaged girl sitting on the fountain out front. An auburn-haired girl.

Miles looked closer, squinting in his intensity. Good God, it was Julianna! She couldn't have been more than sixteen, wearing shorts that showed off her long, tanned legs and a tight T-shirt with no bra on underneath. She looked saucy and innocent at the same time. And she was beautiful. That photo had to have been taken twenty years ago, Miles thought, but someone had kept it tucked away all those years. The uptight, religious creep Mr. Duncan who had managed la Belle for a quarter of a century until it closed, Miles deduced. The guy whose mouth was constantly pursed with disapproval and righteousness. So he'd secretly lusted for Julianna. She'd even had that sanctimonious twerp itching for her.

Miles started to put the photo back in the drawer, but instead slipped it carefully into his pocket. He grabbed his knapsack and walked from the manager's office through the huge lobby heavy with marble and mirrors, and climbed the spiral staircase to the second floor.

Daylight still shone through the floor-to-ceiling windows at each end of the hall and he didn't need to use his flashlight to find the right room. Number **214**. Juliana said it stood for February 14, her birthday and Valentine's Day. They'd spent their honeymoon night in this room. And she'd been murdered in this room. Miles reached out and ran a long index finger over each number. Then he tore down the yellow crime-scene tape. He knew the police had exhausted all the evidence the room had to give, and they still hadn't come up with Julianna's killer.

Miles placed his hand on the doorknob, then paused. He'd known he would visit this room again, but he hadn't expected to feel reluctant, almost squeamish, about entering the once-beautiful scene of his honeymoon night. He and Julianna had drunk champagne there and flung their glasses into the fireplace. They'd listened to music, and with her in an exquisite blue satin and lace nightgown, they'd danced to "Sweet Dreams." Again and again. They had giggled and caressed and made a fervent promise to love each other until the seas ran dry. It was a trite and hackneyed promise, but nice.

Unfortunately, only one of them had meant it.

Miles wandered over to the bed, forcing himself to look down. The spread and sheets were gone, but the mattress remained. The sight of large, rust-colored stains near the top made his stomach turn. Julianna's life force had drained out through her neck onto that mattress, leaving only brownish mottling behind. He wondered if she had regained consciousness after she'd been stabbed in the neck. If so, had she known she was dying? What had been her last thoughts? Had he even once crossed her mind?

Miles realized he could never know the answers to these questions. Trying to figure out Julianna as she was dying was as futile as trying to figure her out when she was living.

Miles sighed and went to the French doors, opening the draperies closed against them. The sun had set even lower, turning the sky to a glorious flaming copper. He opened the doors, letting the fresh evening air drift into the room. Then he sat down on the soft blue carpet near the windows, unzipped his knapsack, and withdrew three candles in cut-glass jars. He lit them and the sweet scent of jasmine slowly began to waft around him. When they were married, Julianna had kept jasmine-scented candles alight most of the time. He would always associate the smell with her. It was a pleasant, a treasured, association.

Miles closed his eyes and remembered the day he had taken almost fifty photos of Julianna on the grounds of the hotel, photos he would later use when doing miniature portraits of her, one of which he put in a locket and gave to Lottie for her birthday. He remembered the reverence in Lottie's once-beautiful eyes when she'd looked at the tiny painting. He also remembered the hatred in Gail's.

Whisking away that particular memory, he carried the knapsack out on the porch, withdrew a portable CD player from it, stuck in a CD of the Eurythmics singing "Sweet Dreams," and slipped on headphones. Then he opened a tiny bottle filled with brandy Alexander mix, the kind of bottle they gave you on airplanes. Brandy Alexanders had been Julianna's favorite drink. He twisted off the cap, stood and walked out on the porch, then held up the bottle to the dazzling evening sky.

"To you, Julianna. You were my only love. You will always be my only love."

He tilted back his head and let the sweet liquid pour down his throat. He was so engrossed in his toast, in the taste of Julianna's favorite drink, in the sound of Annie Lennox's haunting voice singing "Sweet Dreams," that he didn't hear someone running up behind him. He only felt the thrust of strong hands against his back before he toppled over the railing and fell two stories onto the sturdy, sharp, upturned spikes of a thatching rake.

EIGHTEEN

I

Miss Snow had looked daggers at Adrienne as she ascended to the second-floor bathroom with her dress, makeup bag, and curling iron. The woman considered getting ready for the gala at the French Art Colony a travesty. Adrienne wondered why Miss Snow thought a full bathroom complete with shower and tub had been provided if not for such emergencies. Miss Snow lived only two houses down from the gallery and had marched home to change from one nondescript dark dress to another.

At present, Adrienne was reveling in both Miss Snow's absence and in the warm water pouring down from the shower onto her aching shoulders. She'd lifted quite a few paintings and moved some heavy furniture today. It certainly wouldn't have killed Miles Shaw to help them out, she thought crankily. But leave it to him to sweep in halfway through the show, the great artiste who was far above messing with the drudgery of getting ready for such an event. And who would he bring as his date? Adrienne wondered as she shampooed her hair. Kit? No, Kit had said she couldn't come because of her mother and Gavin. Margaret was dead. Maybe he would come alone, but she couldn't see him missing the event altogether. He was too addicted to the praise his work always elicited.

Adrienne stepped out of the shower and wrapped herself

in a terry bathrobe she'd brought from home. Then she opened the door a crack to clear the room of steam. She couldn't even see her reflection in the mirror. She rummaged through her bag until she found a texturizer she could run through her long hair to control the natural curl on a humid night, then she began an assault with the blow dryer.

In twenty minutes, even Adrienne was amazed at the transformation she had wrought. The turquoise sheath Skye had helped her pick out, the one she'd insisted on "because it's exactly the color of your eyes, Mom," fitted perfectly, stopping just above her knees, with a scoop neck low enough to show off her mother-of-pearl necklace to perfection. She'd swept up her hair to show off her dangling mother-of-pearl earrings. Even the shoes with their four-inch heels, again Skye's choice, didn't feel too uncomfortable. She just hoped they didn't start pinching before the evening was over.

The gala was set to start in forty-five minutes. Already a crew worked in the kitchen, making sure the champagne was properly chilled, preparing petit fours and hors d'œuvres. *Maybe I should have brought some of my blueberry muffins,* Adrienne thought. *Miss Snow would have been horrified.*

She decided to call Skye to make sure all was on schedule at the Hamilton home. She was surprised when Skye answered. "Hi, Mom," she said cheerfully. "Are you all dressed up yet?"

"I sure am. I don't look bad, if I do say so myself, but I hope I don't fall down the stairs in these shoes."

"You won't. I'll bet you look awesome. I can't wait to see you."

"I can't wait to see *you,* but why are you answering the phone? Isn't anyone else home?"

"Nope." Adrienne felt a surge of alarm. "Uncle Philip left right after you called earlier. He said he had some things to do and he'd be back in time to get ready. Aunt Vicky made him promise. But then she waited and waited, and I could tell she was getting nervous. So she left about twenty minutes ago to find him. She said she was fairly sure where he was, but she didn't tell Rachel and me. And then Rachel and I were going to start getting dressed when her favorite lipstick broke off and dropped to the floor. Can you even *believe* it? She said it went perfectly with her dress, so she went to the drugstore to look for a color that was close to the one that broke, even though the lipsticks they have at the drugstore aren't as expensive as what she had. I couldn't go because I was in the bathtub."

"But she still isn't back."

"She just left a few minutes ago, Mom. Picking out the right lipstick can take time," Skye said, as if she were an old hand at choosing cosmetics.

"And Philip and Vicky are gone. What about Miss Pitt?"

"She's not here today."

"So you're there all alone?"

"Mom, will you chill out?" Adrienne heard the exasperation in Skye's voice. "I'm not a little kid. I've got all the doors locked. Besides, Brandon is with me, remember? He'll protect me."

"If something happens, he'll be the first one to hide under the bed. That is, if he can fit under it." Skye giggled. "Well, there's nothing I can do, although I'm not happy about you being there alone. If I wanted you to be alone, I could have left you at home."

"Don't get mad, Mom. It's just for a little while. Rachel will be home any minute. Aunt Vicky and Uncle Philip, too. I'm *fourteen*," Skye said, as if it were *forty*. "I can take care of myself. Look, Mom, I just got out of the tub to answer the phone. I gotta start getting dressed. I'll see you tonight, and I promise everything will be fine."

Before Adrienne could voice more worries or issue further safety instructions, Skye wisely hung up. Adrienne sighed and tucked her cell phone back in her purse. She would just have to hope that all would go well tonight. And tomorrow, she would take Kit's advice and leave town until the increasingly dangerous situation that had developed lately had come to an end.

But right now, she had other, simpler worries to occupy her mind. Miss Snow had just returned, dressed from head to toe in her best evening black, looking angry enough to chew nails.

2

"Miss Snow, what's wrong?" Adrienne asked in alarm. "Are you feeling all right?"

"I am most certainly *not* feeling all right." Miss Snow had added a thirty-six-inch strand of fake pearls to her outfit and she twisted them so hard Adrienne was afraid the string would break. "I called Miles Shaw to make certain he would be attending tonight. Well, it seems that not only will he not be attending the gala, his answering machine says he has left town! I cannot believe it! On the night of the French Art Colony gala, that man *left town*! For *good*! He's *moved*!"

Miss Snow might as well have announced that Miles had blown up the courthouse. She whipped out an ancient black fan, sank down on a straight-backed chair just inside the door, and began furiously waving the fan in front of her flushed face. "Never in the *history* of the French Art Colony has something of this *magnitude* occurred! And I was in charge this year. *I* will be blamed!" She fanned harder. "On my word, I shall *never* forgive that man!"

Oh boy, *now* he's had it, Adrienne thought, almost bursting into laughter. Being suspected of viciously murdering Margaret Taylor could not possibly be as serious as having incurred the infinite and eternal wrath of Miss Snow. Could Miles feel it chasing him like a heat-seeking missile wherever he'd made the foolhardy choice to go except the gallery? If so, he'd better get used to it because Miss Snow would *never* forgive him.

Adrienne dared to touch the woman's frail shoulder. "You seem quite agitated, Miss Snow. May I get you a glass of water?"

"No," the woman barked. "I would like a good, stiff brandy. And please don't dawdle with it."

"Yes, ma'am." *Ma'am?* Adrienne couldn't remember the last time she'd called someone "ma'am," but she scurried off like a frightened parlor maid, rushed into the kitchen, and demanded that someone find her a snifter and a bottle of brandy. "It's not for me," she added unnecessarily to one of the caterers. "I think Miss Snow is on the verge of fainting." Or falling into an apoplectic fit, she thought, torn between apprehension and mirth.

Half an hour later, Miss Snow was on her feet and issuing orders. Again. Adrienne knew Miss Snow lived alone in a large, two-story home that had once housed an extended family, and she wondered if the woman retreated into silence when she closed her front doors, or secretly ordered around long-dead or -escaped relatives. Adrienne thought she'd spied a parakeet in the front window about a year ago, but parakeets weren't known as responsive recipients of domination. Still, the hapless bird would have been someone for Miss Snow to talk to.

"What are you daydreaming about?" the woman snapped behind Adrienne, making her jump. "The gala officially starts in fifteen minutes. People should be arriving soon."

"It's not fashionable to be on time," Adrienne said.

"In my day it was. Punctuality is next to godliness, my father always said."

"I thought that was cleanliness. 'Cleanliness is next to godliness.'"

Miss Snow glared and swept away to the kitchen for one last inspection. At least she's off my back for a while, Adrienne thought. If she'd been Miss Snow's parakeet, she would have found a way to break free of the bars and soar to freedom or die trying.

Adrienne's feet had already begun hurting when the first guests arrived twenty minutes later. She had lingered to the side of one window and watched a couple wait in their parked car until they saw another couple walking toward the gallery. Then they had scrambled from their Mercedes, joined the first intrepid couple, and thereby made a merry little group of four people, supposedly so different from a pathetic straggling of two. Miss Snow nearly ran over Adrienne reaching the front door, welcoming them profusely, giggling girlishly, handing them pamphlets, and pitting her copious application of lavender eau de toilette against the other women's Opium and Intuition.

Six more people had shown up when Drew Delaney strolled through the door looking devastating in a tuxedo. He glanced at Miss Snow rakishly and said, "Why, Miss Petunia, don't you look fine?"

Petunia? Adrienne thought. Miss Snow's first name was *Petunia*?

Miss Snow gave him a frozen look. "How do you do, Mr. Delaney? Are you personally covering our little event for the *Point Pleasant Register*?"

"Yes, ma'am, and it is my honor. I wouldn't assign it to any of my reporters. I just decided to hog the whole event to myself."

"You don't know anything about art," Miss Snow pronounced darkly.

"Now that's not quite true. I've studied up on the subject since my grandmother made me take those china-painting lessons from you when I was ten."

China-painting lessons? *Drew?* Adrienne was choking on a sip of champagne when Miss Snow waved an imperious arm toward her. "I'm quite busy tonight, Mr. Delaney. I hope you don't mind if I turn you over to the capable hands of Ms. Reynolds."

"I would consider it an honor and a *great* pleasure to be in the hands of Ms. Reynolds," Drew drawled, assuming a leer.

Adrienne would have assaulted him verbally if she could have stopped coughing.

"Adrienne, you should drink water if you can't handle spirits," Miss Snow chastised. "When you've recovered, please show Mr. Delaney around."

"I think he's been here before," Adrienne managed.

"Then show him around *again*." Miss Show's voice was pure steel. *"Please."*

"Yes, *please*, Adrienne," Drew said somewhat pathetically. "I can't remember a thing about the place."

"Oh, shut up," she muttered as "Petunia" fluttered back to the front door and Drew stood grinning at her. "Do you want a drink?"

"I don't think I can get through the evening without one," Drew said.

"That makes two of us."

"Really? You looked like that first one might have been too much for you."

"It was a combination of hearing Miss Snow's first name and knowing that you took china-painting lessons from her. Really, Drew. *China* painting?"

"It was the summer my parents were deciding whether or not to get a divorce. They went off and left me with my grandmother, who *forced* me to take the lessons from her good friend. I've never been so embarrassed in my whole life. All my friends were playing baseball. That was in the days before soccer became the rage. Anyway, I've lived in fear the rest of my life that the china-painting episode might leak out, and here it did, right in front of the prettiest girl this side of the Mississippi."

"I'll never be able to look at you quite the same, Drew," Adrienne said in mock seriousness. "That is, if you were good at it."

"I stunk. You heard Petunia. I don't know anything about art."

A waiter passed by with a tray of champagne and Adrienne

lifted off two glasses, handing one to Drew. "I'm almost as shocked to find out her name is Petunia as I am to find out you took china-painting lessons."

"You didn't know her first name is Petunia?" Adrienne shook her head. "My goodness, it's a sweet story," Drew said with a mischievous wink. "It seems she had a rough time at birth and came out with a face sort of bright pink from strain and bluish-purple from all the pulling they'd done on her. Afterward, they wrapped her in a white blanket and handed her to her daddy, who said, 'Why, what a pretty little thing. And colorful, too. Wrapped up in all this white wool, she looks like a petunia in the snow! That will be her name. Petunia Snow!' Now isn't that the cutest thing you've ever heard?"

Adrienne bent double with laughter. She glanced up to see Miss Snow glowering at her for making a spectacle of herself. Meanwhile, Drew stood looking handsome and dignified in his tux with only a trace of a polite smile on his tanned face.

"I think Miss Snow is going to come over here and paddle me if I don't get myself under control," Adrienne said, still gasping with laughter. "Let me take you around to see the paintings."

"I'm only interested in one. Yours. What's it called? Ah, *Autumn Exodus*."

"How do you know the title?"

"I'm a reporter," Drew said mysteriously. "I find out *everything*."

Adrienne took him to the painting and stood by nervously while he studied it, although she knew he was no art expert. Finally he exclaimed that it was "wonderful" and asked where her First Place ribbon was.

"They haven't announced the winners yet," she told him, amused by the vague word of praise only an amateur would use, yet pleased that she saw genuine admiration in his eyes. "They'll make a big production out of it. But I'm not expecting to place, even though Miles Shaw didn't enter anything this time."

"By the way, where is the long-haired, full-of-himself Mr. Shaw?" Drew asked.

"Don't even *mention* his name around Miss Snow," Adrienne said in mock horror, glancing over to where the woman was trying to charm the mayor of Gallipolis. "He's a no-show. And I mean a *real* no-show, as in he seems to have left town. For good."

Drew looked at her in surprise. "Left town for good? No. He's just lying low at Kit's place."

"I don't think so. Miss Snow called him and his phone has been disconnected. I'm sure it's not because he didn't pay his bill. And I doubt very much that he's changing addresses. He loves that loft he lived in with Julianna."

"You don't think he could be moving into Kit's?"

Adrienne shook her head. "I think Kit has real feelings for him, but she's not crazy enough to make that kind of commitment based on a night or two."

"Unlike you, she can be impulsive."

"*I* can be impulsive."

"Not that I've ever seen."

"Well, you haven't seen much of me the last few years."

Drew gave her the warm, intimate smile that had driven her wild ever since she was a teenager. "You're right. I haven't seen *nearly* enough of you. And I know, because you always think the worst of me, you believe I meant that remark sexually. I didn't. Although I wouldn't object to sexually, either."

Adrienne felt herself blushing, then blushed harder because she felt silly and adolescent. "You'll never change, Drew."

"I *have* changed. In all the important ways. Well, most of them, at least. Especially when it comes to knowing that I want only one woman in my life. And that woman is you."

"And what about Skye?"

"She's not a woman yet. But let me amend my earlier

comment. I want one woman and one adolescent girl who will grow up to be the same kind of strong, talented, beautiful woman her mother is. If I hadn't been such an idiot, I would have realized it a long time ago."

Drew's usual cocky smile faded and he looked so deeply into her eyes, she felt as if he could see directly into her soul. "How about being my girl again, Adrienne?"

Adrienne felt as if the room were beginning to spin and the sensation had nothing to do with champagne. She wanted nothing more than to step into Drew's arms, to feel the heat of his body through her thin dress, and to drown in his kiss, oblivious to all the guests at the French Art Colony gala.

Instead, she took a step back from him and said in a shaky voice, "I'll have to think about that." She smiled nervously, then asked abruptly, "Where *is* Skye and the rest of the Hamilton family?"

"Well, I can answer one question for you," Drew said. "Your sister is right behind you."

Vicky tapped her on the shoulder. When Adrienne turned, Vicky hugged her. "Hi! I don't think I've ever seen you look so sexy!"

"Thank you. Skye picked out the dress."

"She told us about twenty times you'd let her pick it out."

Adrienne looked around. "Where is she?"

"She'll be along. It seems Rachel ran out at the last minute to get a lipstick, like she doesn't already own a dozen shades. Philip got tired of waiting for her to come back—he has another appearance to make after this, and he wanted to get moving. So I asked Skye if she minded coming a few minutes later with Rachel and Bruce, and she said that was fine."

"Bruce Allard? Vicky, you didn't tell me Rachel had a date tonight."

"I just assumed you knew. Rachel always has a date." Vicky hesitated. "Actually, Bruce sort of insisted on tonight. I heard Rachel putting up a bit of an argument, but you know how persuasive Bruce can be."

"I know how *pushy* Bruce can be," Adrienne snapped. "Vicky, I believed you, Philip, Rachel, and Skye would be attending *together*. If I'd known Bruce was going to be bringing Skye, I would have come and gotten her earlier."

"Now don't get the worried look on your face. You're making lines between your eyebrows." Adrienne looked closely at her sister. She was too gay, and her cheeks were too pink. Oh God, why did she have to drink *tonight*, Adrienne thought in irritation. She was supposed to be looking after my daughter. "Bruce is always on time. He should have arrived at the house about ten minutes ago," Vicky chattered on. "I'll bet they're on their way, now. And don't you fret about Bruce's driving. He's a *very* good driver."

"Not if he ran over Gavin Kirkwood last night," Drew muttered.

Adrienne looked at him in alarm. "What are you talking about?"

"Gavin and young Mr. Allard got in a bad quarrel at The Iron Gate bar last night right before Gavin left and got flattened by a hit-and-run driver."

"What?" Adrienne's voice was so loud that several people turned to look. "Kit didn't say a word about that when she came by my house this afternoon."

"Maybe she had other things on her mind," Vicky offered.

"Other things on her mind?" Adrienne demanded. "What could be more important?"

Vicky patted her arm in what was supposed to be a gesture of comfort. "You're getting yourself all upset over nothing. Bruce wouldn't do a thing like that. It's crazy!"

Adrienne looked frantically at Drew. "Did you know about Bruce and Gavin having a fight?"

"Yes, but it was only an argument, not a fistfight. And right after Gavin left the bar, Allard made a phone call. Then he finished his drink. Several people vouch for him still being at the bar right at the time Gavin was run down. Vicky's right—Allard couldn't have done it. If not, he'd have at least been brought in for questioning, which he wasn't." Drew paused. "Didn't Lucas tell you any of this?"

"No, he did not," Adrienne said, suddenly furious with Lucas. How could he not tell her when Skye was going to be in Bruce's company tonight? But then, Lucas didn't know Bruce would be driving Rachel and Skye to the gala. Not even *she* had known.

"I don't like this," she said emphatically. "I have a bad feeling—"

"Oh, you and your bad feelings," Vicky said dismissively. "Ever since you were a kid, you've been having *baaaaad* feelings."

Adrienne ignored her sister. "I'm going to call Skye and tell her *not* to get in the car with Bruce."

"She's probably already on her way," Vicky said. "I'm sure Bruce has picked up her and Rachel by now. Quit worrying. You're being a huge drag."

Adrienne glared at Vicky. "I don't care if I'm being a huge drag. I can't believe I left my daughter in your care. Of course, when I did, I thought you'd have the good sense not to drink all afternoon and lose your common sense!"

"I did *not* drink all afternoon," Vicky snarled. "I had *one* drink to calm my nerves. How dare you accuse me of being drunk and neglectful of a child!"

Philip appeared beside them, a tense smile locked onto his patrician face. "If you two ladies don't lower your voices," he hissed, "I am going to drag you both out. You're making a scene." He scowled at Drew. "What are you doing here, Delaney?"

"Covering the event for the newspaper," Drew said casually. "And I must say, it's turning out to be much livelier than I'd counted on. It should make for good reading tomorrow."

"Oh God," Philip moaned quietly.

At that moment Miss Snow sailed up to them, her smile almost as stiff as Philip's. "Is there a problem?"

"No," Vicky said loudly. "Adrienne's just being difficult."

"Adrienne has a talent for being difficult," Miss Snow said with false sweetness. She held up a small, beaded evening bag. "This was lying on the table by the door. Is it yours, Adrienne?"

"Yes. I forgot to take it upstairs."

"Well, do so now, please. It keeps ringing. It's very distracting."

Adrienne grabbed for the purse and withdrew her cell phone, which was indeed ringing. The number on the digital readout was Skye's. Adrienne turned on the phone and almost shouted, "Skye? Where are you?"

At first, Adrienne heard only a sob. A frightened, wrenching sob. Then Skye cried, "Mommy, you have to come to the Belle. Hurry! Mr. Shaw—Miles—is hurt. Maybe dying. I'm *so* scared—" She sobbed again, "No! Don't!"

The phone went dead.

NINETEEN

I

Adrienne kept repeating "Skye? Skye?" until finally Drew took the phone out of her shaking hand.

"What is it?" he asked tensely.

"She said I had to come to the Belle because Miles was hurt, maybe dead. She said to hurry, she was scared. Then she was shouting *no* and *don't* . . . and then the phone clicked off." Adrienne's entire body had begun to quiver. "Why is she at the Belle with Miles Shaw?"

"Is Rachel with her?" Vicky cried, clapping her hand over her mouth.

"It's a prank," Philip pronounced. "Because of the murder, the kids thought it would be funny to scare us, even though it's in the worst possible taste and Rachel and Bruce should certainly know better at their ages."

"It is *not* a prank," Adrienne nearly shouted at him. "You didn't hear Skye's voice. I have to get to la Belle."

"I'll take you," Drew said, already reaching in his pocket for his keys. "You can call the police on the way."

"The police!" Philip looked horrified. "If this *is* just a prank and Rachel is involved, do you know the bad publicity I could get out of this?"

"Shut up, Philip." Vicky suddenly looked sober and implacable. "Just for once in your life think about Rachel instead of your all-consuming political career. Adrienne is right. Something's wrong. Now are you going with me, or are you going to have all these people know you'd rather stand here glad-handing when your daughter might be in trouble?"

Philip looked stricken for a moment. To Adrienne's horror, she thought he couldn't make up his mind what to do. Then he reached out and took Vicky's arm. "We'll go to the hotel."

After a few words to a baffled Miss Snow, who looked tragic that her whole carefully planned evening seemed to be falling apart, the four of them spilled out of the French Art Colony and headed for their cars.

At nine o'clock daylight saving time the sky had turned to cobalt and amethyst with a streak of coral near the horizon. Philip had not even asked Adrienne if she wanted to ride with him and Vicky, no doubt because Drew clearly meant to accompany her. Drew steered Adrienne toward his Camaro. "Put on your seat belt. I'm not wasting any time getting to la Belle," he said.

As he pulled away from the curb, Adrienne dialed Skye's number again. Skye's phone was turned off. "Oh God, Drew, what do you suppose has happened?" she nearly wailed.

"I have no idea, but you'd better call Lucas."

"I'm so rattled I didn't even think of him." Frantically she punched in the numbers to his cell phone, but she got only his voice mail. She called police headquarters, but his secretary Naomi said she hadn't seen him for hours. "Is something wrong, Mrs. Reynolds?" she asked, trepidation edging her voice. "Nothing bad has happened, has it? To you or your daughter or . . . well, to Rachel?"

"To Rachel?" Adrienne asked sharply. "Why would you think something might have happened to Rachel? I didn't even know you knew her."

"Oh, she comes in now and then trying to dig up a little news. This is supposed to be Bruce Allard's beat, but you know Rachel. She likes to get the scoop."

"But why did you think something might have happened to her?" Adrienne had heard Lucas speak of Naomi a couple of times. He didn't like her, didn't trust her, and planned on getting rid of her as soon as possible. "Do you know something about Rachel, Naomi? If you do, you must tell me because there *could* be something wrong."

"Oh gosh." Adrienne nearly held her breath. Naomi was on the verge of saying something important. Then she changed her mind. "I don't know anything. Certainly not about missing files or photos. I don't know why I even mentioned Rachel except that we're friends. Listen, I'm working overtime and going home soon, but I'll tell the sheriff you're looking for him if he calls in." She hung up.

"Naomi is acting dumb, but she can't even do that right. She mentioned missing files and photos," Adrienne said flatly.

"Naomi? Naomi at police headquarters? Naomi knows how to chew gum and wear tight clothes. That about covers it."

"She thinks she's a friend of Rachel's."

Drew let out a sharp laugh. "That's a joke. If Rachel is nice to Naomi, it's only to get information." He paused, then groaned. "Missing photos."

"Naomi turned over the photo of Trey to Rachel."

"You don't know she gave the picture to *Rachel,* Adrienne. Police headquarters is Bruce's beat."

"And I turned Skye over to Bruce," Adrienne went on stonily.

"You didn't turn Skye over to Bruce. You turned her over to your sister."

"The drunk."

"She didn't look drunk when she dragged Philip out of the gala. Vicky is not irresponsible and she's not an alcoholic. Something is bothering her lately and she's trying to hide behind liquor. God, she's your own sister. Can't you see her for what she really is?"

Adrienne bent her head and put her face in her hands. She

wanted to cry, but tears wouldn't come. "No, I don't know what my sister is. I don't know what anybody is, except that someone around here is a killer and my little girl is in danger. You didn't hear her voice on the phone, Drew. She was *terrified*."

"But alive. Try Lucas at home, and if you can't get him, call Naomi again and tell her to roust out Sonny Keller or some of the other deputies." She looked at him hopelessly. He glared and said harshly, "Don't you dare give me that nervous, incompetent look, dammit. Make the calls!"

Drew's severe tone galvanized her. He was absolutely right. This was no time for hysterics. She had to be strong.

After all, her daughter's life could depend on her.

2

Skye Reynolds thought the scariest time of her whole life was the day she and her mother found Julianna Brent murdered in a bed at la Belle. But it wasn't. That day had been eclipsed by the moment she had bent over the shattered but still living body of Miles Shaw and had gazed in horror at the sharp spikes poking up through his stomach. Automatically she'd reached for her cell phone and, like a little girl, called her mother. While she was talking frantically, she'd glanced at Miles's face just in time to see his green eyes widen. A feeling as painful as an electric shock ran through her, and she'd turned to find a gun pointed in her face before someone ripped the cell phone out of her hand. Someone familiar. Someone she loved.

"I'm sorry this had to happen, Skye."

Still crouching, her right hand bloody from where she'd touched Miles, Skye asked incredulously, "Rachel, what are you *doing*?"

"Something I don't want to, but I have to, now." Rachel paused, sadness filling her blue eyes, the breeze wafting silky ash-blond hair around her beautiful face. "Stand up, Skye."

Skye looked at her cousin in disbelief, then wariness. "Rachel, I know this is some kind of trick, but it's not funny. Mr. Shaw is hurt really bad. And you're scaring me. Please don't point that gun at me."

"Stand *up,* Skye!"

"But—"

"Stand up *now!*" Rachel's face was deadly white, her eyes turning cold and hard. "Dammit, Skye, don't make this any worse than it is. Do what I say!"

Abruptly, Skye stood. Rachel still pointed the gun at her head, and Skye had the sickening feeling that her cousin had gone crazy. Either that or she'd been drugged. Skye latched onto the last idea with a vengeance. That was it. Someone had drugged Rachel. She didn't know what she was doing.

Earlier, Bruce had come by the Hamilton house to pick up Rachel, but she still hadn't come home, even though she'd said she was only going out to buy lipstick. That had been over an hour ago. Skye explained this to an annoyed Bruce, who'd managed to wait another half hour before he'd blown up and said he knew damn well where Rachel was. The place she'd become obsessed with. In a rage, he'd headed for his car, and worried about her cousin, Skye had jumped in Bruce's car with him. To the Belle they'd raced, Skye terrified they were going to wreck.

When they'd reached the hotel, Bruce had glanced at Miles, then run inside. Skye thought she heard a noise, like a firecracker, but she'd ignored it and gone to Miles. Horrified by his wounds, she'd called her mother. And now Rachel was standing over her with a gun.

Yes, Rachel was drugged. Skye didn't know how it could have happened, but it was the only answer. She wanted to help Rachel, but she realized Rachel wasn't in control. Skye knew drugged people had no idea of what they were doing. Skye also knew it was very important for her not to upset Rachel, because she was temporarily crazy and she could do something that, in her normal state, she would *never* do in a million years. The only way she could help was to make Rachel feel calm and safe and like everything was cool.

"It's okay, Rachel," she said in the mildest voice she could manage. "I'll do whatever you say. But could we get some help for Mr. Shaw? I think he's in lots of pain."

Rachel looked down at Miles without a trace of sympathy. "He deserves to be in pain."

"Oh," Skye said, then understood completely. "You think he murdered Julianna."

Rachel looked at her quizzically for a moment. "Whatever made you think that?" Then she smiled her beautiful, girl-next-door smile. "No, Skye. Miles didn't murder Julianna. *I* did."

3

"I called 911," Adrienne told Drew as she turned off her cell phone. "I hope they get someone here fast, even if it's Keller." Adrienne's hands had begun to perspire. "I don't understand why my daughter is at la Belle."

"Because Bruce and Rachel took her there."

"*Why?* They were supposed to come to the gala. What are they doing at the hotel?"

Drew was silent for a moment, as if thinking. "How about this? Somehow one of them got word that Lottie Brent was seen around the hotel. *Everyone* is looking for Lottie Brent. Bruce and Rachel are reporters. Naturally they wanted to be in on the excitement. Hell, maybe they thought they'd capture her themselves."

"But why take Skye with them?"

"Skye is fourteen. Do you think she'd remain quietly at home while those two went roaring off on an adventure? My guess is that she planted herself in the car and refused to move."

"That sounds like Skye," Adrienne said slowly, knowing she was grasping at straws. "She thinks she's all grown-up. And she also thinks she loves danger. She at least loves excitement."

"There you go." Drew smiled. "Mystery solved."

"Oh, Drew, it is not," Adrienne said desolately. "We're just guessing."

"I think it's a good guess."

Adrienne closed her eyes against the last of the fading daylight. "I hope so, because if anything happens to Skye, it will be all my fault. And I can't live with that. I *won't* live with that."

4

"Come into the hotel, Skye," Rachel said gently. "There are some things I want to explain to you."

Skye glanced at Miles Shaw. His eyes were closed, but he was breathing. Please let him live until my mom gets here, she prayed. Please let me do the right thing to help Rachel.

Feeling as if she were sleepwalking, Skye stood up and moved slowly toward the front entrance of the hotel, knowing Rachel still pointed the gun at her, not certain whether or not she would actually use it. Skye climbed the front steps onto the wide porch. "The police had the doors sealed," she said. "Did you open them, Rachel?"

"Yes. Why?"

"I just wondered. I wouldn't have nerve enough to open a door sealed by the police, but you were always a lot braver than me."

"I didn't think about being brave," Rachel said offhandedly. "I just did what I wanted."

"Yeah, that's cool. That's the kind of thing Buffy the Vampire Slayer would do or the girls on *Charmed*." Skye hesitated at the hotel entrance. "You want me to go *inside*?"

"That's what I said. We can sit down in there. It will be more comfortable. Don't worry. You won't get in trouble. I won't let anyone punish you."

"Thanks, Rachel. You've always been my very best friend, not just my cousin. I know you'll take care of me. You're so good to me, even though I'm younger."

"I like you. I guess I love you, like I'd love the little sister I never had." Inside the dim lobby, Skye banged her thigh against the corner of an end table by a settee. "Be careful," Rachel said. "Just keep walking straight to the staircase. We're going to the second floor."

We're not going *there*, Skye thought in dread. We can't be going *there*. But once they reached the second floor, she saw candlelight flickering out into the hallway from one of the rooms—the room where Julianna Brent had been murdered. Skye shuddered, hoping Rachel didn't notice, but walked on without hesitation. She knew she had to do what Rachel wanted. She had no choice.

When they reached the doorway, Skye stopped. Knowing what Rachel wanted her to do was one thing. Making her body cooperate was another. "Rachel, can't we just talk about things here in the hall?" she asked. "I mean, well, that room has some pretty bad memories for me."

"We have to go in." Rachel's voice sounded patient but determined. "No one is in there. And memories can't hurt you. Go on, Skye. We'll talk things out, and then everything will be fine."

Skye felt as if Rachel could hear her mind screaming, "Mom! Mommy! Where are you? Help me!" But of course Rachel couldn't hear. Not unless she could read minds. Neither could Skye's mother. But hadn't her mom said that sometimes there was a link between the minds of a mother and child? Or was she just imagining that because she was so scared? She didn't know anymore. All she knew was that Mommy was nowhere around and Rachel had a gun. Choking down her rising panic, Skye said, "The candles are pretty, Rachel."

"Miles only lit three of them, but I found a couple more in his knapsack. I hate the smell of jasmine, but I lit them anyway. They *look* pretty, at least. No wonder Julianna liked to put them everywhere. They say women appear more beautiful by candlelight. Julianna would have thought of that, particularly since she was getting older and wouldn't want her wrinkles to show."

"But Julianna didn't have wrinkles," Skye protested, then immediately sensed her mistake. "Well, she *was* as old as my mom. She must have had wrinkles. I guess she just covered them up. Models know how to do tricks with makeup."

"Julianna knew *many* tricks, Skye. Many more than you can even guess."

"She did? Well . . ." Suddenly the situation had become too much for Skye. She felt as if she were going to faint. Or cry. Or scream. Any such disruption could be fatal though. "Can we sit down, Rachel?" she asked sweetly. "You said we were going to talk, but I can't even see your face with you standing behind me. You don't have to worry. I'm not going to run away. This is sort of an adventure."

"I'm glad you see it that way," Rachel said pleasantly. "Okay. Let's sit on the floor facing each other like we do up in my room. I wish we had some Cokes and potato chips."

"Yeah," Skye said faintly as she sank down to the floor, her head beginning to spin. Cokes and potato chips. Something to snack on would sure make things cozy right about now. Jeez, Rachel, she thought. Just how screwed up are you?

"Where's Bruce?" Skye blurted in a little burst of fear.

"Oh, around," Rachel said vaguely. "We're not going to worry about him. He's not worth it. I never really liked him, you know. I only dated him because my parents wanted me to."

"I didn't like him, either," Skye agreed. "He was kind of snotty." Her comment met with silence. Rachel gazed around the room, almost as if she'd forgotten Skye was with her. Unable to sit quietly any longer, Skye burst out, "Why did you kill Julianna?"

Rachel's blue gaze sliced back to her. "I had a good reason. I know you liked her, Skye, but she wasn't a good person. Not good at all."

Skye could not believe this of Julianna, but she thought it wise to nod her head. "I see. What did she do?"

"She was having an affair with my father," Rachel said harshly. "I guess Dad got involved with her because she was so beautiful and he and Mom weren't very happy together, but it was a mistake." Her eyes seemed to turn inward, as if she were searching for a story, the way she did when she was trying to entertain Skye with scary or romantic tales late at night when they were having a sleepover. Skye had always thought Rachel was *excellent* at making up stories. "But that's all the affair was on Dad's part—a mistake. A mistake that he wanted to fix," Rachel went on. Then her eyes livened, as if she'd just had an inspiration. "He wanted to break things off with Julianna, but she wouldn't let him. She threatened him, Skye. She told him if he didn't keep seeing her, she'd tell everyone they'd been having an affair and then his career would be ruined."

"Oh gosh," Skye said meekly, pretending she believed every word although she could always tell when Rachel was fibbing.

"But it was worse than that." Rachel's voice had picked up pace and volume. "Dad said he didn't care who she told—Mom and I were more important to him than his career. He wanted to keep his family together more than anything in the world, even more than he wanted to be governor. So . . . so Julianna said if he didn't stay with her, she would *kill* Mom!"

"Julianna said she would *kill* Aunt Vicky?" Skye gasped with what she hoped was appropriate horror. "I didn't think Julianna would kill anybody."

Rachel's eyes narrowed. "She had you fooled just like

everybody else. She was *evil*, Skye. She would have done it.
Dad was a nervous wreck. That's why he's been so *mean*
lately. He was trapped, you see. He either had to stay with
Julianna, who by now he hated, or risk her killing Mom. It
was awful for him!"

Skye merely stared, heartsick. Rachel was lying to her.
They were cousins and best friends and Rachel said Skye
was like her little sister, but now she was telling this crazy
story and expecting Skye to believe it.

"I went to Julianna's apartment one night. I'd confronted
her before, but this time I meant to really threaten her. I'd
been following her all evening, trying to get up my nerve.
She knew I was following her and she locked herself in her
apartment, but I had a spare key I'd gotten from my dad's
desk drawer. I just walked in on her. We argued. She told me
to leave her alone or else. I guess she meant she'd kill Mom
and me. Then she said someone was coming over, a man
who would protect her, but she was lying just to get me to go
away, because nobody ever came. Just in case, though, I
stayed until about midnight. I thought I'd put a big enough
fright in her to drive her away from Dad." Rachel shook her
head. "But I hadn't. I followed Dad and he went to la Belle
where he always met her."

"Why did they always come here?" Skye asked.

"Privacy. And Julianna had managed to get a key from
Kit's mother, Ellen, without Ellen even knowing it. She was
really sneaky."

Skye thought it had been pretty sneaky of Rachel to steal
her father's key to Julianna's apartment too, but she didn't
say anything. She sat perfectly still, hoping desperately that
her mother would come—her mother and a whole bunch of
police—to save her. In the meantime, she listened.

"That morning I waited until after Dad left, then I came
into this room. I picked up the lamp by the bed and hit her
with it. You know how strong I am from all the sports I play.
You saw that killer serve of mine when we played tennis this

afternoon. Anyway, the base of the lamp was heavy and it knocked her out.

"I bent over her, but she was still breathing," Rachel went on. "The bitch was *still* breathing. So I looked around and on the floor I saw a wine bottle. And beside it was a corkscrew. A big, long corkscrew with a really sharp point." Rachel's eyes seemed to glaze at this point. "I picked up that wicked-looking corkscrew, and I pushed Julianna's hair back, and with all my might I plunged the corkscrew in her neck, right into the carotid artery." Skye winced, feeling nauseated. "There was so much blood, I could hardly believe it. It was all over the sheets and her hair and running down her shoulder. I waited a while, just watching the blood pour out of her." Rachel looked at Skye and smiled. "And then I pulled out the corkscrew neat as you please and it was all over. Just like that!"

Skye's stomach roiled dangerously. Throwing up would not be a good thing to do now, she thought. Rachel wouldn't like it. She'd be offended. Frantic, Skye remembered hearing on some TV show that smiling suppressed the gag reflex, so she smiled brightly at Rachel. She smiled and smiled, which Rachel took as a sign of approval. "I knew you'd understand," Rachel said. "You've always understood me, little cousin.

"Everything would have been cool," she went on, "except that then there was a big crash down on the highway. That awful wreck. Claude Duncan was out of his cabin in a flash, running all over like the lunatic he was. I couldn't get back down to the road without him or the people involved in the wreck or the cops seeing me. I couldn't go *up* the hill because that's where Lottie Brent lives and she's always out early in the mornings. So I hung around in the woods. Then, of all things, you and your mom and Brandon came. God, it was like the whole world decided *this* was the place to be. Brandon came tearing into the woods after me. He seemed to think we were playing a game."

"That's why he was acting so weird!" Skye said suddenly. "He was bounding around like a puppy. It was because of *you*! He loves you!"

"I love him too, but I could have done without him right then. And to make matters worse, while I was dodging around trying to avoid Brandon and you, Aunt Adrienne started snapping photos like there was no tomorrow." She looked at Skye sadly. "That's why I had to get the camera from your mom before she had those pictures developed. She might have gotten a good shot of me."

"*You* hit her when she was going to Photo Finish?"

"Yes. I'm sorry, Skye. I didn't want to hurt her. I love Aunt Adrienne. But I *had* to get the film in that camera."

"Oh yeah, well, I can understand that," Skye said, still trying to sound like she truly did understand and sympathize with everything Rachel had done.

One of the candles made an odd, sizzling noise, then died out. "Wow, I wonder why that happened?" Rachel mused.

A stranger's voice said, "Water in the wax."

Both girls looked up to see Lottie Brent standing in the doorway of the room where her daughter had been murdered.

TWENTY

I

Dressed in near rags, her white hair streaming around her high cheekbones, Lottie fixed her cloudy amber eyes on Rachel and said in her bell-like voice, "You evil, misbegotten girl. Everything you've said about my daughter's intentions toward Philip is a lie."

Skye's dry lips parted in surprise and her heart thudded against her ribs. Rachel stood up, and Skye was certain she would point the gun at Lottie and fire. Instead, the blood drained from Rachel's face and the gun wavered slightly in her hand. Then she drew a deep breath and seemed to get hold of herself again.

"You're Julianna's mother. You'd say anything to defend her. But she *was* having an affair with my father!"

"I know she was," Lottie said calmly. "She told me all about it. She also told me how much she loved your father, and Julianna wasn't one to frighten or threaten someone she loved, or *anyone* for that matter."

Rachel glanced at Skye, as if judging her reaction to what Lottie was saying. Then she glared back at Lottie. "She was going to kill my mother if my father didn't leave her. I killed Julianna to protect my mother!"

"That is absurd and Skye knows it's absurd. I can see it in her eyes," Lottie said, her voice steady and positive. "Rachel, you killed Julianna because your father loved her deeply, more than anyone in the world, and you were jealous."

"My father did *not* love that whore!" Rachel shouted, pointing the gun at Lottie. "He *didn't*!"

"I saw you the morning you killed her," Lottie went on in a strange, placid voice. "I'd awakened with a dark feeling about Julianna. I knew where she was. I came to warn her. But I saw you. Rather, I saw a woman about your height with the same color hair. My eyes aren't good. Cataracts. You even had on a sweatsuit like my other daughter wears. I was certain you were Gail." She closed her eyes. "I came into the hotel and I found Julianna. There was nothing I could do to save her, but I could make her look presentable. I laid her properly in the bed, pulled up the sheet and blanket, put a clasp in her hair, the favorite Austrian crystal clasp she always kept in her purse. And I kissed her on the forehead." A tear ran down Lottie's pale cheek. "I kissed my darling good-bye.

"Then I left the hotel. I couldn't go to the police and tell them Gail had murdered her own sister. But I knew I'd been seen, I thought by Gail. She's an odd girl, a heartless person like her father. I was afraid she'd kill me too, and all this time, I thought I was hiding from her. But it was you who saw me. I was really hiding from you." She gave Rachel an unwavering look. "You would have killed me, wouldn't you?"

"I *tried* to kill you. I thought I finally had you when I was on Aunt Adrienne's patio and I heard her call the sheriff and tell him you were at the cabin, but you left before I could get there. You're a slick old lady. Slick and sneaky like Julianna."

Skye cringed at the ugly tone in her cousin's voice. She'd never heard Rachel talk so cruelly before. She almost didn't sound human, and the thought of such malevolence pouring from her cousin's mouth made Skye feel sick. She wished she'd wake up and find that this was all a nightmare, but she knew it wasn't.

"And what about Claude?" Lottie asked. "Did he see you, too?"

"Yes. It seems the whole world was up that morning. But he had better eyesight than you, Lottie. He knew who I was. And he decided to blackmail me." She shook her head. "He was even more stupid than he seemed if he thought he was a match for me. And pardon my use of the word *match*. It's what I used to burn him up. First, a dose of Numorphan I snatched from all the medicines left over from when my Great-aunt Octavia was dying, then a good dousing of bourbon, and then matches. The cottage made a beautiful fire."

"You burned a man alive, Rachel," Lottie said coldly.

"He brought it on himself." Rachel's jaw tightened. "What are you doing here, anyway?"

"I saw Miles's truck outside. I knew he'd come here, probably to Julianna's room. Miles always loved Julianna. I wanted to tell him that I knew he would never have hurt Juli, no matter what people suspected of him. As soon as I entered the hotel, you came in. I hid, but I followed you here. I got close enough to realize you weren't Gail. And I saw you push him off the balcony."

"I *loved* Miles," Rachel cried. "I protected him by telling him I had information about Julianna's death and to meet me at Heaven's Door the night of Margaret's murder. That way he had an alibi when *I* freed him from Margaret."

"Rachel, you killed Margaret, too?" Skye asked in a small, shattered voice.

"I had to. She knew I killed Julianna. She knew it from the start, but she didn't say anything. After all, she'd been afraid Dad's affair with Julianna would come to light and his campaign would be ruined. I'd taken care of that worry for her. But she also started using what she knew to try to scare me." Rachel paused. "She wanted Miles. She couldn't have him. I decided he was mine as soon as I met him. I'm sure he only started seeing her to hide his feelings for me. The day before she left on that last campaign trip with Mom and Dad, she told me she knew how I felt about Miles and it was ridiculous and if I didn't stop following him around like a lovesick puppy, she'd tell everyone I killed Julianna. She said she had proof, but she wouldn't say what proof. She probably didn't have anything, but I couldn't be sure. So I *had* to kill her.

"I waited until I was sure Miles had made it to Heaven's Door, took off all my clothes, put on some house slippers so I wouldn't leave tracks, a hairnet, a pair of underpants, and I killed her. Then I went home. Nearly *naked*." Rachel almost laughed. "I took a shower and all that blood went down the drain. I'd dumped the slippers, the hairnet, and the pants down a storm drain along the way back to the house."

Rachel's eyes grew troubled. "But Mom heard me slip in through my window. She came into my bathroom and opened the shower door. She saw all that blood still on my legs and going down the drain. I said, 'I started my period.' She just stared at me like she didn't believe me but didn't say a word. The next morning, after she heard about Margaret, she looked dreadful. I knew she suspected the truth. Mrs. Pitt made me call Aunt Adrienne to come to the house. I didn't want to because I thought Mom might tell Adrienne about me. But she didn't."

"She kept quiet just like I kept quiet about Gail," Lottie said. "That is what a mother's love can do. Keep you silent in the face of the most heinous crimes your child commits. But it isn't right, Rachel. I was finally going to tell the police what I thought Gail had done. I called Sheriff Flynn this evening and told him I had to confess something awful. But now it seems I will have something else to tell him. Something about you."

Rachel's face changed into something vicious, almost feral, and Skye cringed, horrified. "You won't tell anything to anyone, old woman, because you will be dead. You'll be lying down there beside Miles, and people will think you blamed him for killing Julianna and fell when you pushed him off the porch."

"And what about your cousin?" Lottie asked softly. "I know you're not capable of much love, Rachel, but you do love Skye. What about her?"

Rachel looked desperately at Skye. "Skye understands me. She understands why I had to do all of these things. She won't tell on me. You'll stand by me, won't you, Skye? You'll protect me, just like I'd protect you."

"I . . . I can't . . ." Tears streamed down Skye's face. "I don't want anyone to hurt you, Rachel, but all the terrible things you've done . . ." A sob racked her chest so hard she lost her breath. "Please, Rachel, tell me you didn't mean any of it. Tell me you were on drugs or you have a brain tumor and you'll go to a hospital and get well and . . ."

"Go to a *hospital*!" Rachel shouted. "Are you insane? I'm not going anywhere except back to school and then on with my life just like I planned it, just like it's supposed to be."

"You can't," Skye said, crying. "Rachel, it can't be that way. You have to tell someone. You have get somebody smart, maybe like a psychiatrist, to help you. You have to *stop*!"

"I *don't* have to stop," Rachel snarled. "And no one can *make* me stop. Not after all I've been through."

"I can make you stop." Lucas Flynn stood in the doorway, a 9 mm gun trained on Rachel. "I can make you stop and I *will* make you stop."

"Oh no you can't," Rachel hissed.

"I have to," Lucas said sadly. "It's my duty, and not just because I'm the sheriff. It's because of what I am to you."

Rachel stared at him for a moment, her eyes seeming to turn glassy. Then, in a strangled voice, she said, "So you're him. Of all people, *you* are my real father."

2

Drew's Camaro kicked up dust as they sped up the road to la Belle Rivière. When they reached the front of the hotel, they immediately spotted Bruce Allard's black GTO. Empty. "Where are they?" Adrienne cried.

Drew didn't answer. His gaze was fixed on something on the ground beside the lowest hotel porch. Without a word, he opened his door and started running. Adrienne immediately followed, then slowed as they got nearer and she saw the body of Miles Shaw splayed on the ground, spikes poking through his abdomen. Drew bent over him, then called, "He's alive. Dial 911 and get an ambulance, Adrienne." She stood immobilized by shock, gazing at the big man who lay moaning, drenched in blood.

Where is Skye? her mind screamed. Where is my daughter? "Adrienne, dial 911 before he bleeds to death!" Drew shouted. "Do it *now*!"

Adrienne snapped back to life as Drew stood and moved away from Miles, going toward the hotel. Adrienne fumbled with shaking fingers in her ridiculously tiny purse for her cell phone, which she immediately dropped. She stooped beside Miles, retrieving the phone. Just as she grabbed it, Miles opened his eyes. His stare was so intense, she froze. "Miles?" she said softly. "Miles, you'll be all right. I don't know what happened, but—"

"Rachel," he ground out, his face contorting with pain. "Rachel did all of it. I didn't know at first . . . I was scared of her when I figured it out. I hid at Kit's and then I was running away like a coward . . ."

"Rachel?" Adrienne gasped. Her mind shut down against the impossibility of what he was saying. "Miles, you're delirious. You don't know what you're talking about. Save your breath. I'm calling for help—"

He grabbed her arm with a bloody hand. Instinctively, she tried to pull back, but he held her with remarkable strength. "She has Skye, Adrienne. Rachel has Skye inside the hotel and she's going to kill her."

3

"What are you *saying*?"

Adrienne had been so absorbed with Miles that she hadn't even heard Philip and Vicky drive up. But now Vicky stood behind her, reaching past her in an effort to grab Miles as Adrienne shouted again, "What are you saying about my daughter?"

Philip pulled Vicky back and Adrienne stood, placing her hands on Vicky's shoulders. "He says Rachel has Skye inside."

"And she's going to *kill* her?" Vicky shrieked. "He's crazy!"

"Philip, keep her off Miles," Adrienne ordered. "I have to get into the hotel."

Adrienne couldn't understand how her voice emerged so strong and commanding when it felt as if everything inside her were quivering in absolute terror. What Miles had said *did* sound crazy, but if he was right . . .

She kicked off her spike-heeled shoes and ran into the hotel. The darkness of the lobby immediately blinded her. Drew called out to her. "I'm behind the registration desk. I just found the light switch. I hope the electricity is still on."

"It is," Adrienne said, remembering turning on the lights the morning she and Skye found Julianna. In a moment, the beautiful chandelier overhead bloomed to life, glowing on the Oriental rugs and elegant Queen Anne furnishings of the lobby. Drew dashed up the stairs toward the second floor. Adrienne followed, hearing Philip and Vicky pounding across the porch and through the double doors.

The injured Miles flashed briefly in Adrienne's mind. In her fear for Skye, she hadn't called 911 asking for an ambulance, but her daughter was more important to her.

She caught up with Drew on the stairs. He took her arm, pulling her along so she could keep up with him. When they reached the second floor, the scent of jasmine hit Adrienne like a splash of perfume. Tastefully muted ceiling lights burned under faceted crystal globes, but Adrienne could still see the flicker of candlelight spilling from one of the rooms—the room where Julianna had died.

"Drew," she whimpered, pointing.

"I see it," he said, just above a whisper. "Stop running. Approach the room slowly and *don't* raise your voice when we get there. If Rachel has Skye, we don't want to startle her. She may have a gun."

"A *gun*!" Adrienne almost cried out, then caught herself. Drew had said to be quiet. Right now he seemed far more in control than she was. She felt more secure following his judgment than hers.

But no amount of good judgment could have prepared Adrienne for what she saw in Room *214*. Skye sat huddled on the floor, her face wet with tears, her eyes wide and terrified. Above her stood Rachel holding a gun, switching it back and forth between a frail, wild-haired Lottie and Lucas Flynn, pointing an even larger revolver at the girl's head.

Adrienne felt as if every bit of air had been sucked from her lungs. She held tightly to Drew's arm, knowing he was all that kept her standing. She stared at the bizarre tableau, too frightened to say anything. Then, from behind her, Vicky moaned, "Oh, my God."

Rachel looked at her mother. "Why didn't you ever tell me the truth, Mom?"

"T-the truth?" Vicky faltered. "What truth?"

"That Philip Hamilton wasn't my real father."

She's lost her mind, Adrienne thought. Rachel has gone

completely over the edge. But Vicky began to cry and asked, "How did you find out?"

"Blood," Rachel answered flatly. "When I had the car wreck two summers ago, I needed a transfusion. I found out you have type A blood and Dad has type O. I have AB. It's not possible for parents with A and O blood to have a child with AB."

"The doctor wasn't supposed to tell you that," Vicky said in a small, crushed voice. "He promised."

Rachel gave her a rueful smile. "Oh, he kept his promise. But this bitchy nurse whose daughter I'd beaten a week earlier in the local tennis championship told me for spite. God, did she gloat!" Rachel's smile faded. "But I knew before then. I think I've always known."

She looked at Philip, who seemed turned to granite. "I always adored you, Daddy. But unless we were in public, you either ignored me or treated me like you couldn't stand me. You could barely *look* at me. I tried so hard to please you. But I couldn't—not with the good looks everyone said I had, not with good grades, not with my athletic achievements or all the other honors I got in school. Nothing seemed to matter. I was *so* hurt. I felt like nothing, worse than nothing.

"After I found out that because of the blood, I couldn't be your biological daughter, I tried to tell myself I was adopted. But I'm good with research. It didn't take long for me to realize I hadn't been adopted. Mom had given birth to me, but I wasn't *yours*. That's why you didn't love me. What I want to know now is exactly what happened. How did I come to be, Mom?"

"Rachel, I can't . . . don't do this to me, *please*," Vicky wavered.

Rachel pointed the gun at her. "Don't you dare stand there looking delicate and sickly and helpless. For once in your life, stand up and tell the truth. Tell me how you betrayed

Dad with another man and gave birth to his child. Lucas Flynn's child!"

Adrienne and Lucas locked stares. She couldn't believe what she'd just heard until she saw the truth in his gray eyes. She barely felt Drew's hand touch hers. He's trying to comfort me, she thought distantly. Drew thinks I'm hurt. But I'm only surprised.

Adrienne tore her gaze away from Lucas's and looked at Skye, huddled on the floor, her tears dried, her face desolate. Adrienne ached with the need to cuddle the girl in her arms, but she knew any movement on her part could be dangerous, so she simply tried to stand still and calm in the maelstrom that swirled around her.

"Tell me, Mother!" Rachel commanded again.

"All right!" Vicky sobbed. "All right. Just try to understand, Rachel. I love you. I always have." Rachel glared at her, and Vicky drew a deep breath. "It was three years after Philip and I married. I'd already realized he didn't love me. He was never mean to me. It would almost have been better if he had been. At least that would have meant he felt *something* about me. But there was nothing except this vague kindness, especially in public. I couldn't stand it, Rachel. I was crushed because I loved him so much. I felt desperate for attention—for *love*—and there was Lucas. He was working on one of Philip's campaigns back then. We were together a lot. We talked. I liked him immensely. And he *loved* me. I knew it even before he said it. And one night, when we'd both had a little too much to drink . . . well, you can guess the rest."

"Oh, you were drunk," Rachel said sarcastically. "Next you'll tell me he raped you."

"No. Nothing like that. Actually . . . well, I gave him the impression I wanted to leave Philip. I don't know what got into me. I was just so angry, so hurt—"

"So *needy,* as always," Rachel snapped.

"Yes. Lucas and I were together several times and then I told him I'd made a mistake. I knew I'd hurt him, but I just couldn't leave Philip. The problem was that I realized too late. I was pregnant."

Rachel looked at her mother contemptuously. "You'd already deceived Dad by committing adultery. Couldn't you pass me off as *his* child, too? Or were you too honorable?"

"No," Vicky said weakly. "I wasn't honorable even then. I told him I was pregnant. I said, 'Isn't it wonderful? We're going to have a child!' And he gave me this cold, stony look and said, 'I'm sterile. I've known for years.' He didn't get furious, he didn't ask who the father was, he didn't show one *trace* of emotion. He just walked out of the house. He came back two days later and said, 'We're going to pretend this baby is mine. I don't want you to tell your mother, your sister, *anybody* that it isn't. And I don't want to know who the father is. End of subject.'" Vicky laughed raggedly. "End of subject! Can you believe it? I couldn't."

"But you did what he said." Rachel looked at Philip. "Why, Dad? Or should I say Philip? Why did you play out this act? And don't lie to me now, not after all you've put me through. Tell me the truth or I will put a bullet in your head."

Philip barely paused before saying in a stiff, dry voice, "I had planned a career in politics since I was a child. I couldn't expect to further my aims by divorcing my pregnant wife. There would have been a scandal. It would have been the end."

"Not if there hadn't been a child at all," Rachel said. "If you were determined not to divorce Mom, why didn't you insist she get an abortion? She would have done what you wanted, no matter how she felt about getting rid of an unborn child."

"Abortion has always been abhorrent to me."

"Since when?" Rachel asked disdainfully. "As I recall, you've always been pro-choice, although as a stalwart Republican you never broadcast your views on that subject."

Another pause before Philip said, "Considering abortion in the abstract is different than the reality of your own wife having one. I did not want to put your mother through it."

Rachel's eyes narrowed and a sardonic smile formed on her face. "You're very convincing when you lie to the public, Dad, but not to me. I can tell when you're lying. Now, because I intend to keep everyone in this room until questions are answered to my satisfaction, why don't you try telling the truth?"

The silence in the room seemed to swell until Adrienne thought she would scream. Didn't Philip realize that Rachel was on the edge, capable of anything, even of shooting him? Why wouldn't he answer? What would happen if he refused to answer? She closed her eyes and felt Drew's grip on her hand tighten. She clung to his hand as if he were the only thing in the world that could save all of them. Including Skye.

"Answer her, Philip," Drew finally said, his voice steely. "If you don't answer and keep putting all these people at risk, I swear I'll choke you to death before Rachel has a chance to shoot you."

"Shut up, Delaney," Philip said, seething. "This is none of your business."

"Answer her!" Lucas commanded.

Philip looked at him with naked hatred. "You son of a bitch. I gave you a job. I was good to you. I had no idea—"

"It doesn't matter now," Lucas said coldly. "Just tell Rachel what she wants to know."

Adrienne could feel Philip breathing hard behind her. He'd probably never felt so cornered and powerless in his whole life. "All right, Rachel. If you want the truth, you'll get it. I'm not going into specifics, but when I was fourteen, I got an injury. A very private injury inflicted by none other than Great-aunt Octavia. I'd broken a Ming vase. It wasn't the first time she'd beaten me with her cane, but it was the worst. I never said anything about it, or about any of the other beatings, because I was ashamed of what an old woman could do to me. I also had nowhere else to go. My parents were dead. There were no other close relatives. She filled my head with stories about the horrors of foster homes and orphanages." His head tipped down slightly. Adrienne wasn't sure, but she thought she saw a look of remembered terror on his face. But in a moment he looked up again, his face expressionless. "Later, when the pain in my groin wouldn't go away, I got worried and went to the doctor. I made an excuse for the injury. He wanted to test me, and I let him. That's when I discovered I was sterile."

His reverence for the imperious, cruel-eyed Octavia had always mystified Adrienne. Now she realized that what Philip had felt wasn't reverence—it was fear. And he'd been in the old harridan's care since he was six.

"I was ashamed of being sterile," he went on. "I kept hoping some miracle would happen. But after your mother and I had been married for three years, she still wasn't pregnant. So I knew it was true. And I also knew that other people would begin wondering what the problem was. They might think Vicky was barren, but what if they suspected the problem lay with me? What if they thought I wasn't a *man*?"

Good God, Adrienne thought. Octavia must have planted that idea in his mind. She must have made him doubt his manliness and proving it had become an obsession with him.

"So when Vicky told me she was pregnant, I knew the baby wasn't mine. My first impulse was to get rid of it. But I went away and thought about it for a couple of days. And I decided that this was the way to save my reputation. People would think there was nothing wrong with me. After all, I had a child, didn't I? My marriage would stay intact and I would have a child. I'd be the perfect political candidate—the man with a spotless reputation. A family man."

Rachel looked at him incredulously. "You accepted me because you thought it was good for your *career*?"

"Yes," Philip said simply. "It made perfect sense."

"Dear Lord," Vicky whispered. "Even I didn't know your true reason for wanting to keep the baby. Without one, you were afraid people would think you weren't a *real* man, a *virile* man?"

"Well, you didn't think it was because I cared about the kid, did you?" Philip asked viciously.

"I thought you really didn't want to put me through an abortion because you knew I hated the idea. And I thought you could come to love the baby," Vicky said weakly.

"Love? *Her?*" Philip almost snorted. "Every time I looked at her, I thought of what you'd done. You had *me,* Philip Hamilton, and you still turned to another man. I didn't know it was Lucas, but I knew it *had* to be someone inferior to me." Or *superior,* Adrienne mused, because he could father a child. "And then came the most galling part of all," Philip went on. "Watching another man's child grow into something special. Beautiful. Intelligent. Someone who excelled at almost everything. Music. Tennis." He laughed harshly. "Even that damned rifle team she was on for a while."

The rifle team, Adrienne thought. She'd forgotten all about how worried Vicky had been that Rachel would get hurt handling the guns. But she'd been a champion. A champion who had shot at Lucas and at her at Lottie's cabin. A champion who could have killed both of them if she'd really wanted to.

"Daddy," Rachel said pathetically, "I tried to excel at everything because of *you.* I thought if I could just make you proud enough of me, you'd finally love me."

"Love you?" Philip scoffed. "You killed Claude and Margaret and, worst of all, Julianna. Julianna was the only person in my whole life that I *loved*!" Vicky swayed as if she were going to faint, but Philip didn't even glance at her. "You tried to kill Gavin Kirkwood, didn't you? I remember that call you got from Bruce right before you went tearing out of the house, then claimed you'd had a fender-bender and your car was in the shop. It was Bruce calling you to say he'd gotten some information out of Kirkwood, wasn't it? Information you thought might hurt you. And where the hell is Bruce, anyway? Have you dispatched him, too?"

"No . . . I—"

"I don't *care!*" Philip screamed at her. "I was right about you all along, right not to love you because you were a mistake of nature. You are despicable! You are an abomination!"

"No, Daddy, *please* . . ." Rachel sobbed.

"I-am-not-your-father," Philip spat. "Thank God I am not your father because I will hate you to the depths of my soul until the day I die!"

"Philip!" Vicky cried, but he went on ranting at the girl who stood before him, shaking, crying, seeming to crumble right in front of them.

Lucas stepped forward. "Rachel, don't listen to him," he pleaded. "You are not an abomination. You're a beautiful, talented girl who is troubled. We'll get help for you. *I'll* get help for you. *I* am your father, not Philip Hamilton. And *I* love you, no matter what. I won't let anything happen to you."

Shaking violently, Rachel looked at him wildly. "Get help for me? Like what? I've killed people. You all know it. I'll be put in prison for the rest of my life. I'm not a juvenile. I'll get the death penalty! The *electric* chair!"

"*No,*" Lucas said desperately. "There are other ways this can be handled."

"A mental institution. You'll put me in a crazy house and I'll live there until I rot. Well, I won't do it! I'd rather die. I *will* die! It's the only way. But I'll do it on my terms!"

Rachel raised her pistol and shot at the ceiling. Everyone recoiled and she took advantage of their temporary shock to dash past them, out of the room and down the hall. Lucas was the first to move, tearing along behind her as she ran to the stairs. The stairs leading *upward.* Drew followed Lucas as Adrienne went to Skye, stooping and trying to scoop the girl into her arms. But Skye fought her off. "She's gonna kill herself, Mom!" she shrieked, then with amazing speed stood and ran out of the room. Stunned, Adrienne struggled to her feet as Vicky too ran from the room. Philip stood perfectly still, his expression vacant, as Adrienne pushed past him and followed the others.

She could hear Lucas yelling for Rachel to stop. She could hear Skye crying, calling to Rachel that she loved her. She could hear Drew shouting for Lucas to catch Rachel and get the gun away from her, as if Lucas weren't already trying his best to catch up with a fleet young woman over twenty years his junior. But Vicky was silent except for her rasping breath.

To Adrienne, the trip up the stairs seemed to take an hour. The hotel had become a nightmare full of shouts and yells and shrieks and people running frantically after her niece who carried a gun. They bypassed the third floor and stumbled up the stairs to the fourth. Adrienne and Vicky had just reached the top when they saw Rachel near the end of the hall. An outside light shone brightly through the great, arched floor-to-ceiling window and for a moment, Rachel stood several feet in front of it, bathed in light, a beautiful, tragic girl who only hours ago had seemed to have a wonderful life ahead of her. She turned, looked at her mother, and said, "Tell Daddy good-bye for me."

Vicky screamed at the top of her voice as Rachel ran toward the window. She was fast and strong, and the glass crashed into countless pieces as she hurled herself against the old, thin panes. Lucas sank to his knees, his face contorted in silent horror when his daughter landed with a body-shattering thud on the concrete walkway below.

EPILOGUE

"It's only late August, but I'm sure I can smell autumn in the air," Kit said.

She, Adrienne, Drew, and Brandon sat in the gazebo at The Iron Gate. At eleven A.M., a cloudless sapphire-blue sky hung over them and a warm breeze wafted through the gazebo, a breeze rife with subtle smells that sent Brandon's nose twitching furiously. Looking at him, Drew said, "I wonder if cats have as many olfactory glands as dogs."

Kit laughed. "I have no idea, but speaking of cats, I really miss Calypso. I never wanted a pet, but I got used to her after just a few days. I didn't tell Lottie that when I took Calypso home, though. I know Lottie and she'd want to give me the cat, but she needs Calypso for company more than I do right now."

"At least Lottie's safe. And unnecessarily apologetic for the shooting incident at her cabin. After all, she didn't tell me where she was, but she did tell me absolutely not to look for her." Adrienne sipped her mimosa, feeling relaxed and almost decadent. Skye was at Sherry's for the day. With Sherry's help, and that of the good-looking Joel on whom Skye had developed a crush, she slowly seemed to be emerging from the depths of depression over her cousin's death five weeks ago. "I'm surprised poor Lottie didn't die hiding out in the woods for days. Instead, she came through it with only a case of bronchitis."

"I told you she was tough," Drew said, smiling. "You'll probably turn out just like her."

"Living in a cabin by myself in the woods and having visions?" Adrienne asked in mock horror.

"Tough and wily," Drew corrected.

"I don't feel tough and wily. I feel like one big, dumb bruise. I can only imagine how Vicky feels, but she refused to let me go to Canada with her. She said if I was along, we'd just talk about Rachel and she wouldn't even begin to heal. She thought she needed time alone."

"And where is the ex-gubernatorial candidate?" Kit asked. "I know he fled town right after he made an obligatory appearance at Rachel's funeral."

"He's touring Europe," Adrienne said. "In his public statement he made a big deal about being unable to stay in the town where his 'darling though troubled daughter' had met her death, but he's really just hiding."

Drew scoffed. "Hiding from the Allards, no doubt. They want to sue him for the pain and suffering his daughter caused dear Bruce."

"He's alive, isn't he?" Adrienne asked sarcastically.

"But she shot him in the leg. He might walk with a limp."

"Which will no doubt affect him drastically when he takes over his father's businesses, including the newspaper." Adrienne grinned at Drew. "Just think of it. Someday Bruce will be your boss."

"That is the day I resign as editor and begin work on the Great American Novel."

"It's too bad Miles didn't fare as well as Bruce," Kit said sadly. "But at least he'll live, although his recovery will take months."

Adrienne didn't know what to say. She now knew Kit had loved Miles and she always would. Maybe someday Miles would turn to Kit, but the shadow of Julianna would always hang over them.

"But there's one bright note," Kit said suddenly. "Gavin's

near death scared my mother into realizing how much she still cares for him. They're like teenage lovebirds. It's almost sickening, except that I'm glad to see Mother so happy. I didn't realize how much *her* depression affected *me*. Even considering all the awful things that have happened lately, not having to worry about her constantly has made my life easier."

Brandon raised his head and barked. They all looked around to see Lucas Flynn walking by. He smiled, raised his hand in greeting, then continued along the sidewalk. He looked tall and handsome in his uniform, but even at this distance, Adrienne had seen the sadness in his gray eyes.

"That must have been awkward," Kit murmured.

Adrienne shook her head. "Actually, it wasn't. We had a long talk after Rachel's death." She looked at Drew. "I haven't even told you all the things he said, but I think the time has come."

She reached out and took his hand. "Lucas always knew Rachel was his child, but Vicky didn't want him, so he went away. He never stopped thinking about Vicky *or* Rachel, though, so he came to Point Pleasant to be near them. He had no hope of Vicky leaving Philip for him, or even of her telling Rachel the truth about her father. He just wanted to be part of their lives."

Adrienne smiled regretfully. "That's where I came in. We met and really liked each other. In fact, he came to love Skye and me. Not in the way he loved Vicky and Rachel, but in a warm, caring way. And Skye and I were alone. He thought he could help us, provide us with a more secure life. But his real reason for wanting to be part of our lives was because we were part of Vicky's and Rachel's. He didn't fully realize it at the time, but that's what he wanted—to be close to the romantic love of his life and his daughter."

Drew's dark eyes gazed into hers, full of understanding. And *love,* Adrienne thought joyfully. At one time, Drew may have been selfish and careless, but almost twenty years had changed him. He was truly a man, now. A man full of generosity and capable of genuine love, both for her and for Skye.

"I'm sorry about Lucas," Kit said gently. "I know you cared about him."

"I still care," Adrienne said. "But I'm not in love with him and he wasn't really in love with me. He'll always be a part of my life and Skye's—I wouldn't want it any other way and Drew understands—but there's only one man for me."

Kit smiled. "No disrespect to Trey Reynolds, Adrienne, but there always has been one man for you."

Drew leaned over and kissed Adrienne, a gentle yet passionate kiss that didn't embarrass her one bit even though her mother had always told her public displays of affection were vulgar. Then Drew leaned back, his smile growing even wider. "Hey, kid, we forgot why we came here this morning!"

"I thought it was because you couldn't bear to go another day without seeing me!" Kit joked.

"Well, there's that, but there's also something else," Adrienne said. "Come out to van."

"The van?" Kit echoed. "When did *you* get a van?"

"I rented it for a special purpose," Adrienne said. "It's the red one at the curb."

"It's the *only* van at the curb," Kit said. She looked down at Brandon asleep on her feet. "I hate to disturb your much-needed rest, but let's see what Adrienne has hidden in that rented vehicle."

They walked out to the van and Drew opened the rear doors, then looked at Kit. "I'm afraid I'll need someone to help me unload this, so for now you'll have to step into the van in order to view the surprise."

Kit looked at Drew and Adrienne dubiously. "Are you sure you don't have something horrible hidden in there? Something to scare the daylights out of me just for fun?"

"I swear," Adrienne said, placing her hand over her heart. Then she gave Kit a little shove. "In you go!"

They watched Kit carefully climb into the van, then wait until her vision had adjusted to the dimmer light coming in through the van windows and the open back doors. Finally, she spotted a long object covered in canvas. With a cry of joy, she rushed to it, threw back the canvas, and revealed a six-by-three-foot oil painting of la Belle Rivière.

"Oh, Adrienne, it's *beautiful*!" Kit exclaimed ecstatically. "You haven't mentioned it for weeks and I thought you quit working on it. Then when Mother had the hotel demolished last week, I gave up all hope."

Adrienne entered the van and stooped beside Kit, looking at the painting. "In spite of all the bad things that happened there, there were wonderful things happened, too. La Belle was a fabulous old hotel. I just couldn't let it go unforgotten."

Kit gazed at the painting, a genuine smile of pleasure lighting her face.

Adrienne stared at the painting, too. She looked at the graceful Georgian lines, the glass cupolas reflecting glints of the sun, the weather vanes, the large rooftop clock tower with its Roman numerals, the long porches with their hanging pots of colorful flowers, the glowing stained glass in the double doors. And for a moment, a moment Adrienne could have sworn was not an illusion, the hotel came alive again, its front doors swinging open as it welcomed guests into its beautiful, haunted halls.